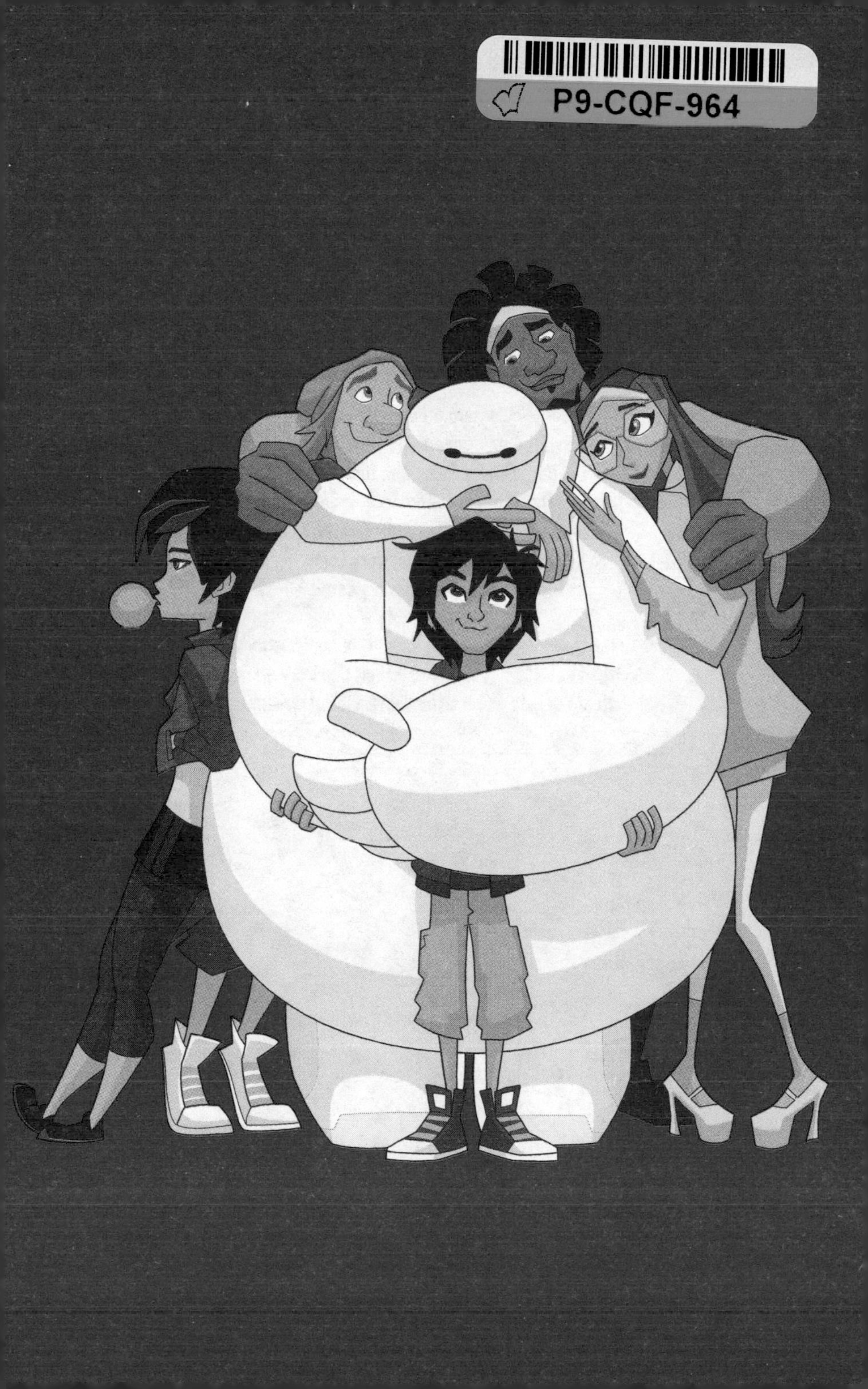

ALSO FROM JOE BOOKS

Disney Big Hero 6 Cinestory Comic
Gravity Falls Shorts Comic Collection Vol. 1: Just West of Weird
Disney Darkwing Duck Comics Collection: Orange Is the New Purple
Disney Darkwing Duck Comics Collection: Tales of the Duck Knight
Disney Tangled Before Ever After Cinestory Comic
Disney • Pixar Coco Cinestory Comic
Disney DuckTales Cinestory Comic

Star Wars: A New Hope Cinestory Comic: 40th Anniversary Edition
Spark of Rebellion: A Star Wars Rebels Cinestory Comic
Path of the Jedi: A Star Wars Rebels Cinestory Comic

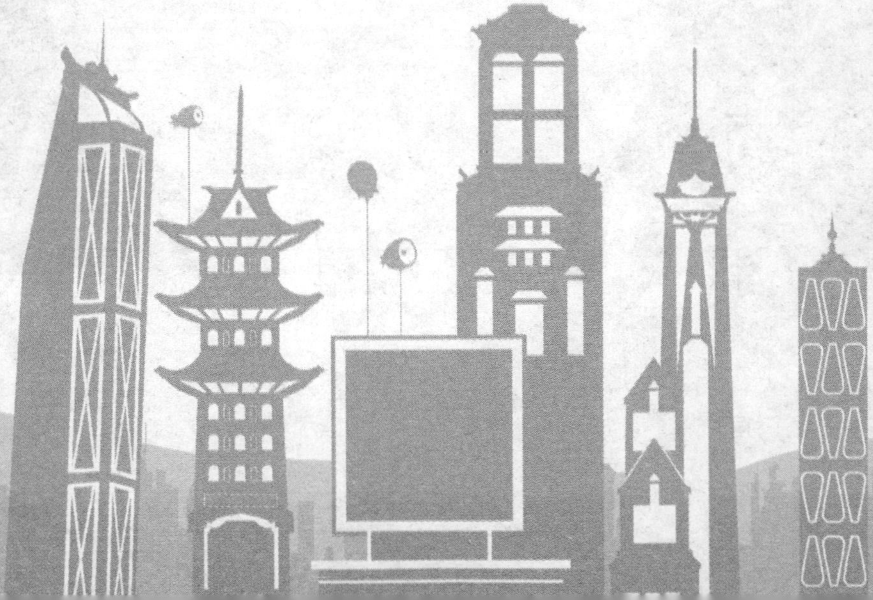

Disney

BIG HERO 6

THE SERIES

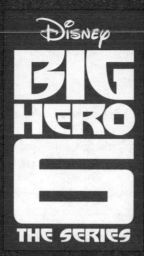

BAYMAX RETURNS

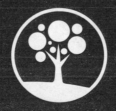

JOE BOOKS LTD

Copyright © 2018 Disney Enterprises, Inc. All rights reserved.

Published simultaneously in the United States and Canada by Joe Books Ltd,
489 College Street, Suite 203, Toronto, ON M6G 1A5.

www.joebooks.com

No portion of this publication may be reproduced or transmitted,
in any form or by any means, without the express written
permission of the copyright holders.

First Joe Books edition: January 2018

Print ISBN: 978-1-77275-498-8
ebook ISBN: 978-1-77275-842-9

Names, characters, places, and incidents featured in this publication are
either the product of the author's imagination or are used fictitiously.
Any resemblance to actual persons (living or dead), events, institutions,
or locales, without satiric intent, is coincidental.

Joe Books™ is a trademark of Joe Books Ltd. Joe Books® and the
Joe Books logo are trademarks of Joe Books Ltd, registered in
various categories and countries. All rights reserved.

Library and Archives Canada Cataloguing in Publication
information is available upon request.

Printed and bound in Canada
1 3 5 7 9 10 8 6 4 2

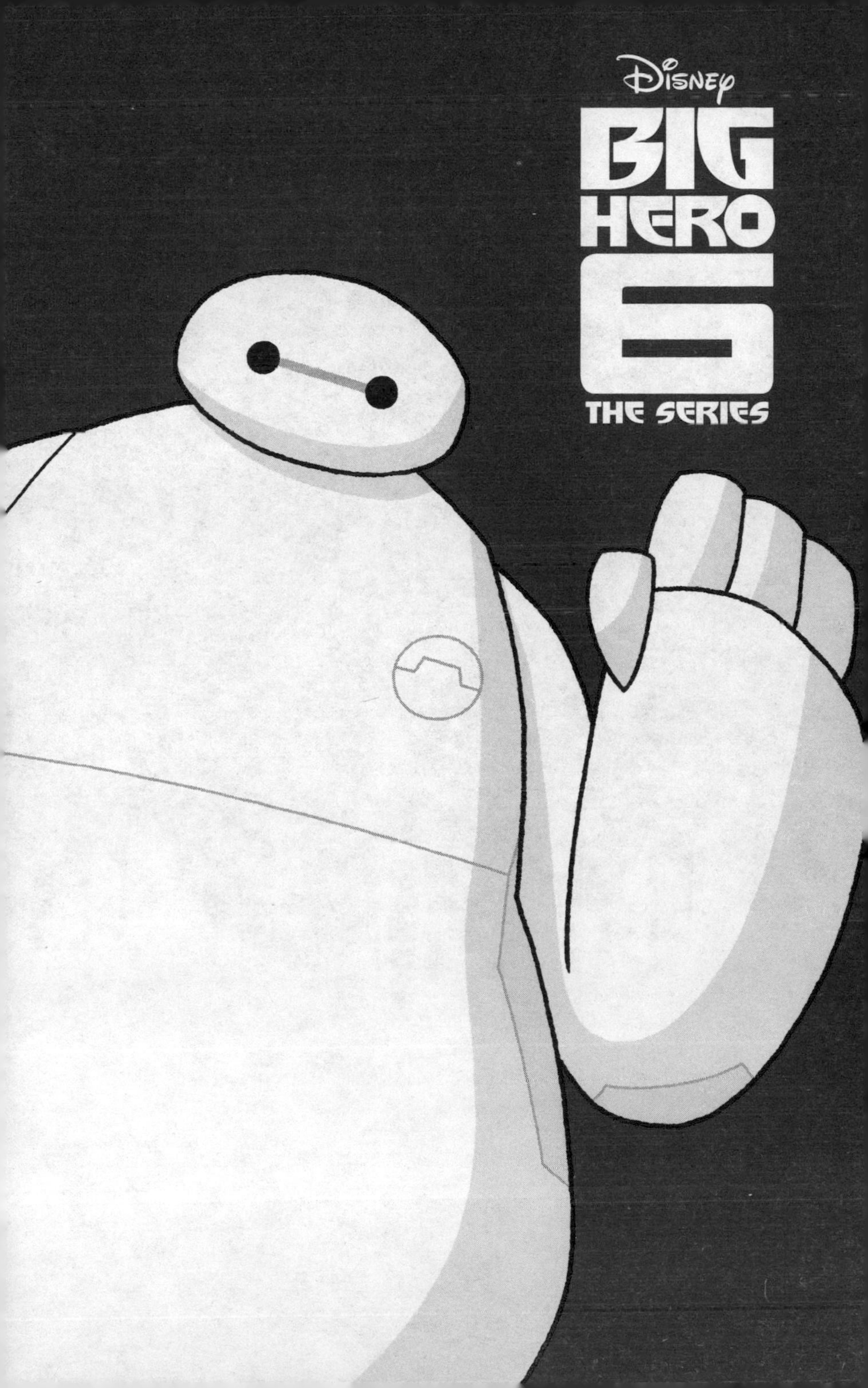
Disney
BIG HERO 6
THE SERIES

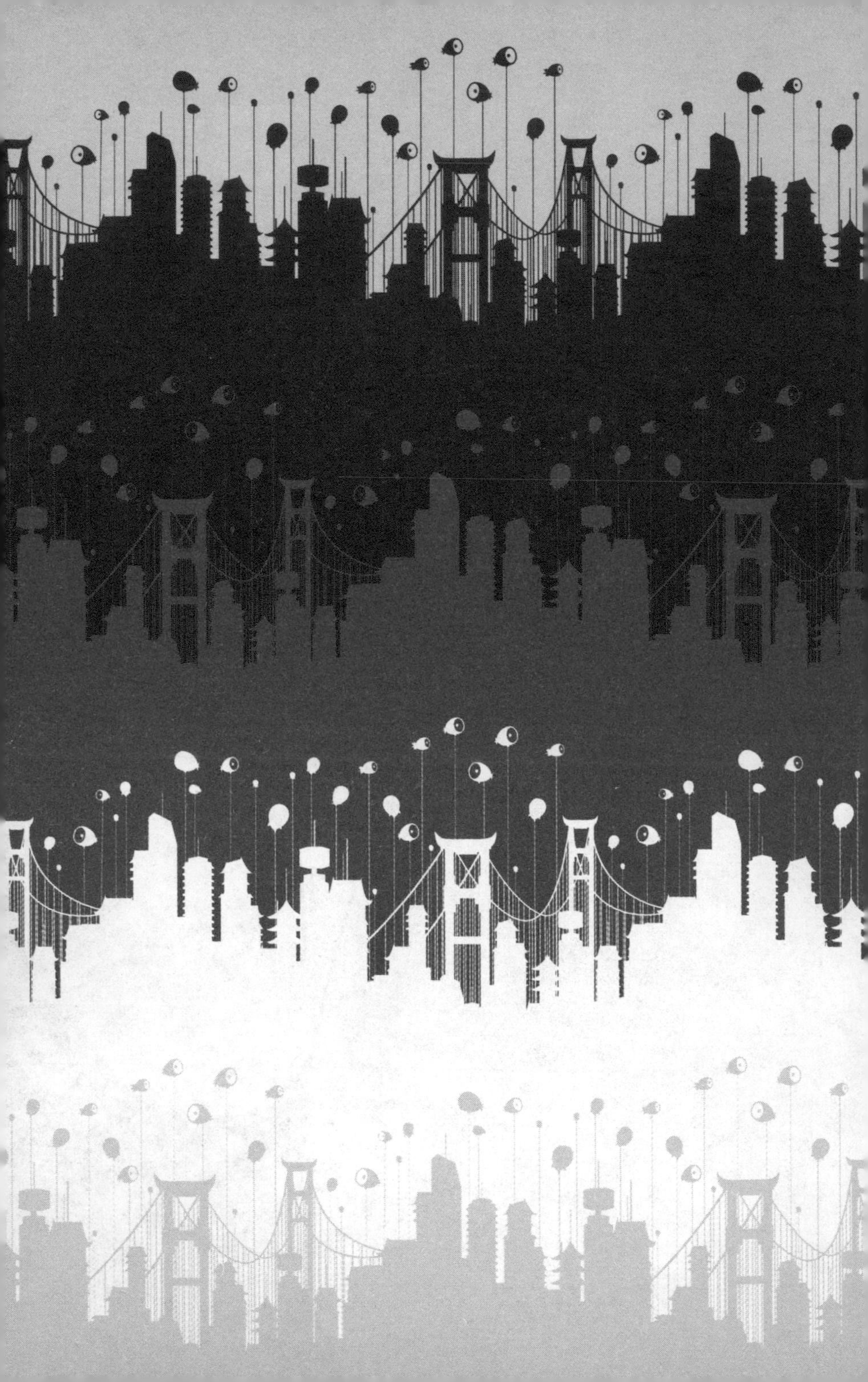

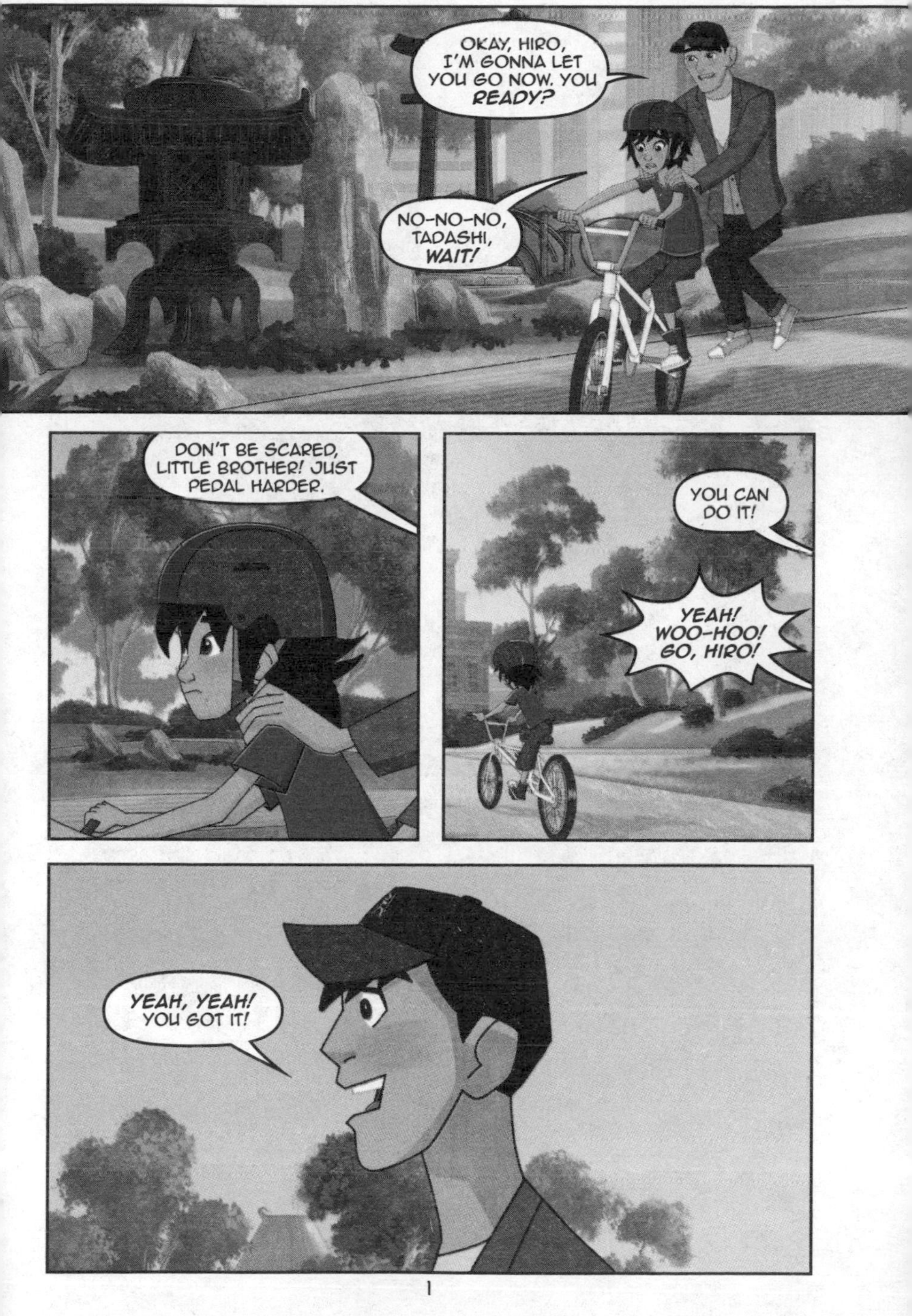
OKAY, HIRO, I'M GONNA LET YOU GO NOW. YOU *READY?*
NO-NO-NO, TADASHI, *WAIT!*
DON'T BE SCARED, LITTLE BROTHER! JUST PEDAL HARDER.
YOU CAN DO IT!
YEAH! WOO-HOO! GO, HIRO!
YEAH, YEAH! YOU GOT IT!

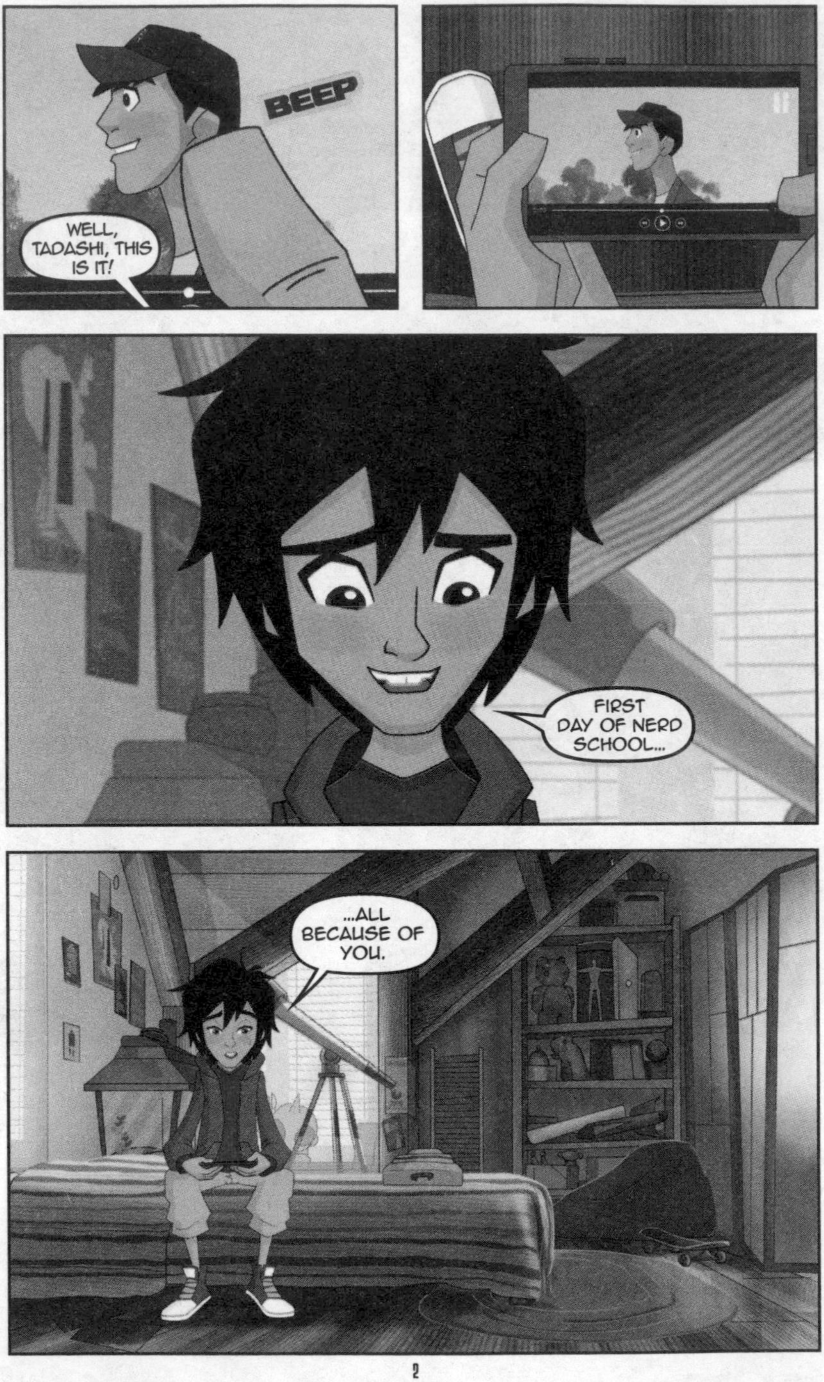
BEEP
WELL, TADASHI, THIS IS IT!
FIRST DAY OF NERD SCHOOL...
...ALL BECAUSE OF YOU.

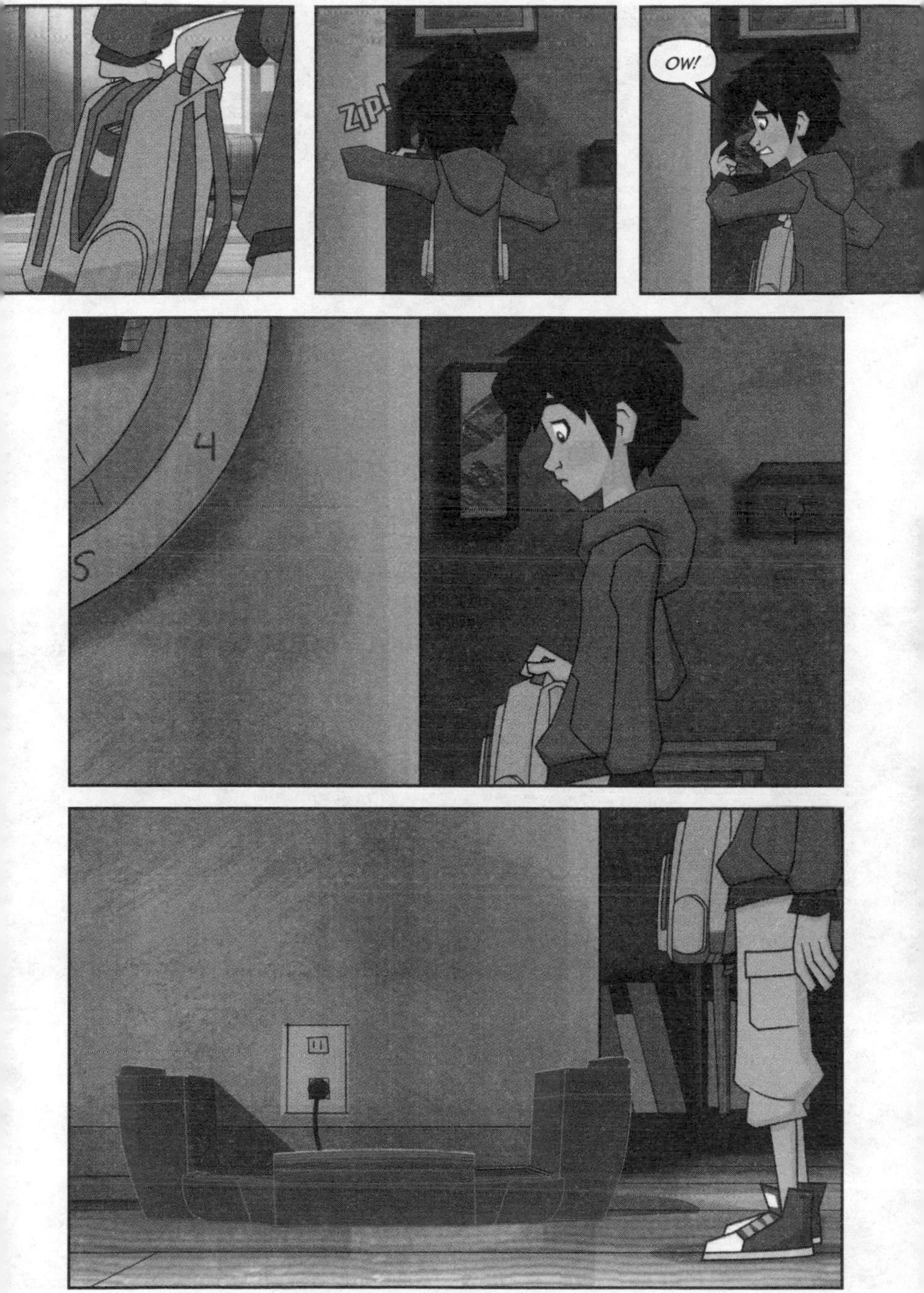
ZIP!
OW!

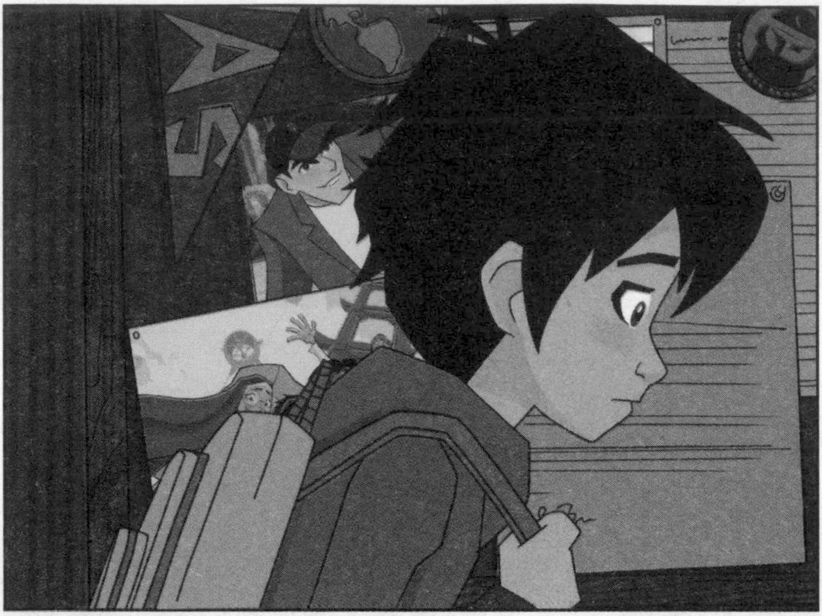
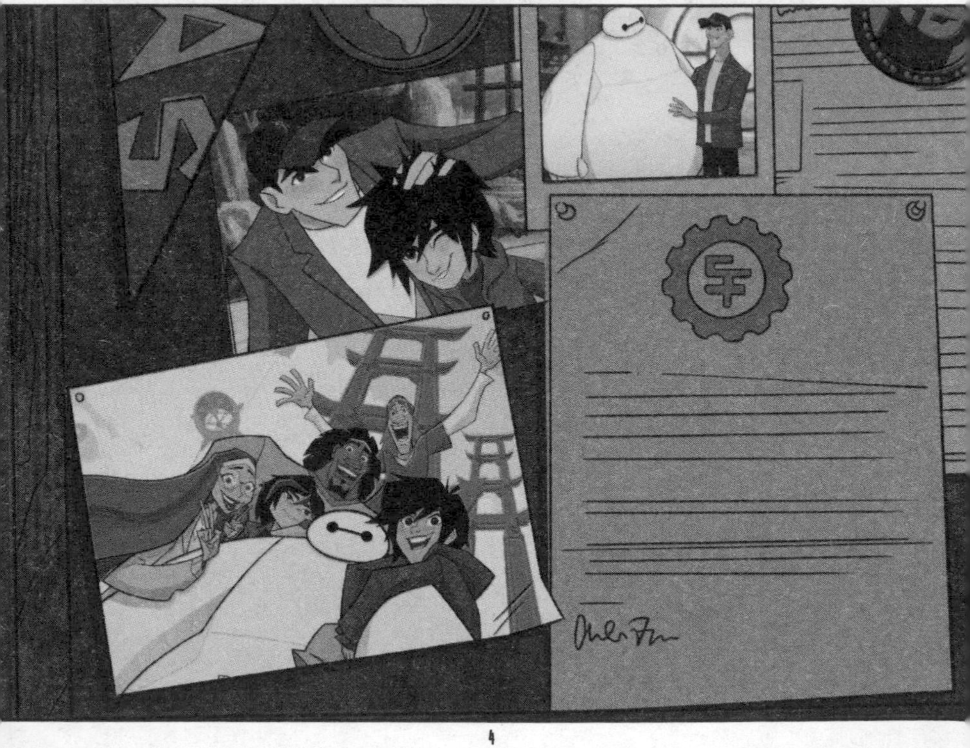

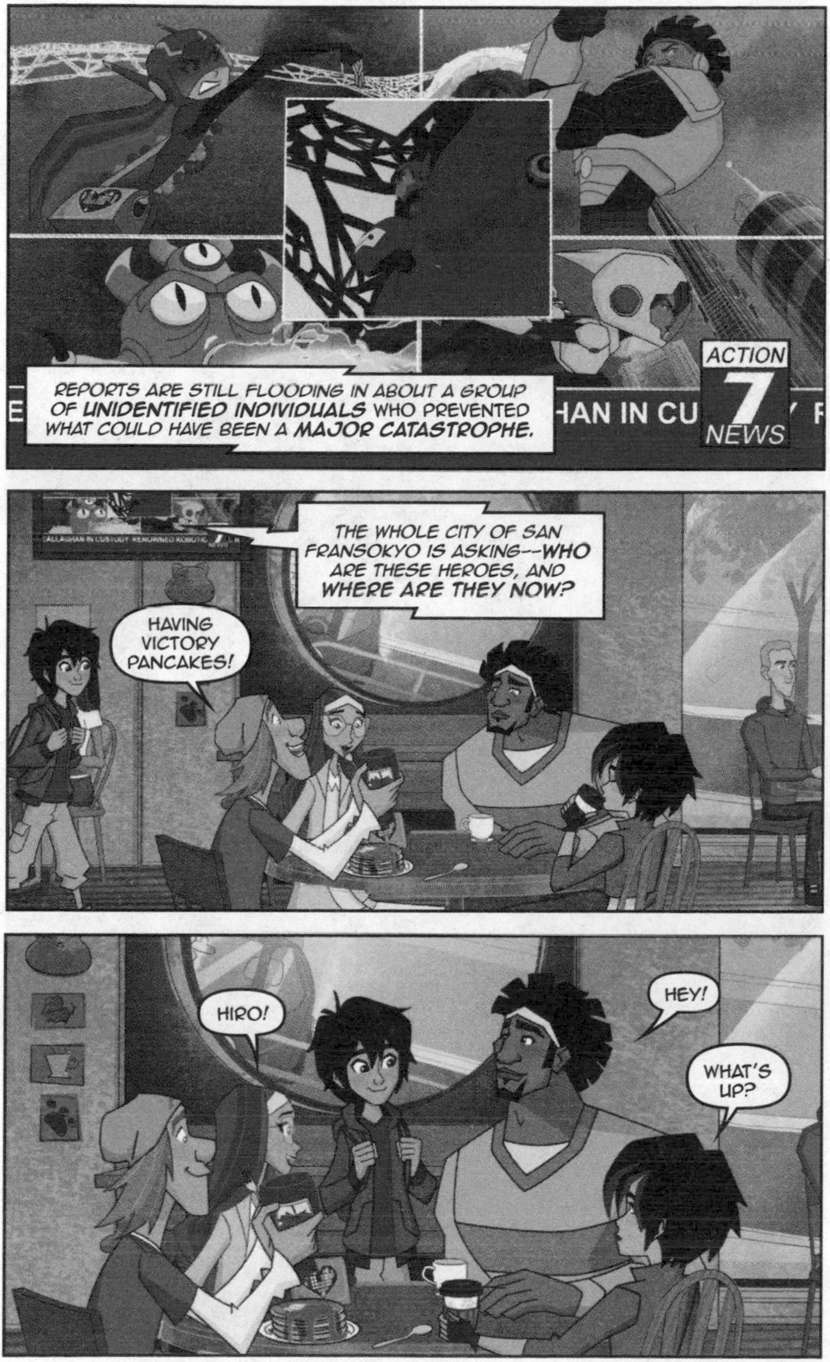
REPORTS ARE STILL FLOODING IN ABOUT A GROUP OF UNIDENTIFIED INDIVIDUALS WHO PREVENTED WHAT COULD HAVE BEEN A MAJOR CATASTROPHE.
HAN IN CU
ACTION 7 NEWS
THE WHOLE CITY OF SAN FRANSOKYO IS ASKING--WHO ARE THESE HEROES, AND WHERE ARE THEY NOW?
HAVING VICTORY PANCAKES!
HIRO!
HEY!
WHAT'S UP?

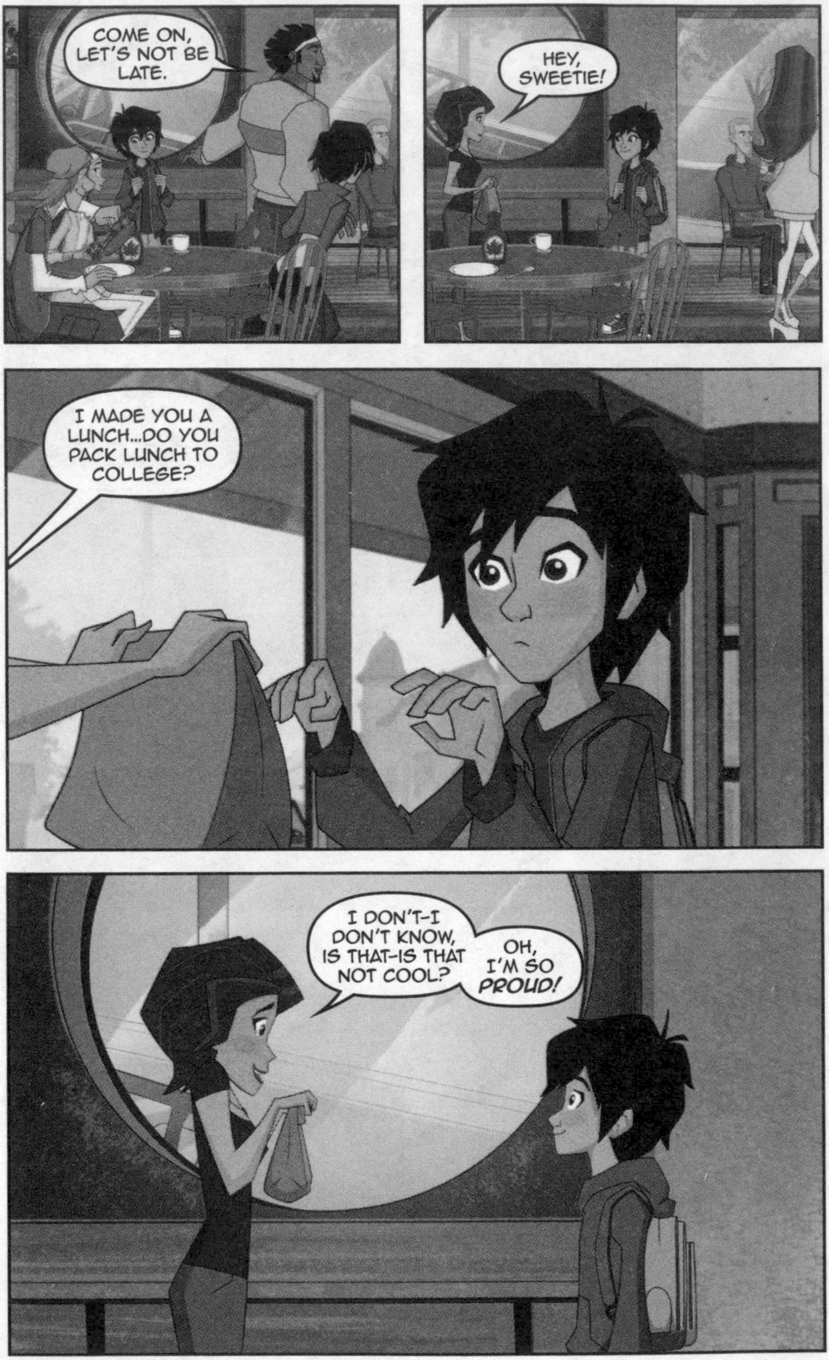
COME ON, LET'S NOT BE LATE.
HEY, SWEETIE!
I MADE YOU A LUNCH...DO YOU PACK LUNCH TO COLLEGE?
I DON'T-I DON'T KNOW, IS THAT-IS THAT NOT COOL?
OH, I'M SO *PROUD!*

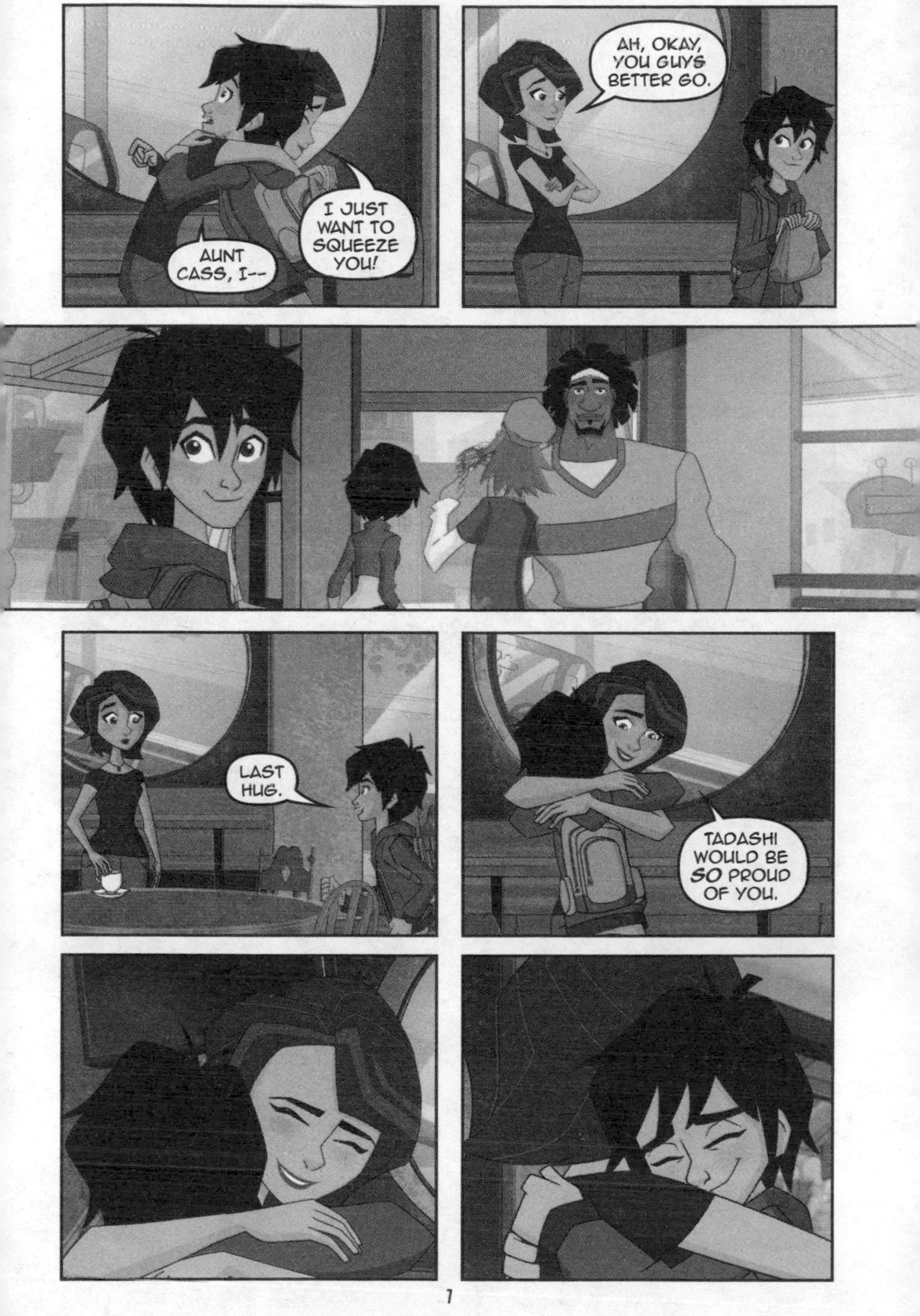
AUNT CASS, I--
I JUST WANT TO SQUEEZE YOU!
AH, OKAY, YOU GUYS BETTER GO.
LAST HUG.
TADASHI WOULD BE SO PROUD OF YOU.

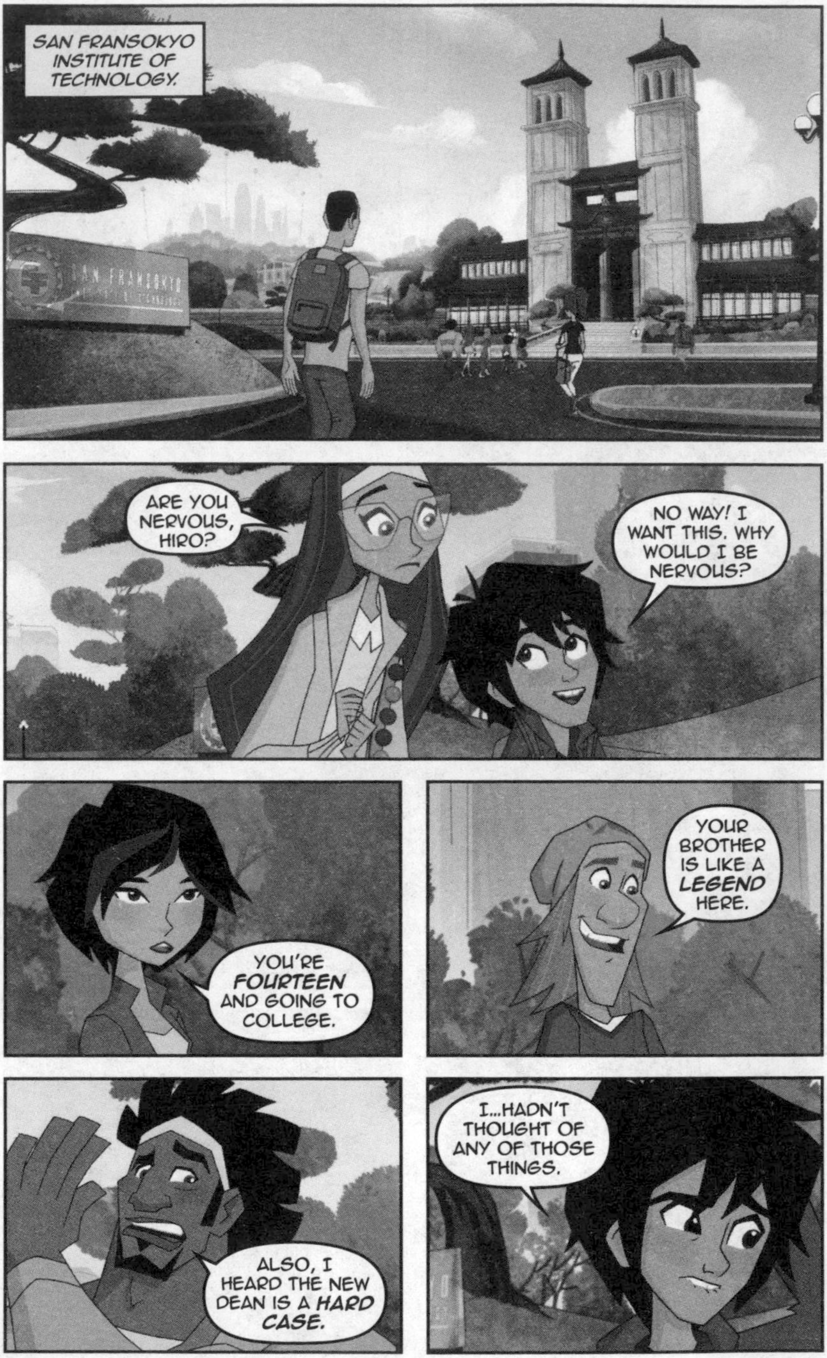
SAN FRANSOKYO INSTITUTE OF TECHNOLOGY.
ARE YOU NERVOUS, HIRO?
NO WAY! I WANT THIS. WHY WOULD I BE NERVOUS?
YOU'RE FOURTEEN AND GOING TO COLLEGE.
YOUR BROTHER IS LIKE A LEGEND HERE.
ALSO, I HEARD THE NEW DEAN IS A HARD CASE.
I...HADN'T THOUGHT OF ANY OF THOSE THINGS.

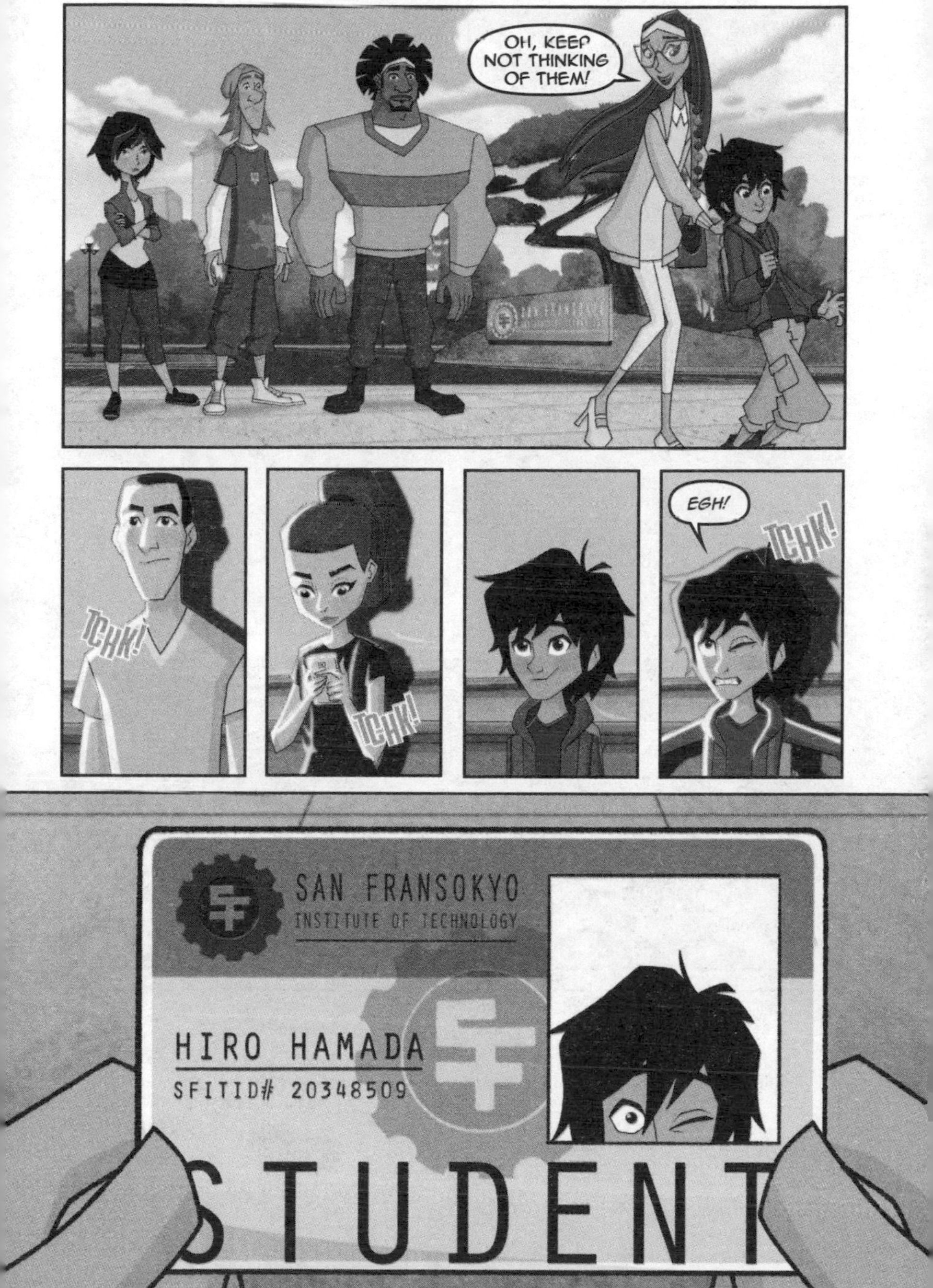
OH, KEEP NOT THINKING OF THEM!
TCHK!
TCHK!
EGH!
TCHK!
SAN FRANSOKYO
INSTITUTE OF TECHNOLOGY
HIRO HAMADA
SFITID# 20348509
STUDENT

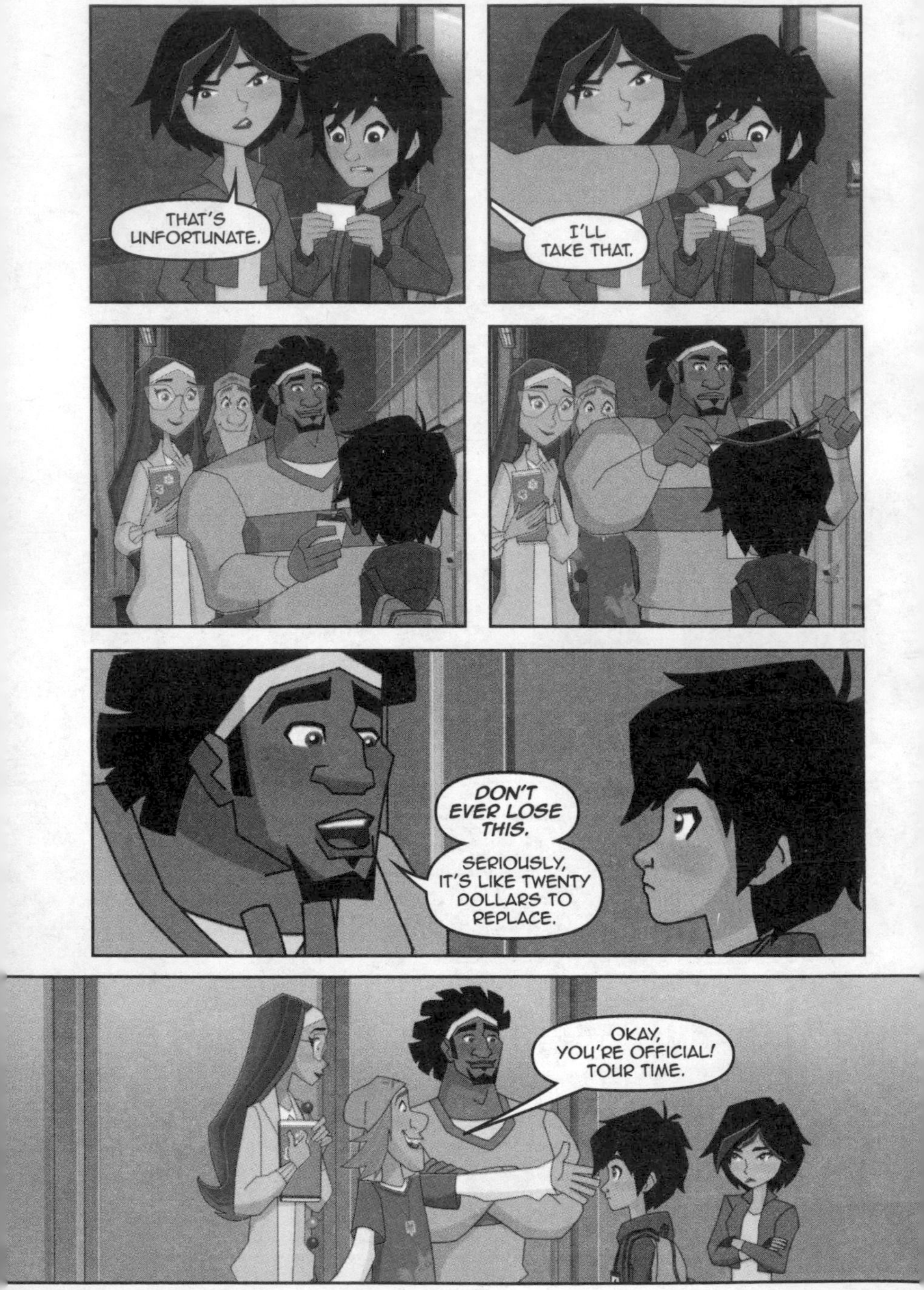

THAT'S UNFORTUNATE.
I'LL TAKE THAT.
DON'T EVER LOSE THIS.
SERIOUSLY, IT'S LIKE TWENTY DOLLARS TO REPLACE.
OKAY, YOU'RE OFFICIAL! TOUR TIME.

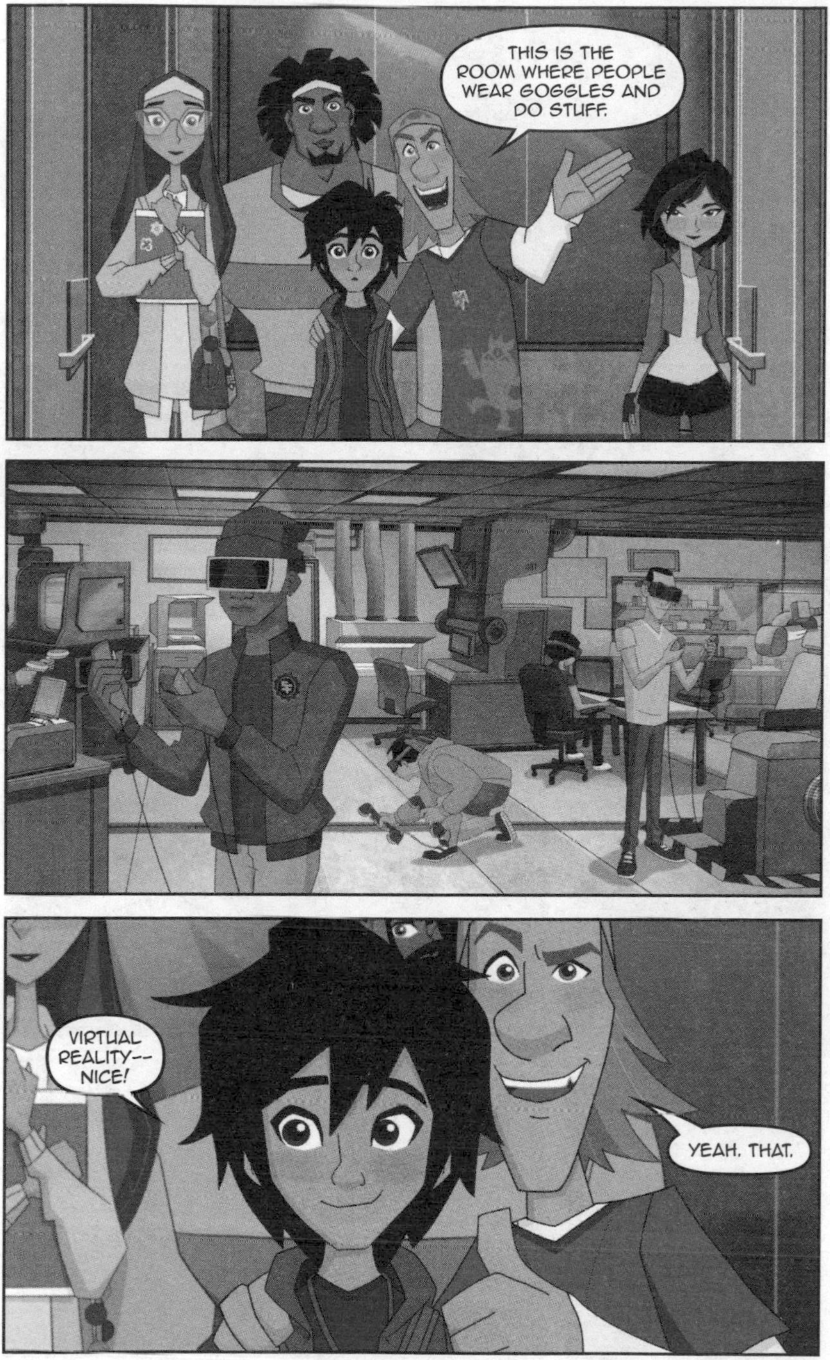
THIS IS THE ROOM WHERE PEOPLE WEAR GOGGLES AND DO STUFF.
VIRTUAL REALITY-- NICE!
YEAH. THAT.

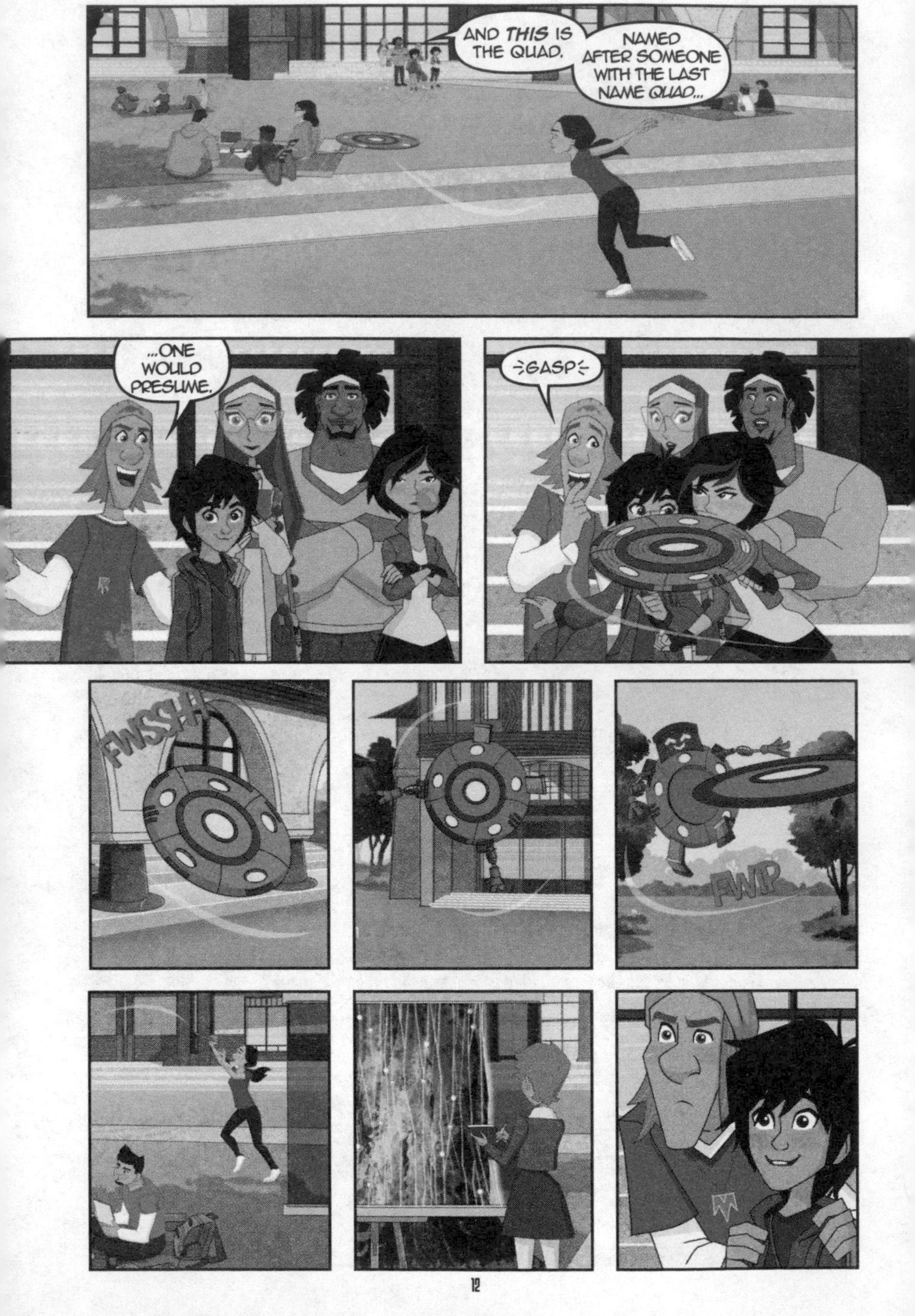
AND THIS IS THE QUAD.
NAMED AFTER SOMEONE WITH THE LAST NAME QUAD...
...ONE WOULD PRESUME.
GASP
FWSSH
FWIP

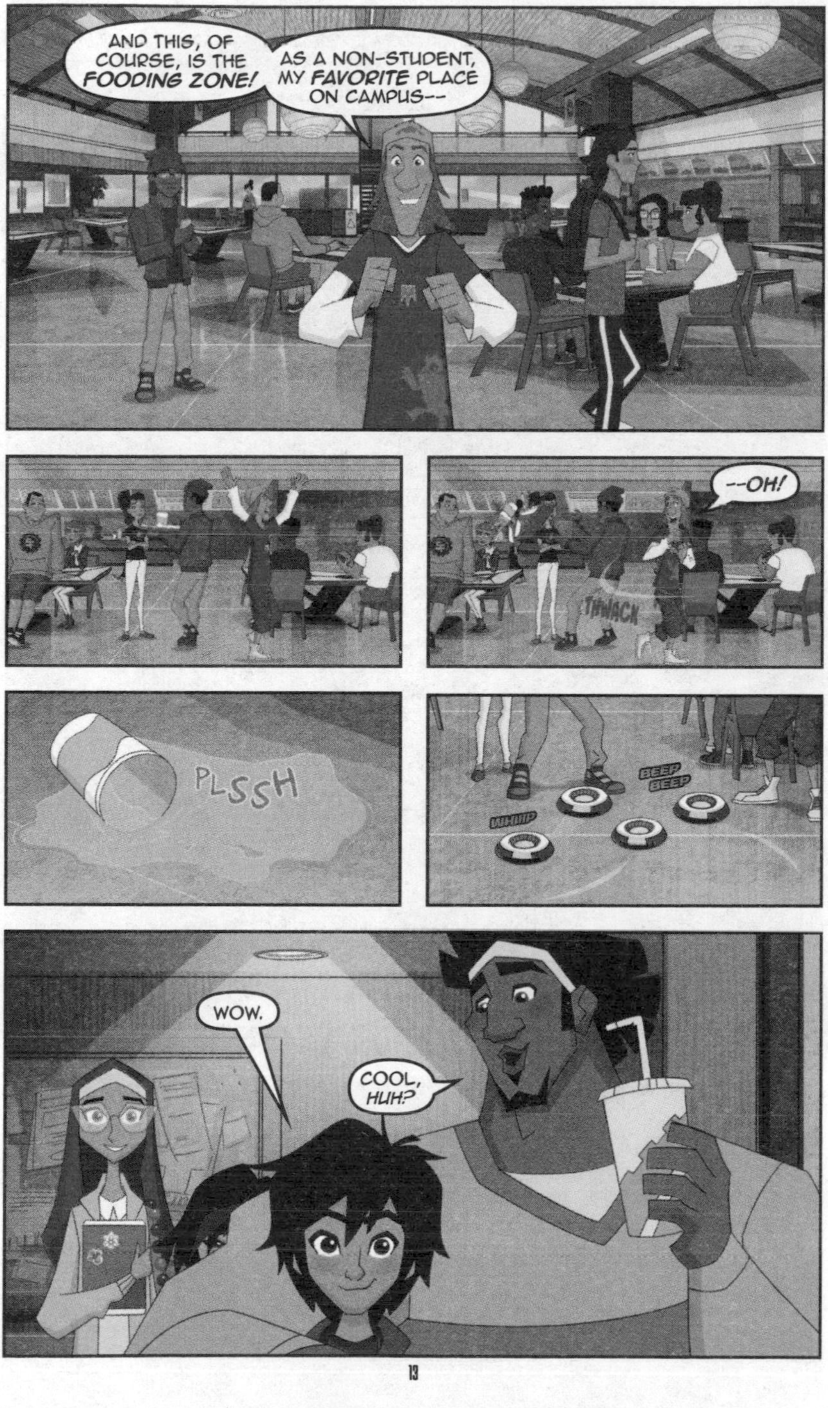
AND THIS, OF COURSE, IS THE *FOODING ZONE!*
AS A NON-STUDENT, MY *FAVORITE* PLACE ON CAMPUS--
--OH!
THWACK
PLSSH
BEEP
BEEP
WOW.
COOL, HUH?

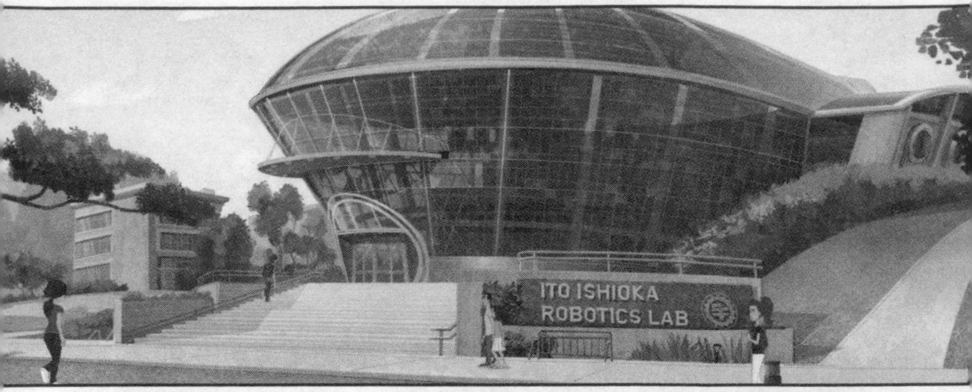
ITO ISHIOKA
ROBOTICS LAB

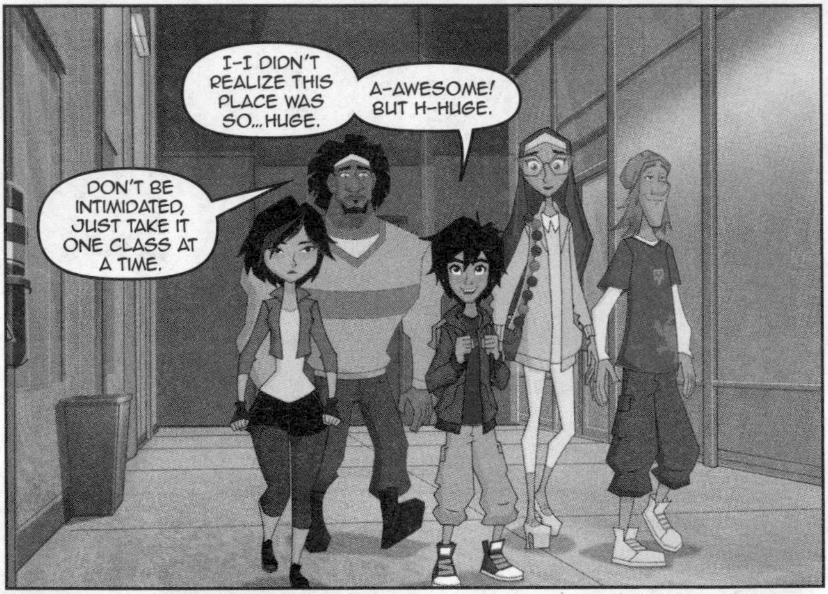
I-I DIDN'T REALIZE THIS PLACE WAS SO...HUGE.
A-AWESOME! BUT H-HUGE.
DON'T BE INTIMIDATED, JUST TAKE IT ONE CLASS AT A TIME.

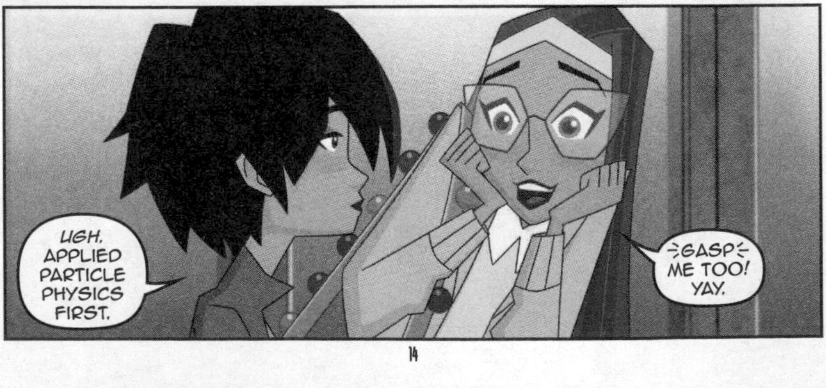
UGH. APPLIED PARTICLE PHYSICS FIRST.
GASP ME TOO! YAY.

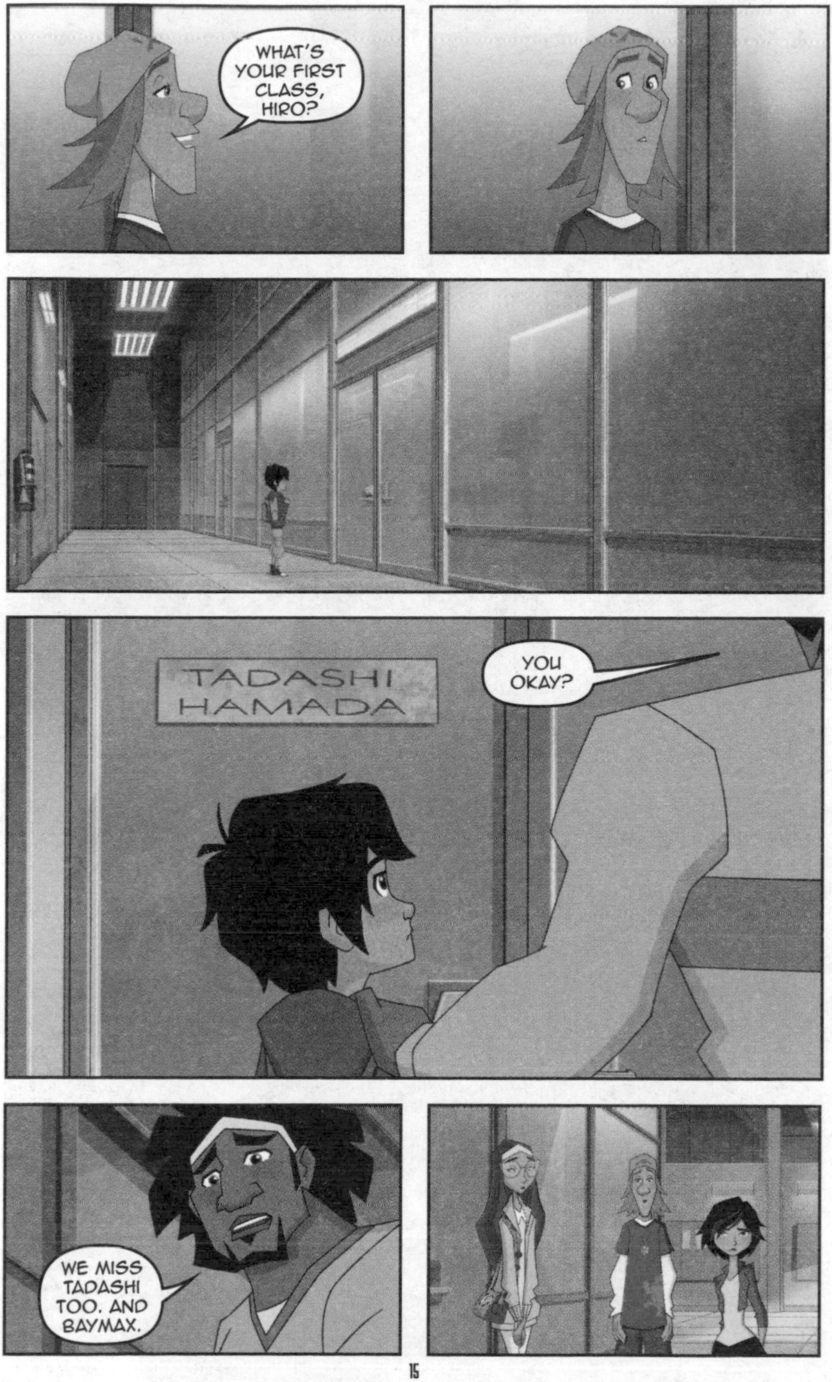
WHAT'S YOUR FIRST CLASS, HIRO?
TADASHI HAMADA
YOU OKAY?
WE MISS TADASHI TOO. AND BAYMAX.

YEAH,
I'LL...UM...

...I'LL CATCH UP
WITH YOU GUYS
LATER.

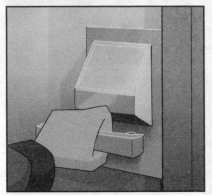

WISH YOU WERE HERE, BIG BROTHER.

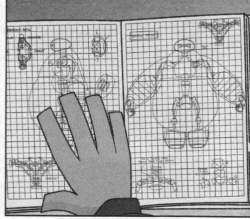

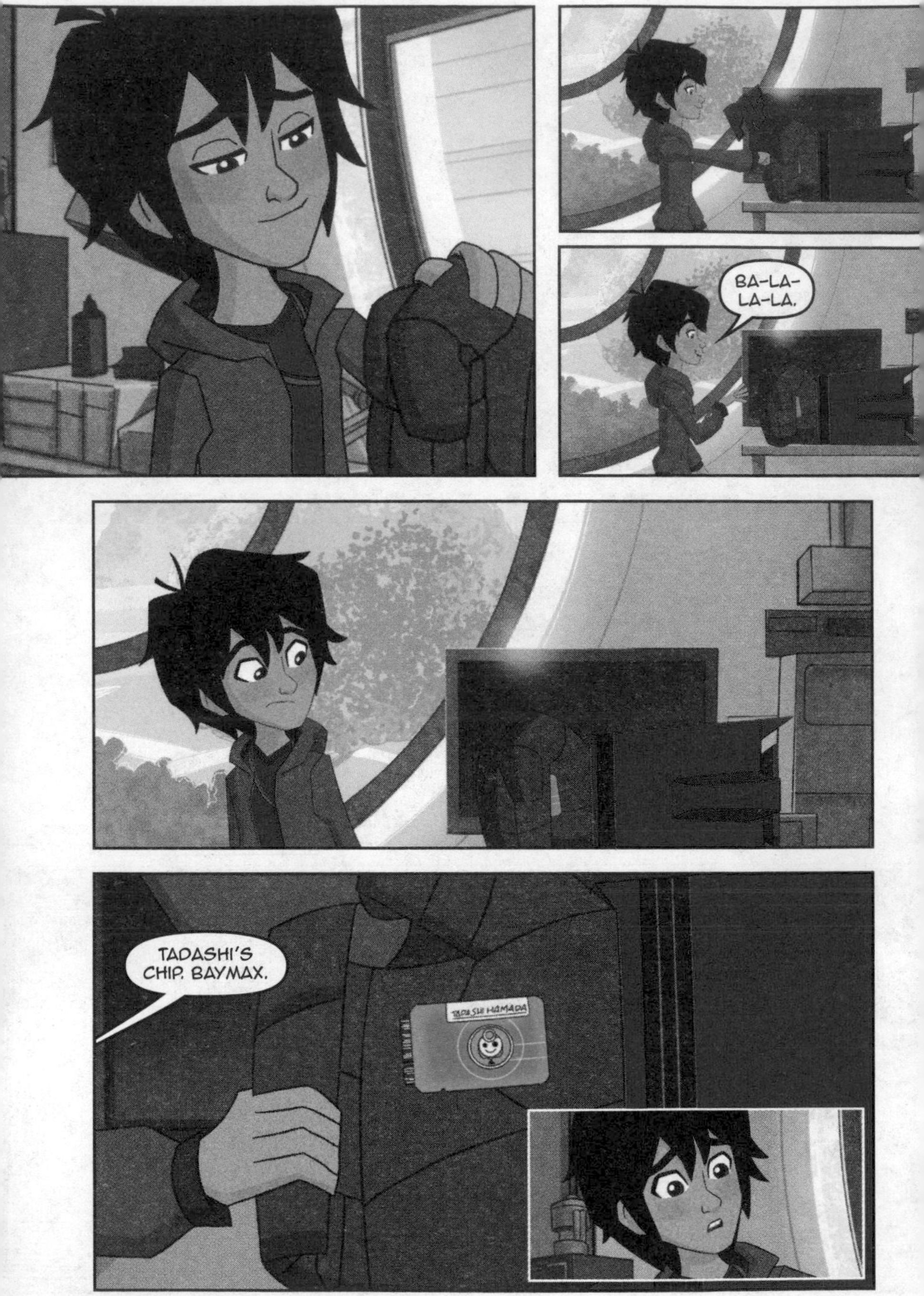
BA-LA-LA-LA.
TADASHI'S CHIP. BAYMAX.
TADASHI HAMADA

UM, O—OKAY, OKAY!

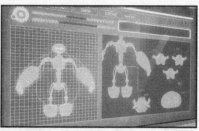

I'M GONNA NEED A CARBON-FIBER SKELETON, ACTUATORS, DEFINITELY GONNA UPGRADE TO SUPER CAPACITORS.

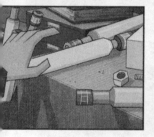

HAH! I CAN DO THIS! I CAN REBUILD YOU, BAYMAX.

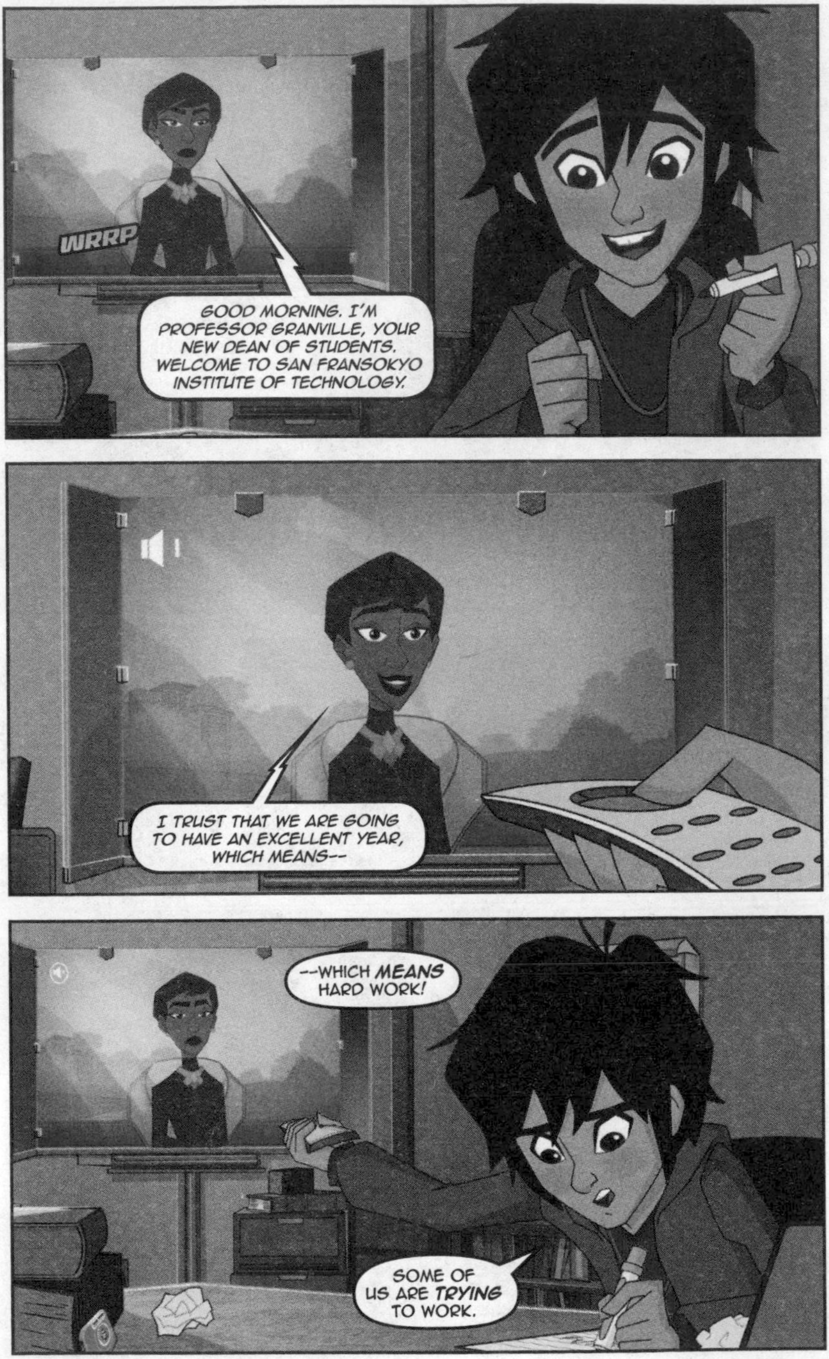
WRRP
GOOD MORNING. I'M PROFESSOR GRANVILLE, YOUR NEW DEAN OF STUDENTS. WELCOME TO SAN FRANSOKYO INSTITUTE OF TECHNOLOGY.
I TRUST THAT WE ARE GOING TO HAVE AN EXCELLENT YEAR, WHICH MEANS--
--WHICH MEANS HARD WORK!
SOME OF US ARE TRYING TO WORK.

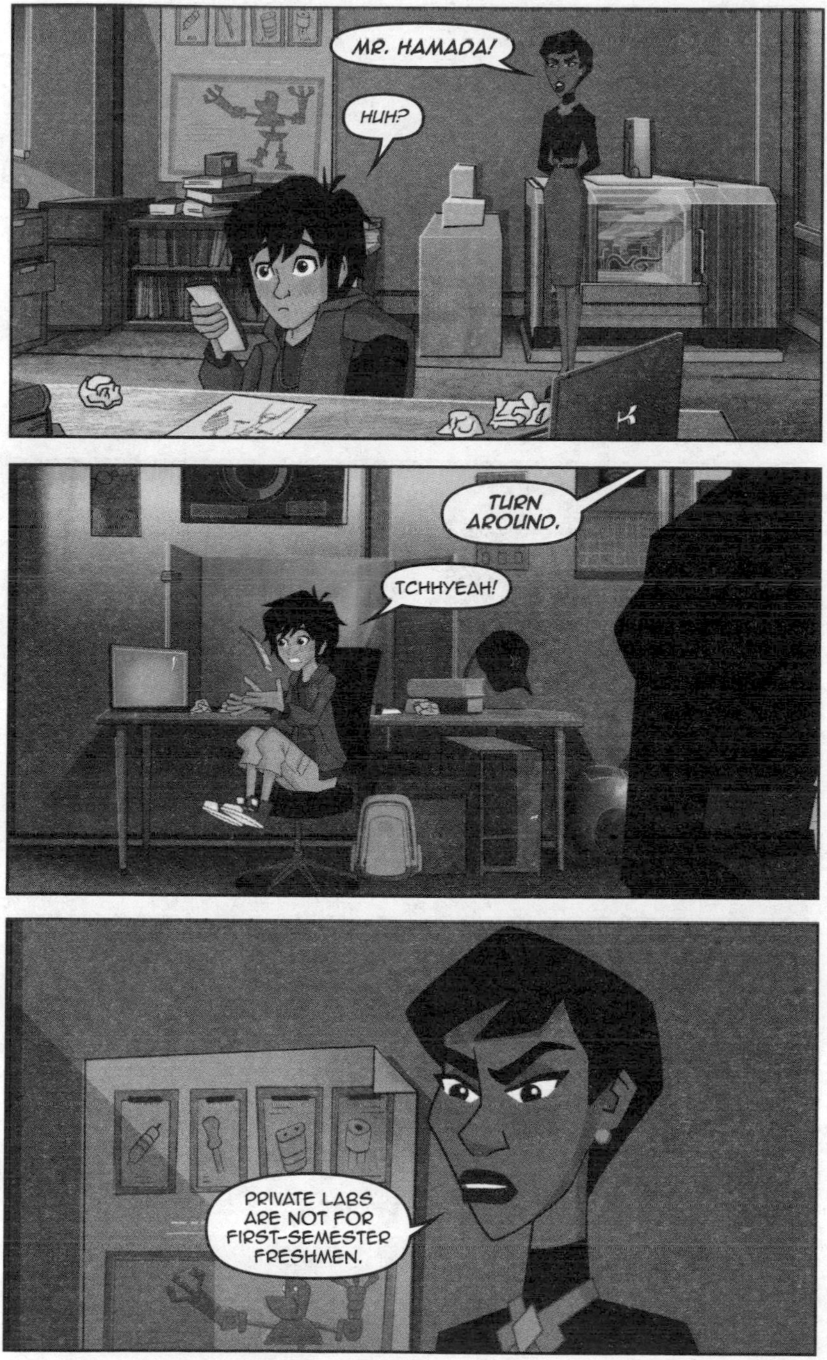
MR. HAMADA!
HUH?
TURN AROUND.
TCHHYEAH!
PRIVATE LABS ARE NOT FOR FIRST-SEMESTER FRESHMEN.

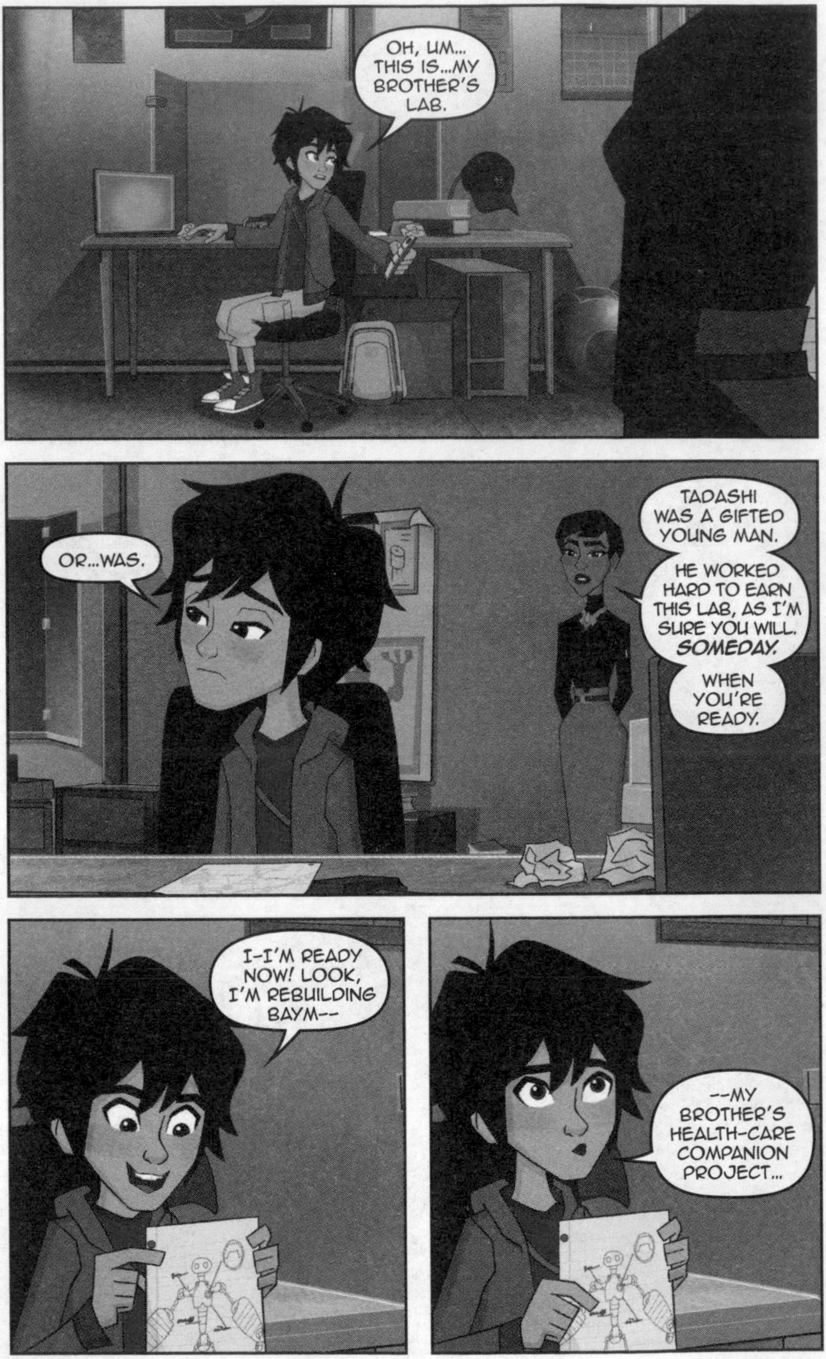
OH, UM... THIS IS...MY BROTHER'S LAB.
OR...WAS.
TADASHI WAS A GIFTED YOUNG MAN.
HE WORKED HARD TO EARN THIS LAB, AS I'M SURE YOU WILL. SOMEDAY.
WHEN YOU'RE READY.
I-I'M READY NOW! LOOK, I'M REBUILDING BAYM--
--MY BROTHER'S HEALTH-CARE COMPANION PROJECT...

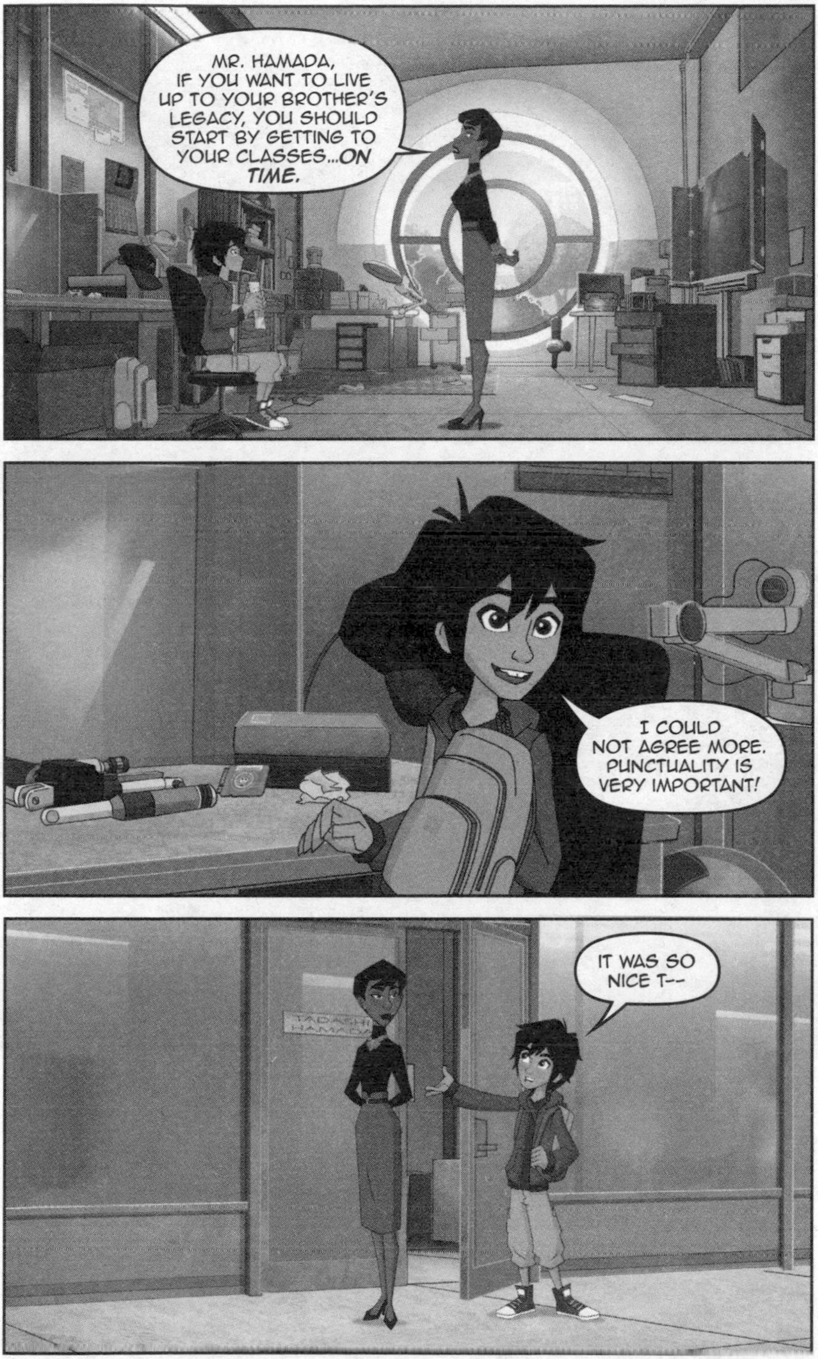
MR. HAMADA, IF YOU WANT TO LIVE UP TO YOUR BROTHER'S LEGACY, YOU SHOULD START BY GETTING TO YOUR CLASSES...*ON TIME.*
I COULD NOT AGREE MORE. PUNCTUALITY IS VERY IMPORTANT!
TADASHI HAMADA
IT WAS SO NICE T--

TICK-TOCK, MR. HAMADA. DON'T WANT TO KEEP YOUR THERMODYNAMICS PROFESSOR WAITING.

I HEAR SHE IS TOUGH, BUT FAIR. *INTERMITTENTLY.*

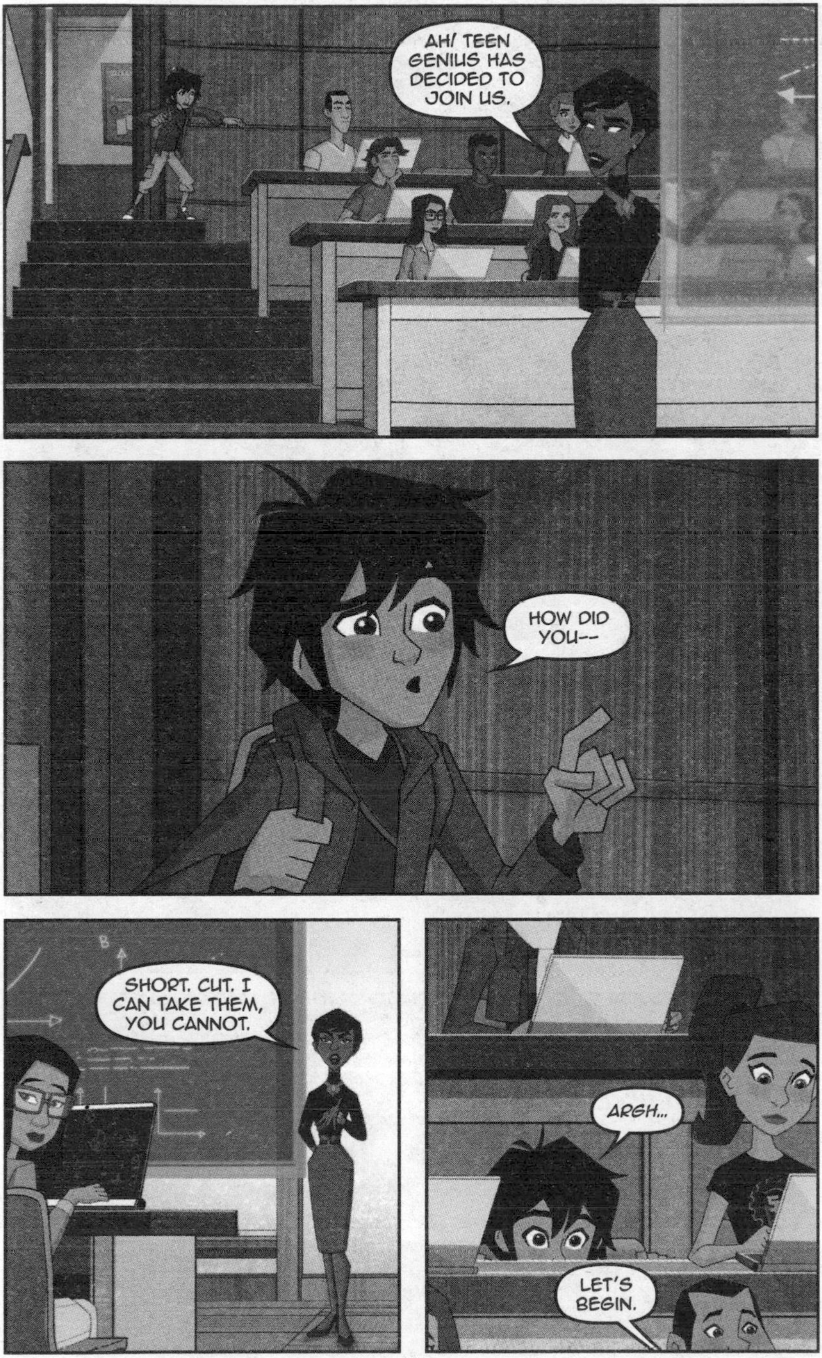
AH! TEEN GENIUS HAS DECIDED TO JOIN US.
HOW DID YOU--
SHORT. CUT. I CAN TAKE THEM, YOU CANNOT.
ARGH...
LET'S BEGIN.

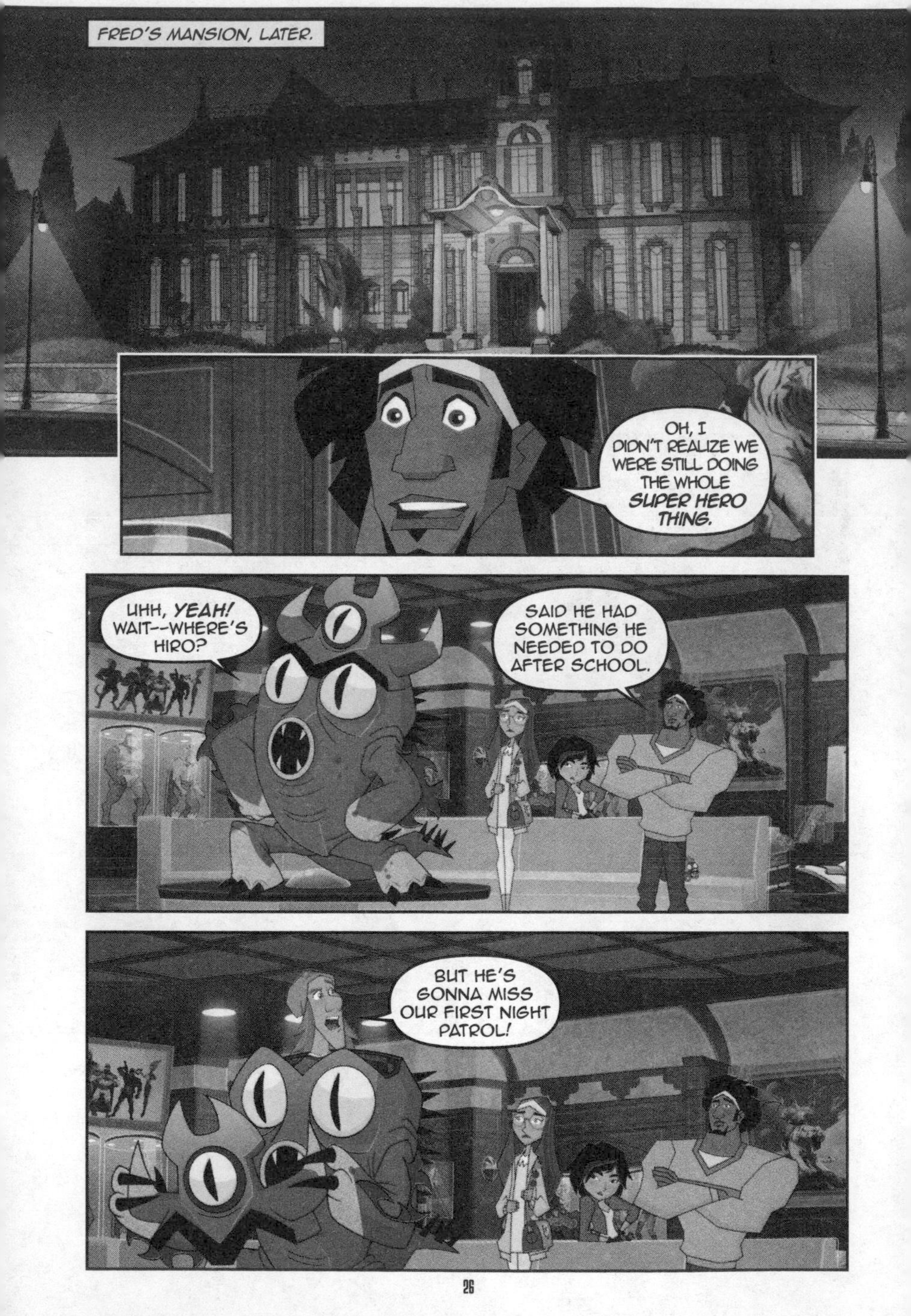
FRED'S MANSION, LATER.
OH, I DIDN'T REALIZE WE WERE STILL DOING THE WHOLE SUPER HERO THING.
UHH, YEAH! WAIT--WHERE'S HIRO?
SAID HE HAD SOMETHING HE NEEDED TO DO AFTER SCHOOL.
BUT HE'S GONNA MISS OUR FIRST NIGHT PATROL!

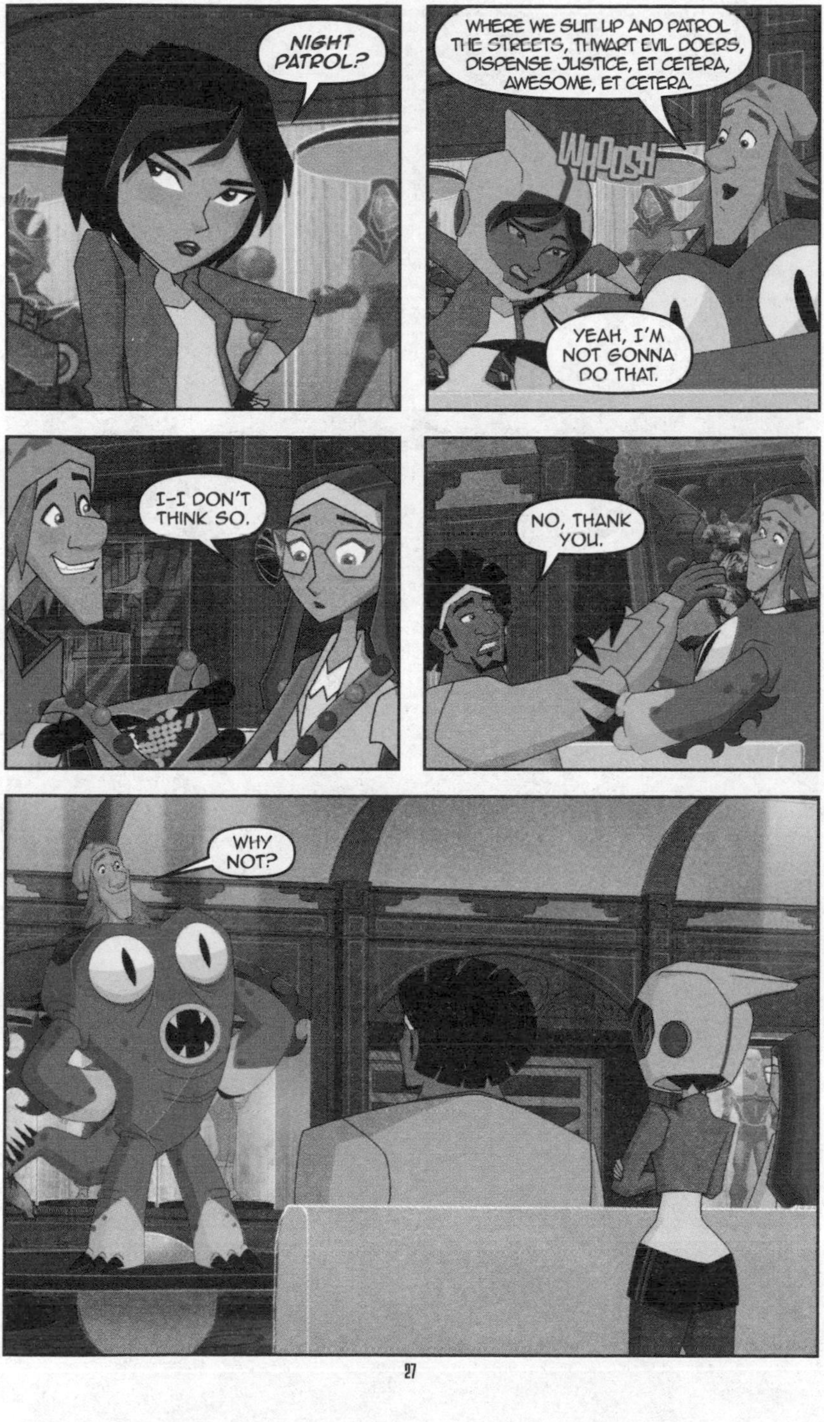
NIGHT PATROL?
WHERE WE SUIT UP AND PATROL THE STREETS, THWART EVIL DOERS, DISPENSE JUSTICE, ET CETERA, AWESOME, ET CETERA.
WHOOSH
YEAH, I'M NOT GONNA DO THAT.
I-I DON'T THINK SO.
NO, THANK YOU.
WHY NOT?

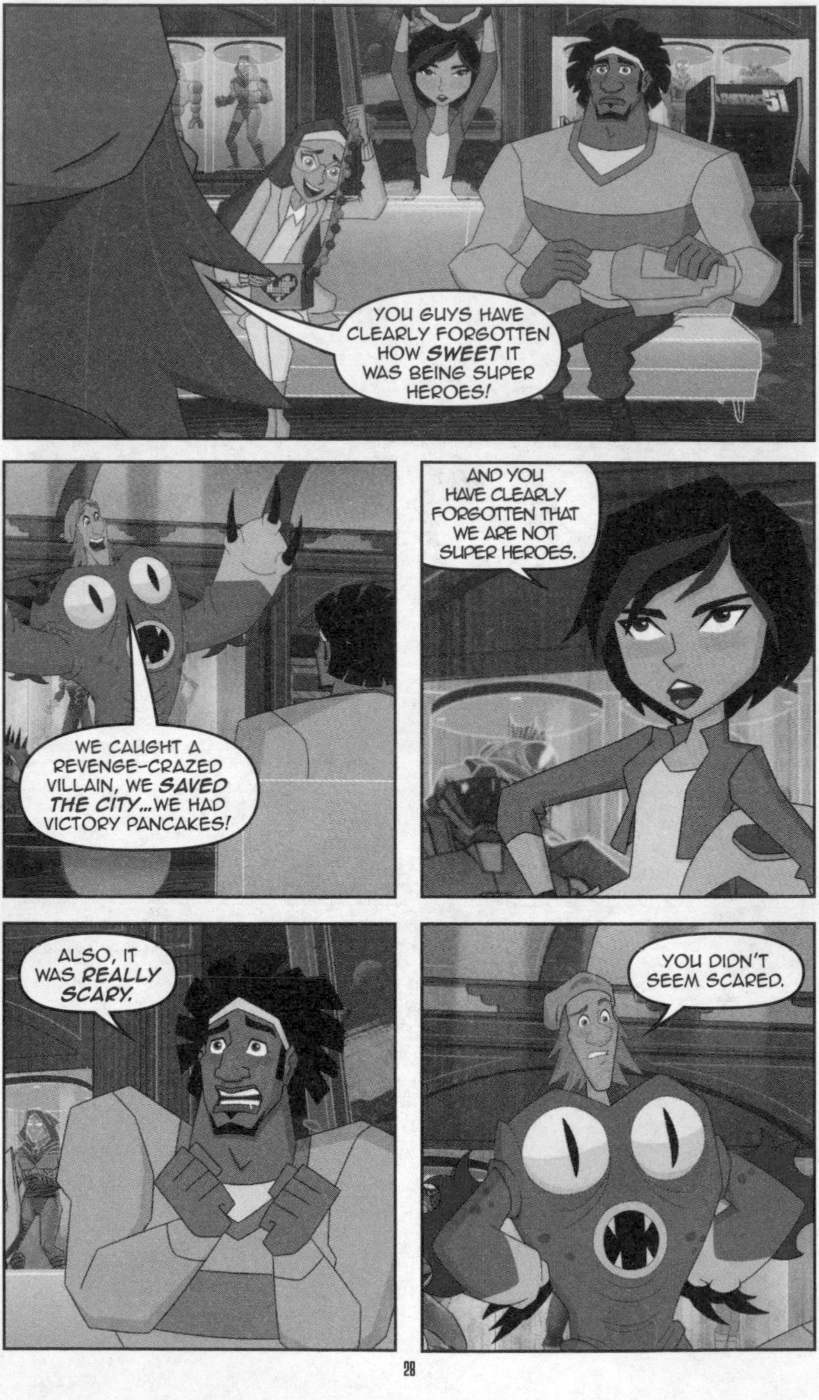

YOU GUYS HAVE CLEARLY FORGOTTEN HOW SWEET IT WAS BEING SUPER HEROES!
WE CAUGHT A REVENGE-CRAZED VILLAIN, WE SAVED THE CITY...WE HAD VICTORY PANCAKES!
AND YOU HAVE CLEARLY FORGOTTEN THAT WE ARE NOT SUPER HEROES.
ALSO, IT WAS REALLY SCARY.
YOU DIDN'T SEEM SCARED.

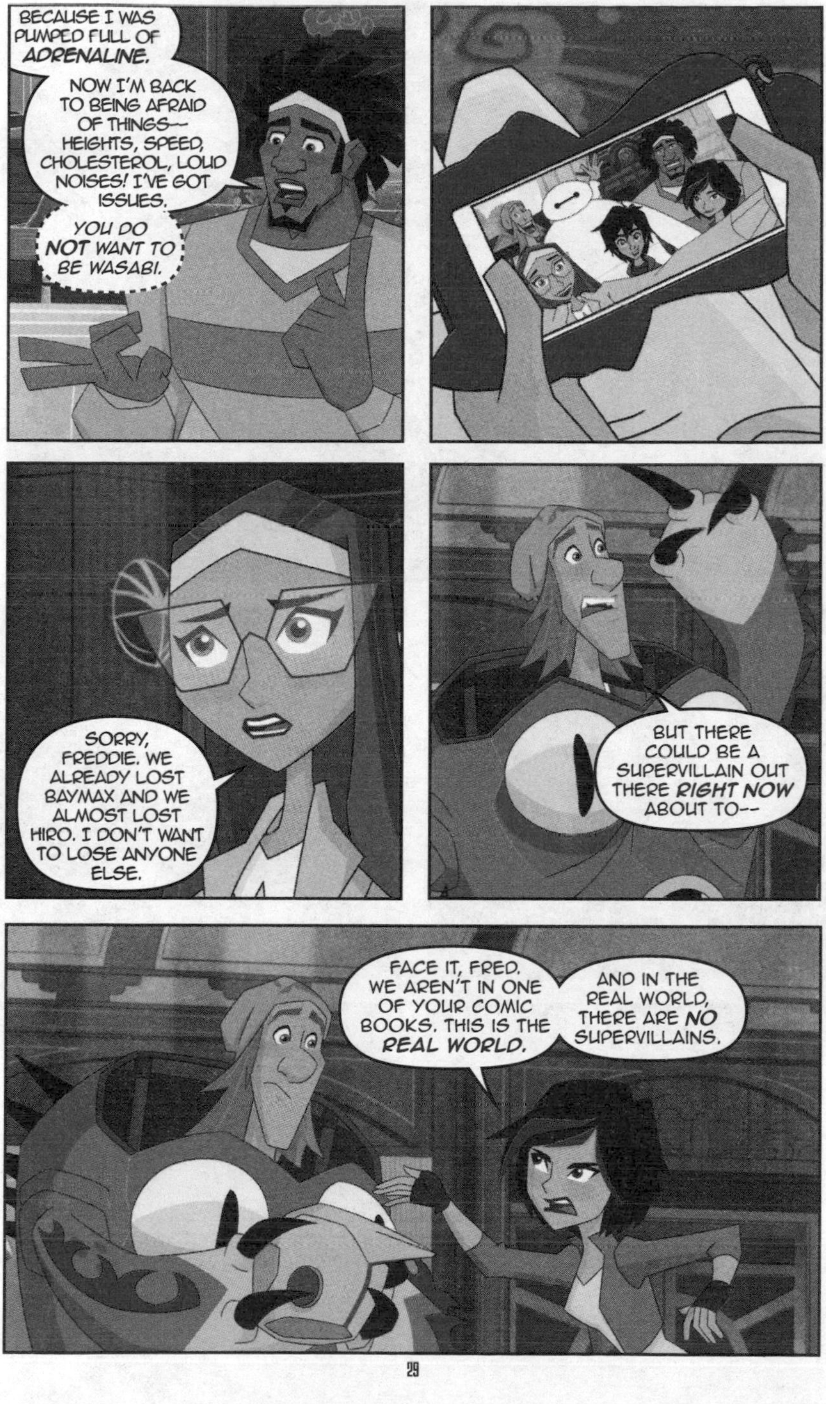

BECAUSE I WAS PUMPED FULL OF ***ADRENALINE.***
NOW I'M BACK TO BEING AFRAID OF THINGS-- HEIGHTS, SPEED, CHOLESTEROL, LOUD NOISES! I'VE GOT ISSUES.
*YOU DO **NOT** WANT TO BE WASABI.*
SORRY, FREDDIE. WE ALREADY LOST BAYMAX AND WE ALMOST LOST HIRO. I DON'T WANT TO LOSE ANYONE ELSE.
BUT THERE COULD BE A SUPERVILLAIN OUT THERE ***RIGHT NOW*** ABOUT TO--
FACE IT, FRED. WE AREN'T IN ONE OF YOUR COMIC BOOKS. THIS IS THE ***REAL WORLD.***
AND IN THE REAL WORLD, THERE ARE ***NO*** SUPERVILLAINS.

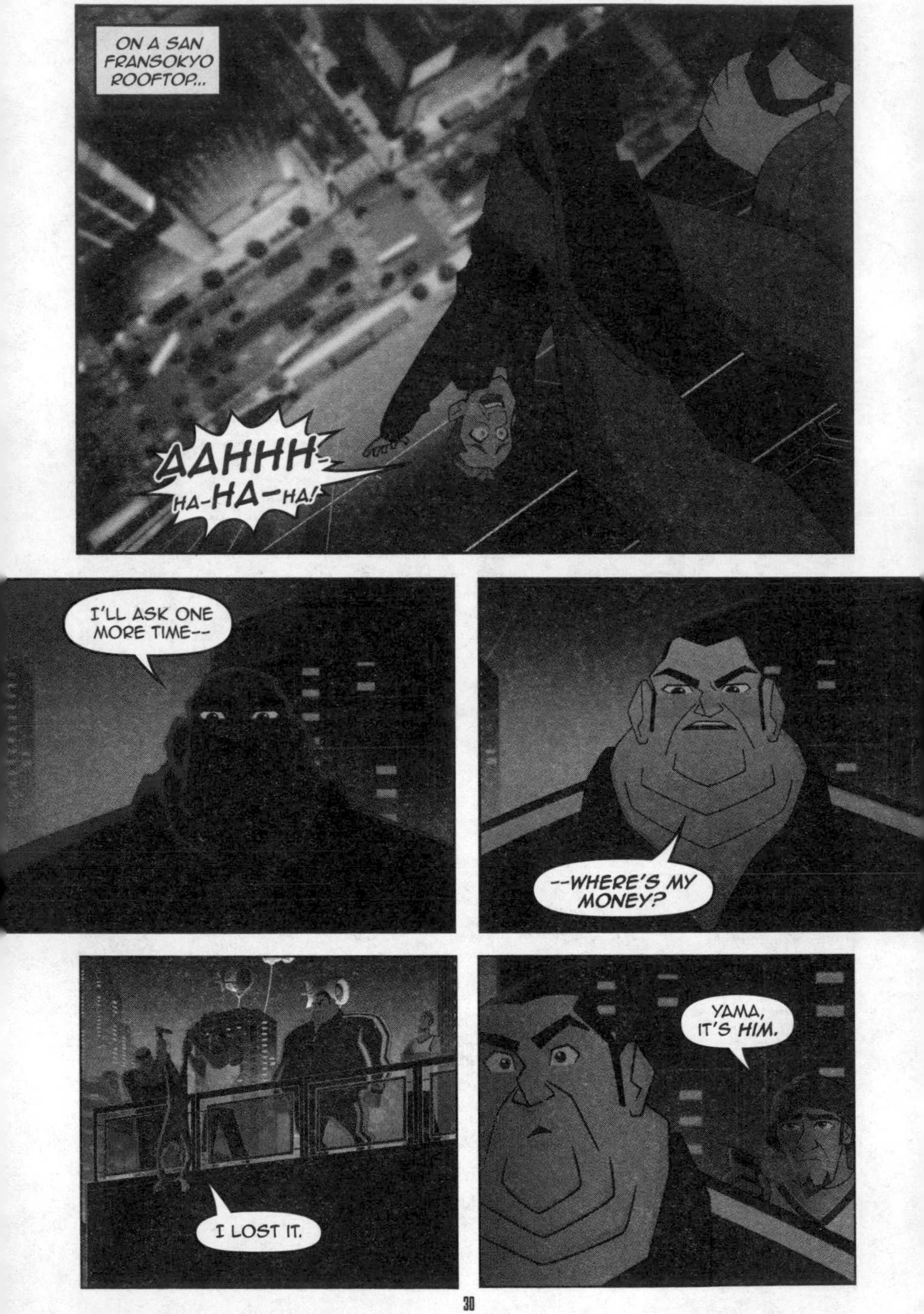
ON A SAN FRANSOKYO ROOFTOP...
AAHHH-HA-HA-HA!
I'LL ASK ONE MORE TIME--
--WHERE'S MY MONEY?
I LOST IT.
YAMA, IT'S HIM.

OBAKE. MMM.

WHATEVER YOU NEED.

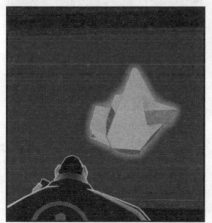

AND WHERE IS IT?

DONE.

SAN FRANSOKYO INSTITUTE OF TECHNOLOGY.

MADA

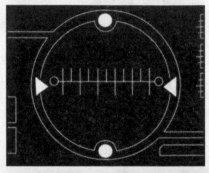

PLEASE WORK, PLEASE WORK...

HELLO, HIRO.

BAYMAX!

YEAH...HUGS, NOT REALLY--WE'LL HAVE TO STICK WITH THIS FOR NOW, BUDDY.

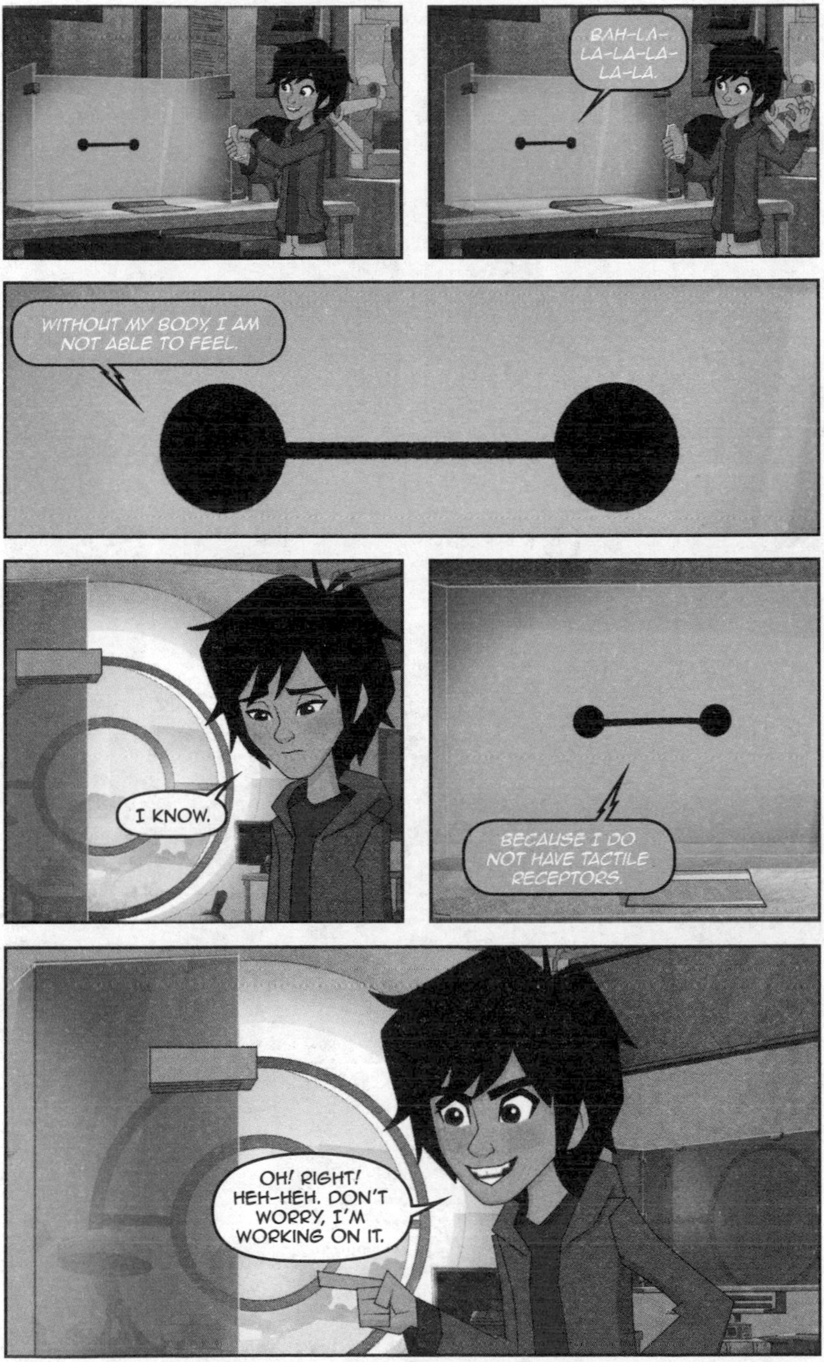
BAH-LA-LA-LA-LA-LA-LA-LA.
WITHOUT MY BODY, I AM NOT ABLE TO FEEL.
I KNOW.
BECAUSE I DO NOT HAVE TACTILE RECEPTORS.
OH! RIGHT! HEH-HEH. DON'T WORRY, I'M WORKING ON IT.

WHRRRRR

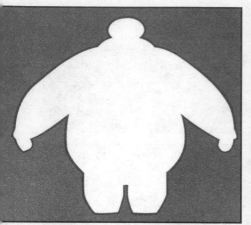

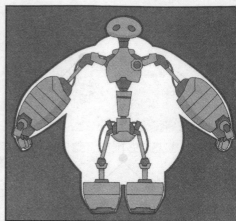

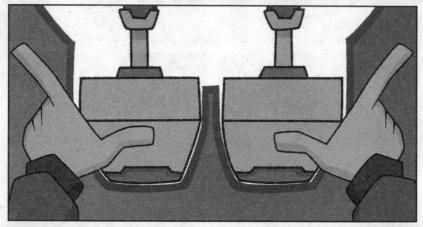

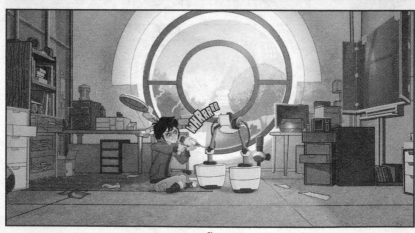

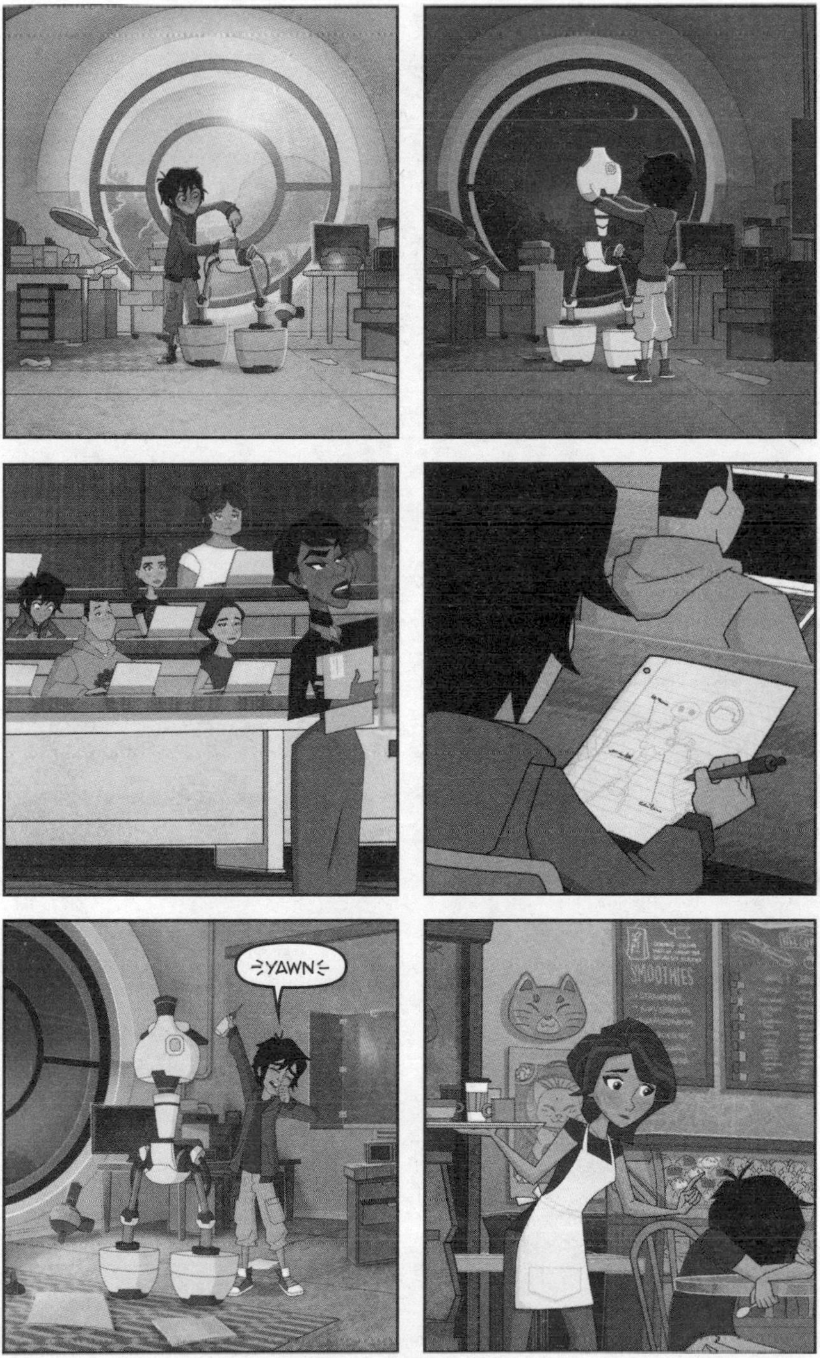
YAWN
SMOOTHIES

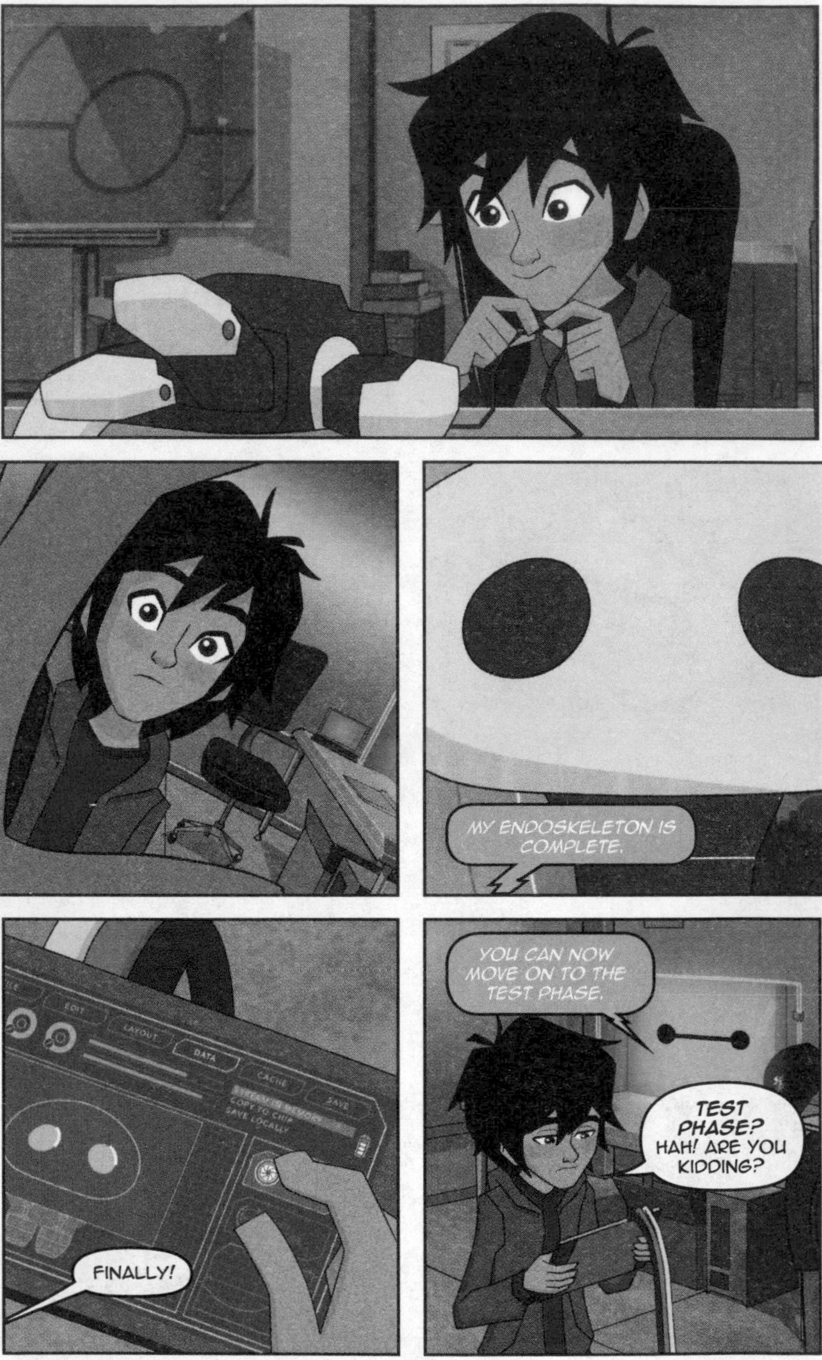
MY ENDOSKELETON IS COMPLETE.
EDIT
LAYOUT
DATA
CACHE
SAVE
COPY TO CHIP
SAVE LOCALLY
FINALLY!
YOU CAN NOW MOVE ON TO THE TEST PHASE.
TEST PHASE? HAH! ARE YOU KIDDING?

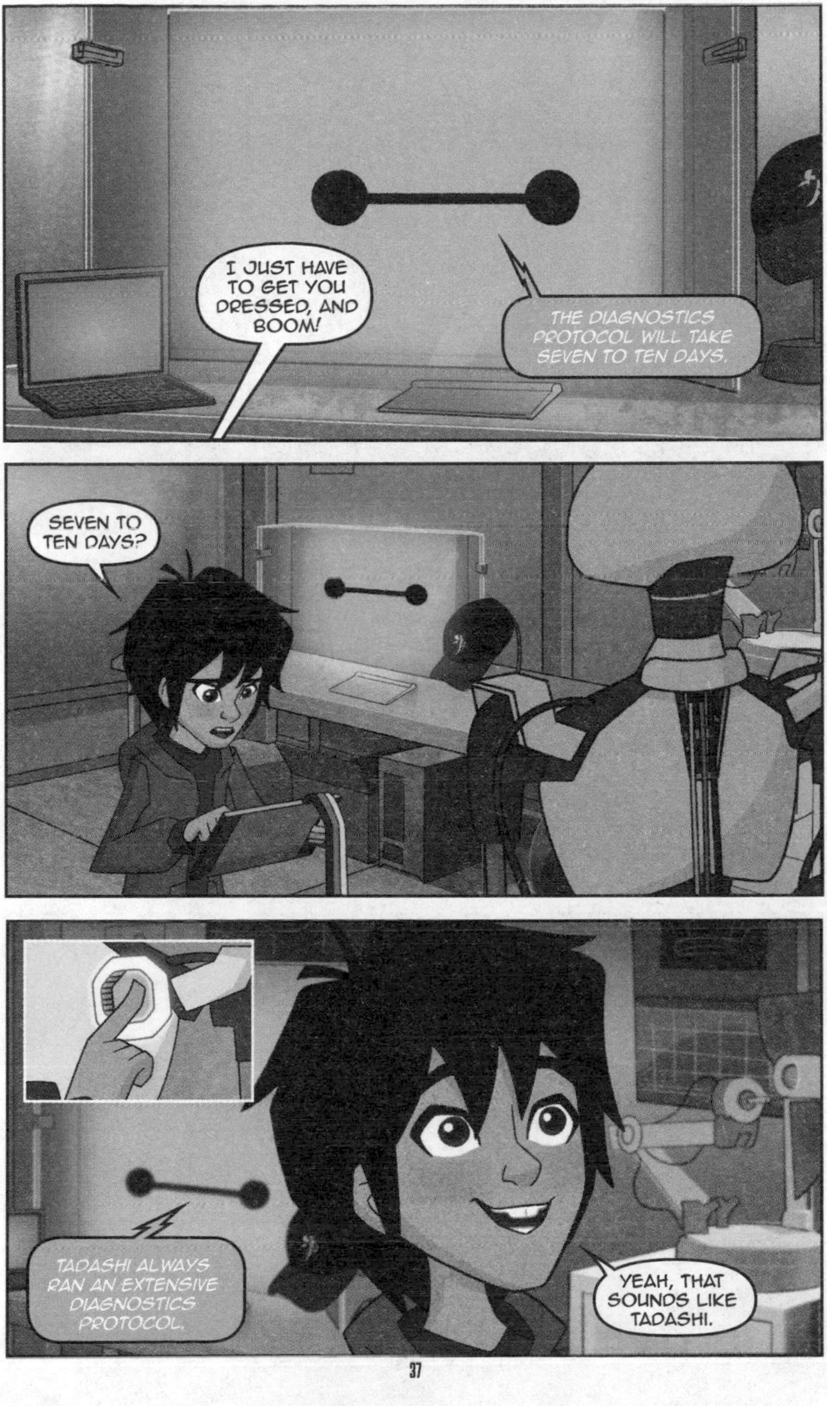
I JUST HAVE TO GET YOU DRESSED, AND BOOM!
THE DIAGNOSTICS PROTOCOL WILL TAKE SEVEN TO TEN DAYS.
SEVEN TO TEN DAYS?
TADASHI ALWAYS RAN AN EXTENSIVE DIAGNOSTICS PROTOCOL.
YEAH, THAT SOUNDS LIKE TADASHI.

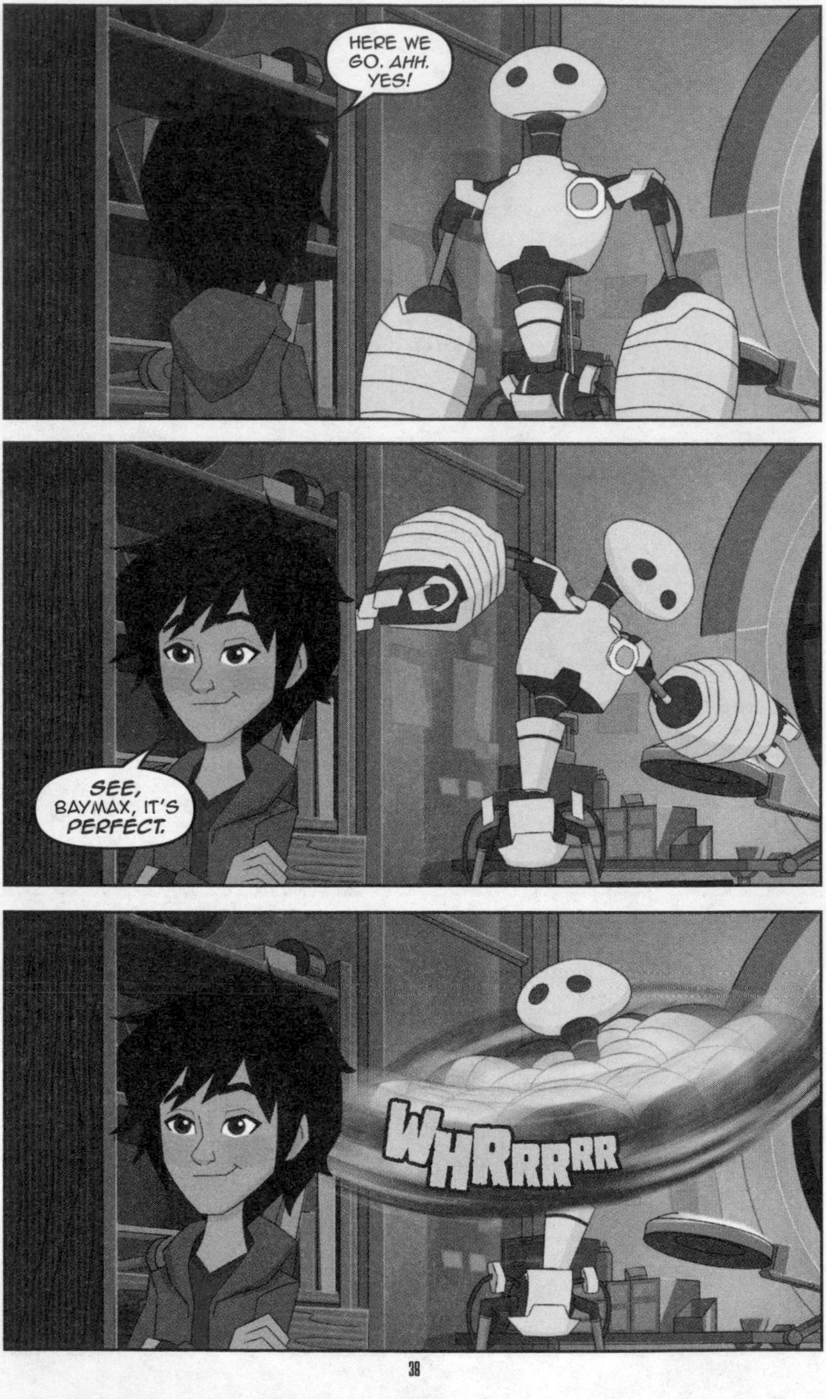
HERE WE GO. AHH. YES!
SEE, BAYMAX, IT'S PERFECT.
WHRRRRR

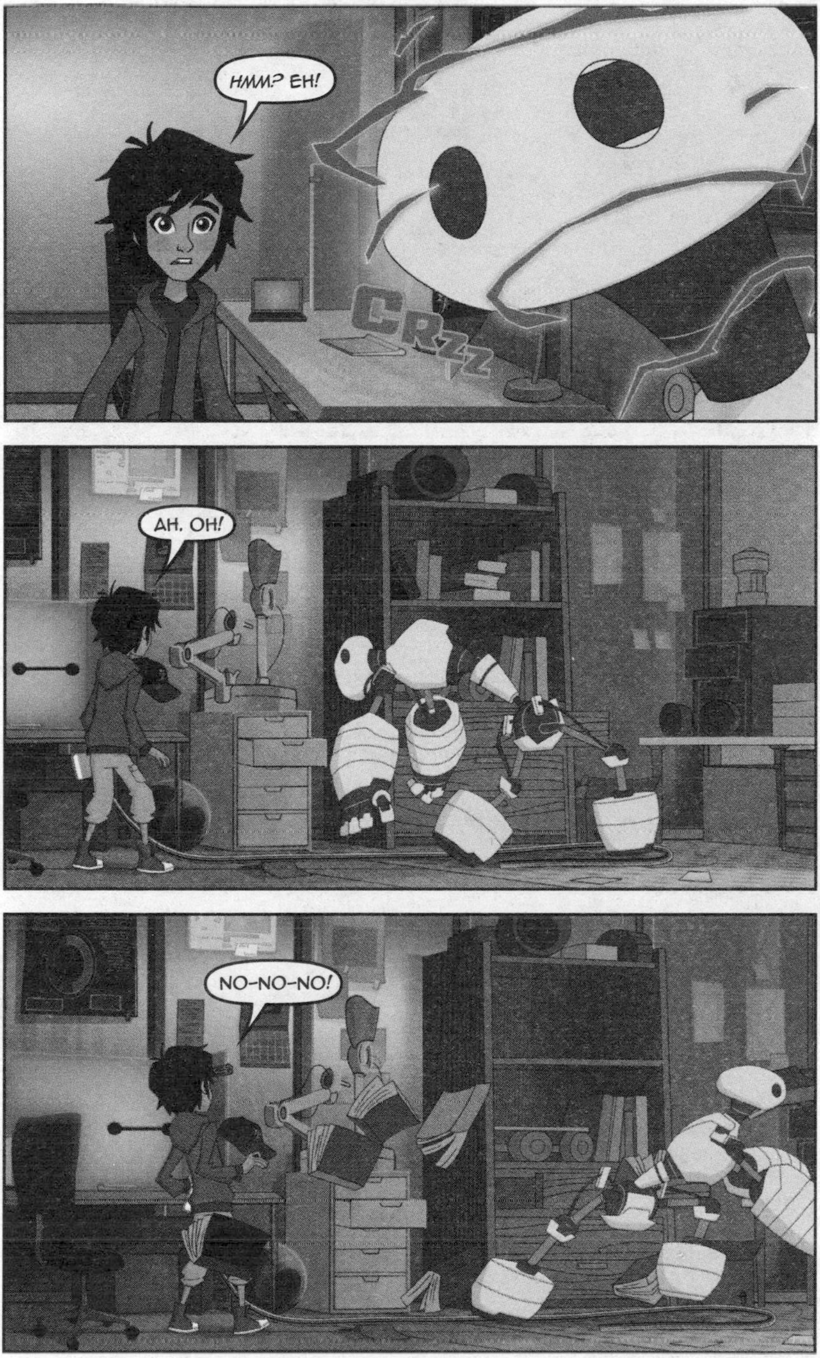
HMM? EH!
CRZZ
AH, OH!
NO-NO-NO!

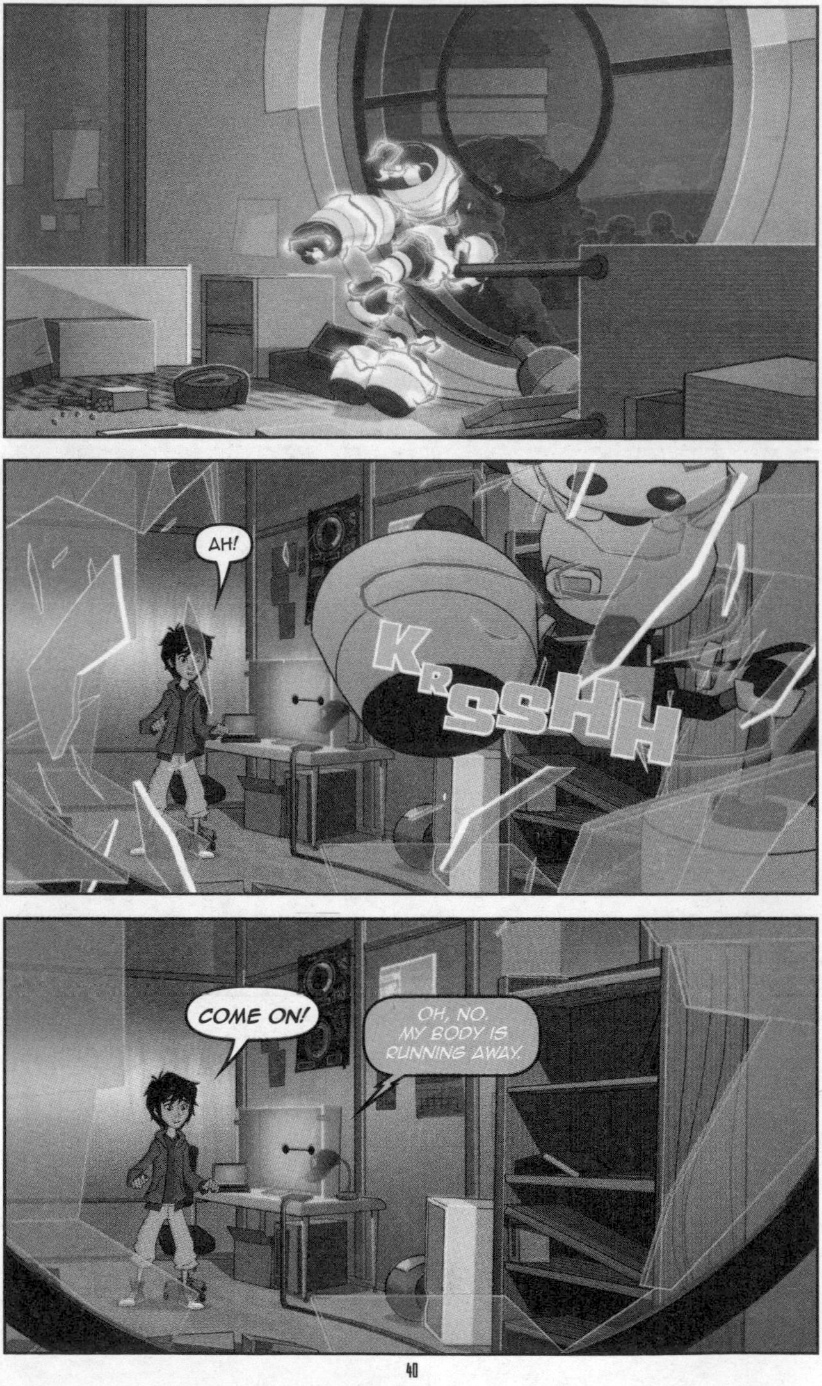
AH!
KRSSHH
COME ON!
OH, NO.
MY BODY IS
RUNNING AWAY.

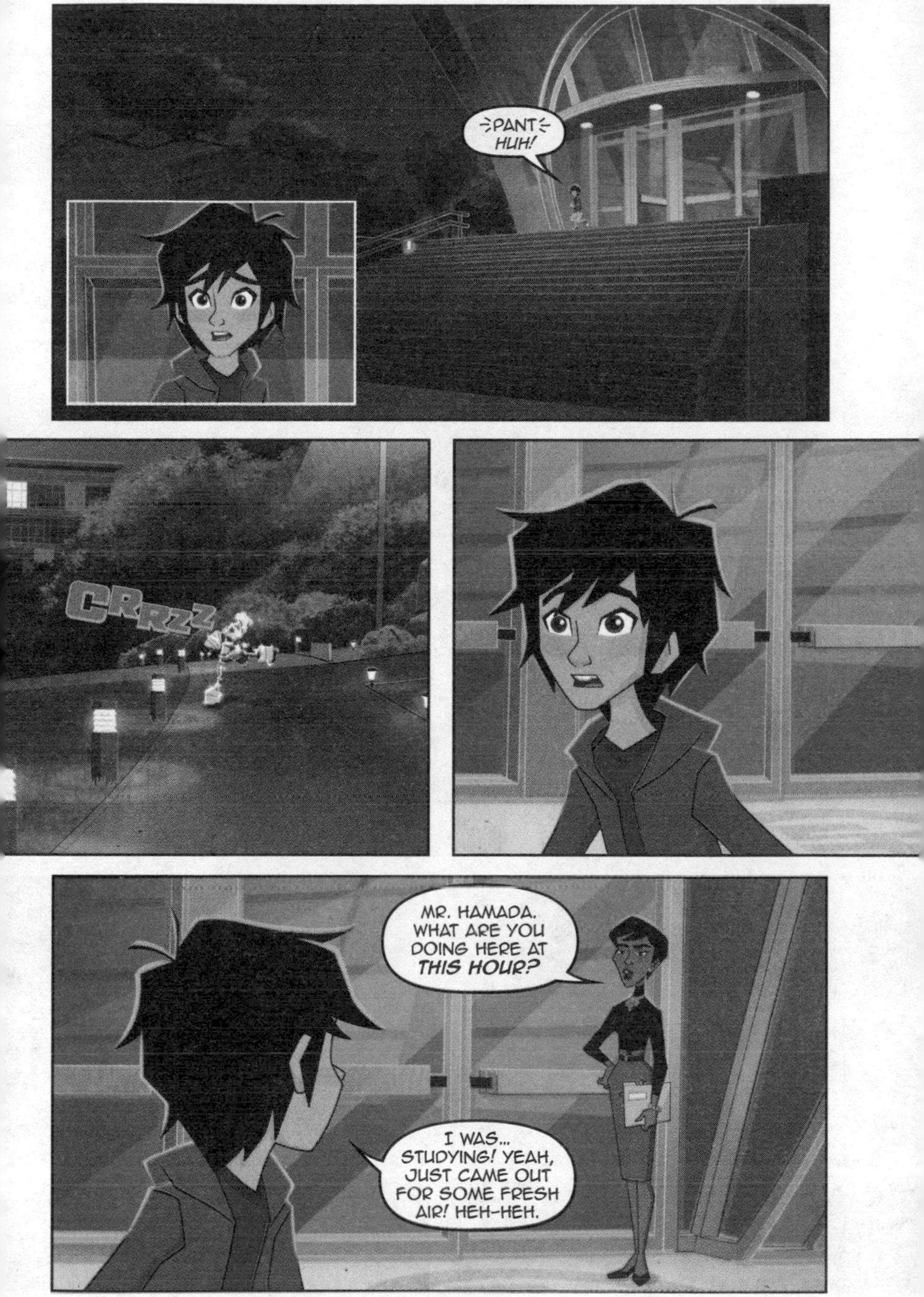
PANT HUH!
CRRZZ
MR. HAMADA. WHAT ARE YOU DOING HERE AT THIS HOUR?
I WAS... STUDYING! YEAH, JUST CAME OUT FOR SOME FRESH AIR! HEH-HEH.

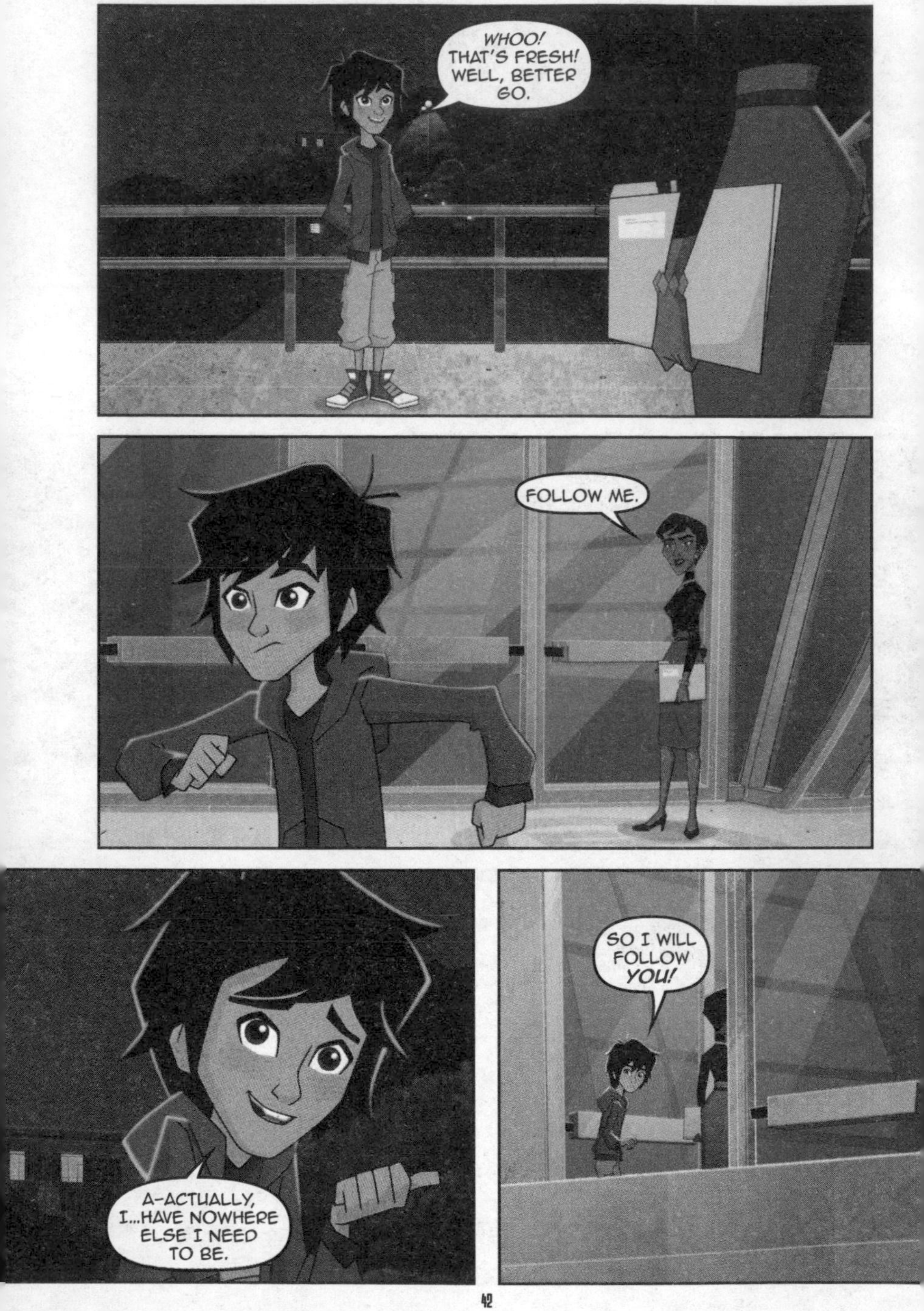
WHOO! THAT'S FRESH! WELL, BETTER GO.
FOLLOW ME.
A-ACTUALLY, I...HAVE NOWHERE ELSE I NEED TO BE.
SO I WILL FOLLOW YOU!

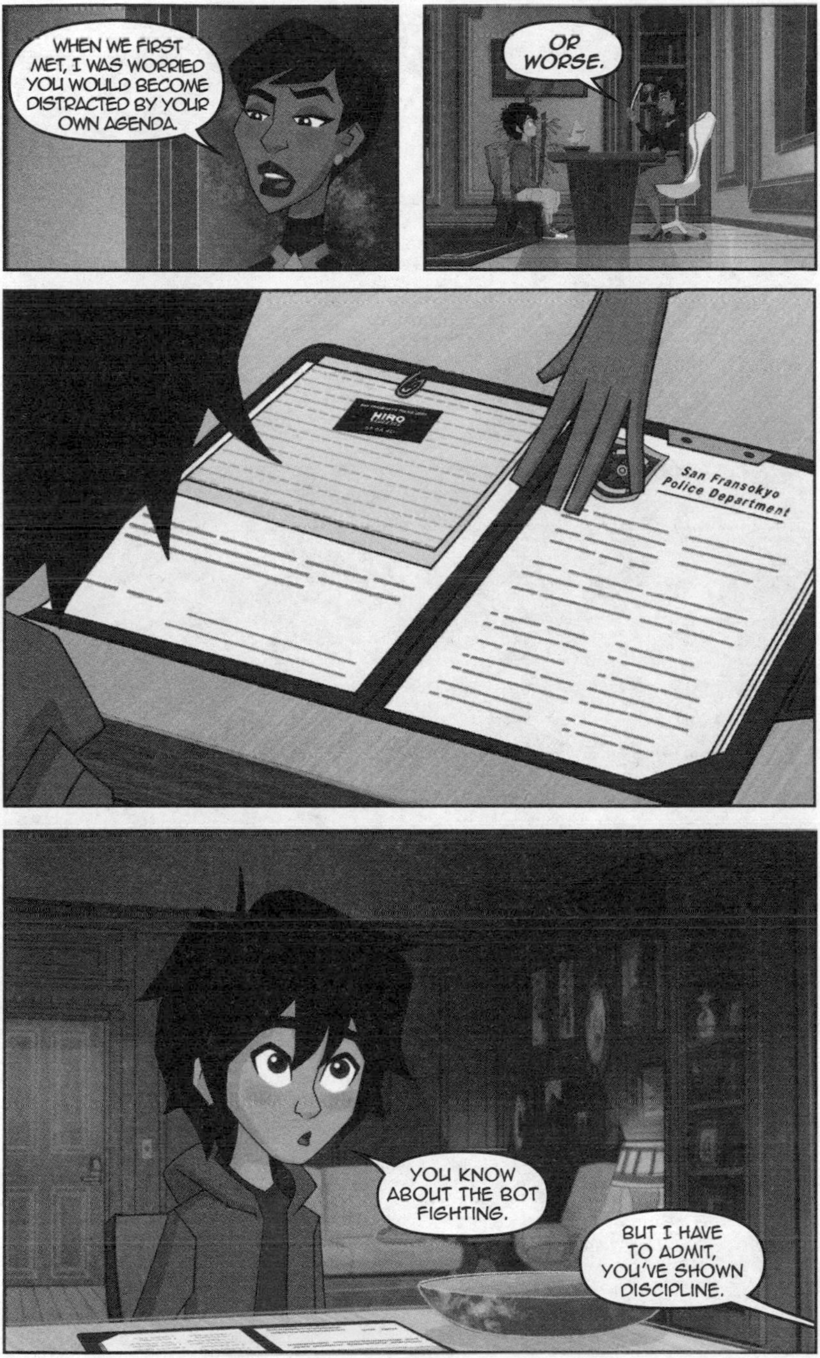
WHEN WE FIRST MET, I WAS WORRIED YOU WOULD BECOME DISTRACTED BY YOUR OWN AGENDA.
OR WORSE.
HIRO
San Fransokyo Police Department
YOU KNOW ABOUT THE BOT FIGHTING.
BUT I HAVE TO ADMIT, YOU'VE SHOWN DISCIPLINE.

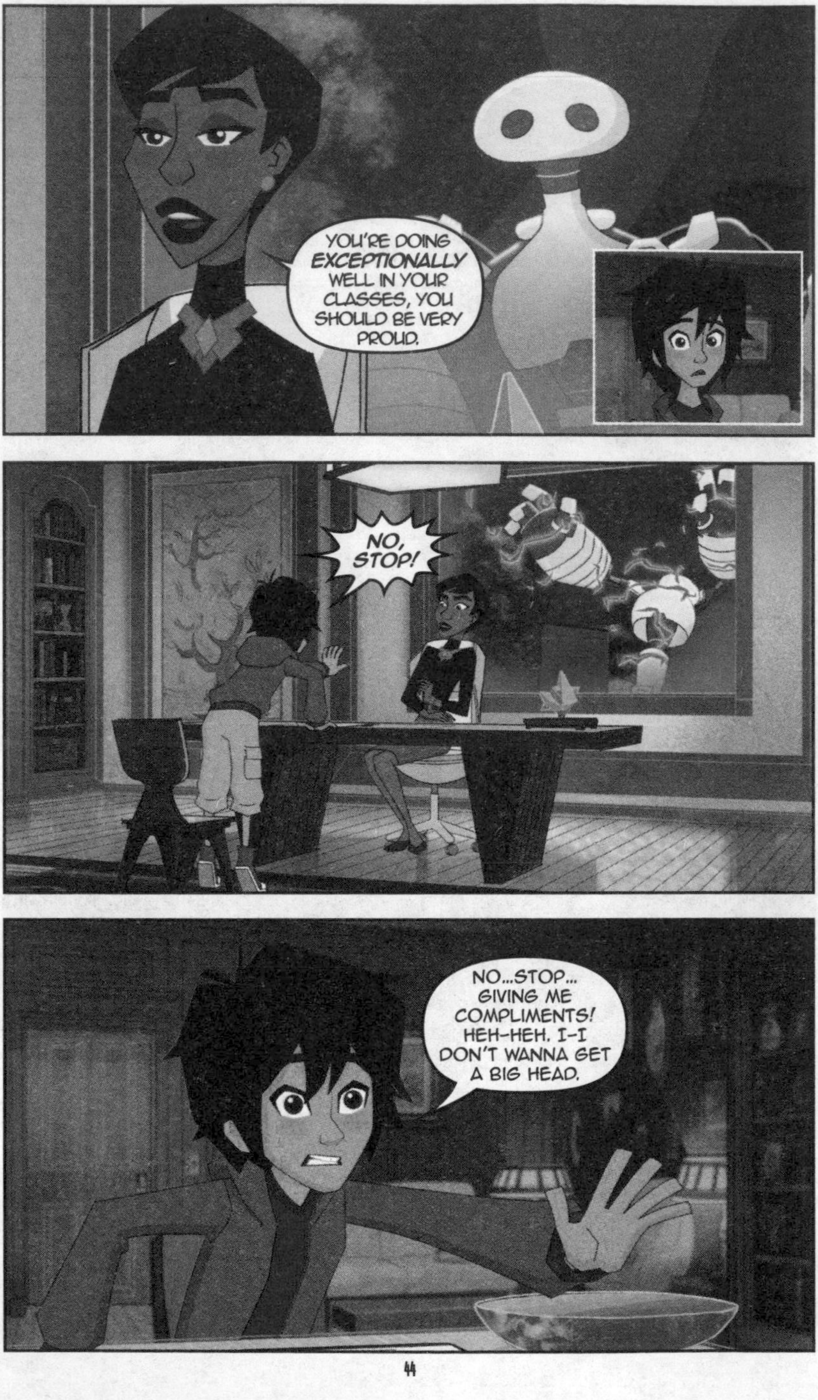
YOU'RE DOING EXCEPTIONALLY WELL IN YOUR CLASSES, YOU SHOULD BE VERY PROUD.
NO, STOP!
NO...STOP... GIVING ME COMPLIMENTS! HEH-HEH. I-I DON'T WANNA GET A BIG HEAD.

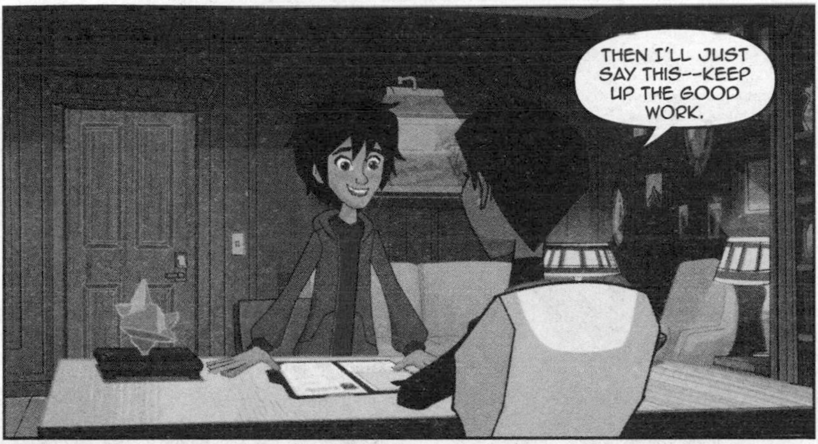
THEN I'LL JUST SAY THIS--KEEP UP THE GOOD WORK.

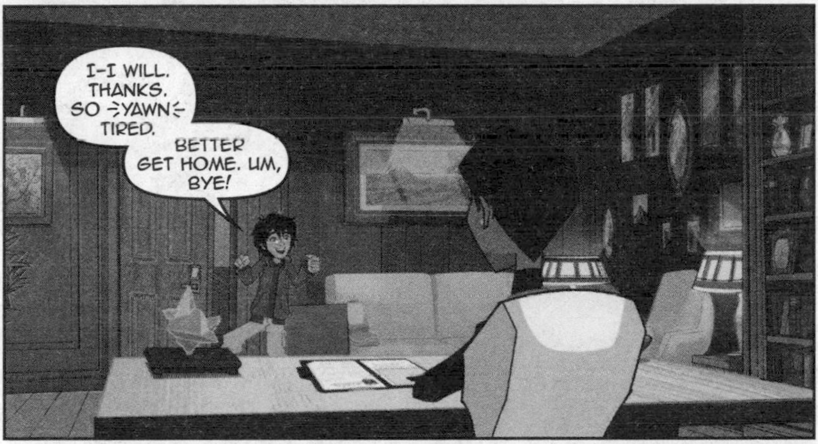
I-I WILL. THANKS. SO ⇛YAWN⇚ TIRED.
BETTER GET HOME. UM, BYE!

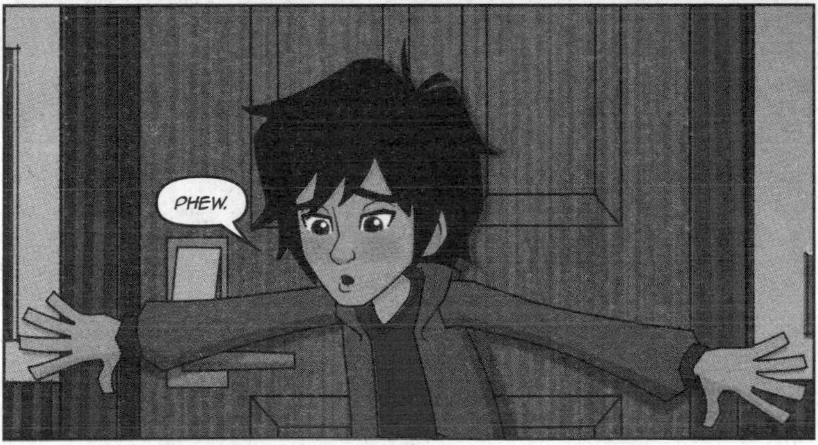
PHEW.

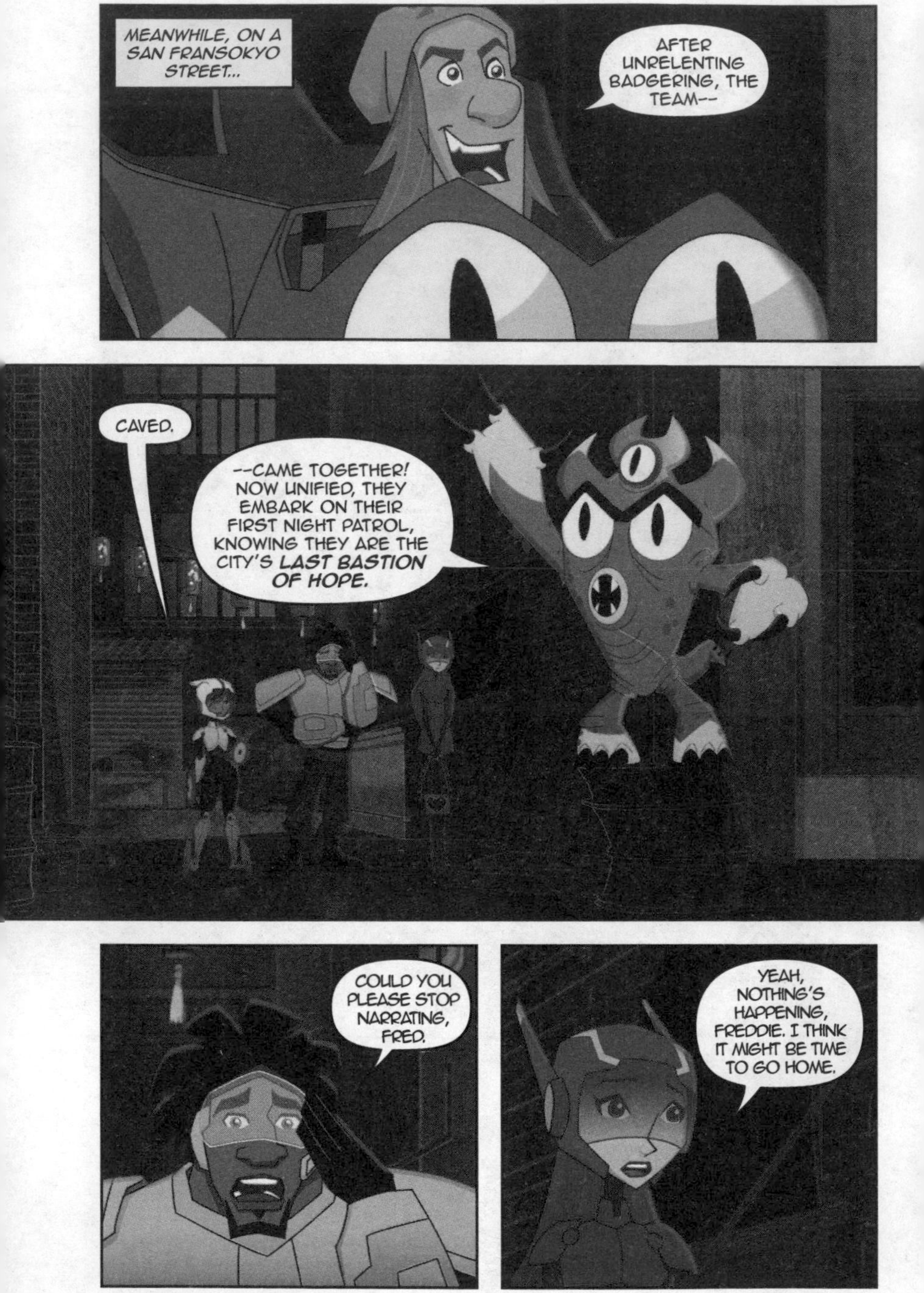
MEANWHILE, ON A SAN FRANSOKYO STREET...
AFTER UNRELENTING BADGERING, THE TEAM--
CAVED.
--CAME TOGETHER! NOW UNIFIED, THEY EMBARK ON THEIR FIRST NIGHT PATROL, KNOWING THEY ARE THE CITY'S *LAST BASTION OF HOPE.*
COULD YOU PLEASE STOP NARRATING, FRED.
YEAH, NOTHING'S HAPPENING, FREDDIE. I THINK IT MIGHT BE TIME TO GO HOME.

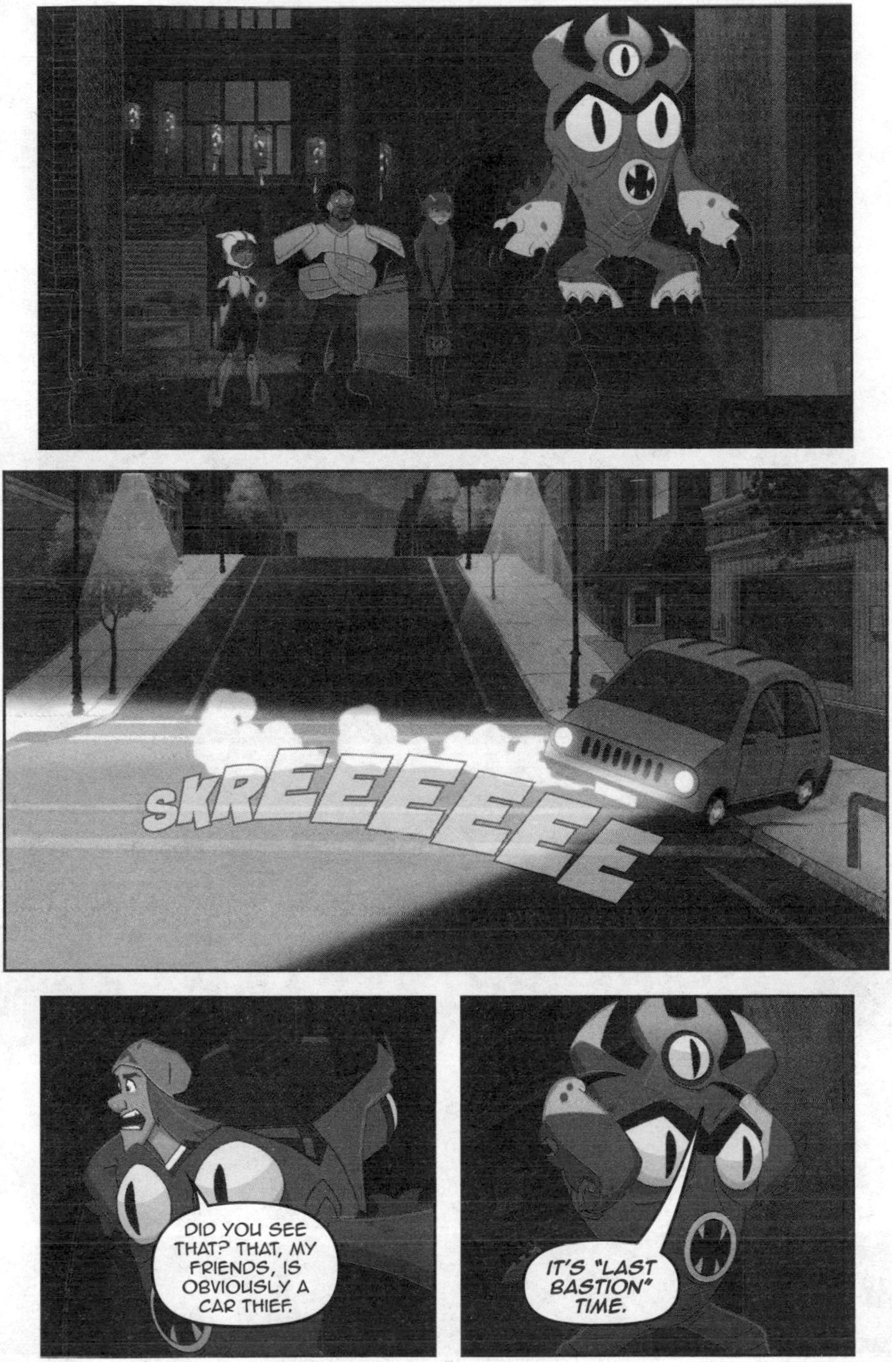
SKREEEEEEEE
DID YOU SEE THAT? THAT, MY FRIENDS, IS OBVIOUSLY A CAR THIEF.
IT'S "LAST BASTION" TIME.

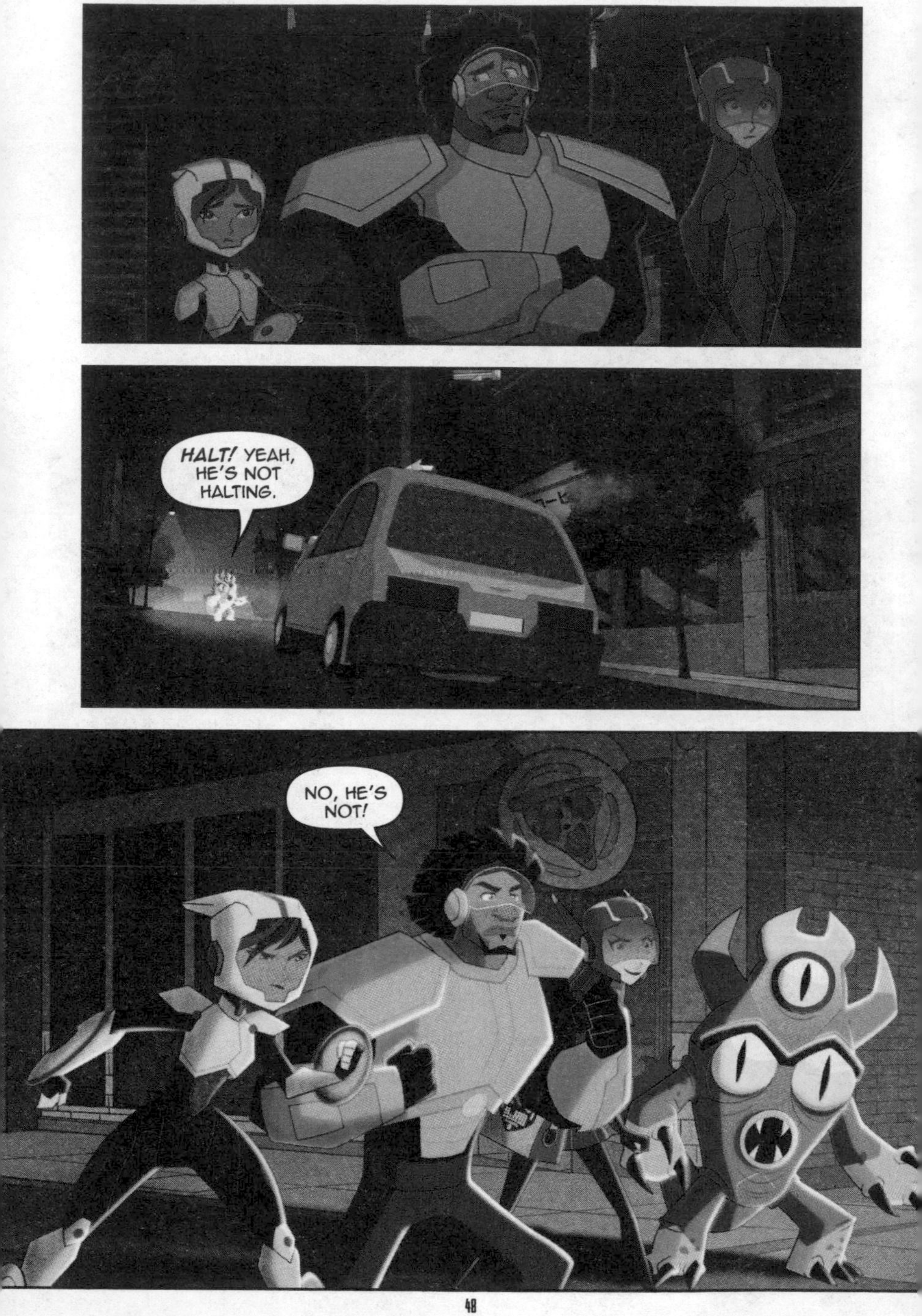
HALT! YEAH, HE'S NOT HALTING.
NO, HE'S NOT!

AAUGH! AHH!
UGH.
THUNK
STOP
MUG

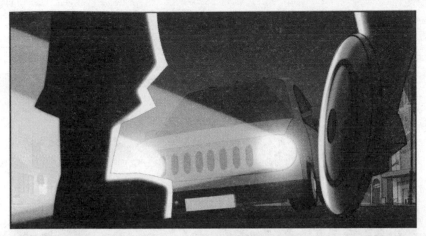

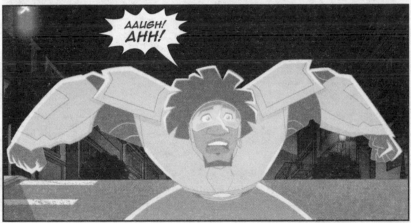

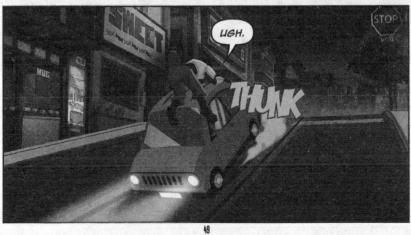

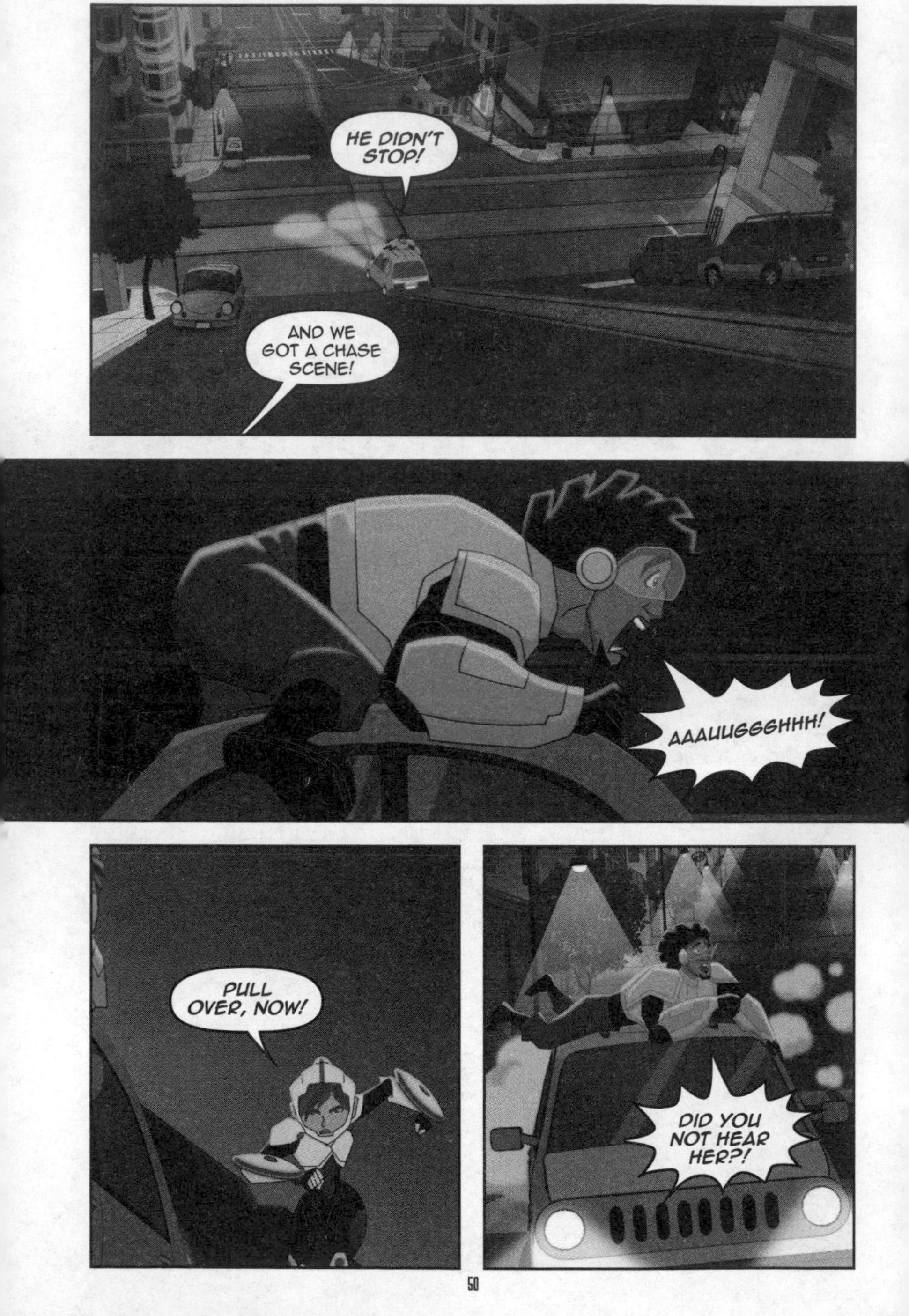
HE DIDN'T STOP!
AND WE GOT A CHASE SCENE!
AAAUUGGGHHH!
PULL OVER, NOW!
DID YOU NOT HEAR HER?!

WE'RE GONNA NEED SOMETHING TO SLOW HIM DOWN.

I HAVE JUST THE THING.

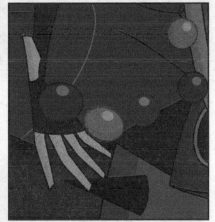

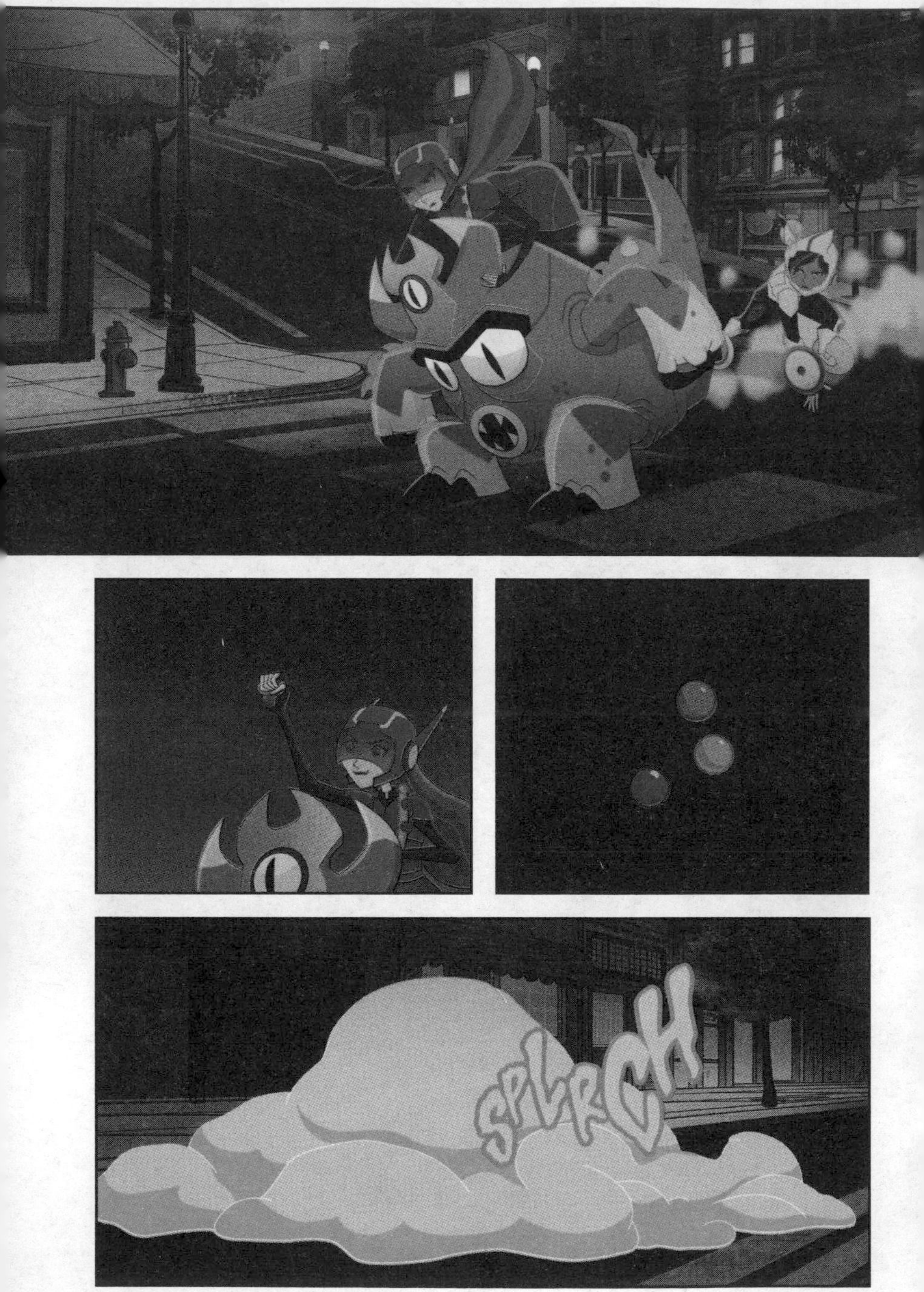
SPLRCH

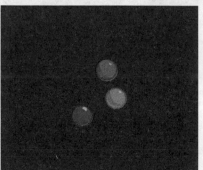

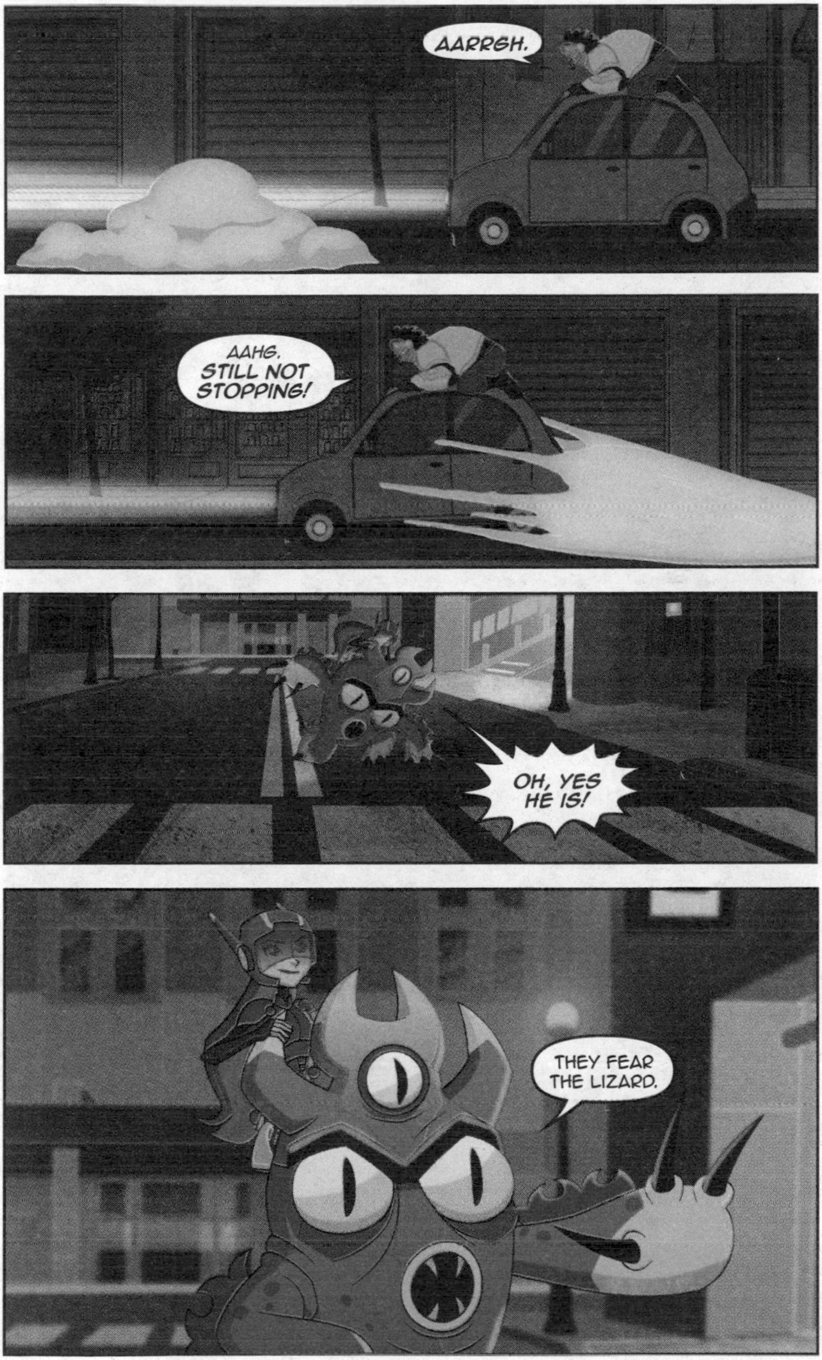
AARRGH.
AAHG. STILL NOT STOPPING!
OH, YES HE IS!
THEY FEAR THE LIZARD.

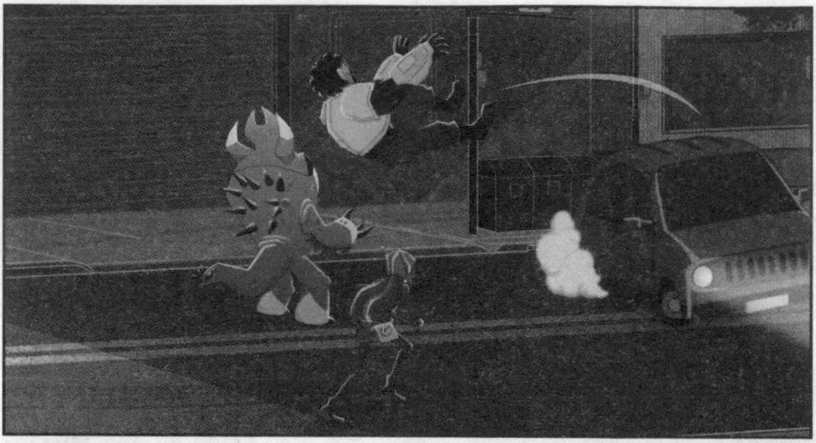

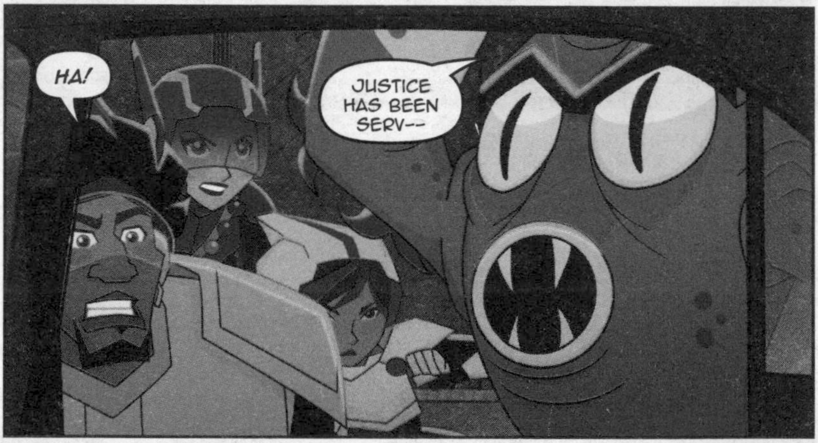
HA!
JUSTICE HAS BEEN SERV--

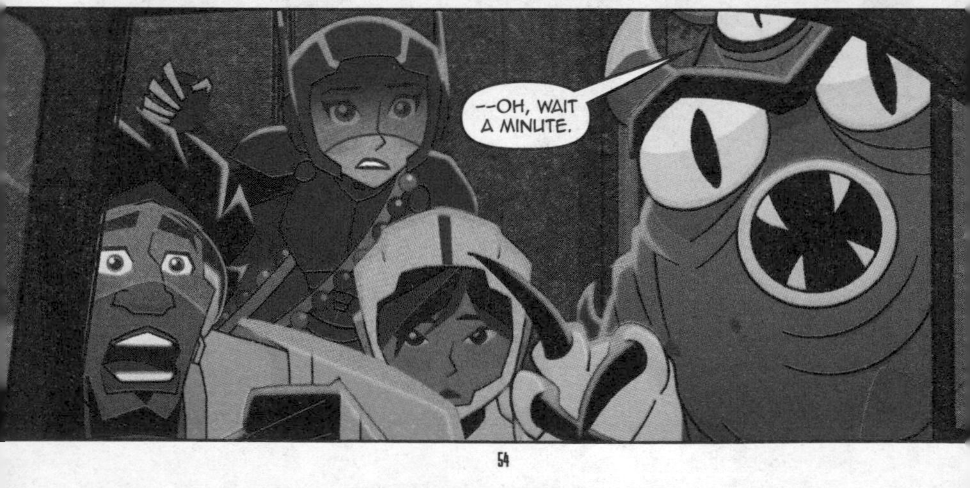
--OH, WAIT A MINUTE.

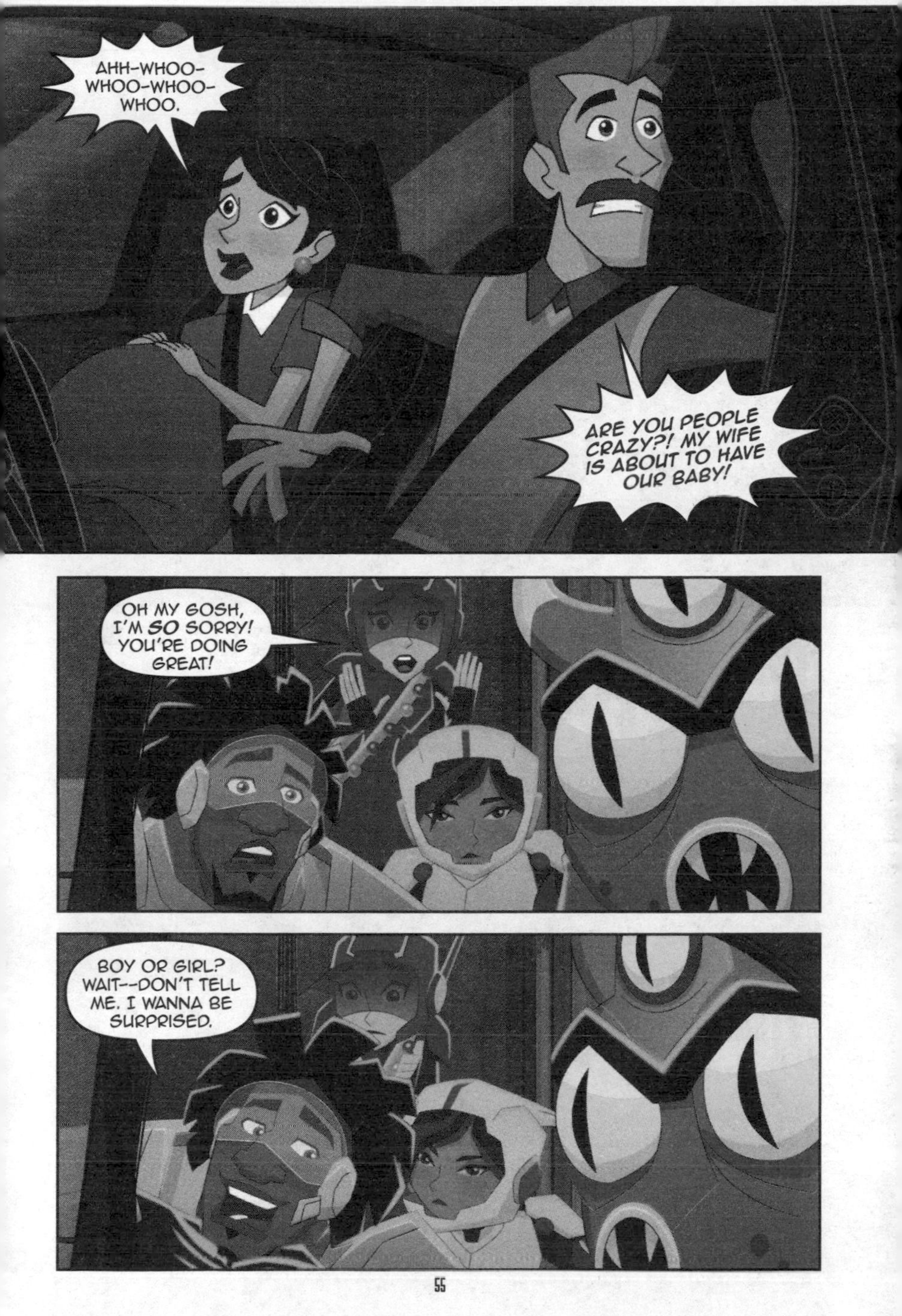
AHH-WHOO-WHOO-WHOO-WHOO.
ARE YOU PEOPLE CRAZY?! MY WIFE IS ABOUT TO HAVE OUR BABY!
OH MY GOSH, I'M *SO* SORRY! YOU'RE DOING GREAT!
BOY OR GIRL? WAIT--DON'T TELL ME. I WANNA BE SURPRISED.

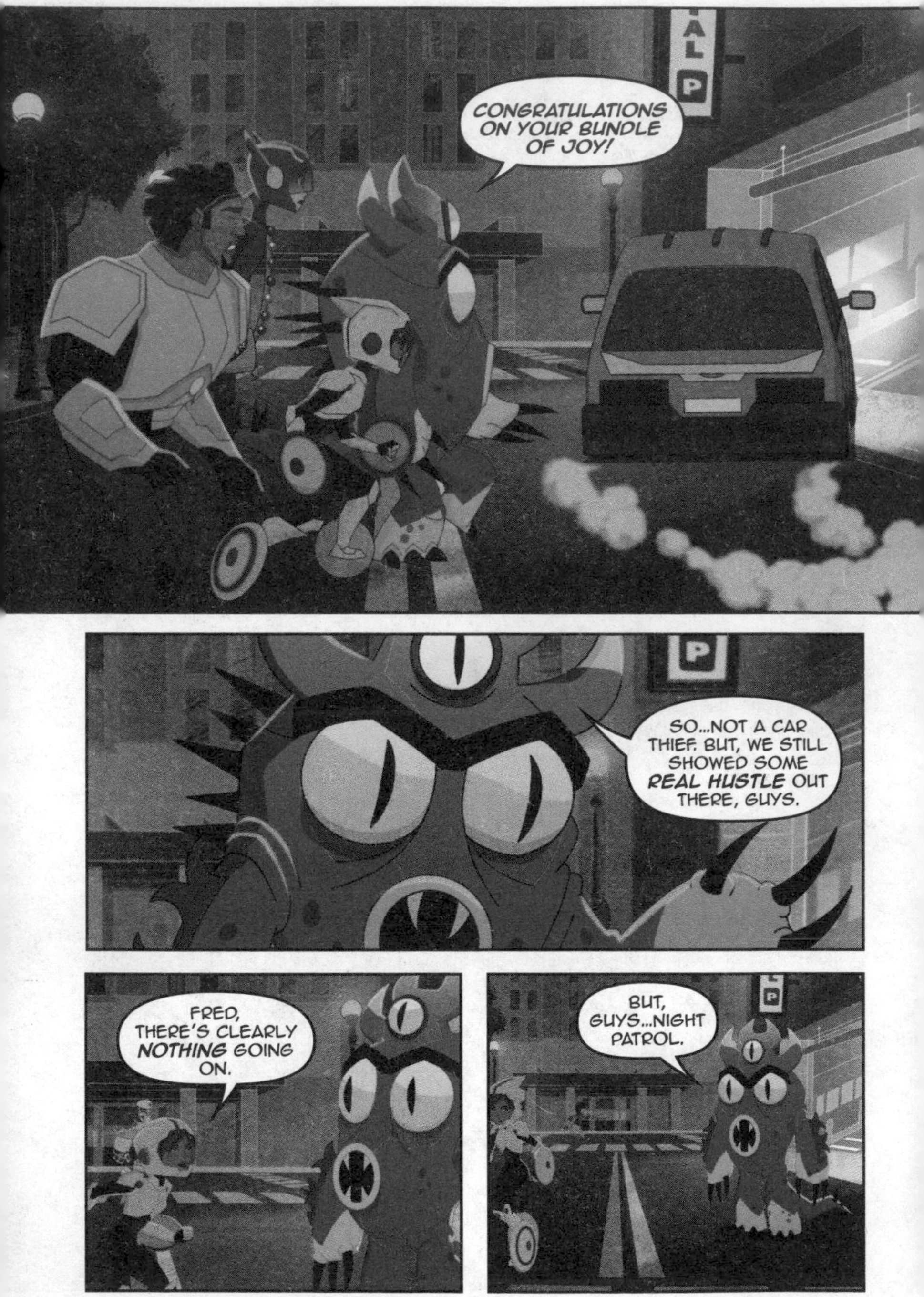
CONGRATULATIONS ON YOUR BUNDLE OF JOY!
SO...NOT A CAR THIEF. BUT, WE STILL SHOWED SOME REAL HUSTLE OUT THERE, GUYS.
FRED, THERE'S CLEARLY NOTHING GOING ON.
BUT, GUYS...NIGHT PATROL.

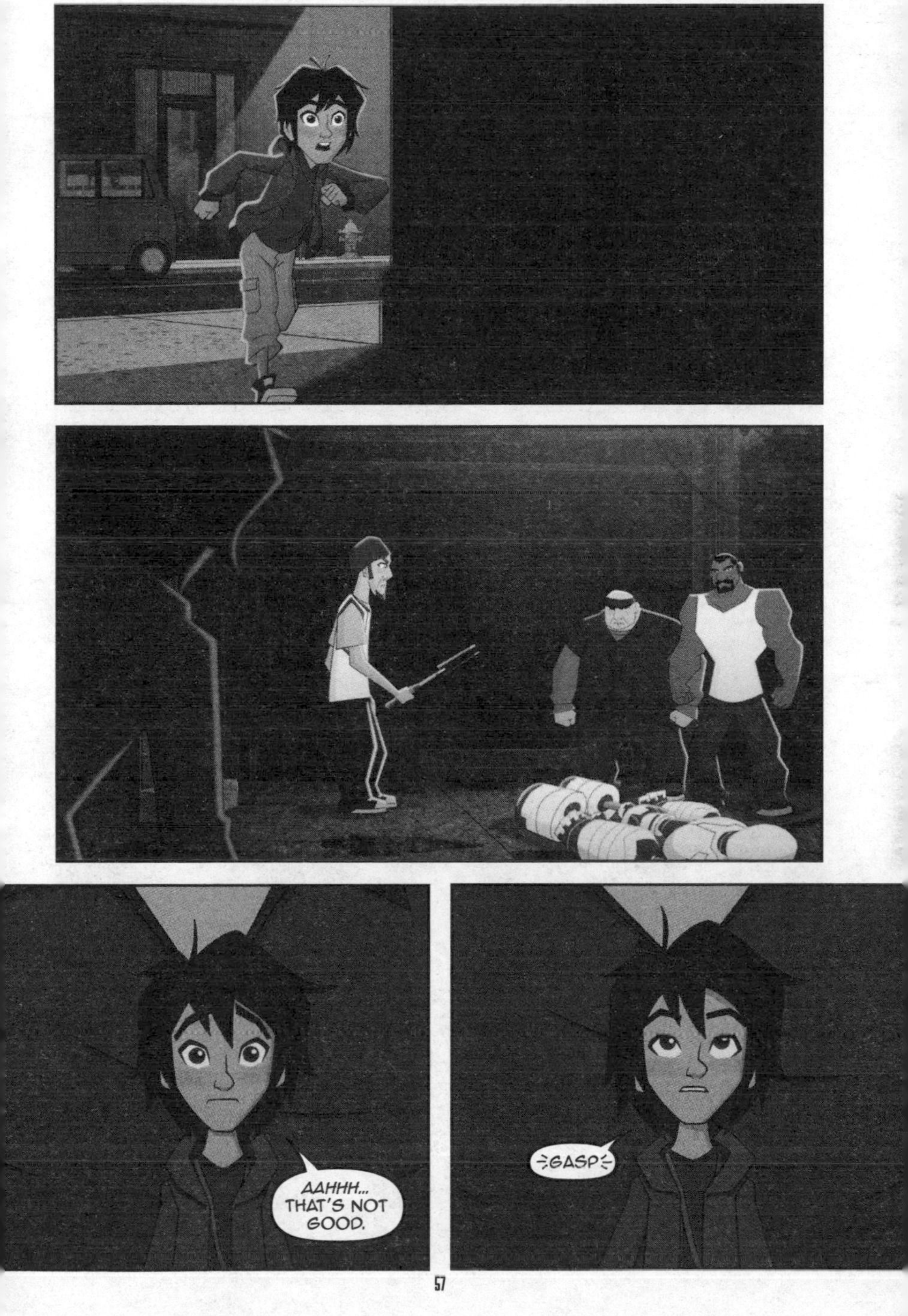
AAHHH... THAT'S NOT GOOD.
GASP

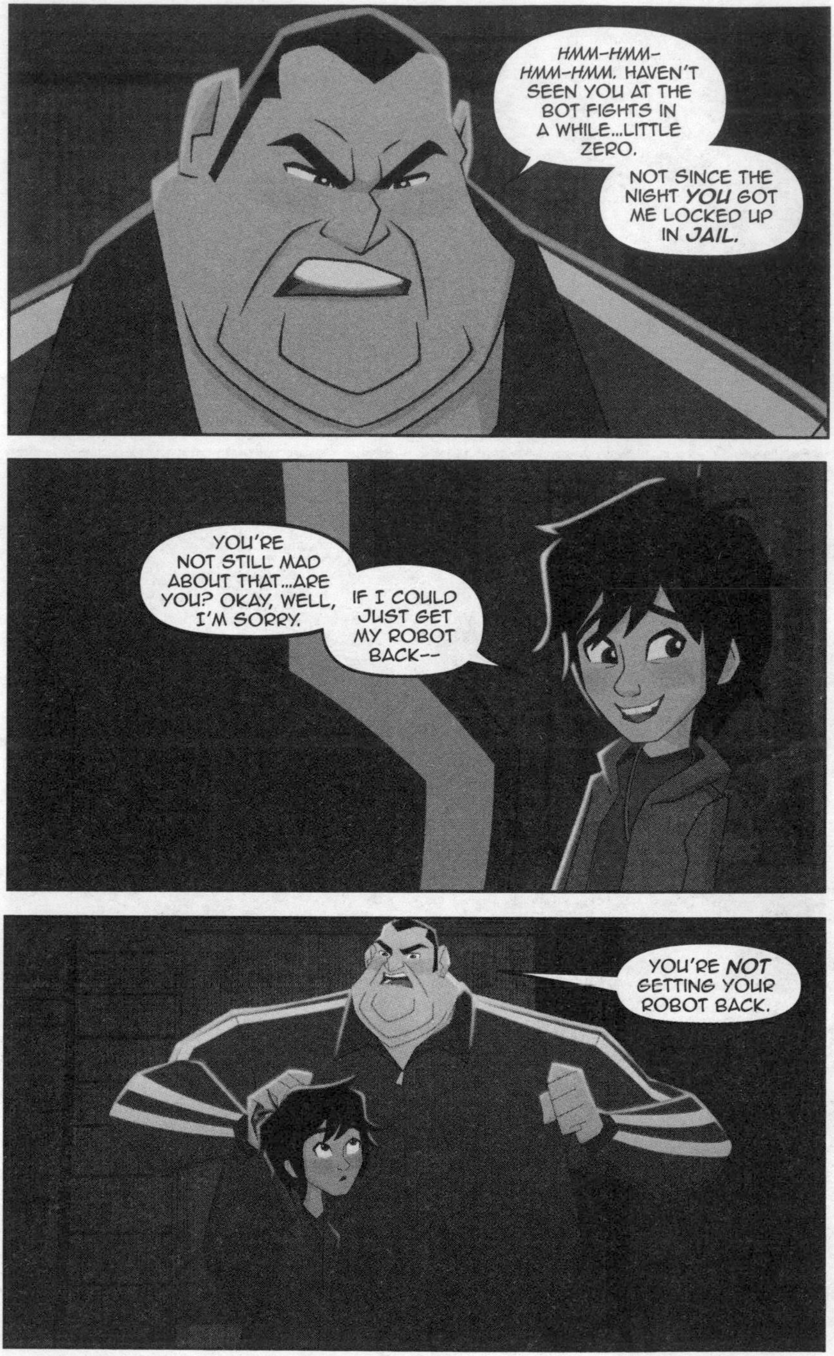
HMM-HMM-HMM-HMM. HAVEN'T SEEN YOU AT THE BOT FIGHTS IN A WHILE...LITTLE ZERO.
NOT SINCE THE NIGHT *YOU* GOT ME LOCKED UP IN *JAIL.*
YOU'RE NOT STILL MAD ABOUT THAT...ARE YOU? OKAY, WELL, I'M SORRY.
IF I COULD JUST GET MY ROBOT BACK--
YOU'RE *NOT* GETTING YOUR ROBOT BACK.

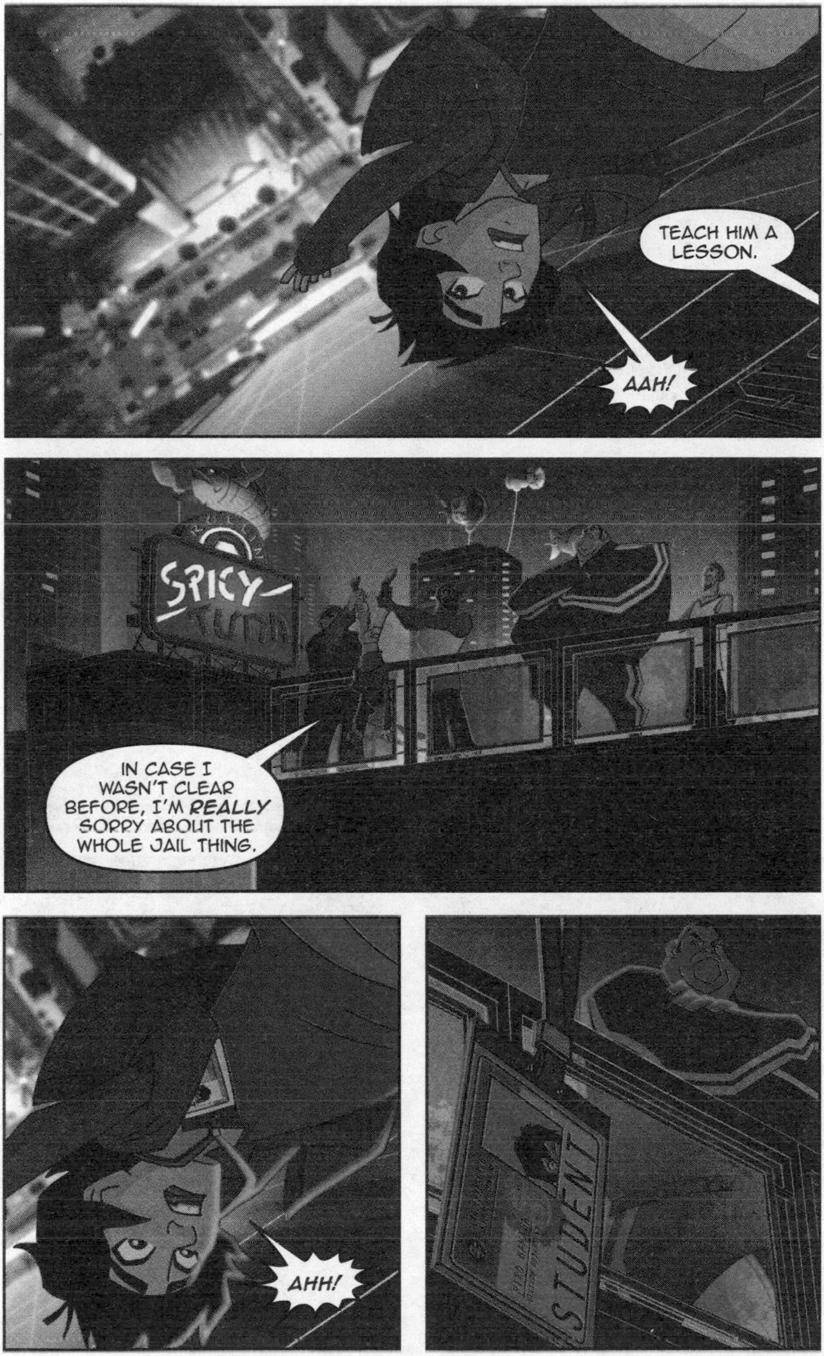
TEACH HIM A LESSON.
AAH!
IN CASE I WASN'T CLEAR BEFORE, I'M *REALLY* SORRY ABOUT THE WHOLE JAIL THING.
SPICY TUNA
AHH!
STUDENT

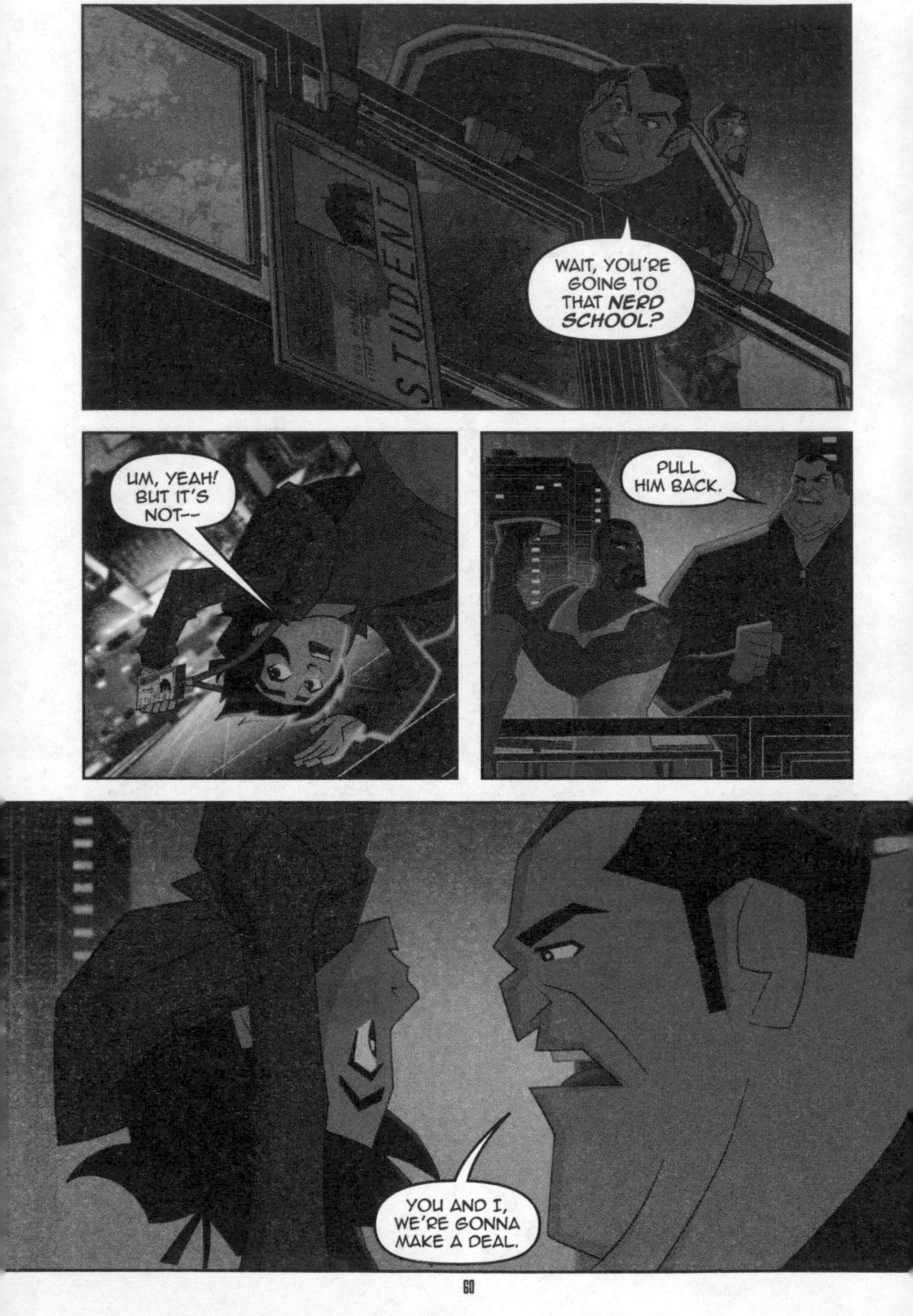
STUDENT
WAIT, YOU'RE GOING TO THAT NERD SCHOOL?
UM, YEAH! BUT IT'S NOT--
PULL HIM BACK.
YOU AND I, WE'RE GONNA MAKE A DEAL.

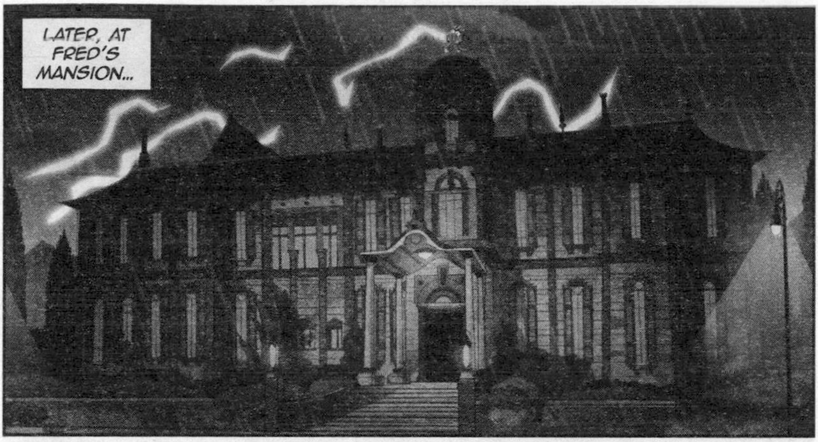
LATER, AT FRED'S MANSION...

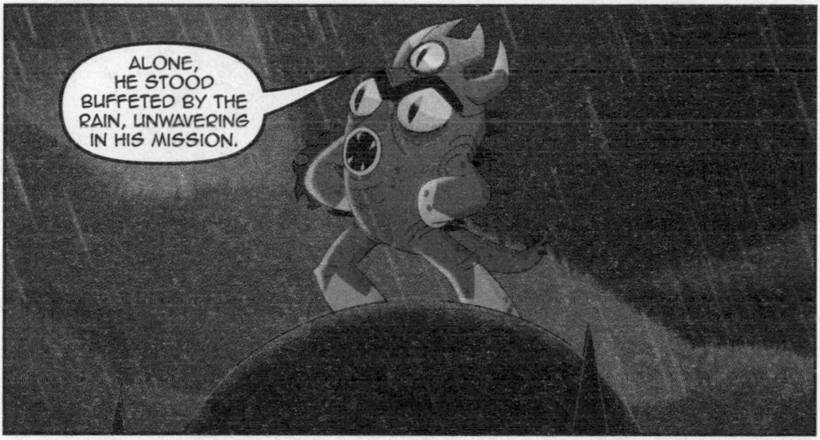
ALONE, HE STOOD BUFFETED BY THE RAIN, UNWAVERING IN HIS MISSION.

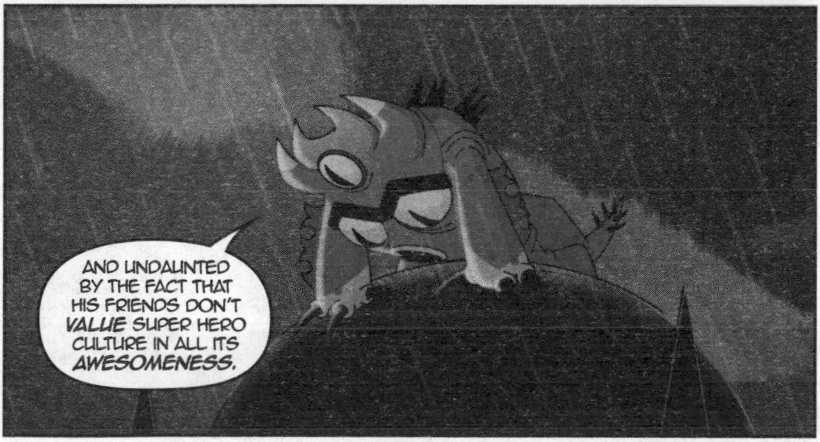
AND UNDAUNTED BY THE FACT THAT HIS FRIENDS DON'T *VALUE* SUPER HERO CULTURE IN ALL ITS *AWESOMENESS.*

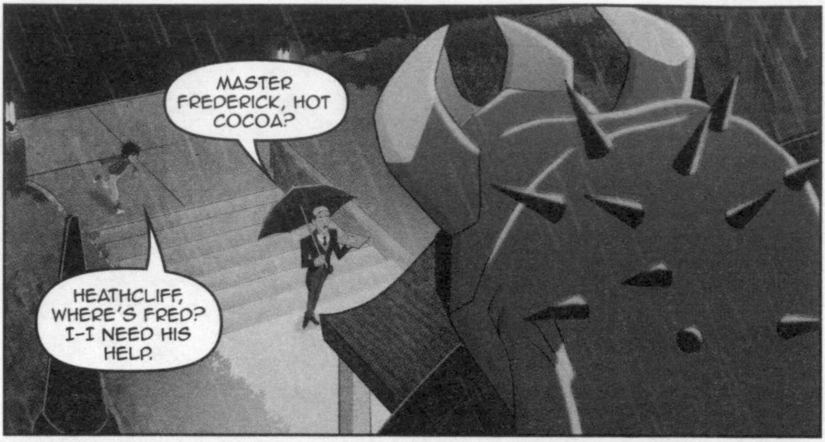
MASTER FREDERICK, HOT COCOA?
HEATHCLIFF, WHERE'S FRED? I-I NEED HIS HELP.

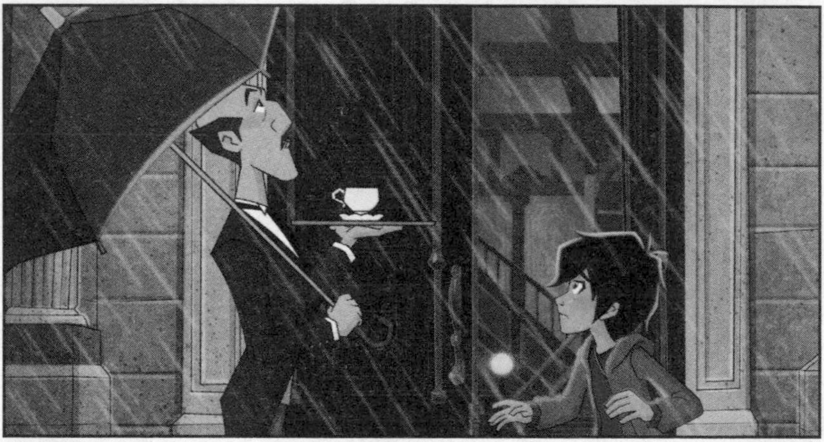

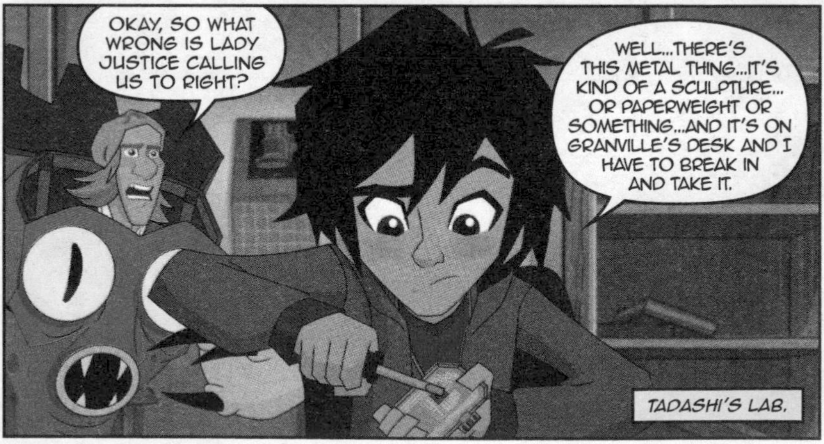
OKAY, SO WHAT WRONG IS LADY JUSTICE CALLING US TO RIGHT?
WELL...THERE'S THIS METAL THING...IT'S KIND OF A SCULPTURE... OR PAPERWEIGHT OR SOMETHING...AND IT'S ON GRANVILLE'S DESK AND I HAVE TO BREAK IN AND TAKE IT.
TADASHI'S LAB.

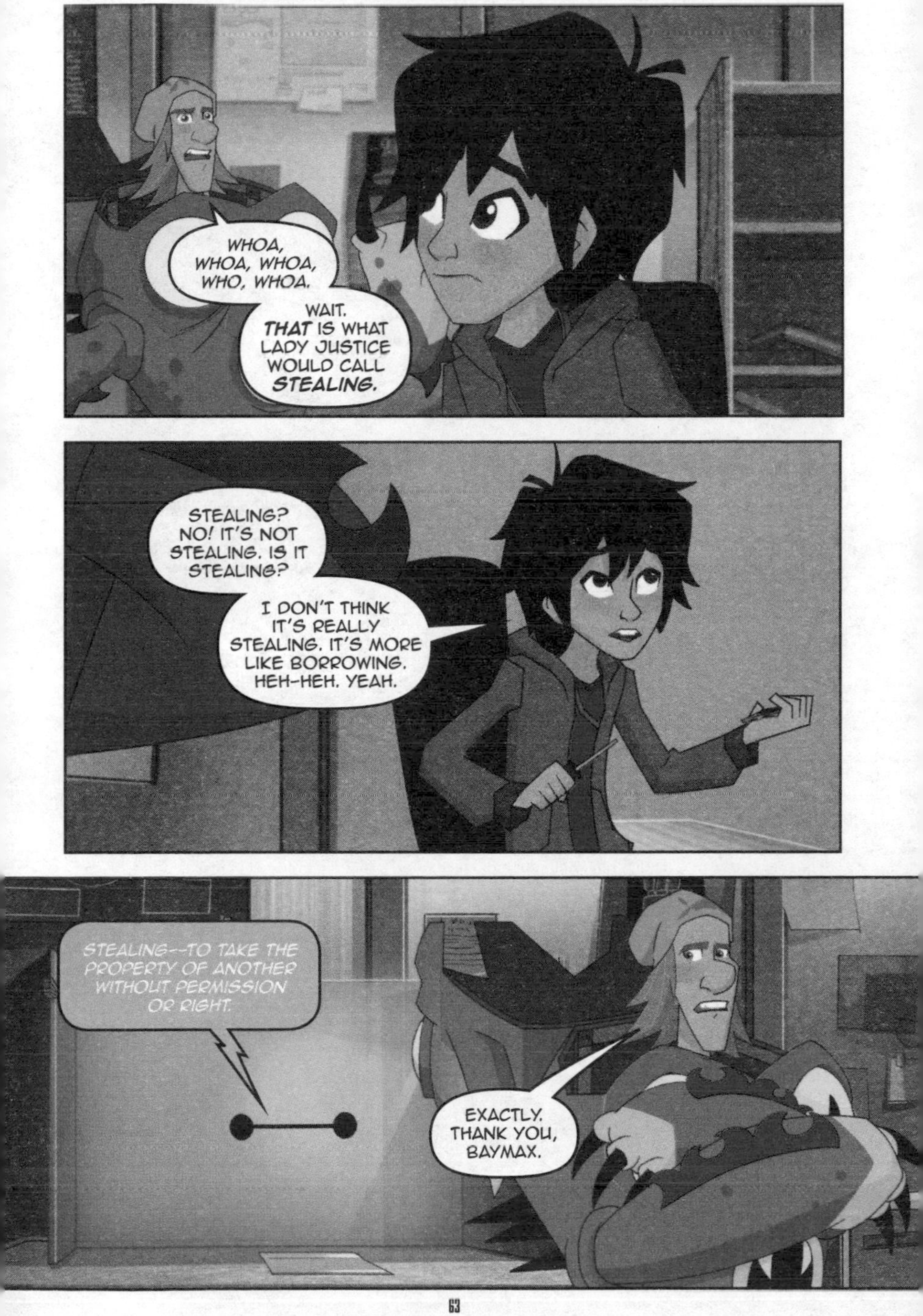
WHOA, WHOA, WHOA, WHO, WHOA.
WAIT. THAT IS WHAT LADY JUSTICE WOULD CALL STEALING.
STEALING? NO! IT'S NOT STEALING. IS IT STEALING?
I DON'T THINK IT'S REALLY STEALING. IT'S MORE LIKE BORROWING. HEH-HEH. YEAH.
STEALING--TO TAKE THE PROPERTY OF ANOTHER WITHOUT PERMISSION OR RIGHT.
EXACTLY. THANK YOU, BAYMAX.

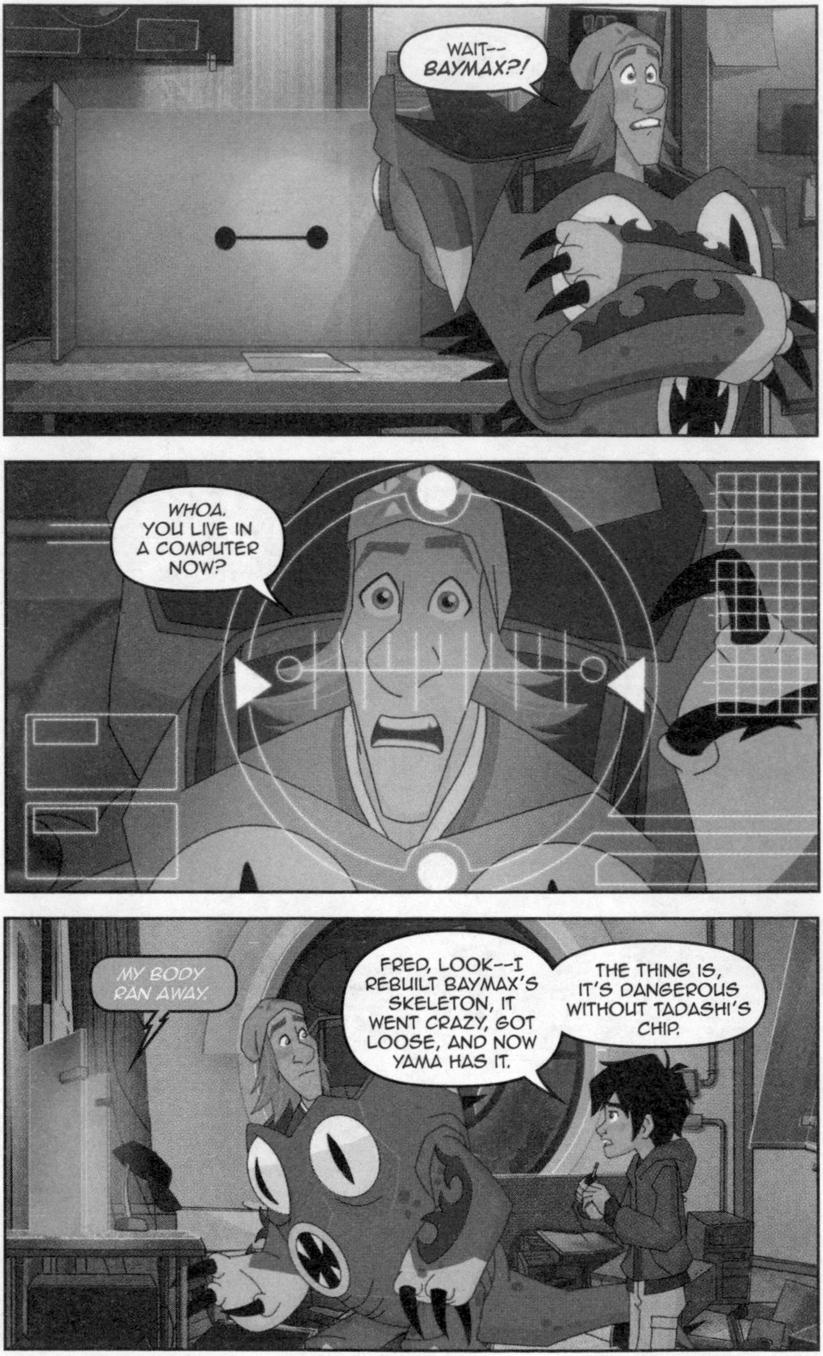
WAIT-- BAYMAX?!
WHOA. YOU LIVE IN A COMPUTER NOW?
MY BODY RAN AWAY.
FRED, LOOK--I REBUILT BAYMAX'S SKELETON, IT WENT CRAZY, GOT LOOSE, AND NOW YAMA HAS IT.
THE THING IS, IT'S DANGEROUS WITHOUT TADASHI'S CHIP.

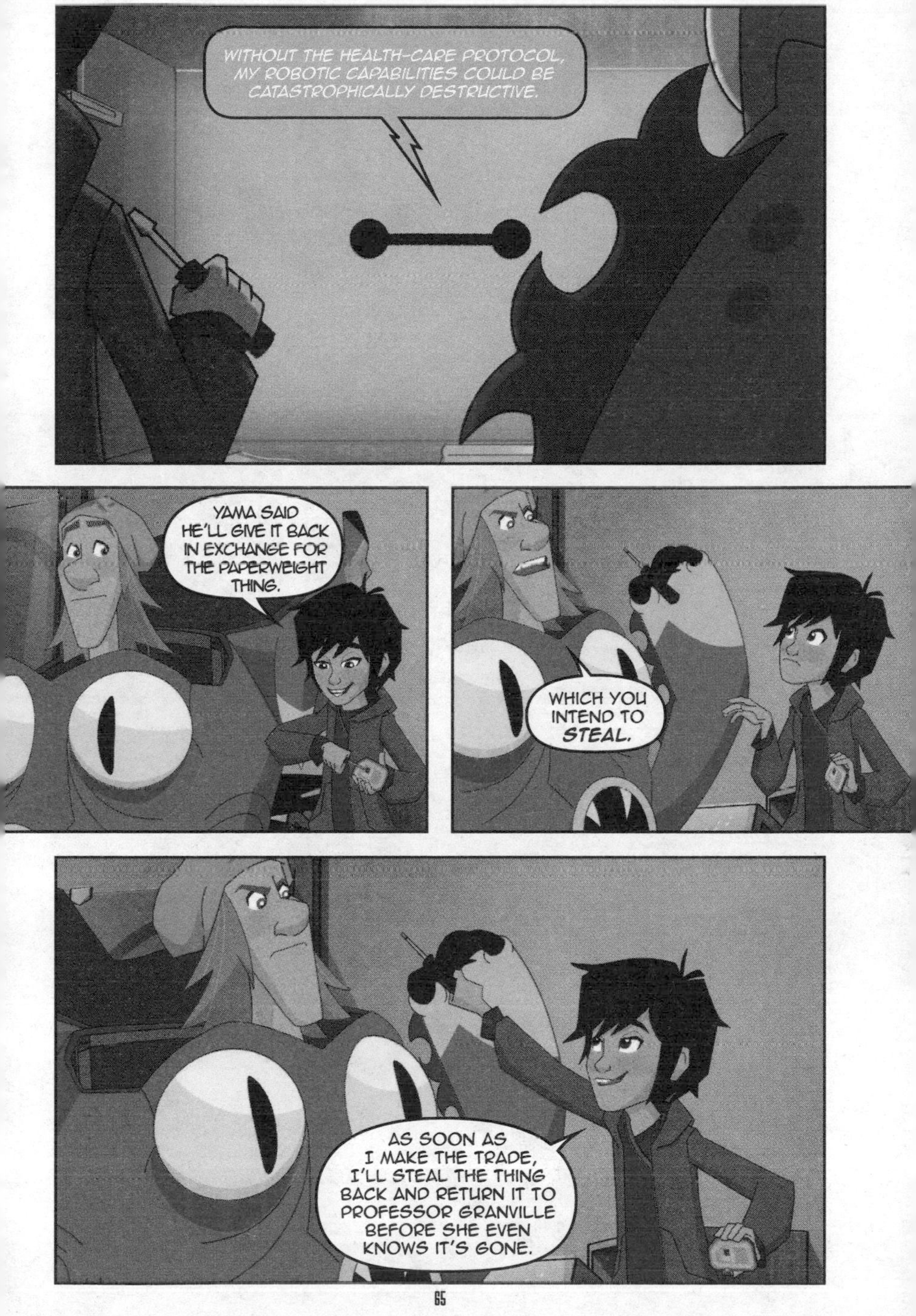
WITHOUT THE HEALTH-CARE PROTOCOL, MY ROBOTIC CAPABILITIES COULD BE CATASTROPHICALLY DESTRUCTIVE.
YAMA SAID HE'LL GIVE IT BACK IN EXCHANGE FOR THE PAPERWEIGHT THING.
WHICH YOU INTEND TO STEAL.
AS SOON AS I MAKE THE TRADE, I'LL STEAL THE THING BACK AND RETURN IT TO PROFESSOR GRANVILLE BEFORE SHE EVEN KNOWS IT'S GONE.

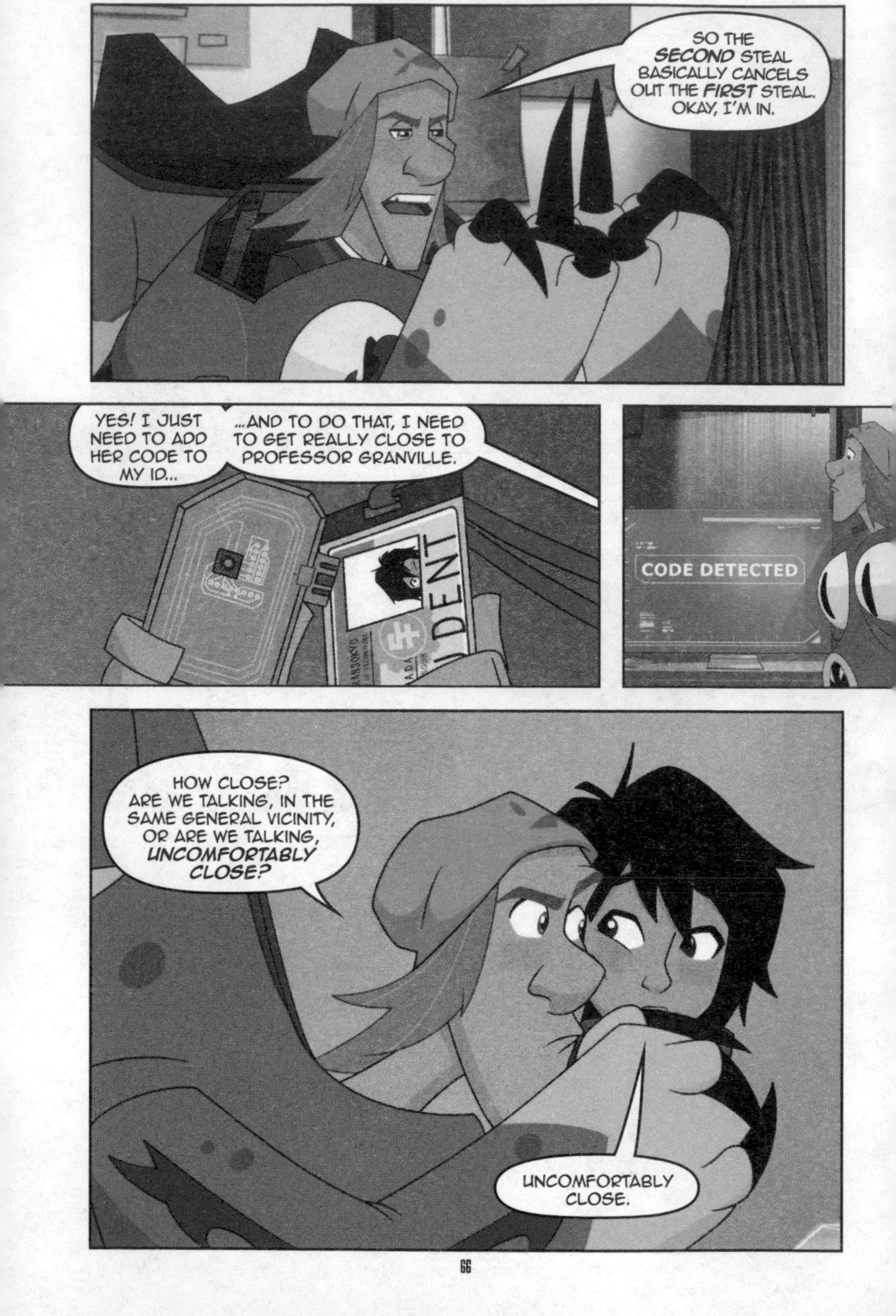
SO THE SECOND STEAL BASICALLY CANCELS OUT THE FIRST STEAL. OKAY, I'M IN.
YES! I JUST NEED TO ADD HER CODE TO MY ID...
...AND TO DO THAT, I NEED TO GET REALLY CLOSE TO PROFESSOR GRANVILLE.
CODE DETECTED
HOW CLOSE? ARE WE TALKING, IN THE SAME GENERAL VICINITY, OR ARE WE TALKING, UNCOMFORTABLY CLOSE?
UNCOMFORTABLY CLOSE.

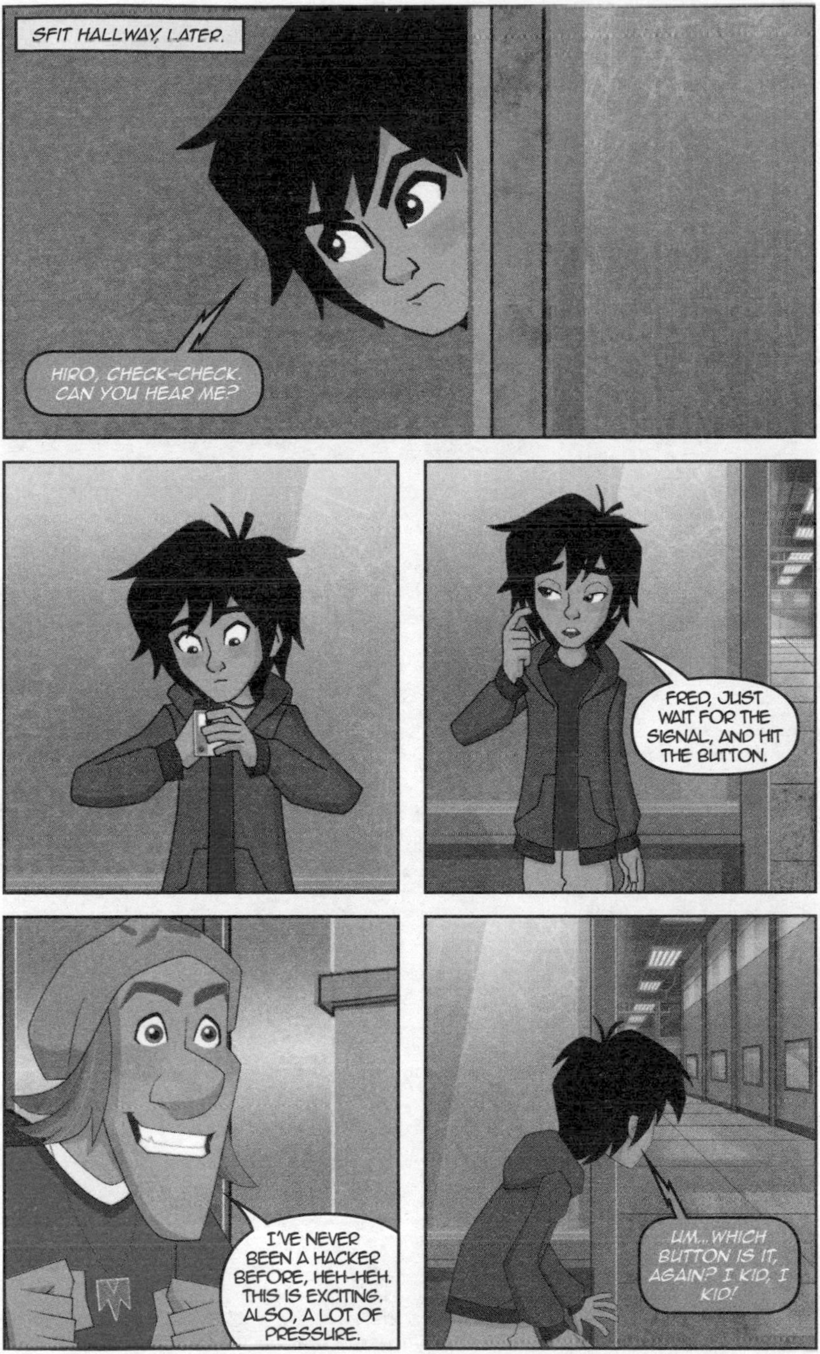
SFIT HALLWAY, LATER.
HIRO, CHECK-CHECK. CAN YOU HEAR ME?
FRED, JUST WAIT FOR THE SIGNAL, AND HIT THE BUTTON.
I'VE NEVER BEEN A HACKER BEFORE, HEH-HEH. THIS IS EXCITING. ALSO, A LOT OF PRESSURE.
UM...WHICH BUTTON IS IT, AGAIN? I KID, I KID!

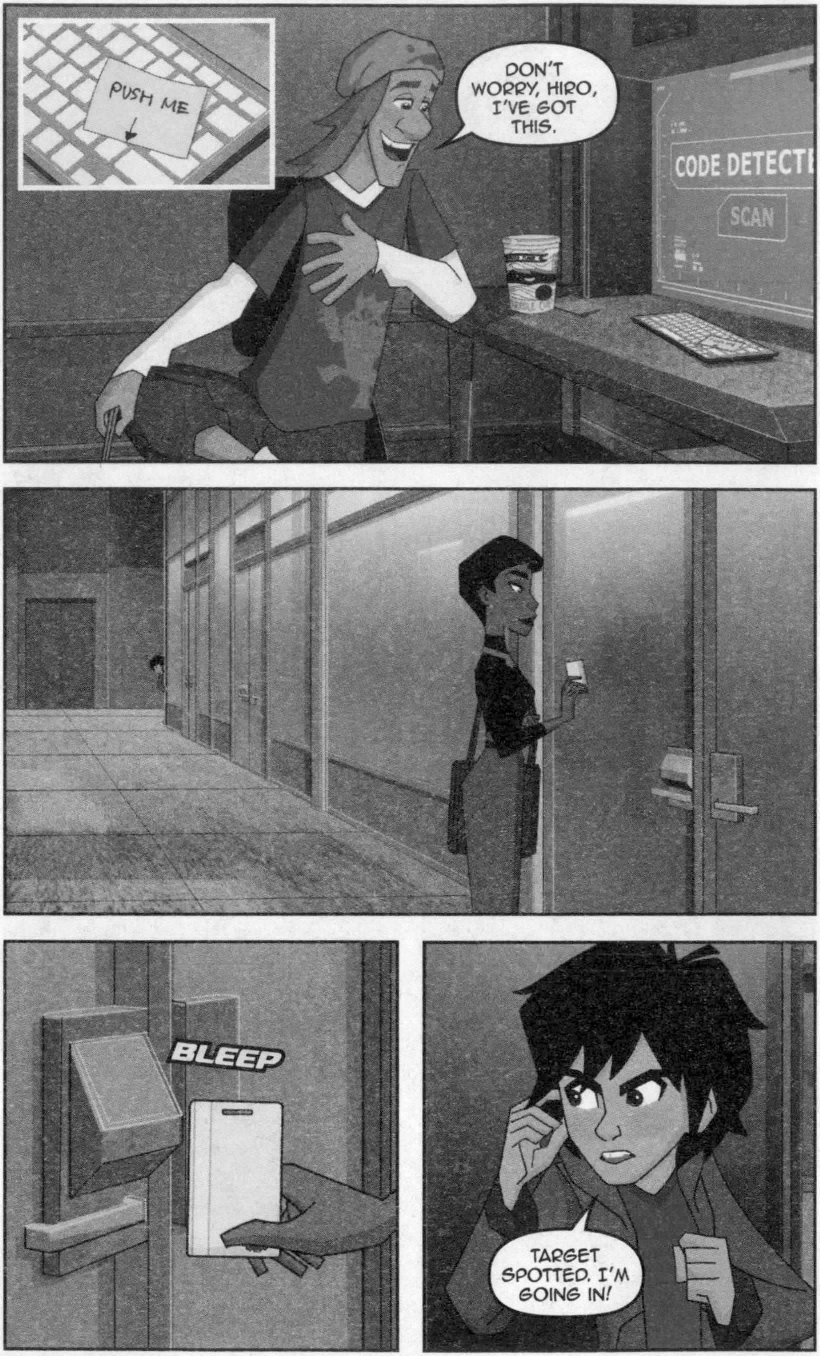
PUSH ME
DON'T WORRY, HIRO, I'VE GOT THIS.
CODE DETECTE
SCAN
BLEEP
TARGET SPOTTED. I'M GOING IN!

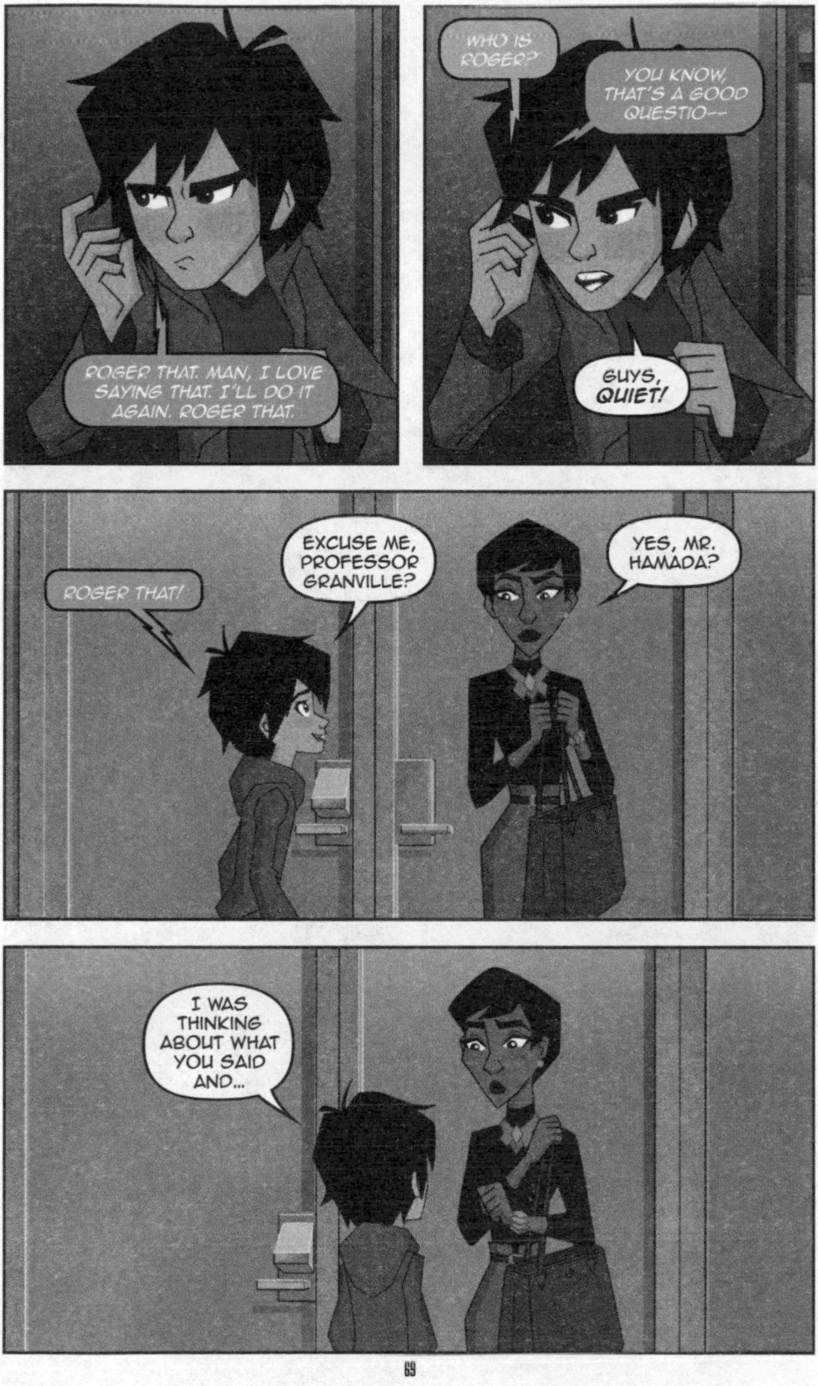
ROGER THAT. MAN, I LOVE SAYING THAT. I'LL DO IT AGAIN. ROGER THAT.
WHO IS ROGER?
YOU KNOW, THAT'S A GOOD QUESTIO--
GUYS, **QUIET!**
ROGER THAT!
EXCUSE ME, PROFESSOR GRANVILLE?
YES, MR. HAMADA?
I WAS THINKING ABOUT WHAT YOU SAID AND...

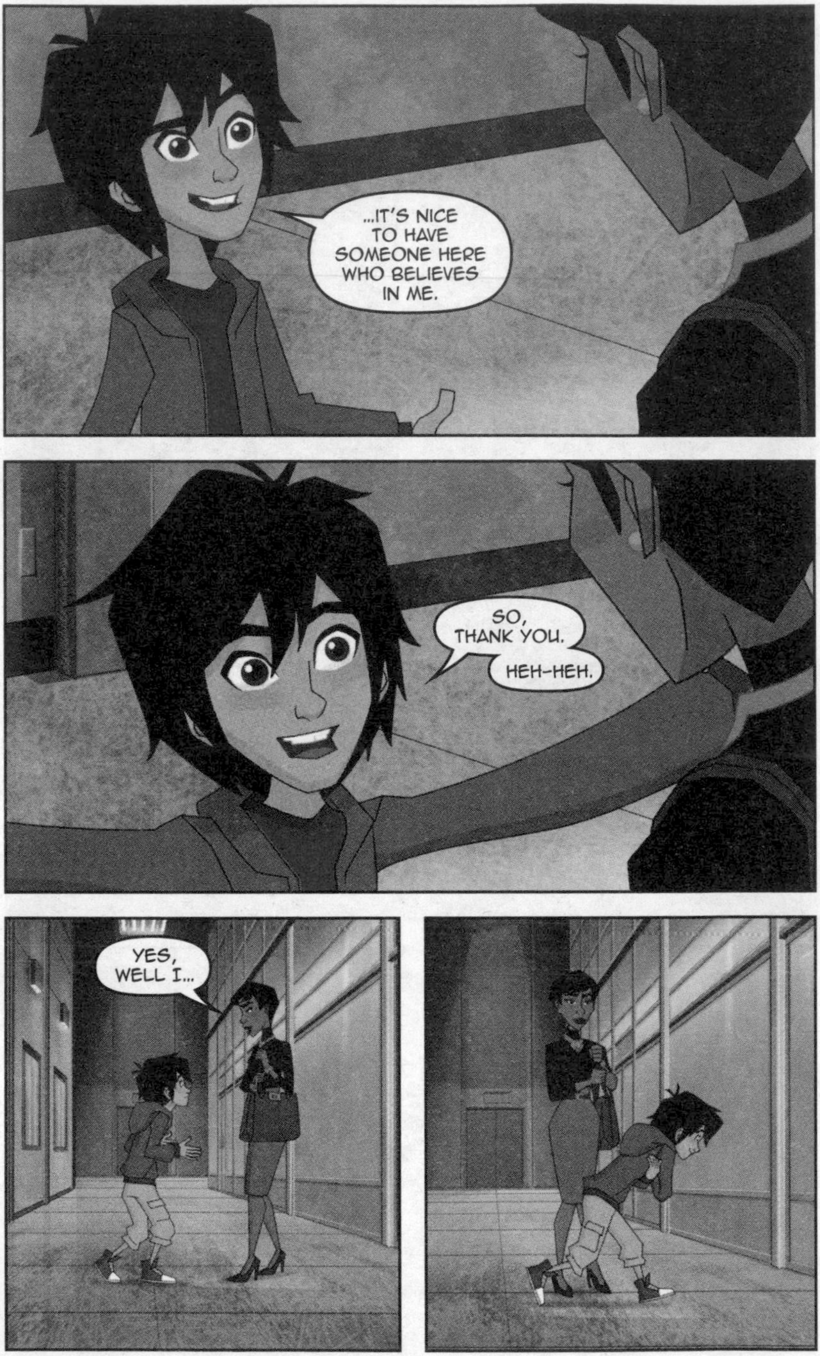
...IT'S NICE TO HAVE SOMEONE HERE WHO BELIEVES IN ME.
SO, THANK YOU.
HEH-HEH.
YES, WELL I...

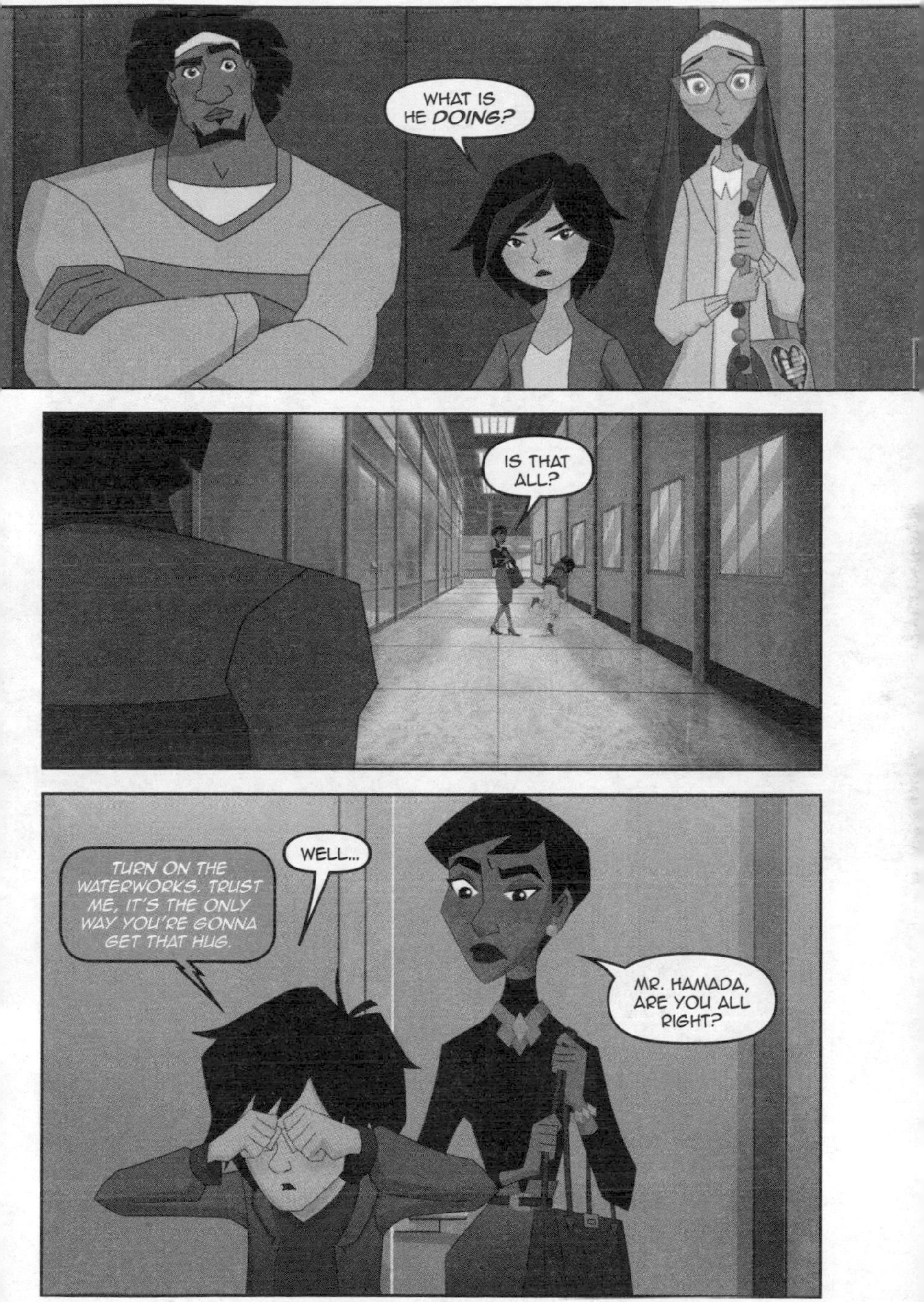
WHAT IS HE DOING?
IS THAT ALL?
TURN ON THE WATERWORKS. TRUST ME, IT'S THE ONLY WAY YOU'RE GONNA GET THAT HUG.
WELL...
MR. HAMADA, ARE YOU ALL RIGHT?

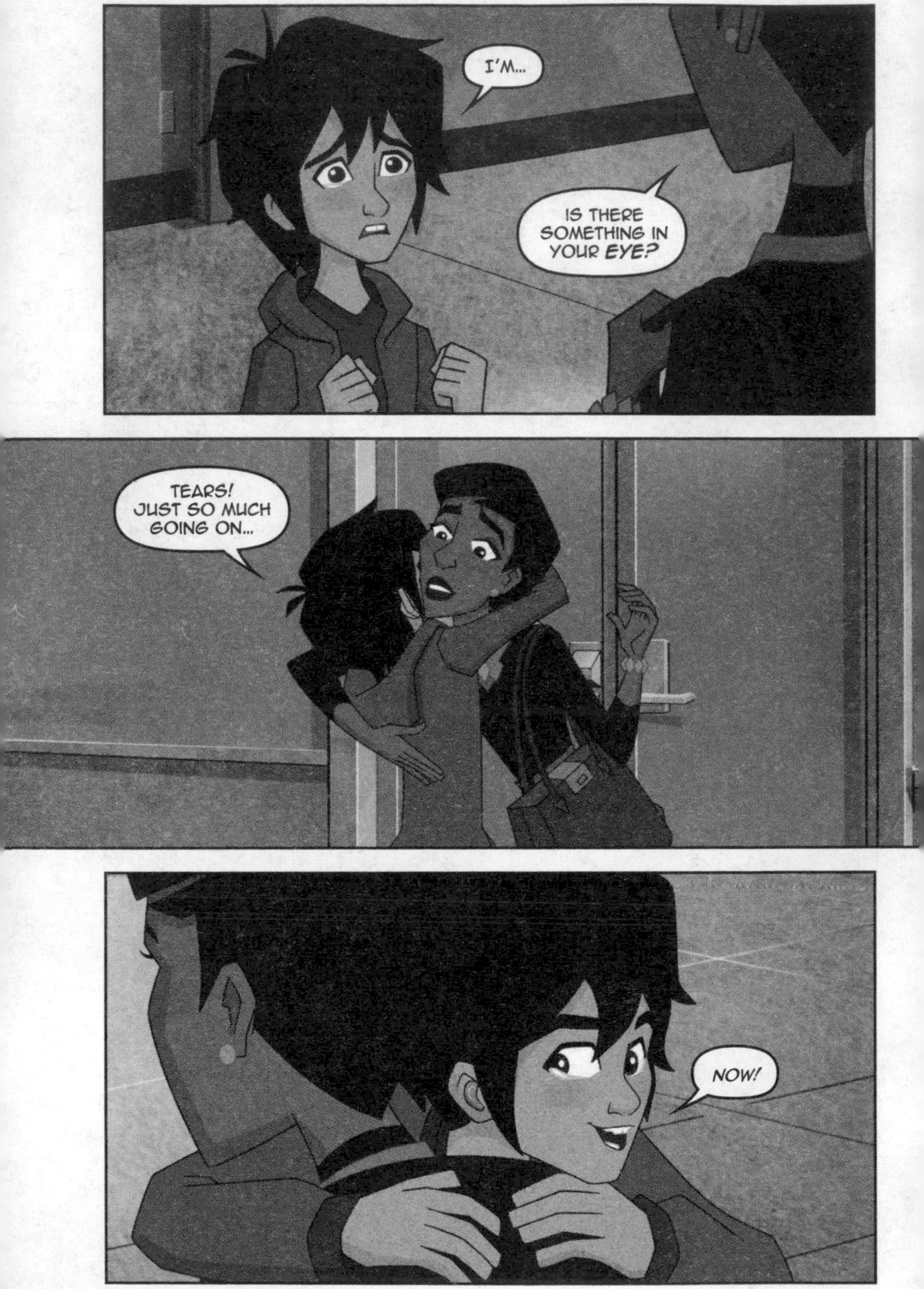
I'M...
IS THERE SOMETHING IN YOUR EYE?
TEARS! JUST SO MUCH GOING ON...
NOW!

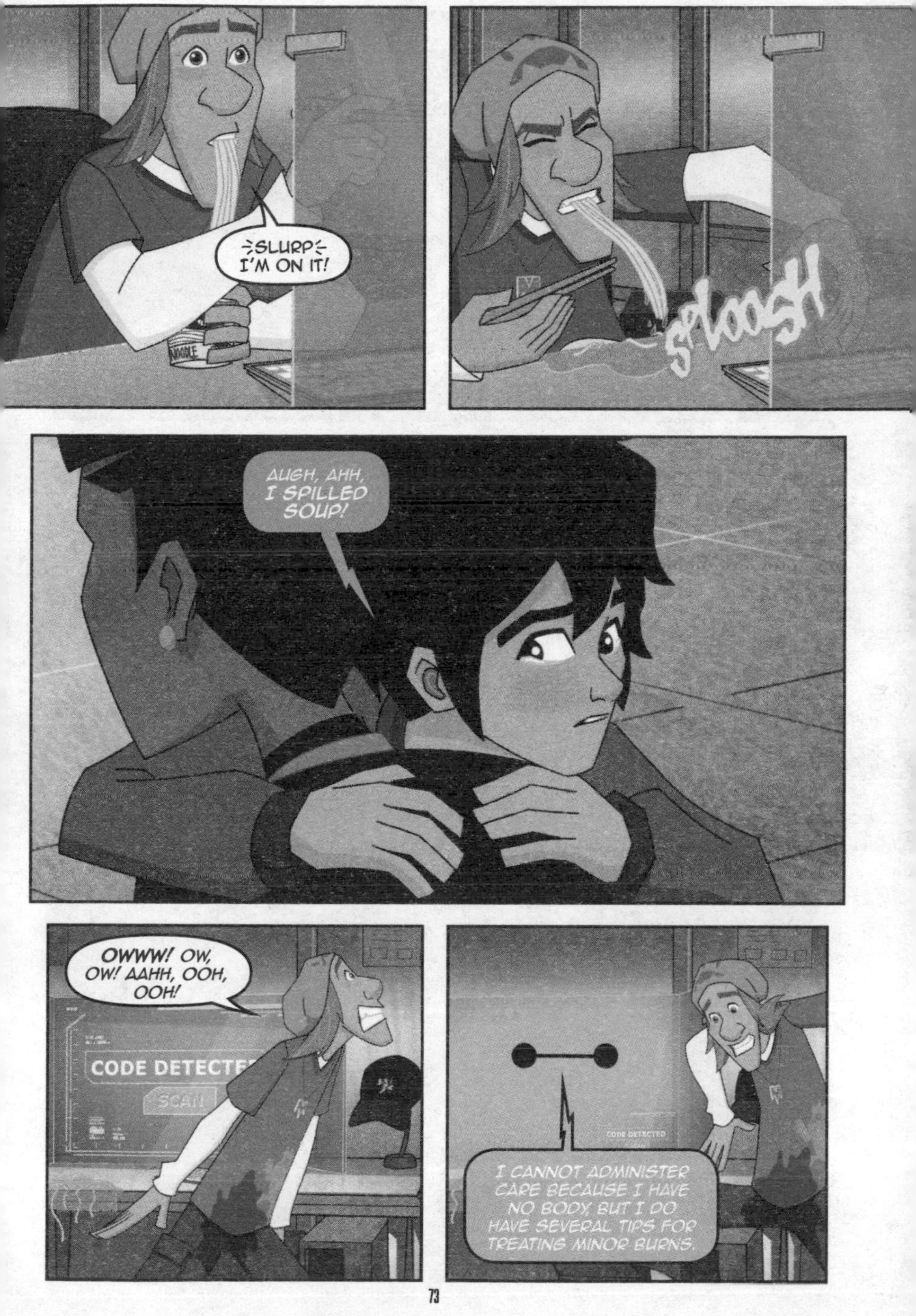

SLURP I'M ON IT!
SPLOOSH
AUGH, AHH, I SPILLED SOUP!
OWWW! OW, OW! AAHH, OOH, OOH!
CODE DETECTED
SCAN
CODE DETECTED
I CANNOT ADMINISTER CARE BECAUSE I HAVE NO BODY, BUT I DO HAVE SEVERAL TIPS FOR TREATING MINOR BURNS.

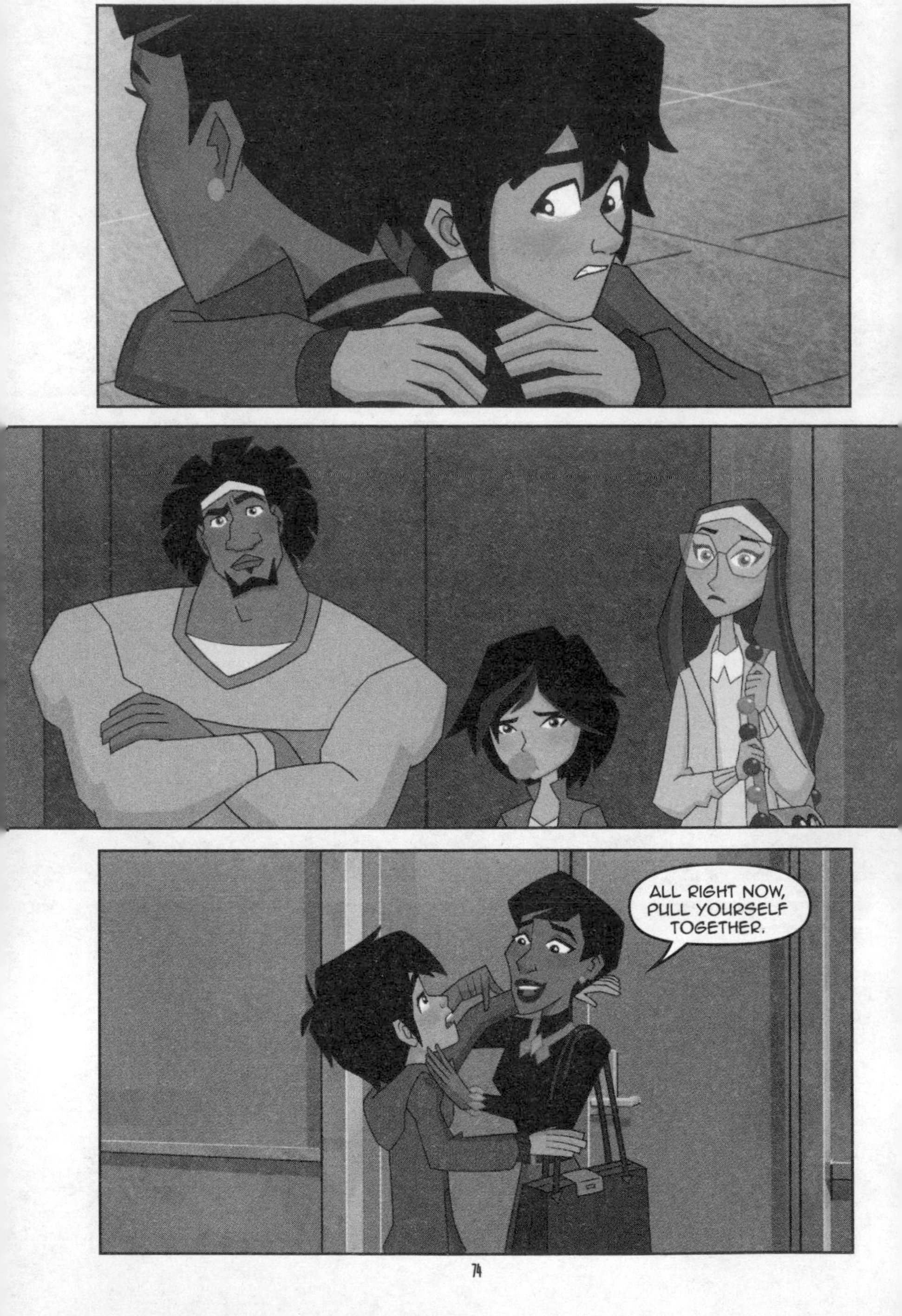
ALL RIGHT NOW, PULL YOURSELF TOGETHER.

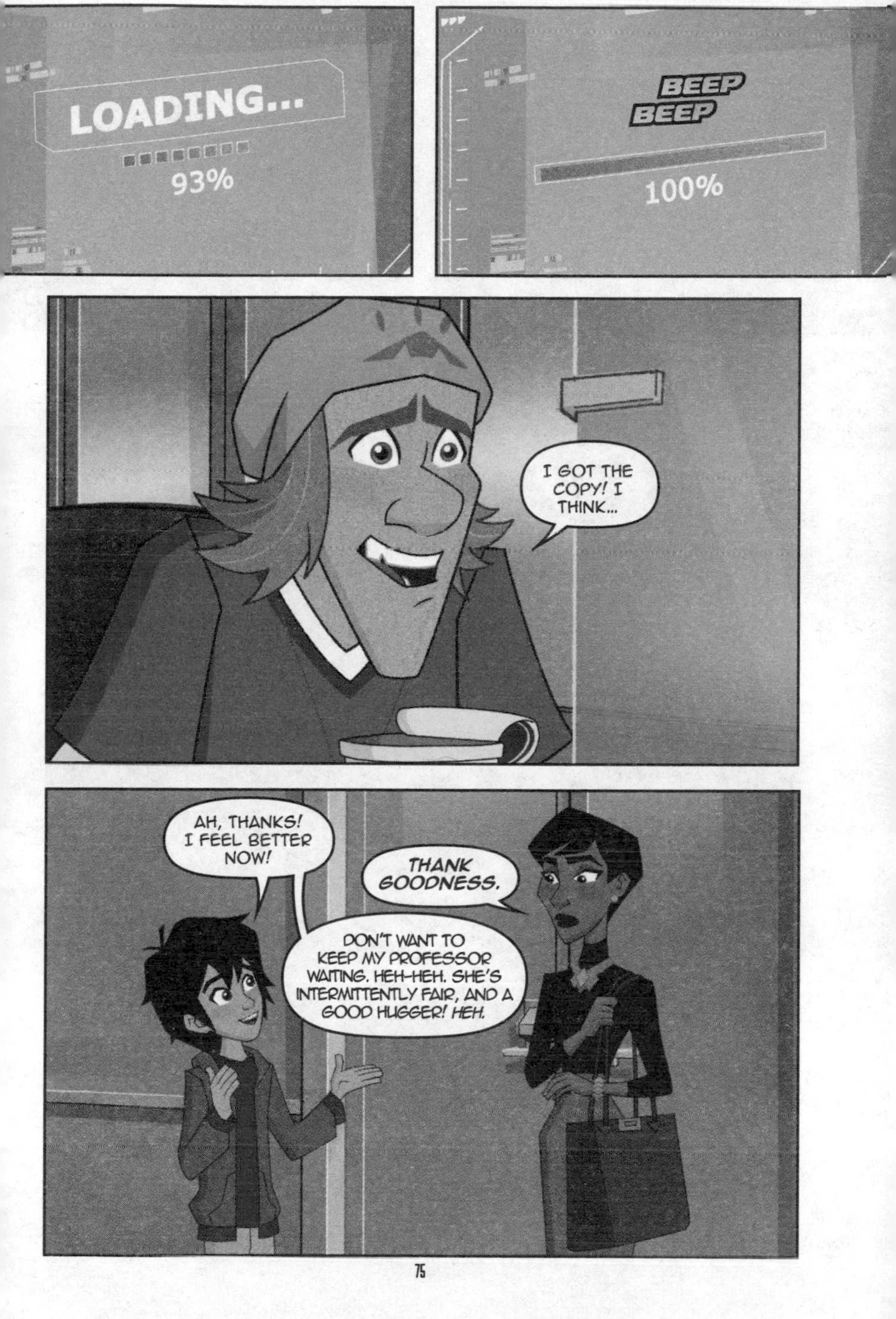
LOADING...
93%
BEEP
BEEP
100%
I GOT THE COPY! I THINK...
AH, THANKS! I FEEL BETTER NOW!
DON'T WANT TO KEEP MY PROFESSOR WAITING. HEH-HEH. SHE'S INTERMITTENTLY FAIR, AND A GOOD HUGGER! HEH.
THANK GOODNESS.

SAN FRANSOKYO INSTITUTE OF TECHNOLOGY, NIGHT.

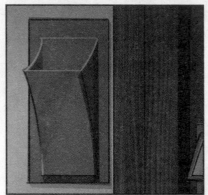

BLEEP

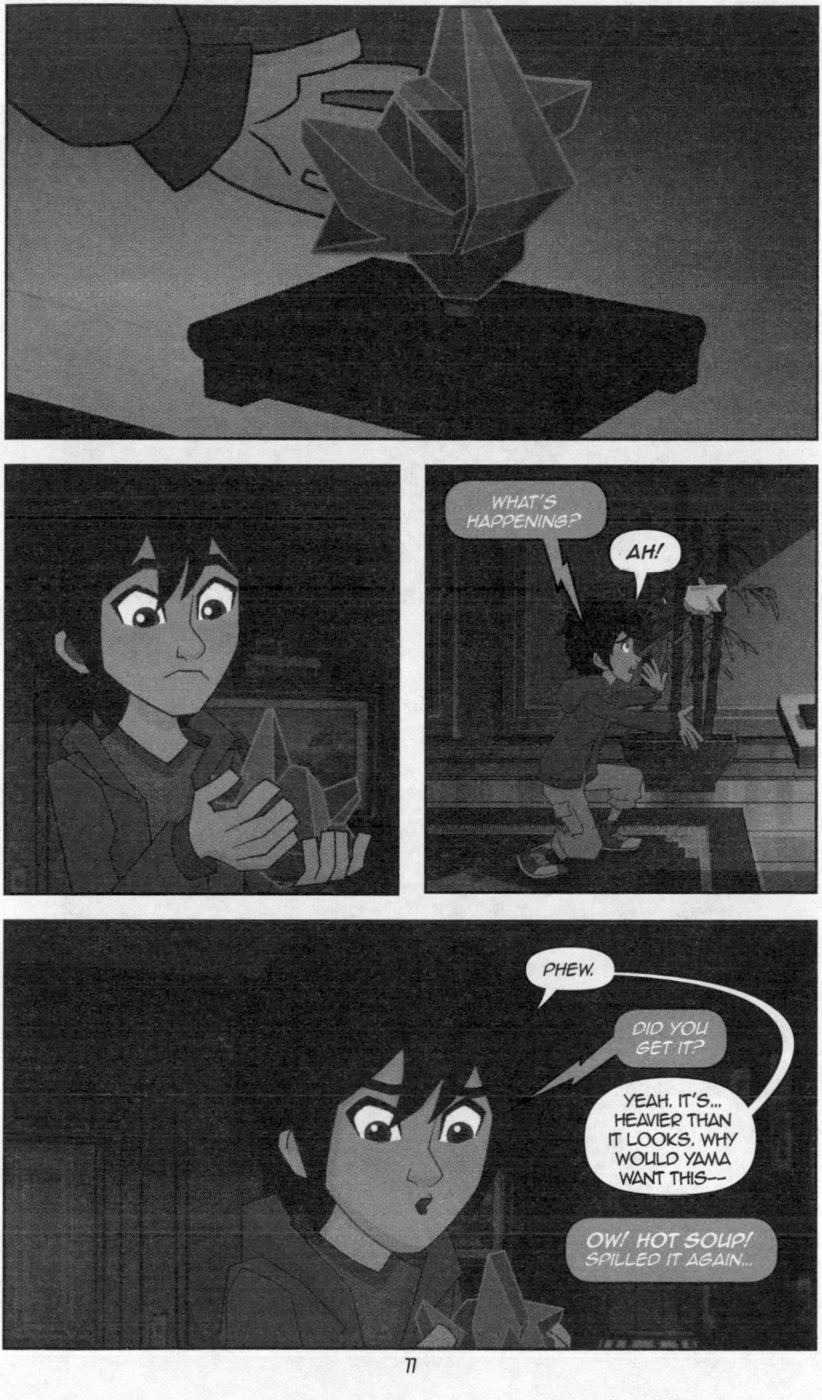
WHAT'S HAPPENING?
AH!
PHEW.
DID YOU GET IT?
YEAH. IT'S... HEAVIER THAN IT LOOKS. WHY WOULD YAMA WANT THIS--
OW! HOT SOUP! SPILLED IT AGAIN...

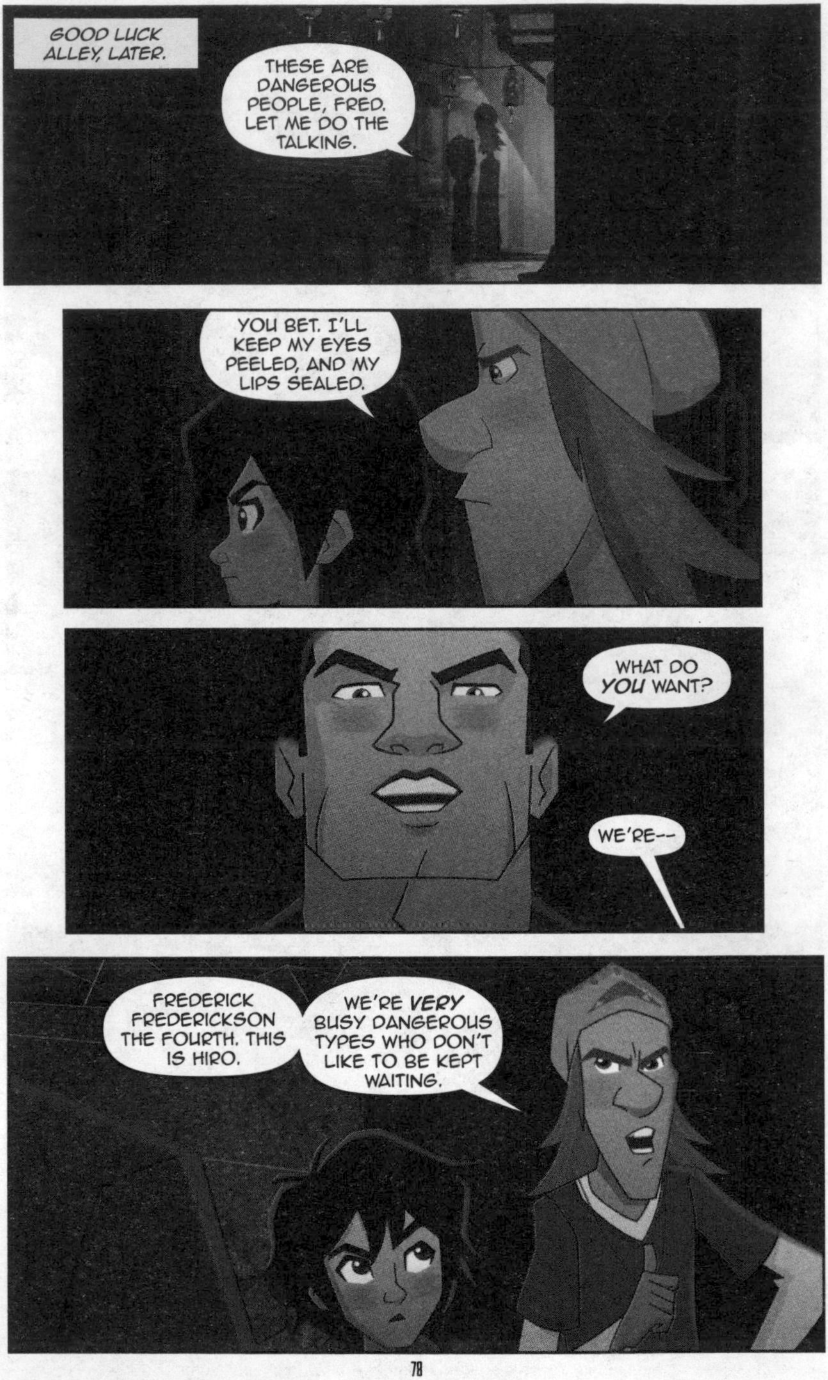
GOOD LUCK ALLEY, LATER.
THESE ARE DANGEROUS PEOPLE, FRED. LET ME DO THE TALKING.
YOU BET. I'LL KEEP MY EYES PEELED, AND MY LIPS SEALED.
WHAT DO *YOU* WANT?
WE'RE--
FREDERICK FREDERICKSON THE FOURTH. THIS IS HIRO.
WE'RE *VERY* BUSY DANGEROUS TYPES WHO DON'T LIKE TO BE KEPT WAITING.

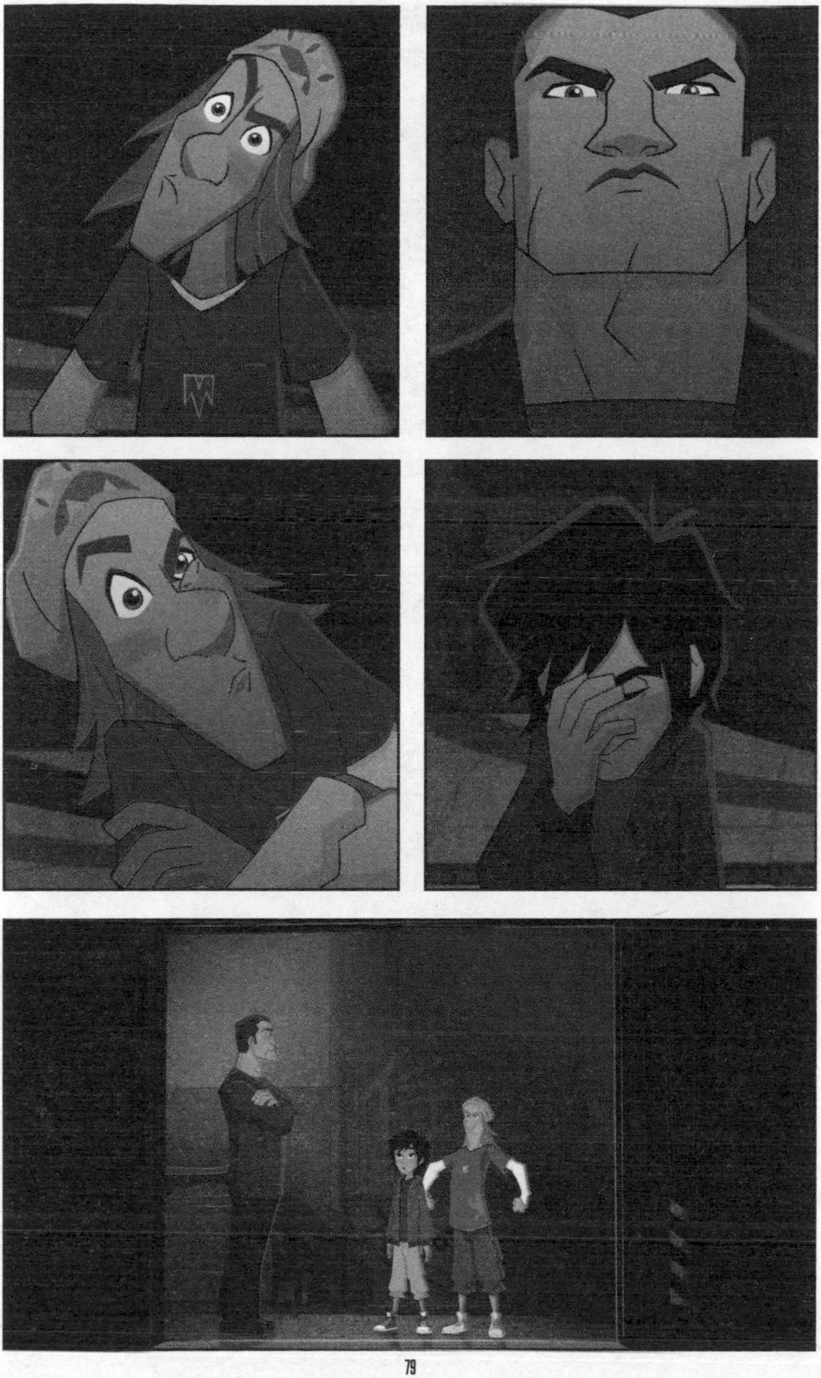

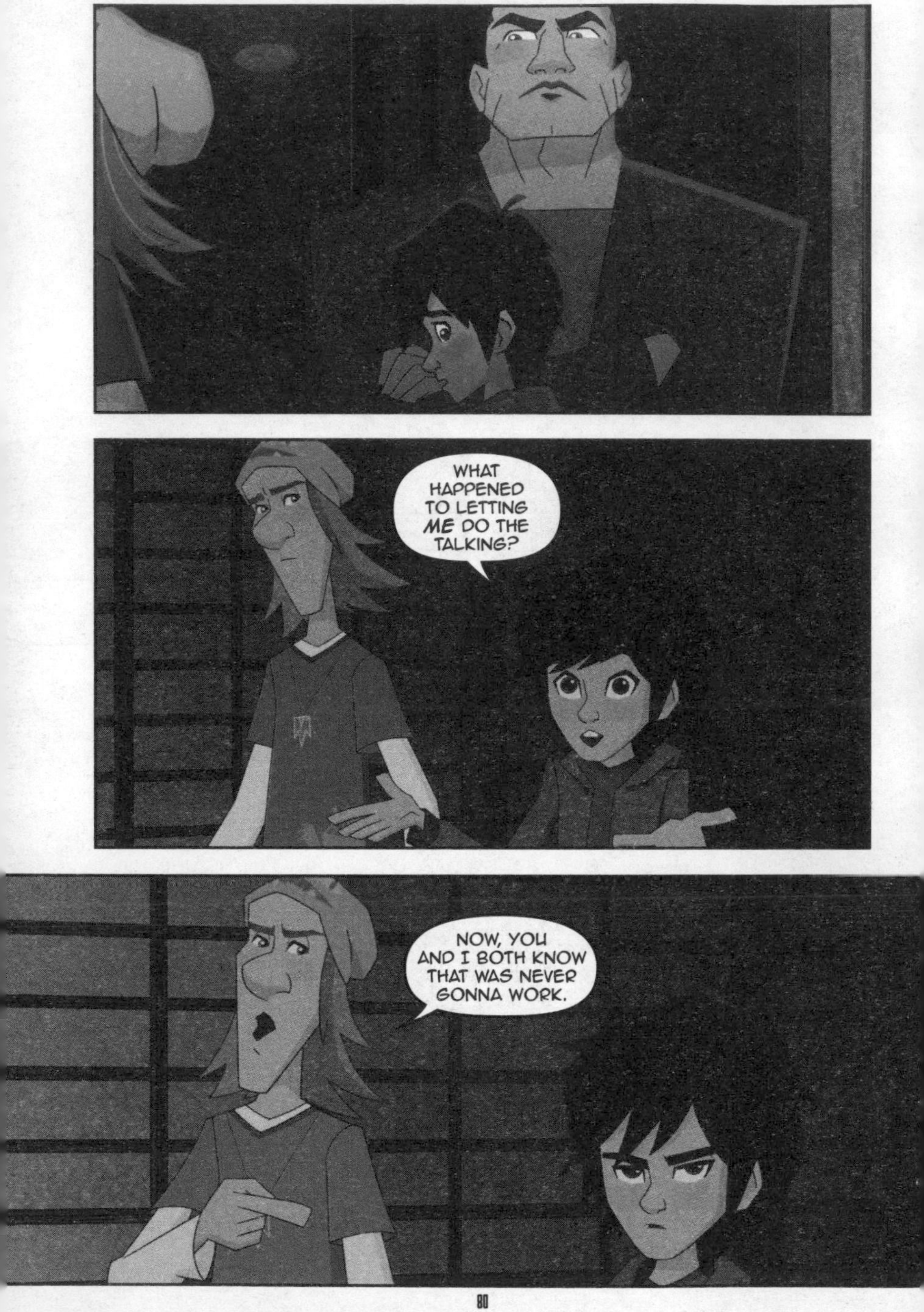
WHAT HAPPENED TO LETTING *ME* DO THE TALKING?
NOW, YOU AND I BOTH KNOW THAT WAS NEVER GONNA WORK.

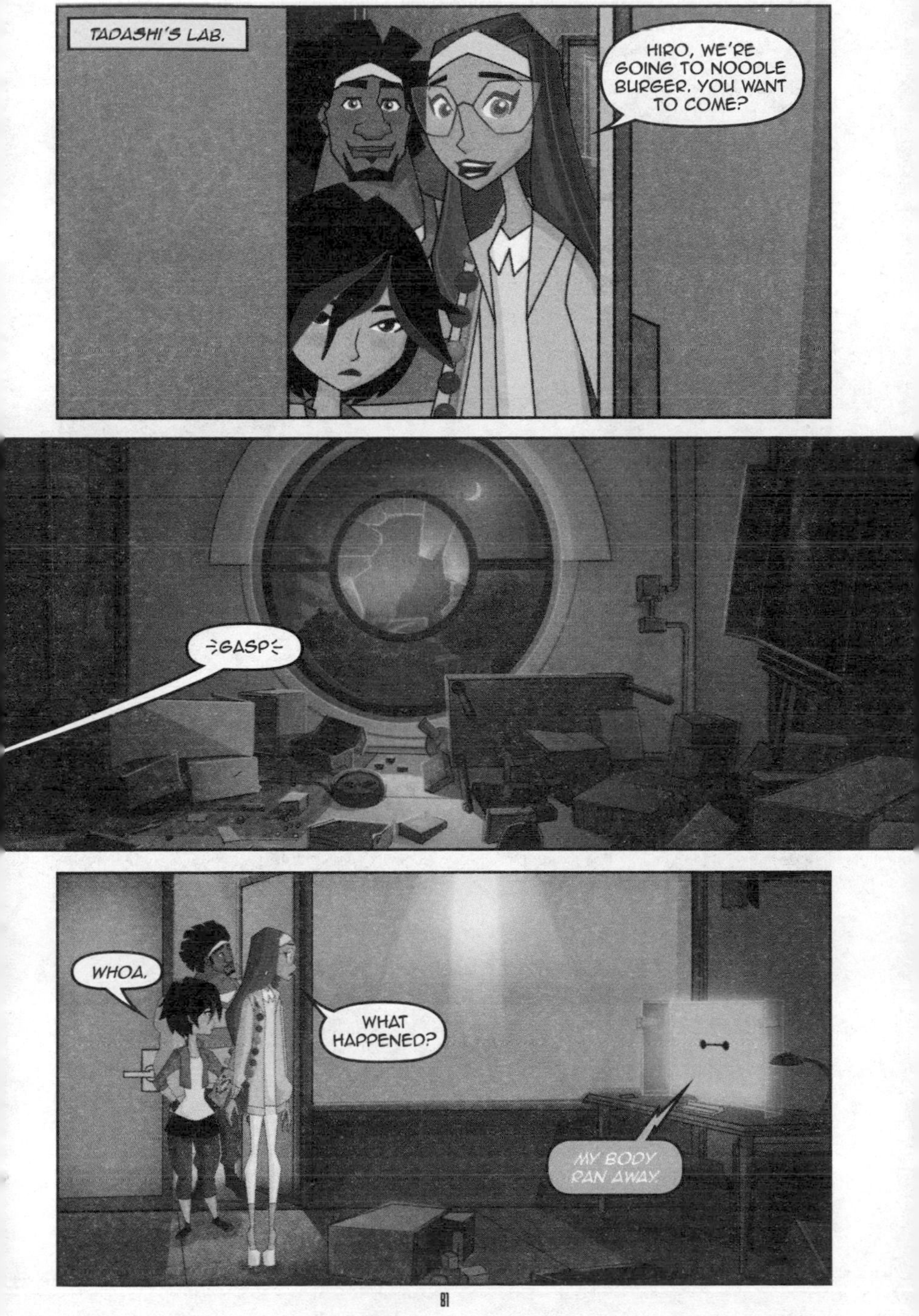
TADASHI'S LAB.
HIRO, WE'RE GOING TO NOODLE BURGER. YOU WANT TO COME?
GASP
WHOA.
WHAT HAPPENED?
MY BODY RAN AWAY.

BAYMAX?!
YOU'RE BACK! WAIT, WHY ARE YOU IN THE COMPUTER? AND WHERE'S HIRO?
HIRO CAN BE FOUND...HERE.
THAT'S GOOD LUCK ALLEY.
WHY DO THEY CALL IT GOOD LUCK ALLEY?
GOOD LUCK...GETTING OUT ALIVE.

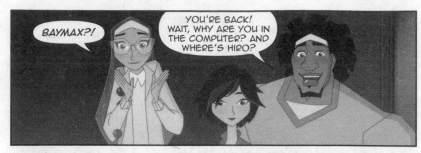

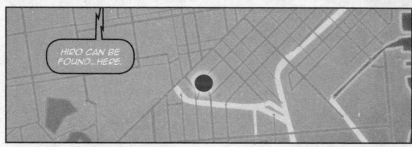

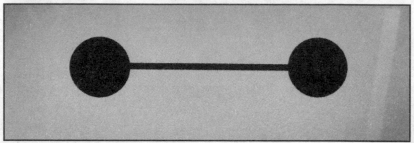

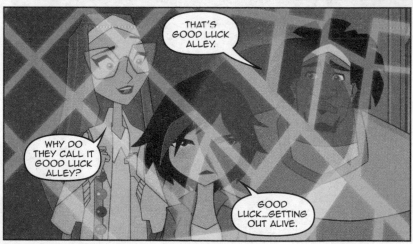

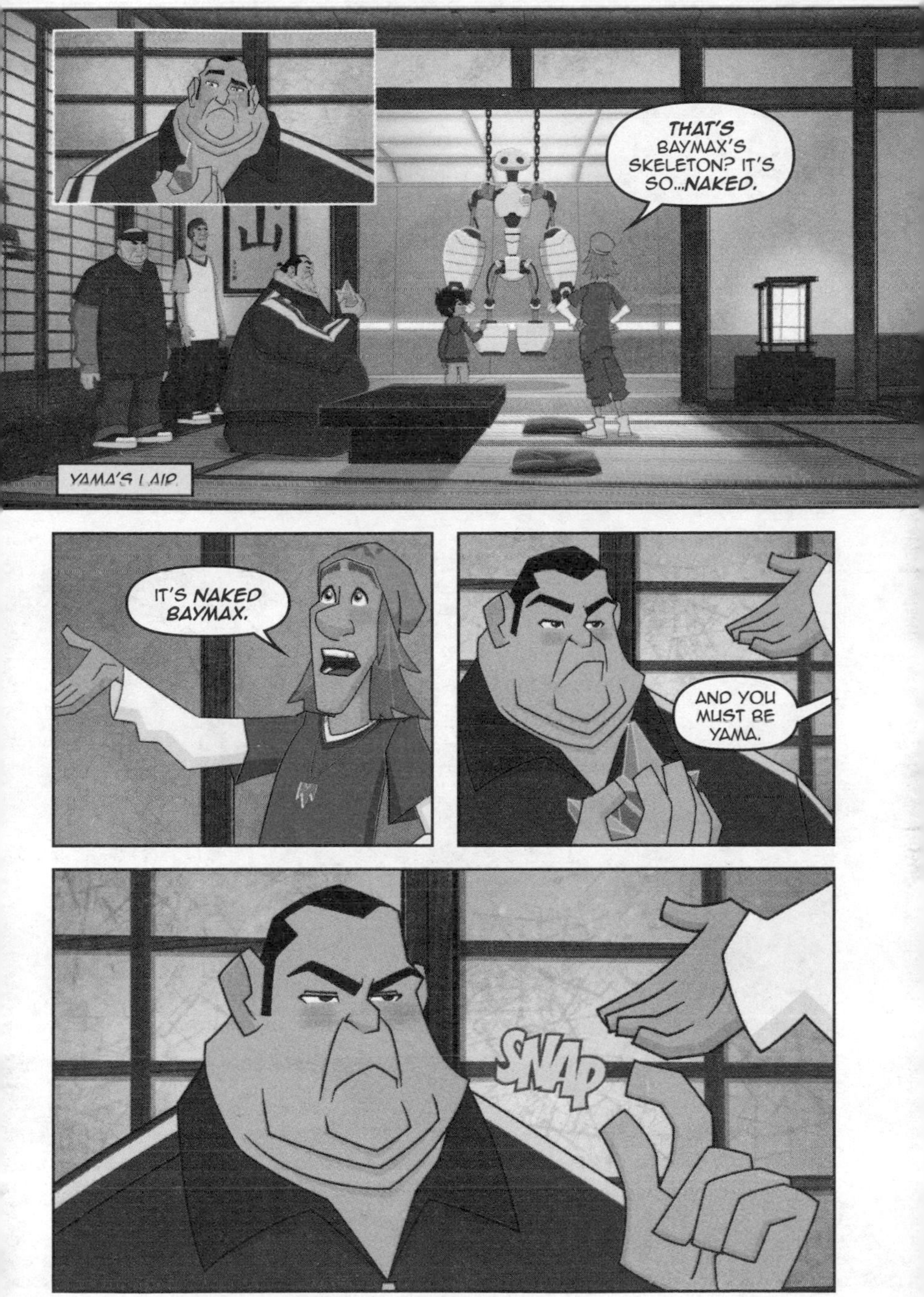
THAT'S BAYMAX'S SKELETON? IT'S SO...NAKED.
YAMA'S LAIR.
IT'S NAKED BAYMAX.
AND YOU MUST BE YAMA.
SNAP

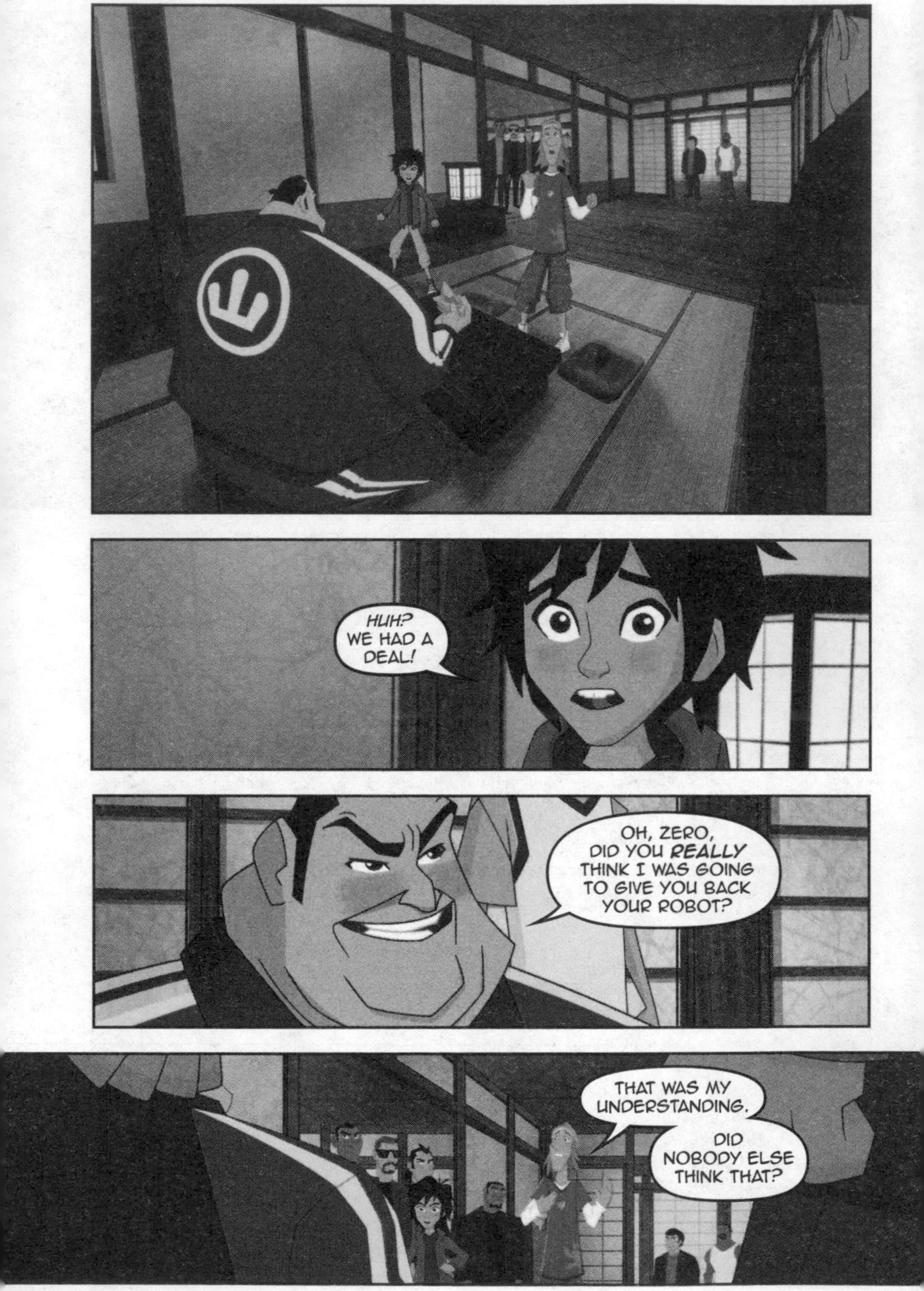
HUH? WE HAD A DEAL!
OH, ZERO, DID YOU *REALLY* THINK I WAS GOING TO GIVE YOU BACK YOUR ROBOT?
THAT WAS MY UNDERSTANDING.
DID NOBODY ELSE THINK THAT?

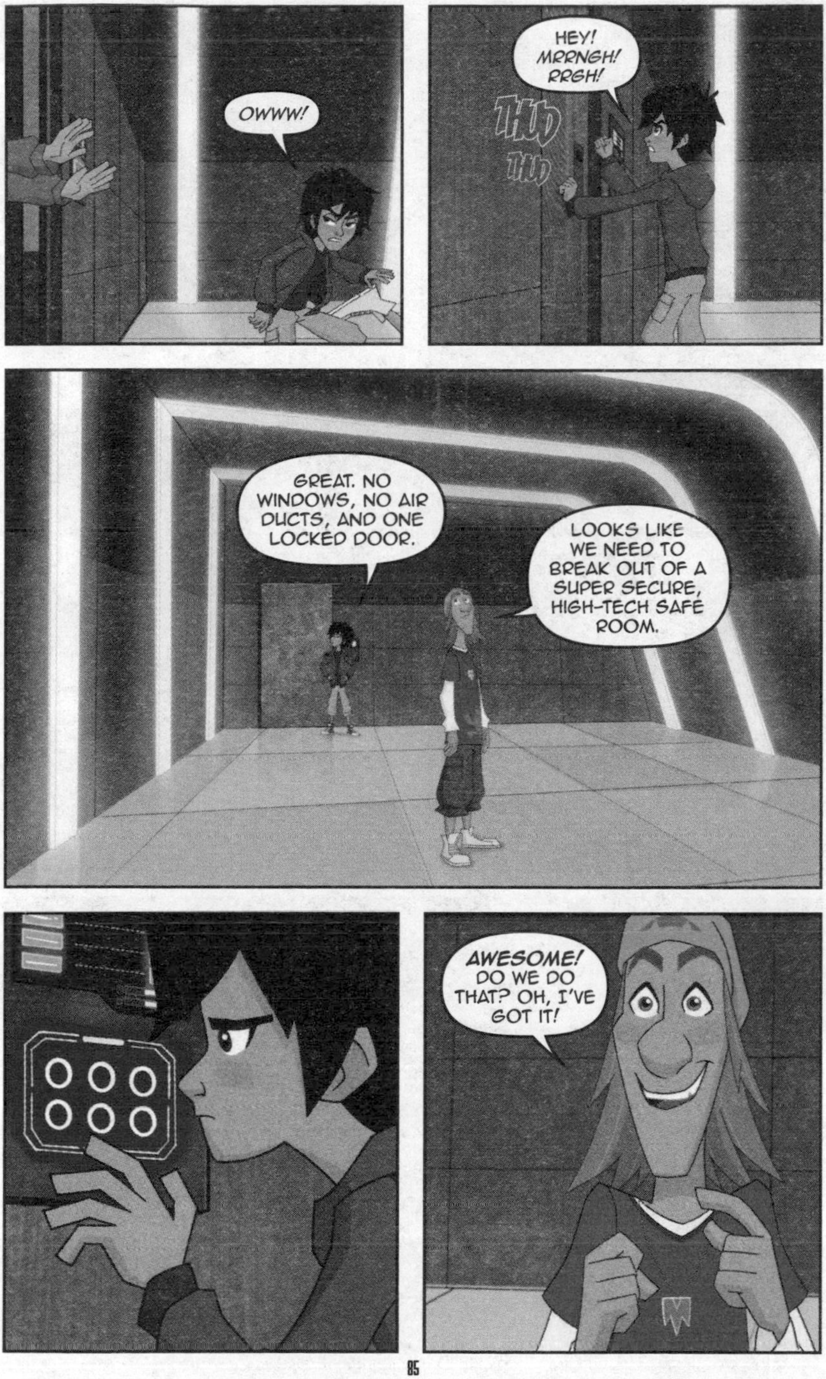
OWWW!
HEY! MRRNGH! RRGH!
THUD
THUD
GREAT. NO WINDOWS, NO AIR DUCTS, AND ONE LOCKED DOOR.
LOOKS LIKE WE NEED TO BREAK OUT OF A SUPER SECURE, HIGH-TECH SAFE ROOM.
AWESOME! DO WE DO THAT? OH, I'VE GOT IT!

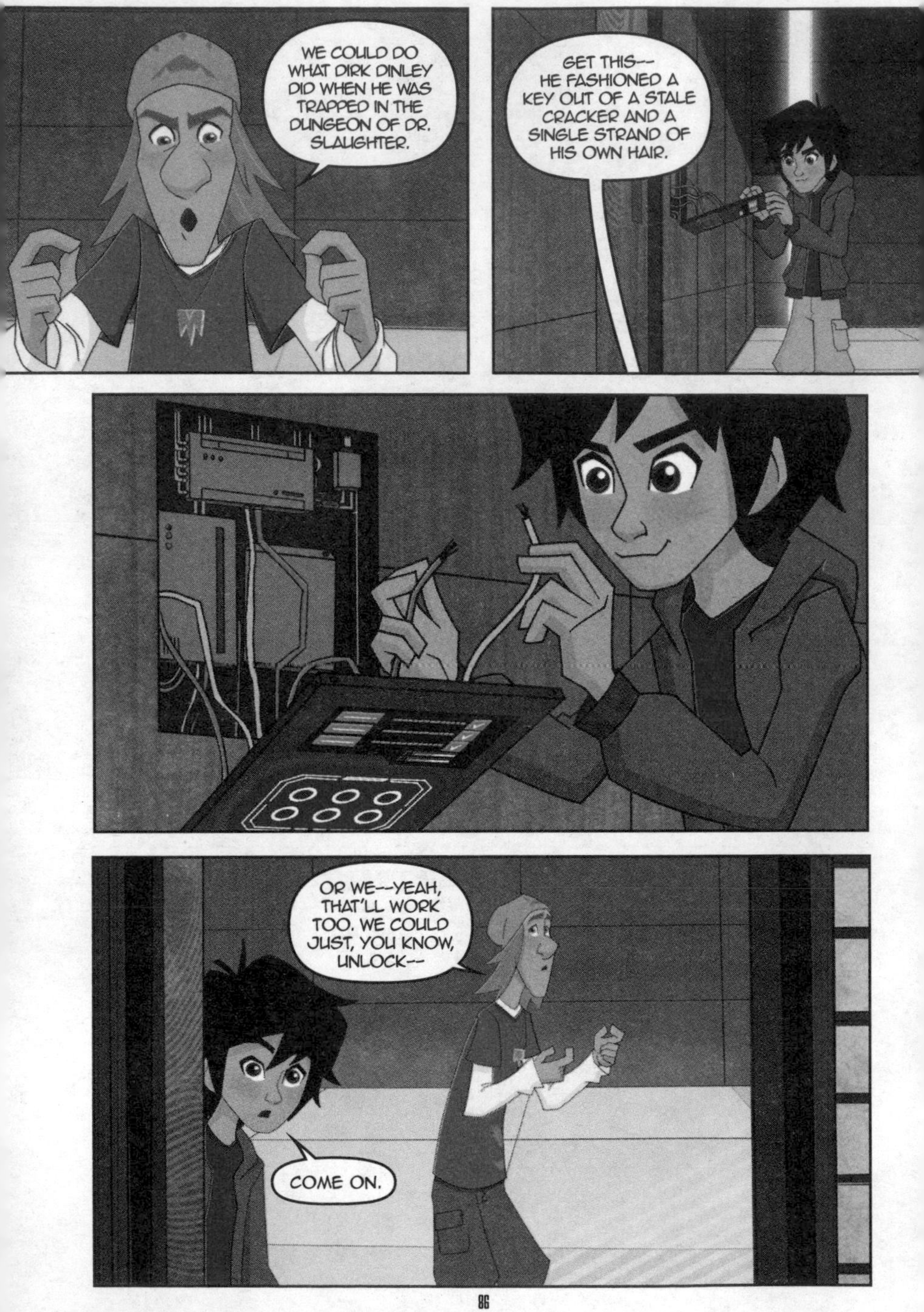
WE COULD DO WHAT DIRK DINLEY DID WHEN HE WAS TRAPPED IN THE DUNGEON OF DR. SLAUGHTER.
GET THIS-- HE FASHIONED A KEY OUT OF A STALE CRACKER AND A SINGLE STRAND OF HIS OWN HAIR.
OR WE--YEAH, THAT'LL WORK TOO. WE COULD JUST, YOU KNOW, UNLOCK--
COME ON.

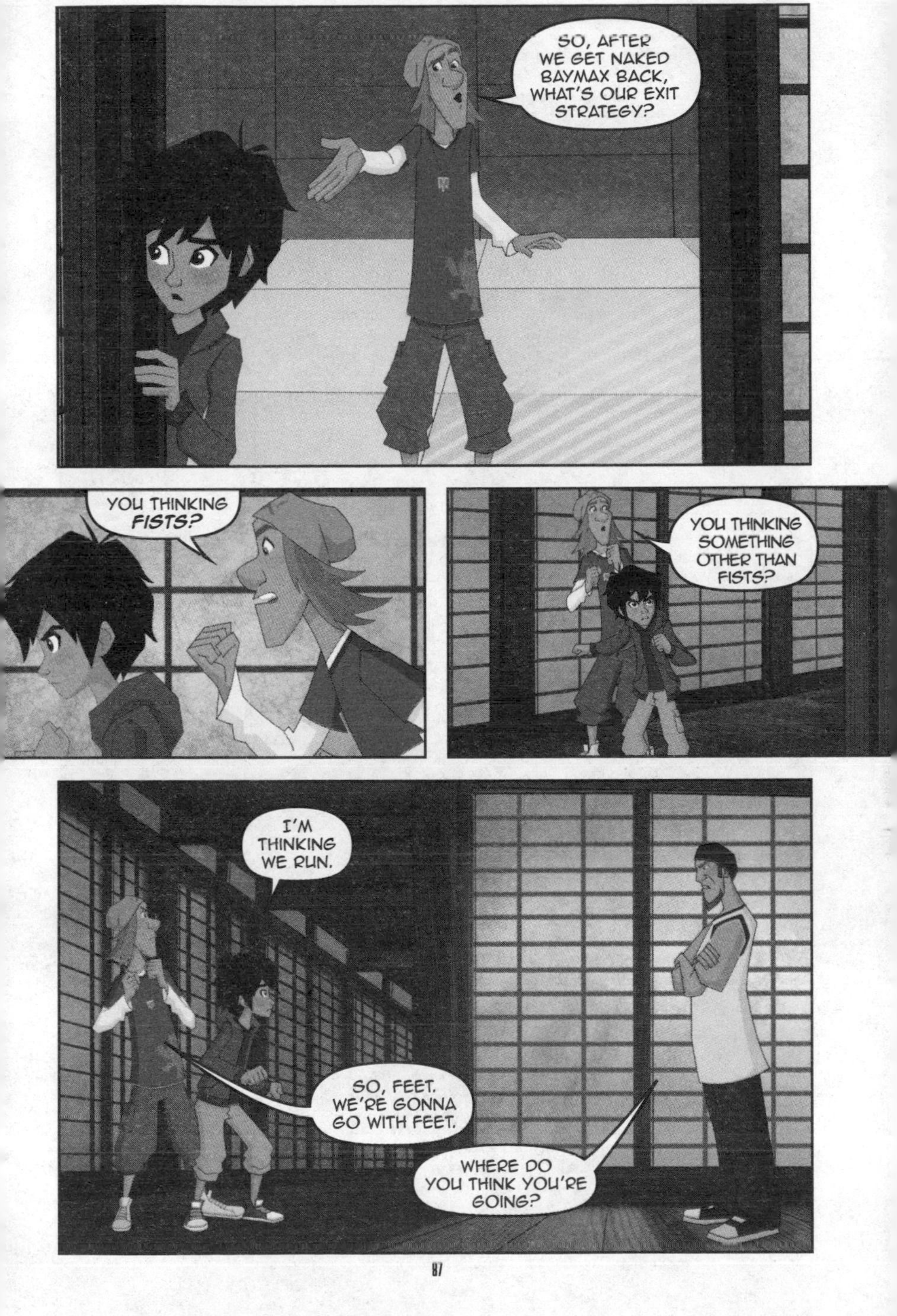
SO, AFTER WE GET NAKED BAYMAX BACK, WHAT'S OUR EXIT STRATEGY?
YOU THINKING *FISTS?*
YOU THINKING SOMETHING OTHER THAN FISTS?
I'M THINKING WE RUN.
SO, FEET. WE'RE GONNA GO WITH FEET.
WHERE DO YOU THINK YOU'RE GOING?

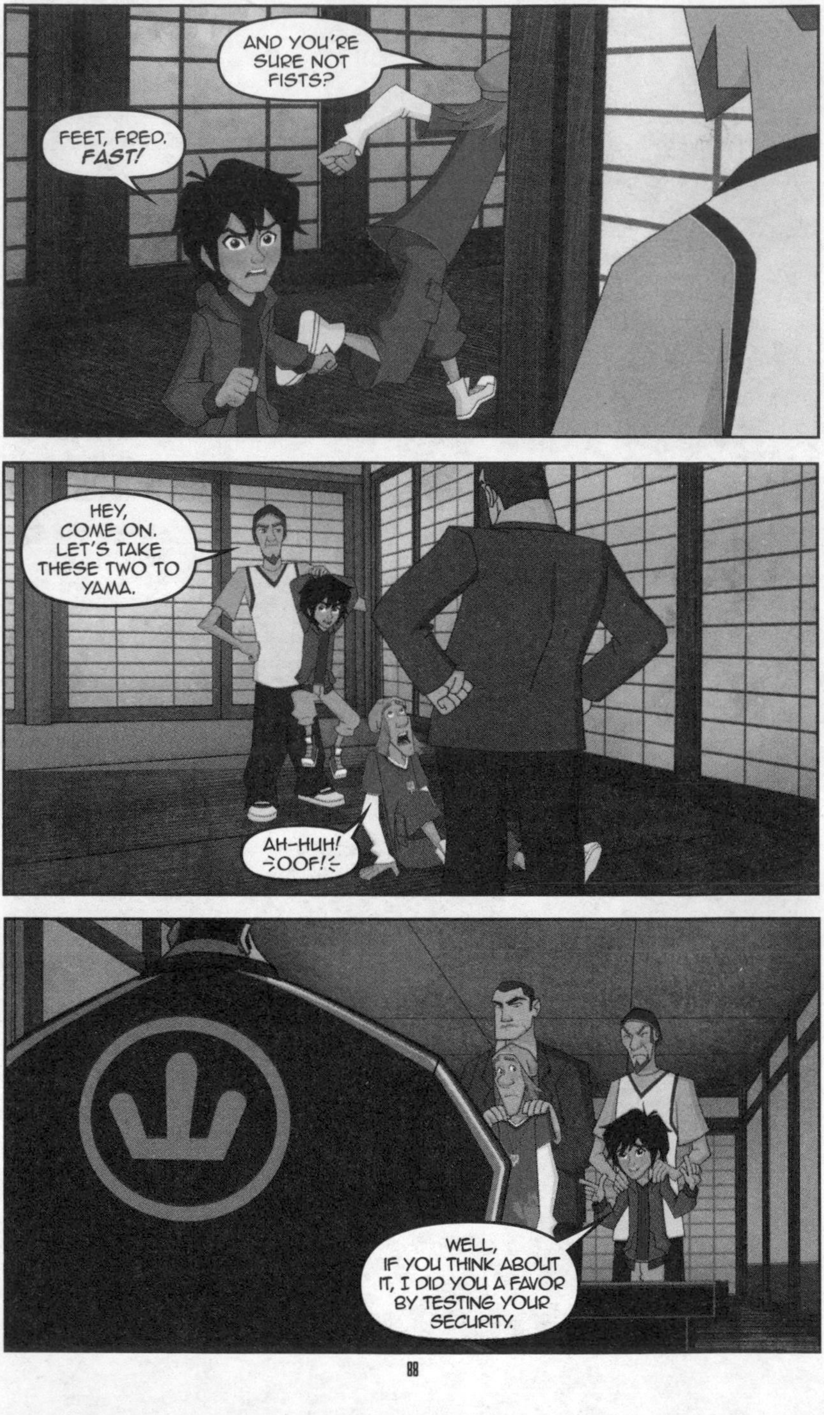
AND YOU'RE SURE NOT FISTS?
FEET, FRED. FAST!
HEY, COME ON. LET'S TAKE THESE TWO TO YAMA.
AH-HUH! OOF!
WELL, IF YOU THINK ABOUT IT, I DID YOU A FAVOR BY TESTING YOUR SECURITY.

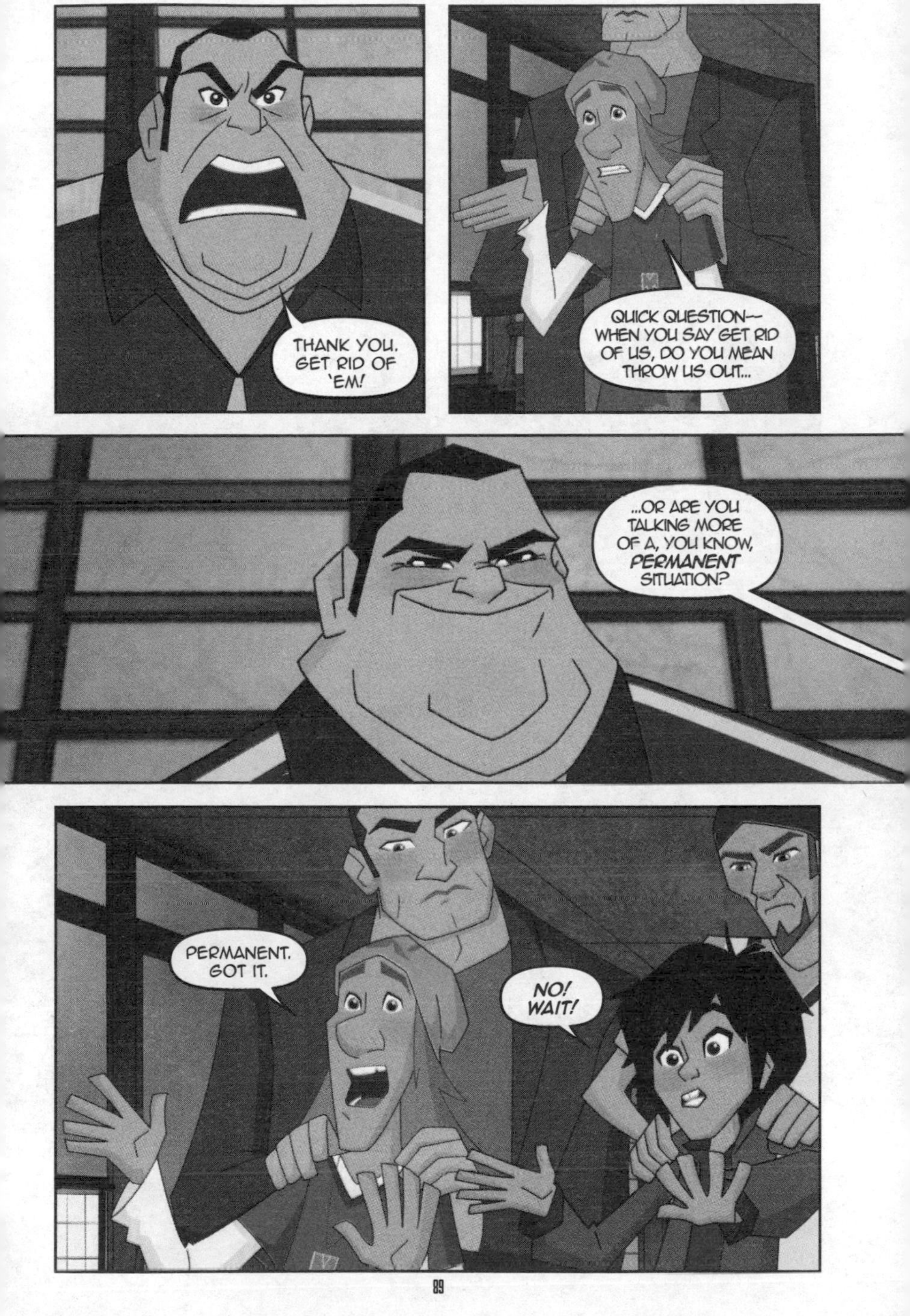
THANK YOU. GET RID OF 'EM!
QUICK QUESTION-- WHEN YOU SAY GET RID OF US, DO YOU MEAN THROW US OUT...
...OR ARE YOU TALKING MORE OF A, YOU KNOW, PERMANENT SITUATION?
PERMANENT. GOT IT.
NO! WAIT!

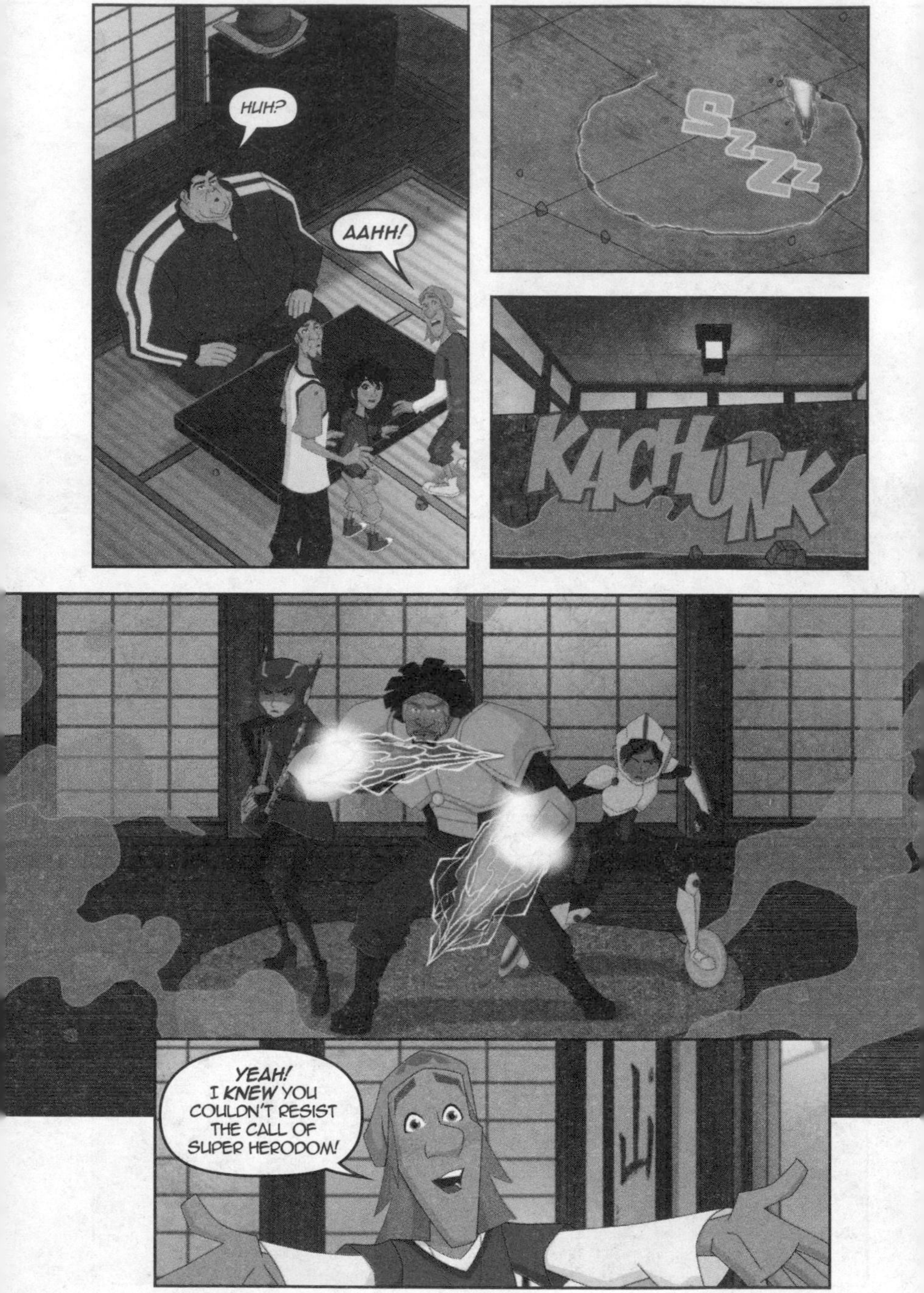
HUH?
AAHH!
SZZZ
KACHUNK
YEAH! I KNEW YOU COULDN'T RESIST THE CALL OF SUPER HERODOM!

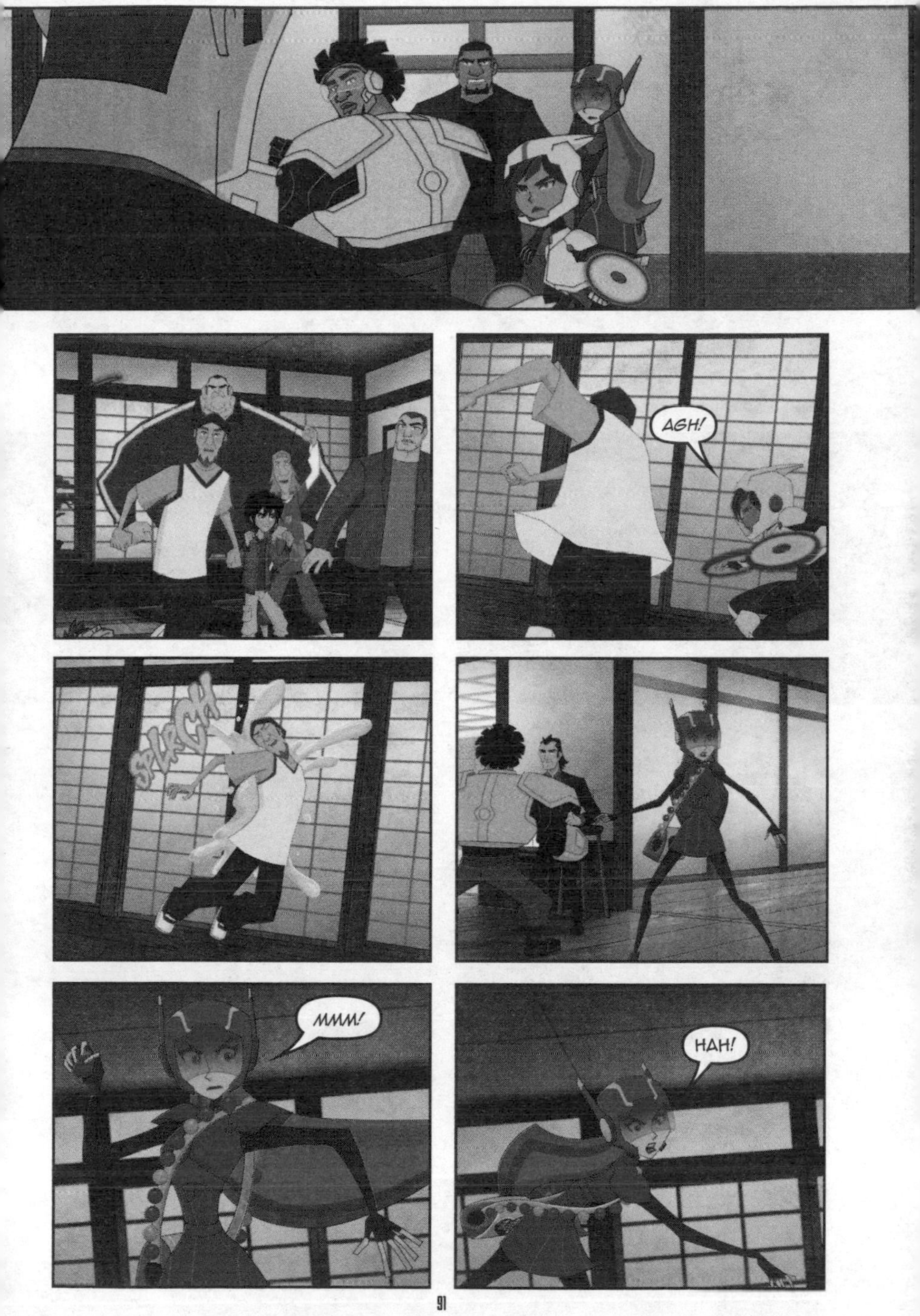
AGH!
MMM!
HAH!

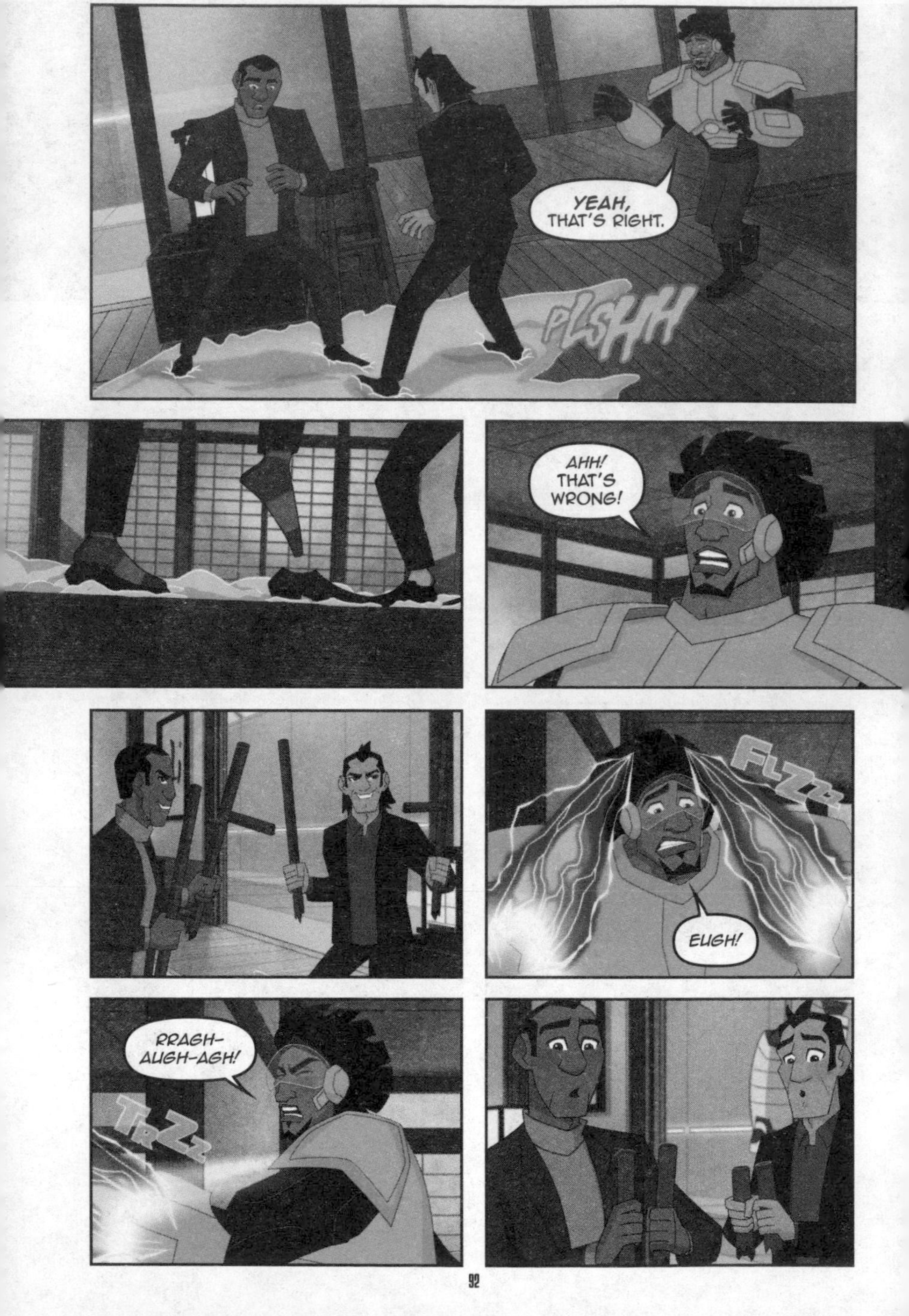
YEAH, THAT'S RIGHT.
PLSHH
AHH! THAT'S WRONG!
FLZZZ
EUGH!
RRAGH-AUGH-AGH!
TRZZ

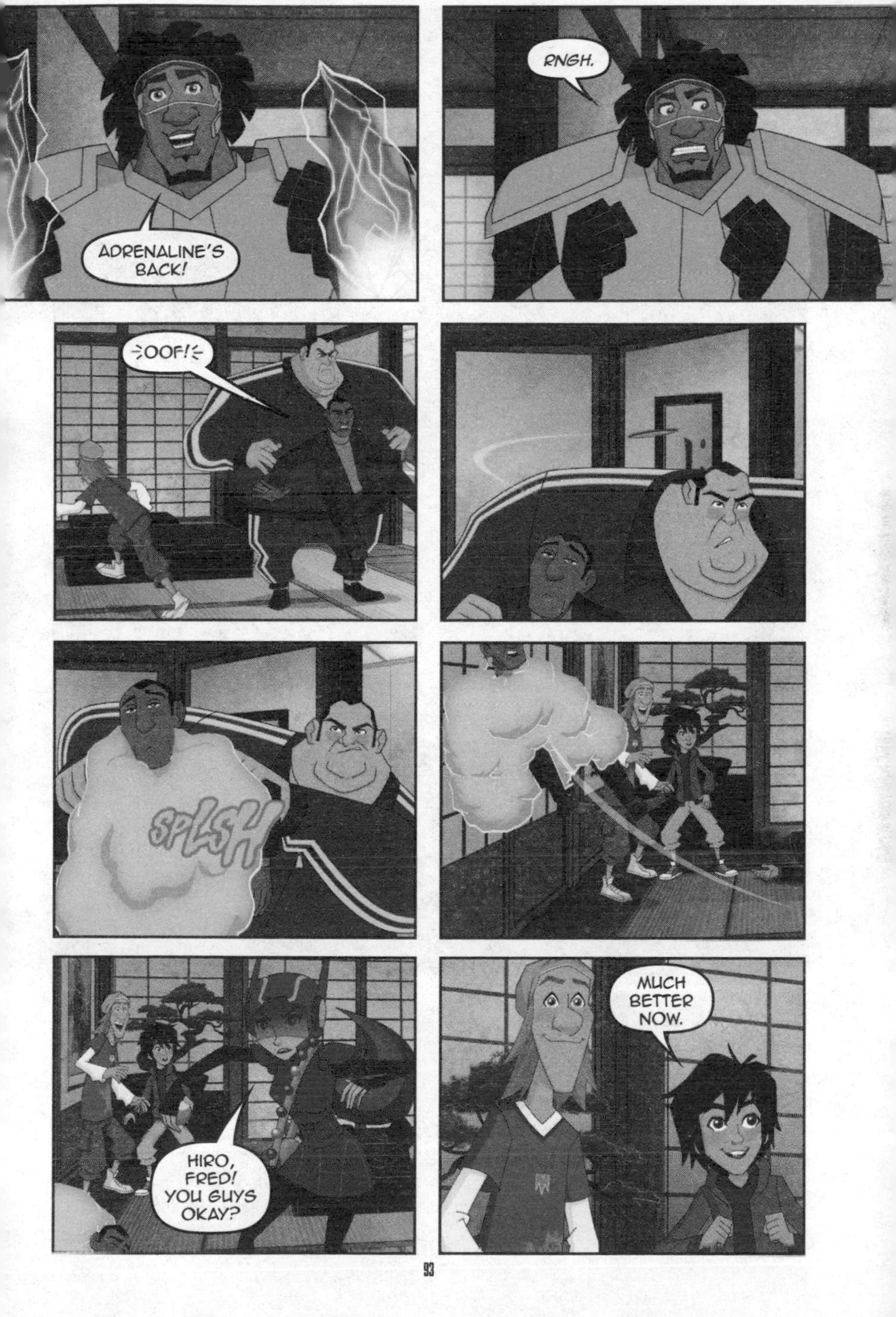
ADRENALINE'S BACK!
RNGH.
OOF!
SPLSH
HIRO, FRED! YOU GUYS OKAY?
MUCH BETTER NOW.

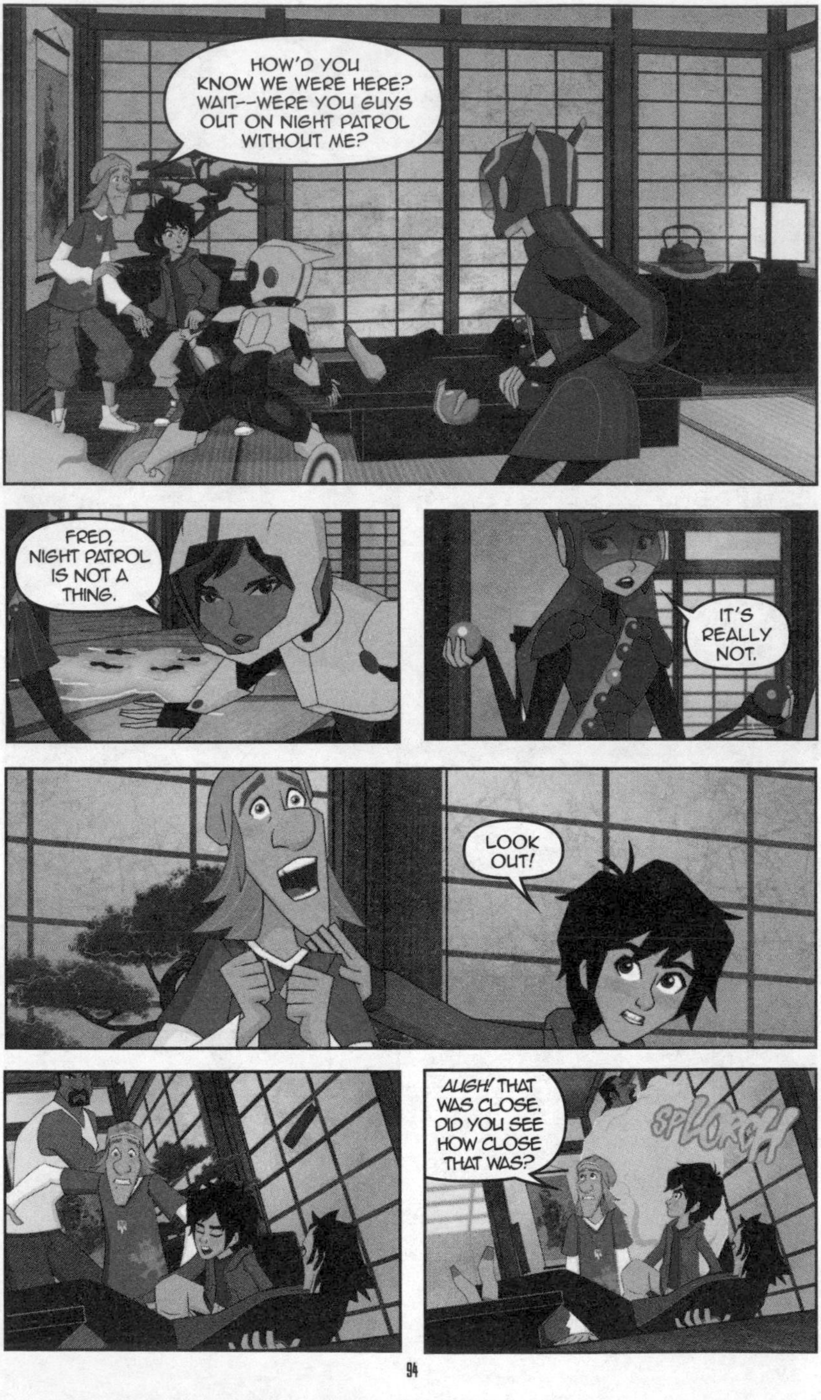
HOW'D YOU KNOW WE WERE HERE? WAIT--WERE YOU GUYS OUT ON NIGHT PATROL WITHOUT ME?
FRED, NIGHT PATROL IS NOT A THING.
IT'S REALLY NOT.
LOOK OUT!
AUGH! THAT WAS CLOSE. DID YOU SEE HOW CLOSE THAT WAS?
SPLORCH

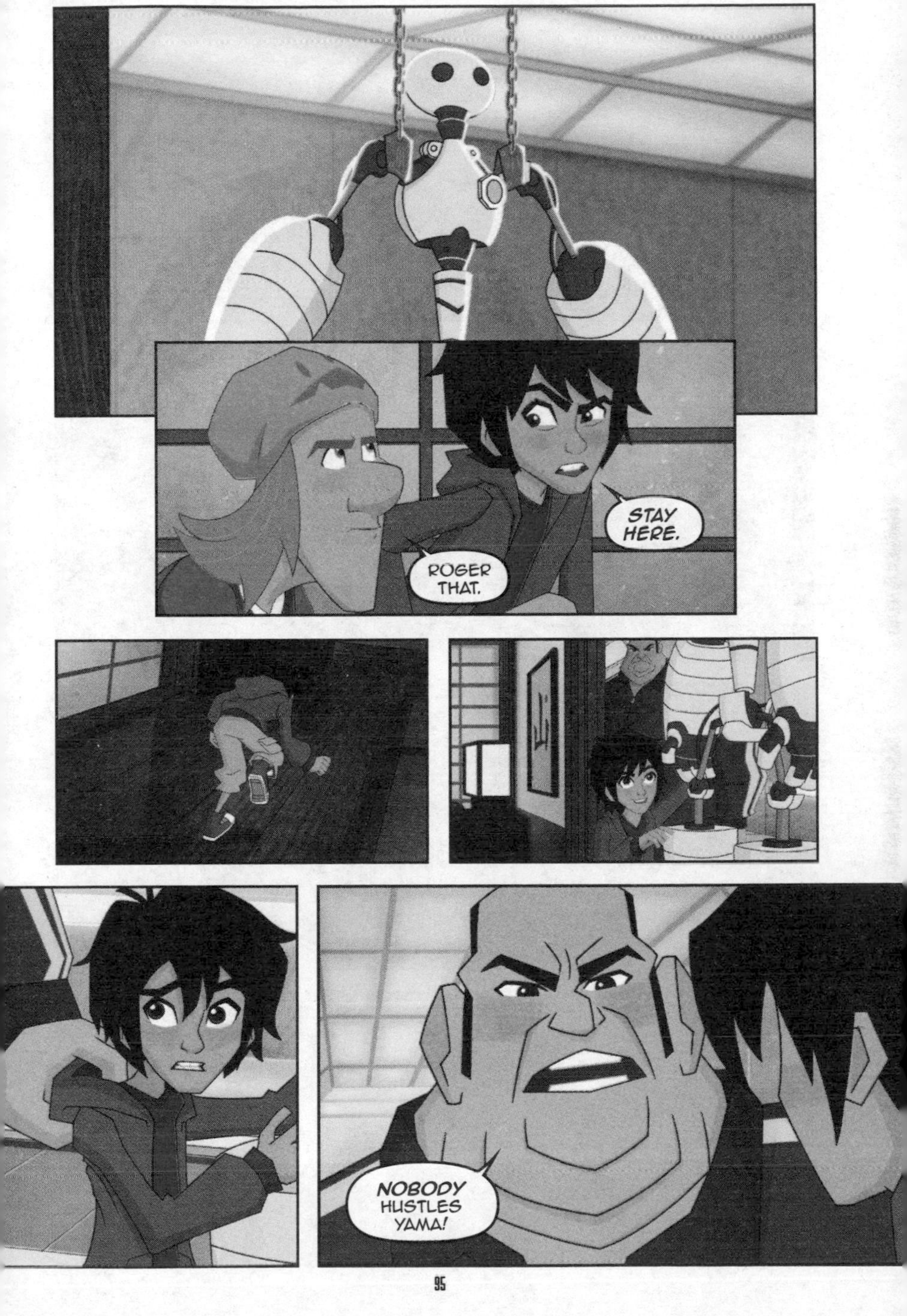
STAY HERE.
ROGER THAT.
NOBODY HUSTLES YAMA!

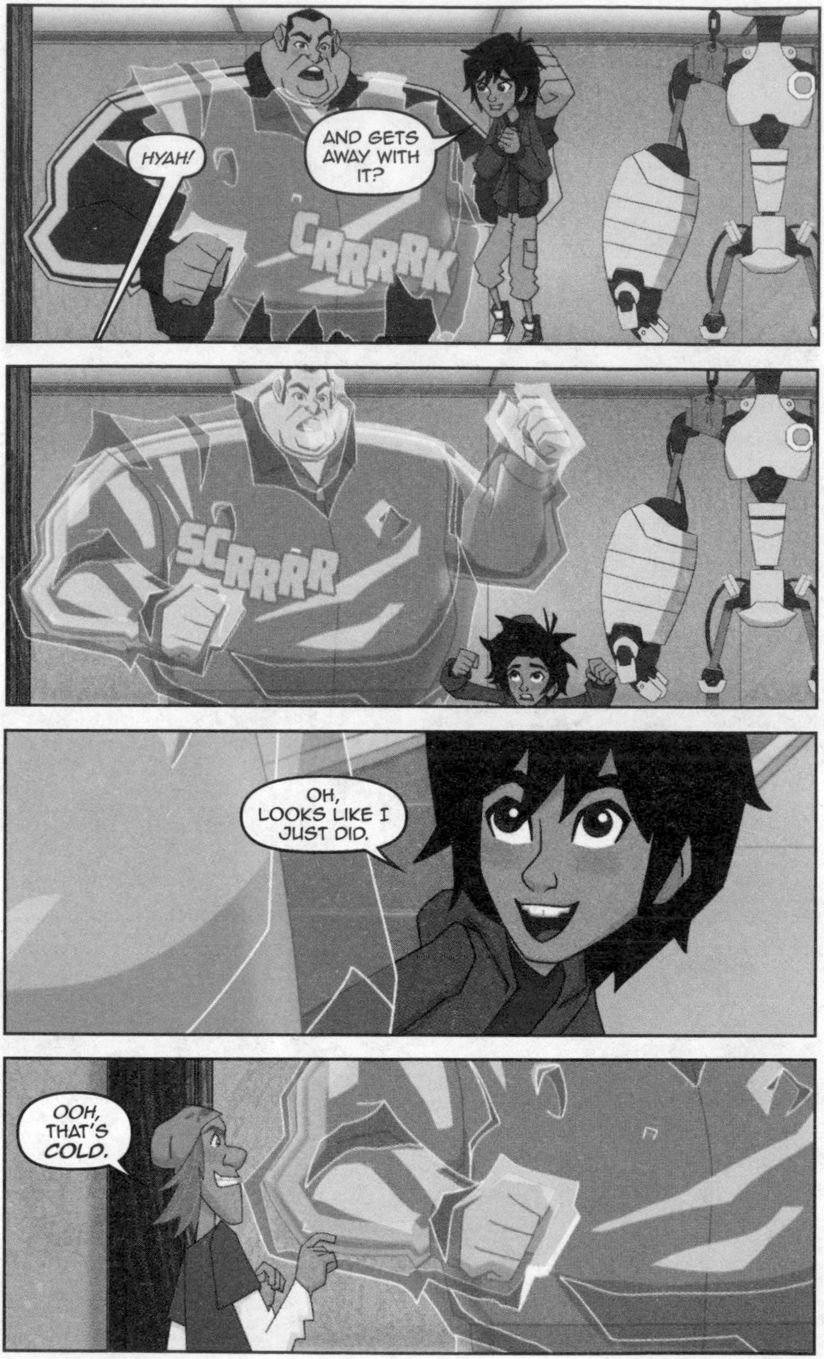
AND GETS AWAY WITH IT?
HYAH!
CRRRRK
SCRRRR
OH, LOOKS LIKE I JUST DID.
OOH, THAT'S COLD.

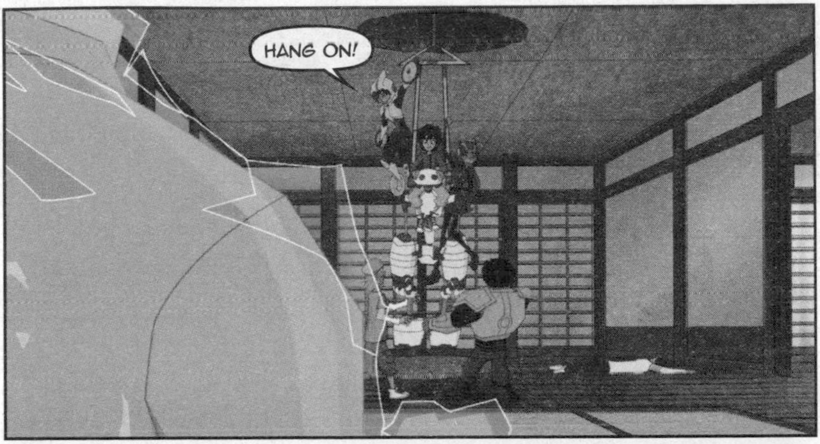
HANG ON!

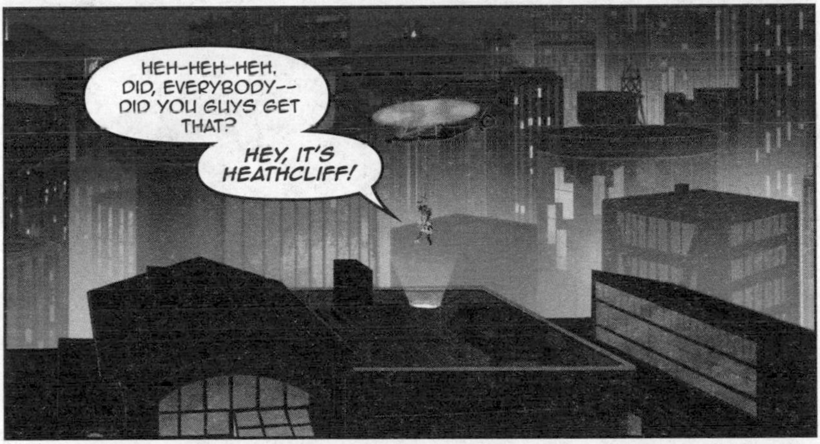
HEH-HEH-HEH. DID, EVERYBODY-- DID YOU GUYS GET THAT?
HEY, IT'S HEATHCLIFF!

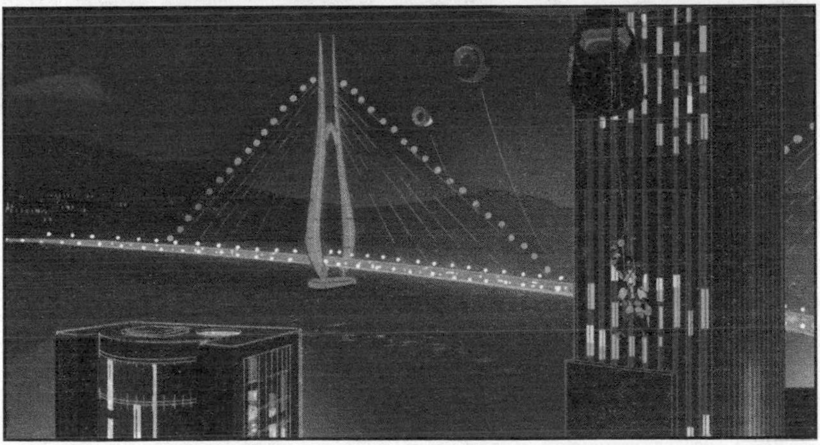

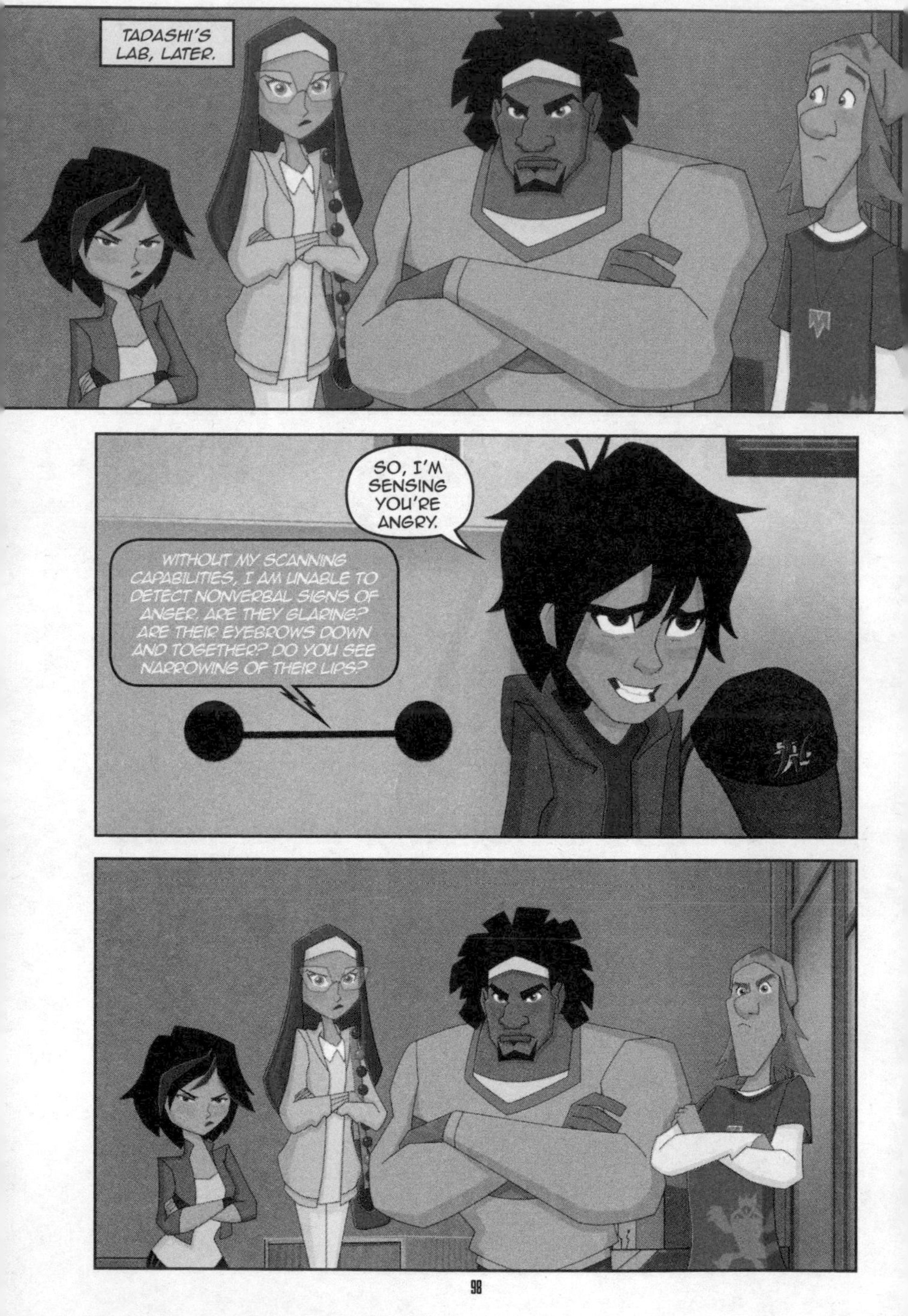
TADASHI'S LAB, LATER.
SO, I'M SENSING YOU'RE ANGRY.
WITHOUT MY SCANNING CAPABILITIES, I AM UNABLE TO DETECT NONVERBAL SIGNS OF ANGER. ARE THEY GLARING? ARE THEIR EYEBROWS DOWN AND TOGETHER? DO YOU SEE NARROWING OF THEIR LIPS?

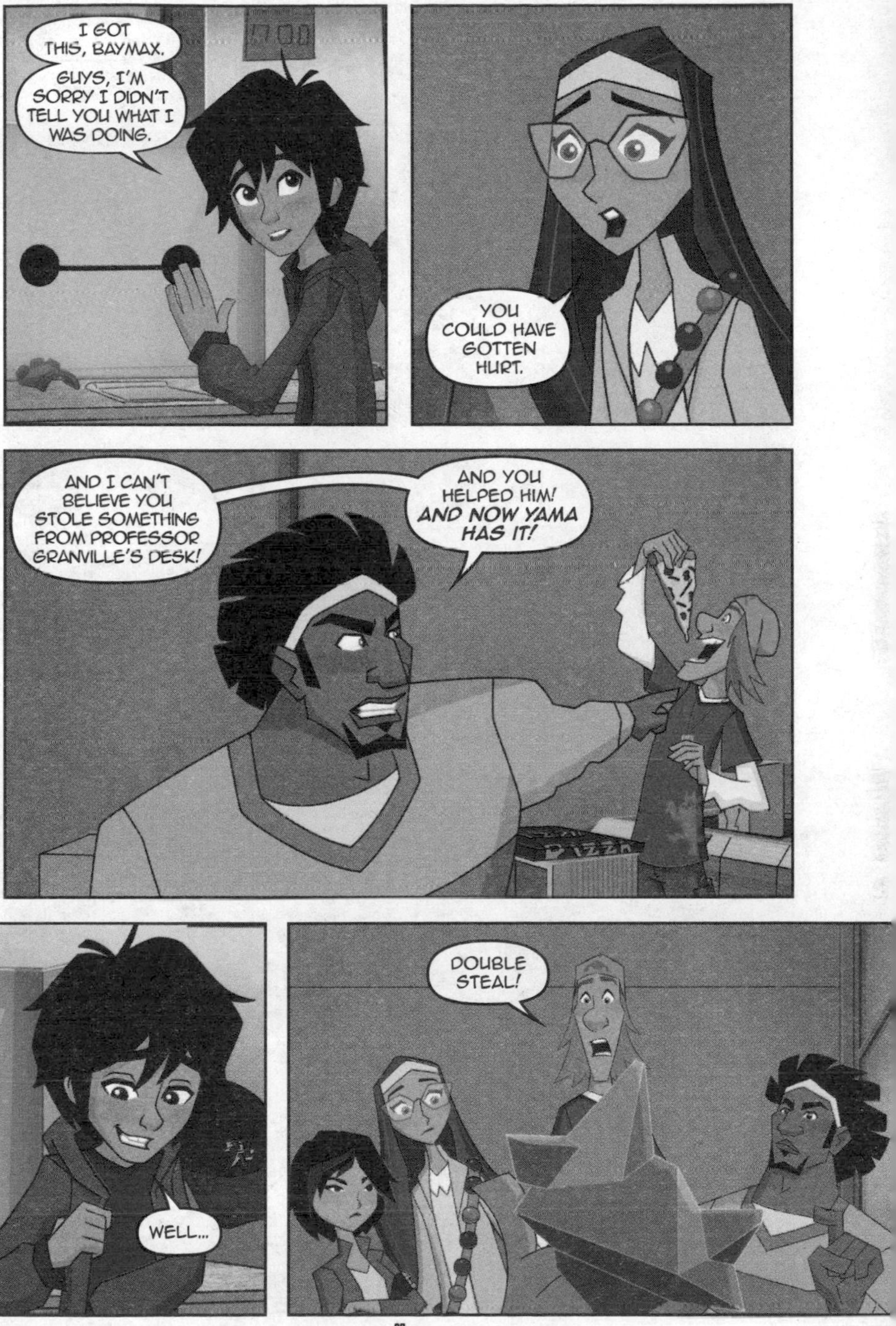
I GOT THIS, BAYMAX.
GUYS, I'M SORRY I DIDN'T TELL YOU WHAT I WAS DOING.
YOU COULD HAVE GOTTEN HURT.
AND I CAN'T BELIEVE YOU STOLE SOMETHING FROM PROFESSOR GRANVILLE'S DESK!
AND YOU HELPED HIM! ***AND NOW YAMA HAS IT!***
WELL...
DOUBLE STEAL!

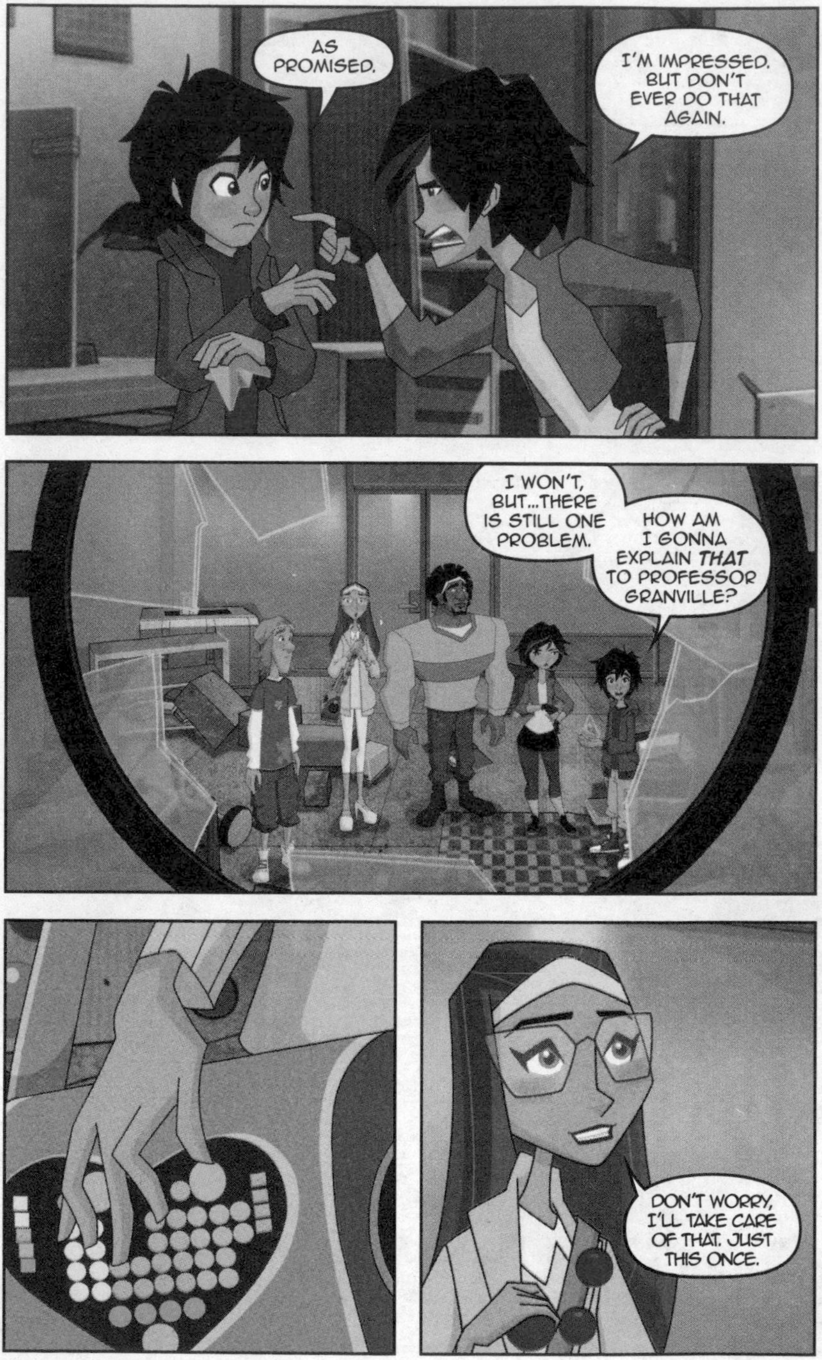
AS PROMISED.
I'M IMPRESSED. BUT DON'T EVER DO THAT AGAIN.
I WON'T, BUT...THERE IS STILL ONE PROBLEM.
HOW AM I GONNA EXPLAIN *THAT* TO PROFESSOR GRANVILLE?
DON'T WORRY, I'LL TAKE CARE OF THAT. JUST THIS ONCE.

GRANVILLE'S OFFICE, NIGHT.

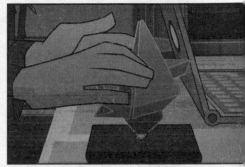

TADASHI'S LAB, THE NEXT DAY.

DIAGNOSTICS
IN PROGRESS

99%

COME ON,
COME ON,
COME ON.

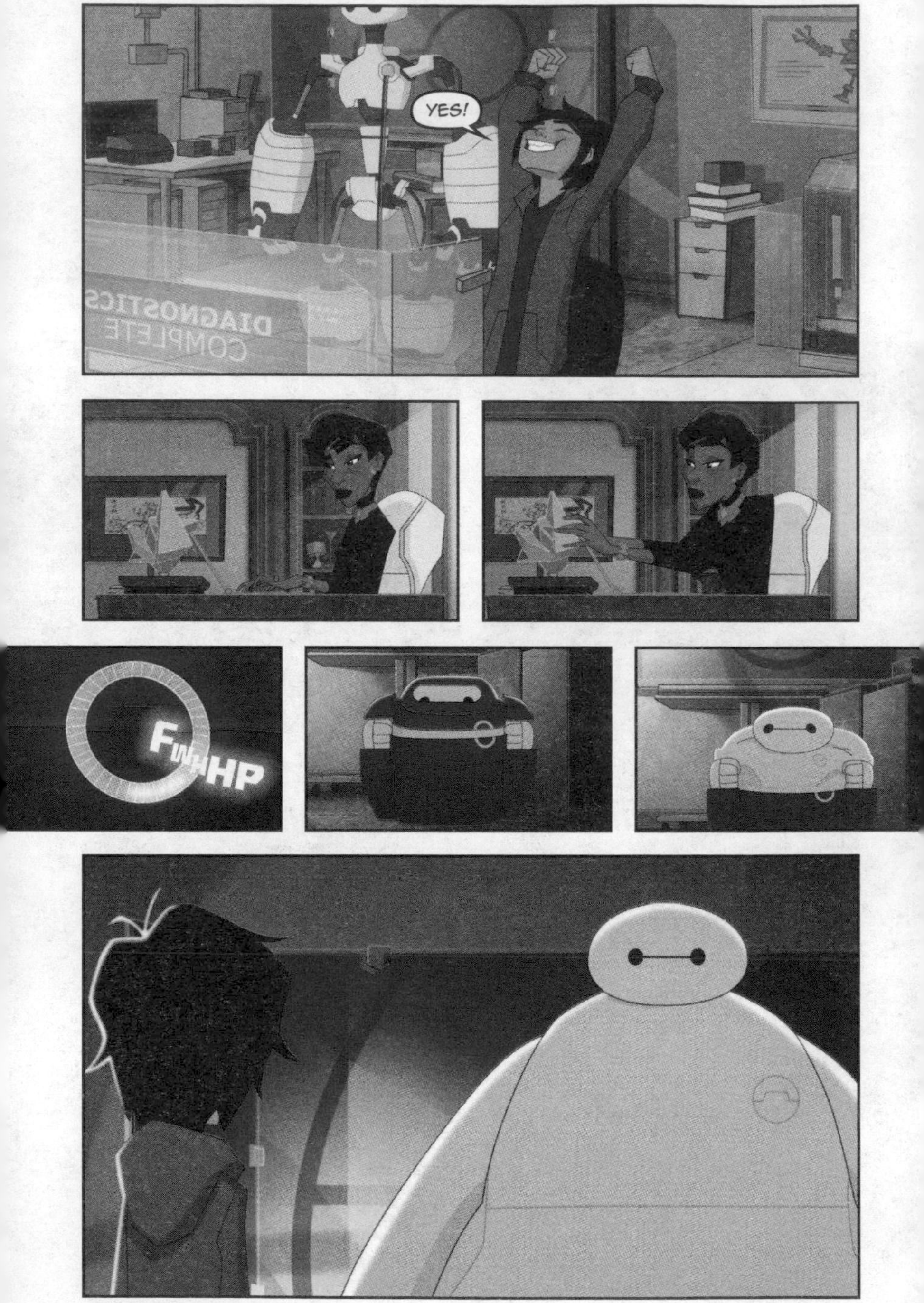
YES!
DIAGNOSTICS
COMPLETE
FWHHP

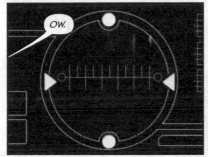

TADASHI HAMADA
TADASHI
OW.
I AM BAYMAX, YOUR PERSONAL HEALTH-CARE COMPANION.
HELLO, HIRO.

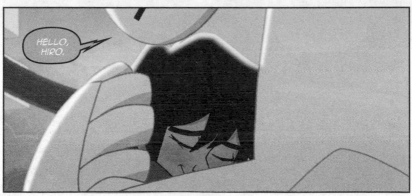

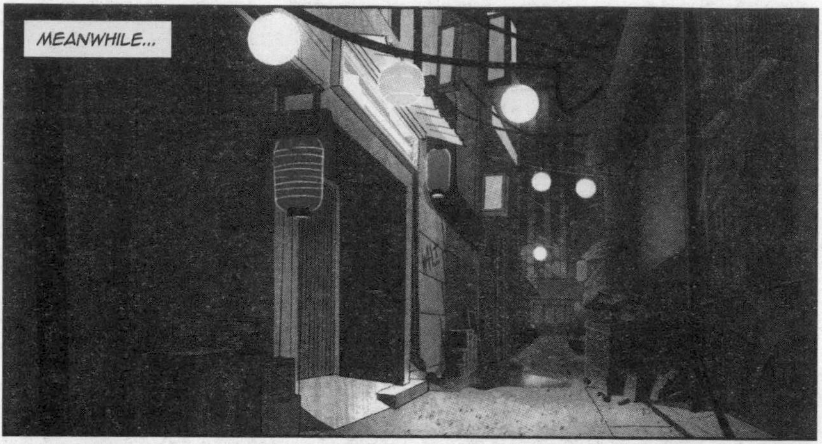
MEANWHILE...

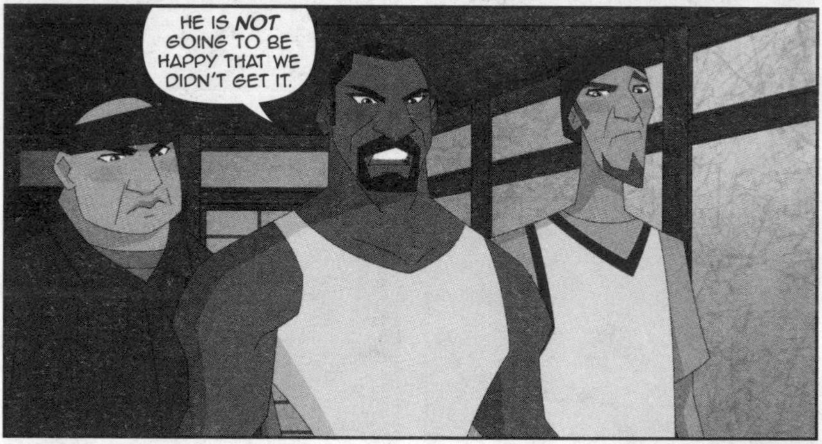
HE IS **NOT** GOING TO BE HAPPY THAT WE DIDN'T GET IT.

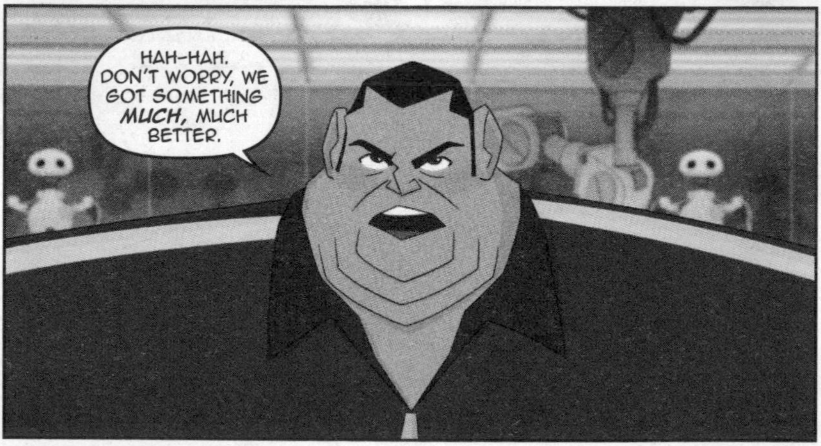
HAH-HAH. DON'T WORRY, WE GOT SOMETHING **MUCH,** MUCH BETTER.

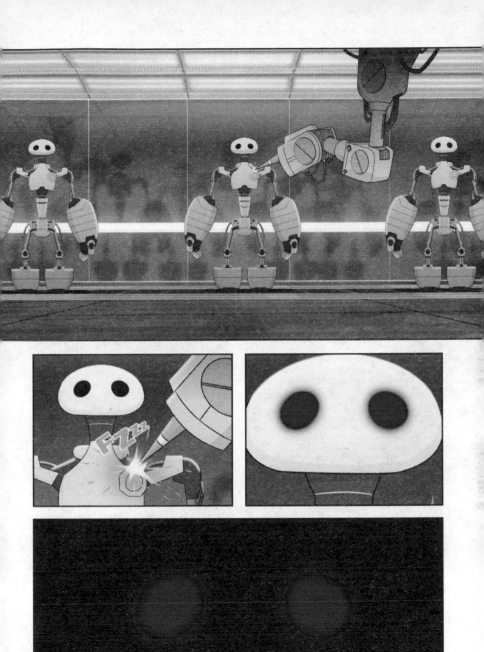

FZzz

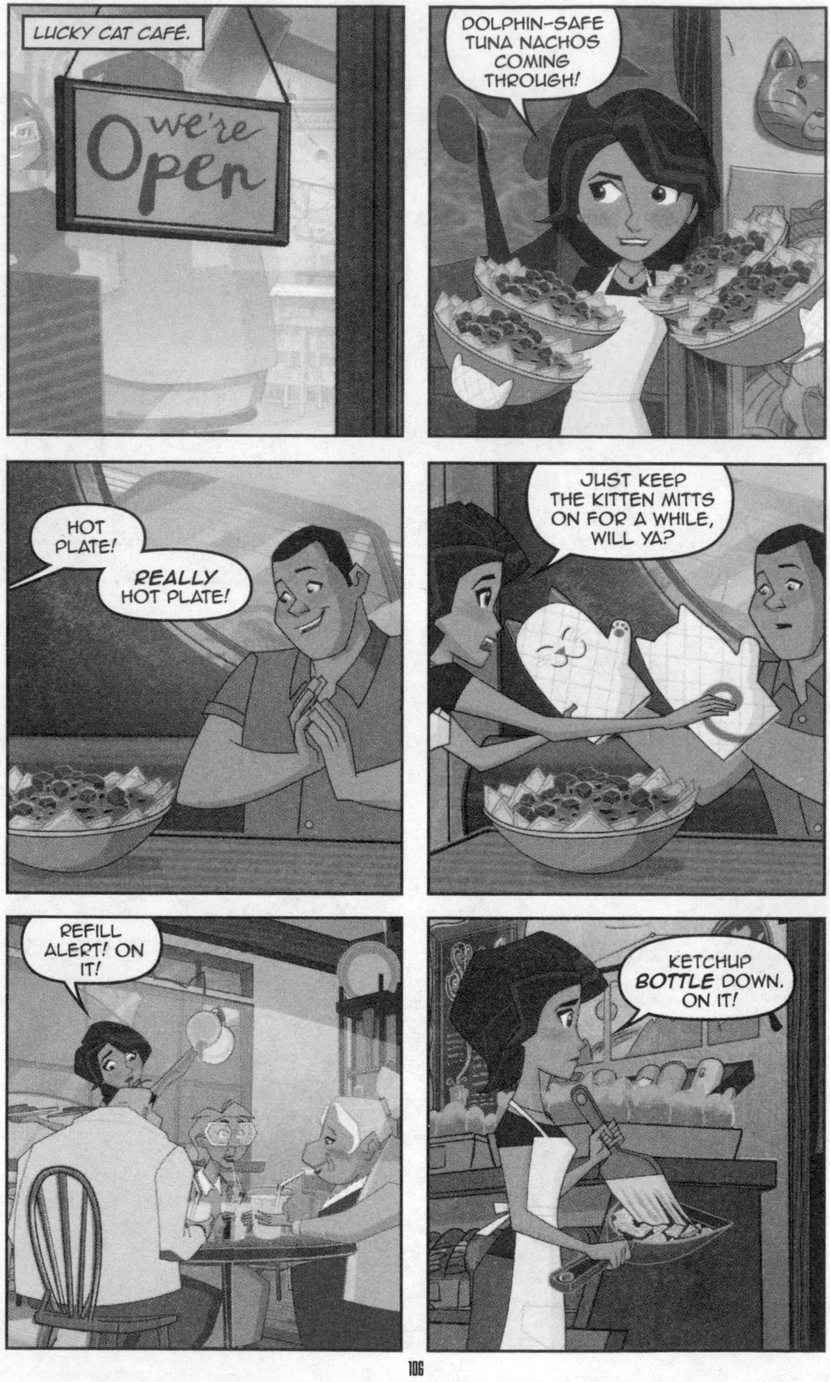
LUCKY CAT CAFÉ.
We're Open
DOLPHIN-SAFE TUNA NACHOS COMING THROUGH!
HOT PLATE!
REALLY HOT PLATE!
JUST KEEP THE KITTEN MITTS ON FOR A WHILE, WILL YA?
REFILL ALERT! ON IT!
KETCHUP BOTTLE DOWN. ON IT!

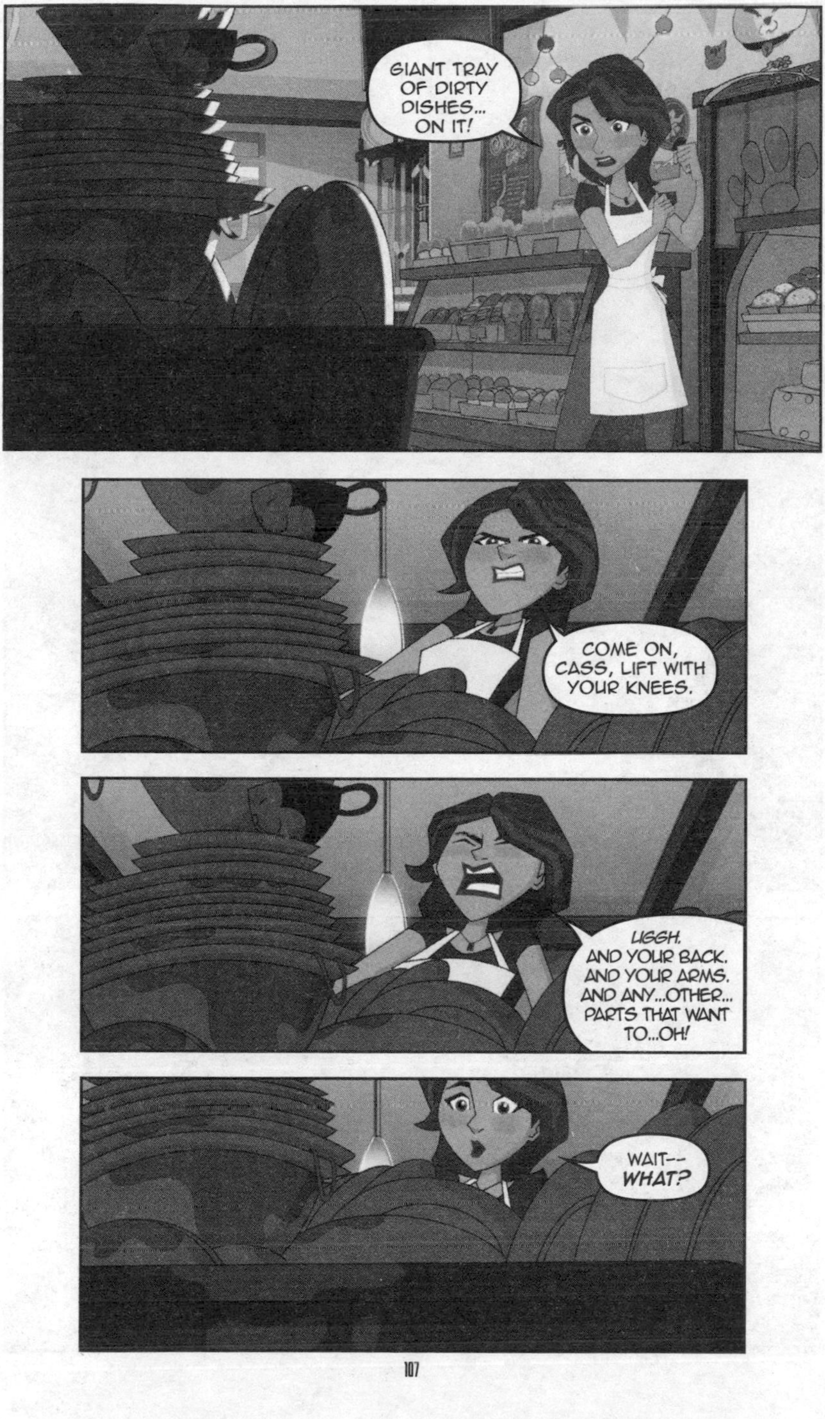
GIANT TRAY OF DIRTY DISHES... ON IT!
COME ON, CASS, LIFT WITH YOUR KNEES.
UGGH. AND YOUR BACK. AND YOUR ARMS. AND ANY...OTHER... PARTS THAT WANT TO...OH!
WAIT-- WHAT?

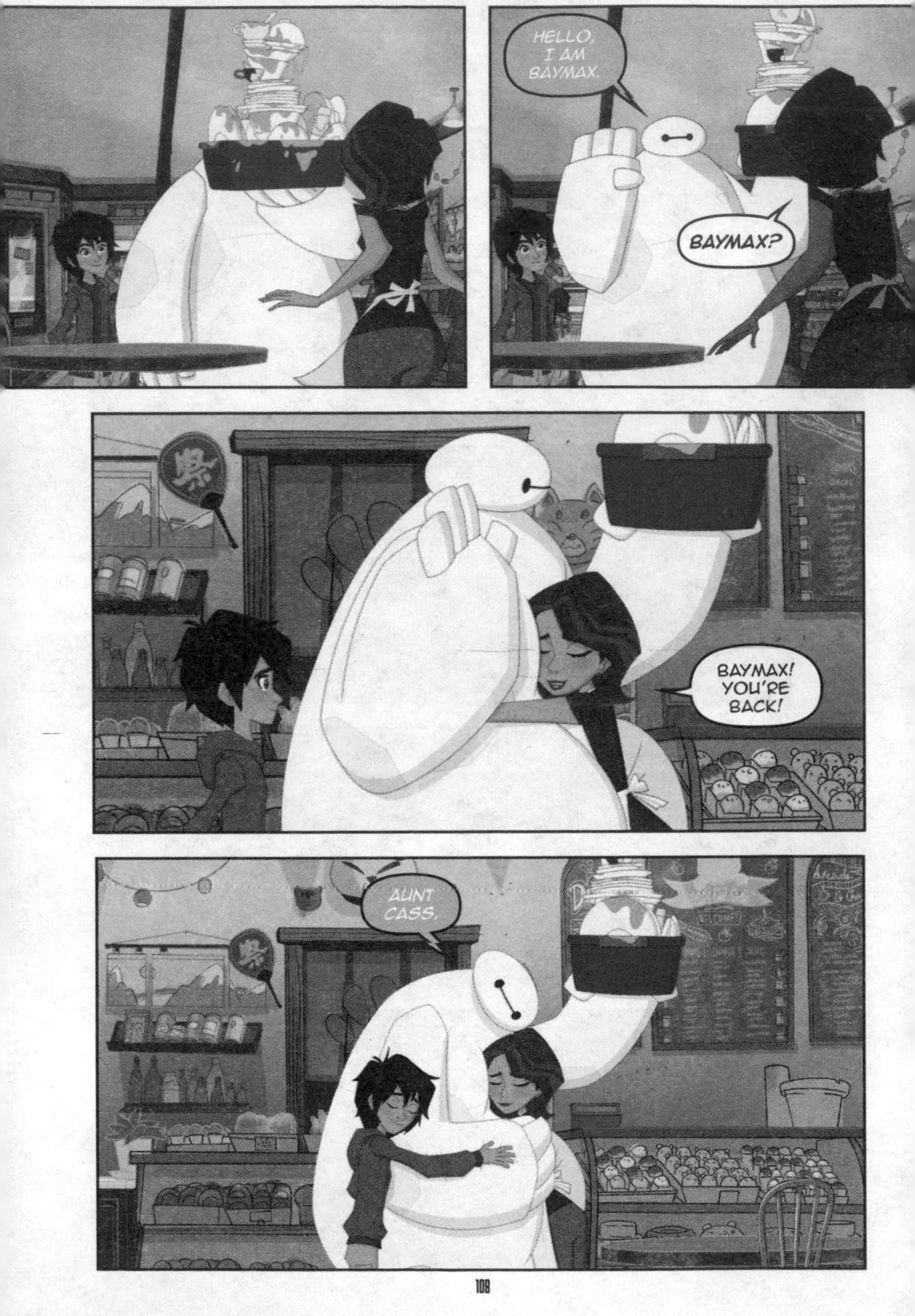
HELLO, I AM BAYMAX.
BAYMAX?
BAYMAX! YOU'RE BACK!
AUNT CASS.

YAMA'S BUILDING.
プラザ

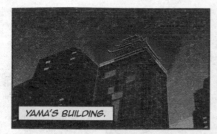

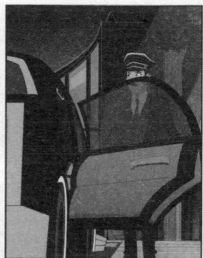

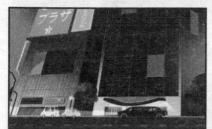

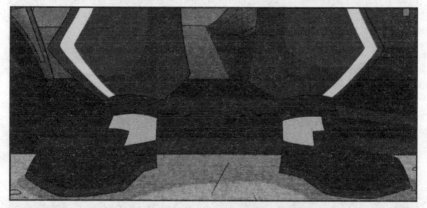

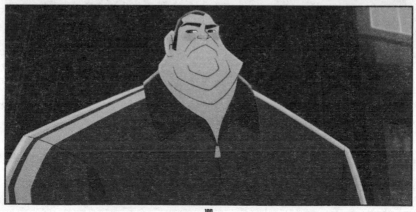

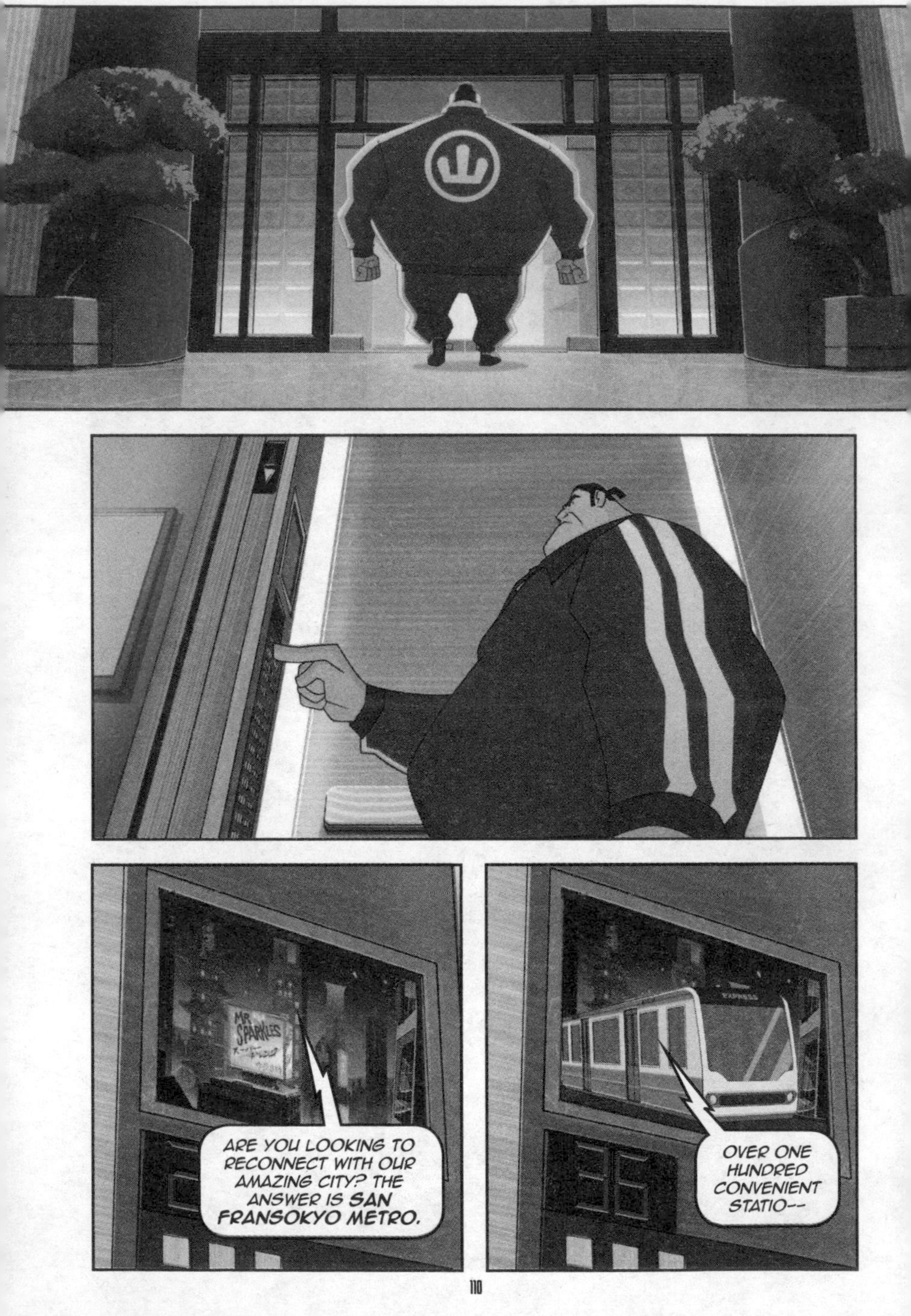
MR SPARKLES
ARE YOU LOOKING TO RECONNECT WITH OUR AMAZING CITY? THE ANSWER IS SAN FRANSOKYO METRO.
OVER ONE HUNDRED CONVENIENT STATIO--

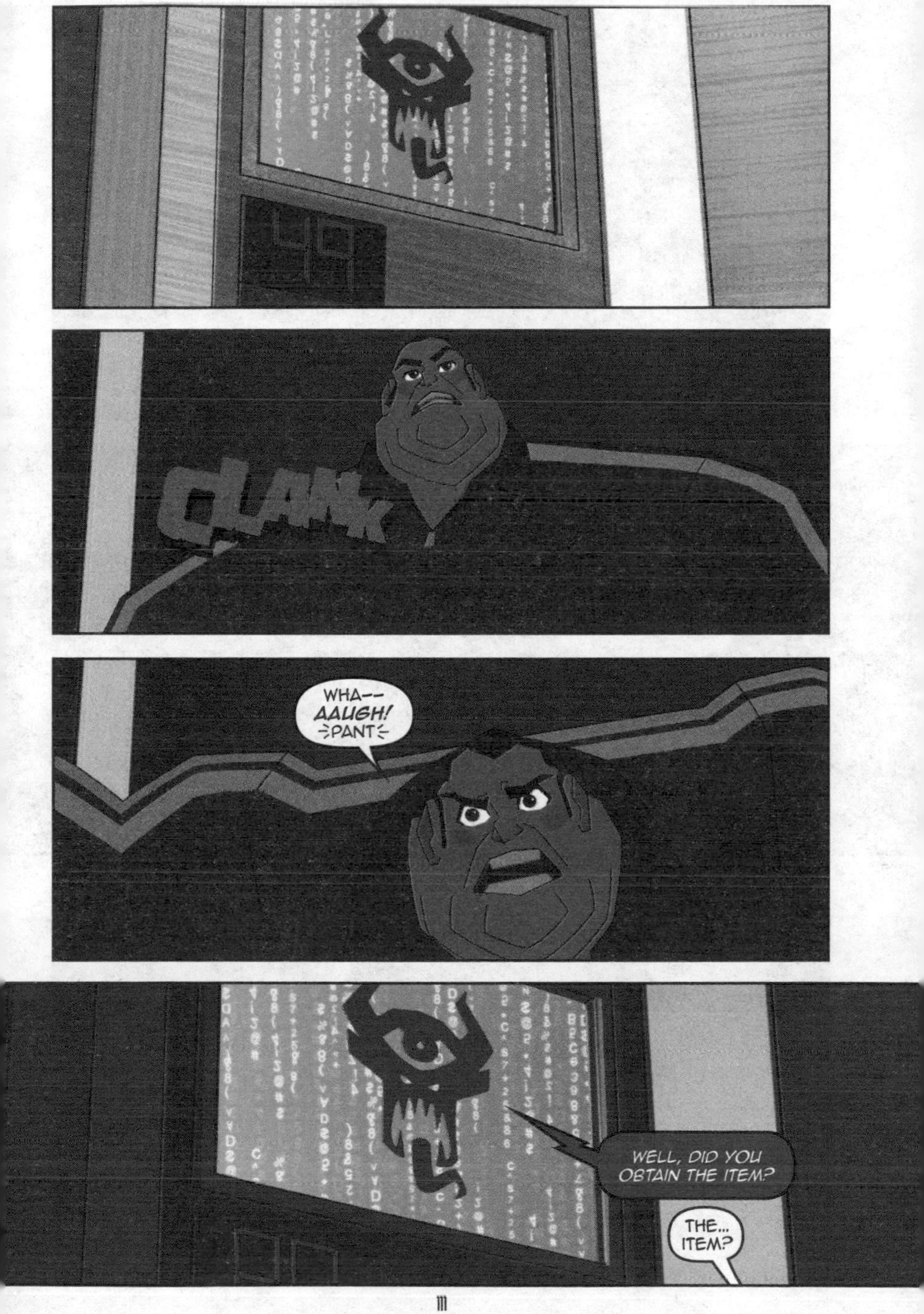
CLANK
WHA-- AAUGH! PANT
WELL, DID YOU OBTAIN THE ITEM?
THE... ITEM?

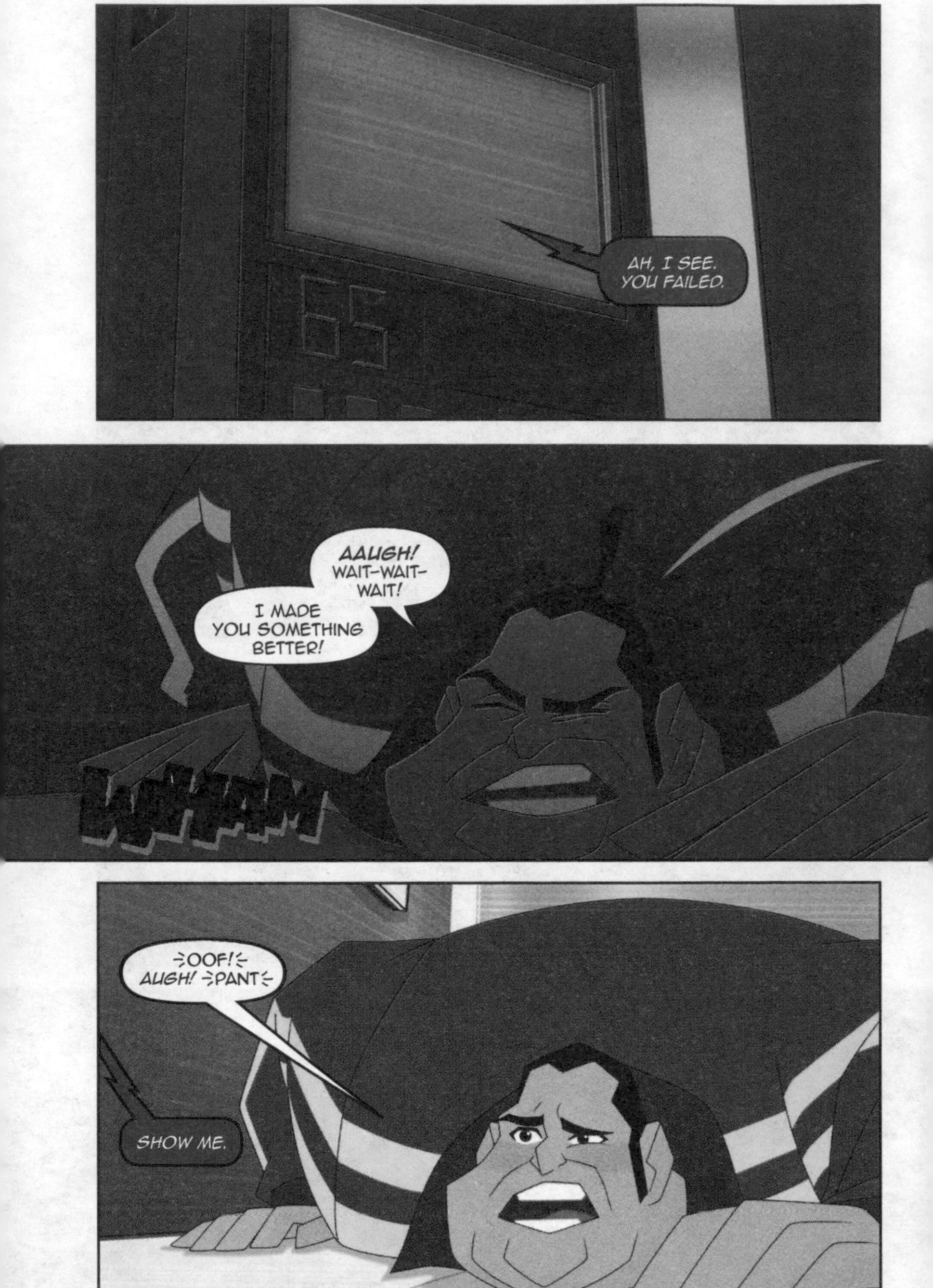
AH, I SEE. YOU FAILED.
AAUGH! WAIT-WAIT-WAIT!
I MADE YOU SOMETHING BETTER!
WHAM
OOF! AUGH! PANT
SHOW ME.

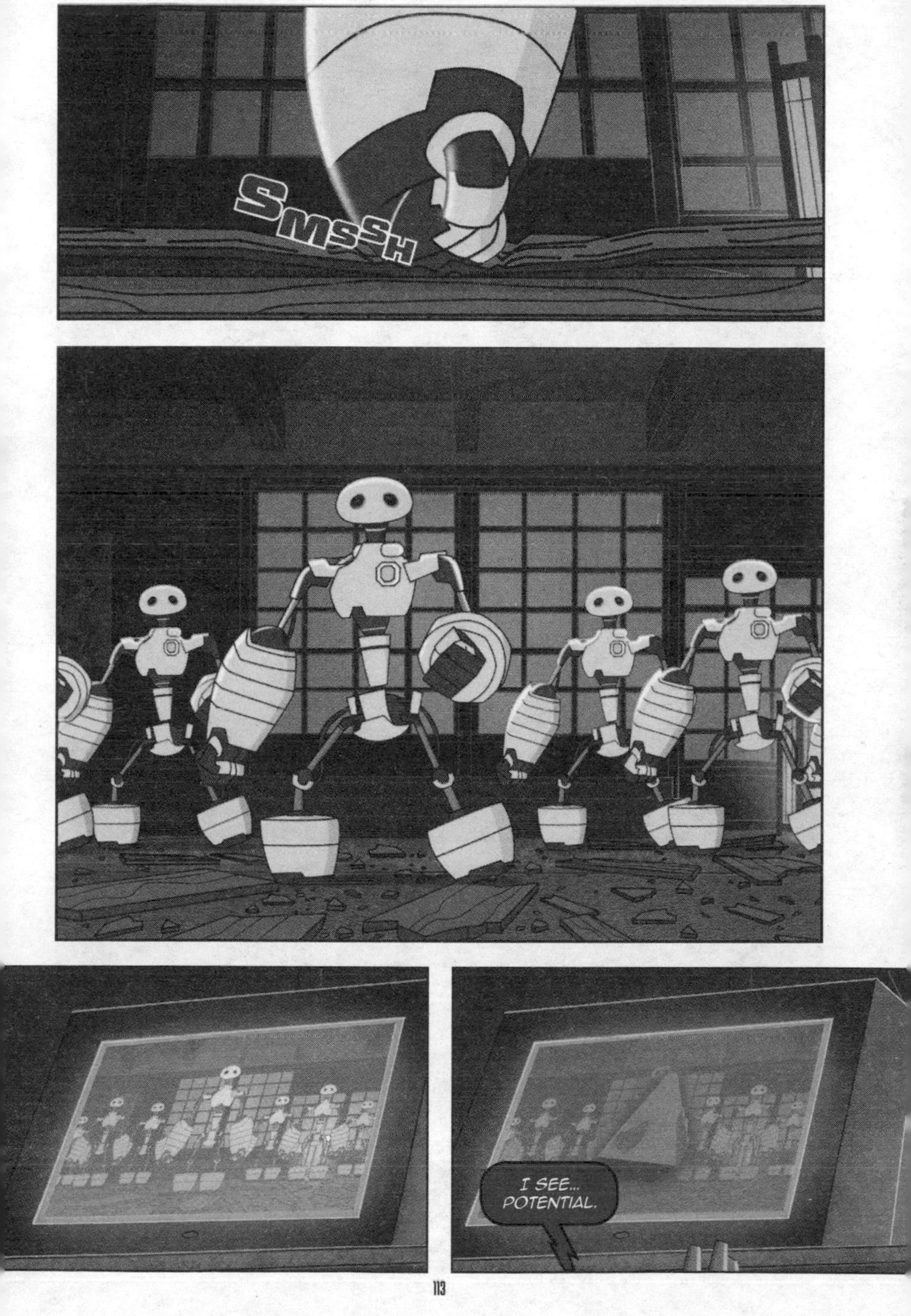
SMSSH
I SEE... POTENTIAL.

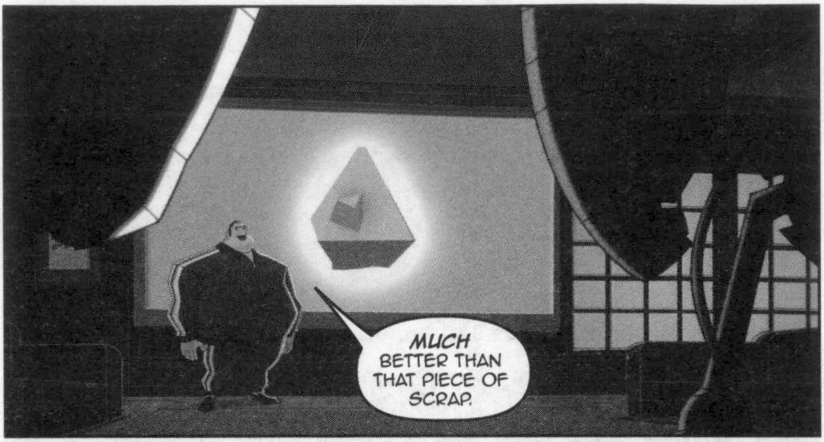
MUCH BETTER THAN THAT PIECE OF SCRAP.

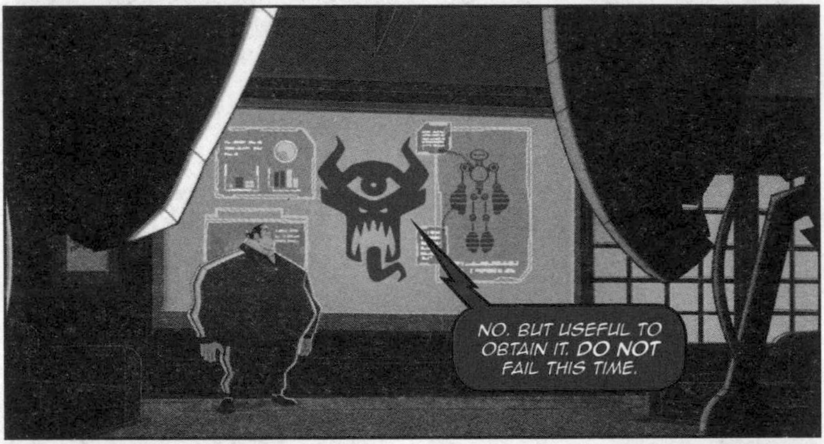
NO. BUT USEFUL TO OBTAIN IT. DO NOT FAIL THIS TIME.

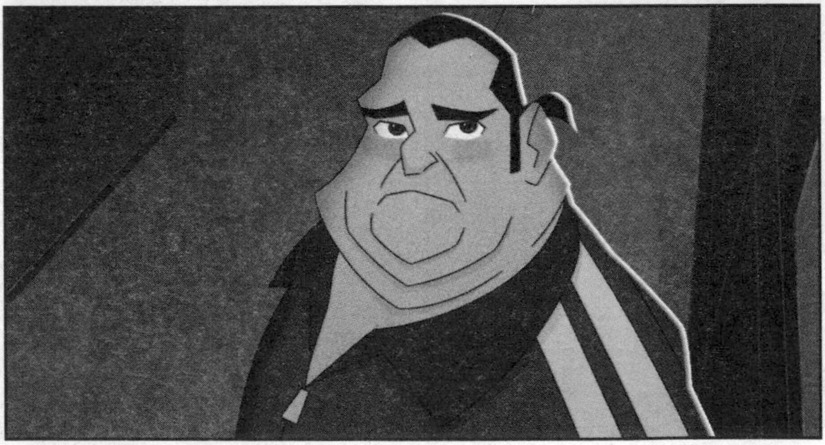

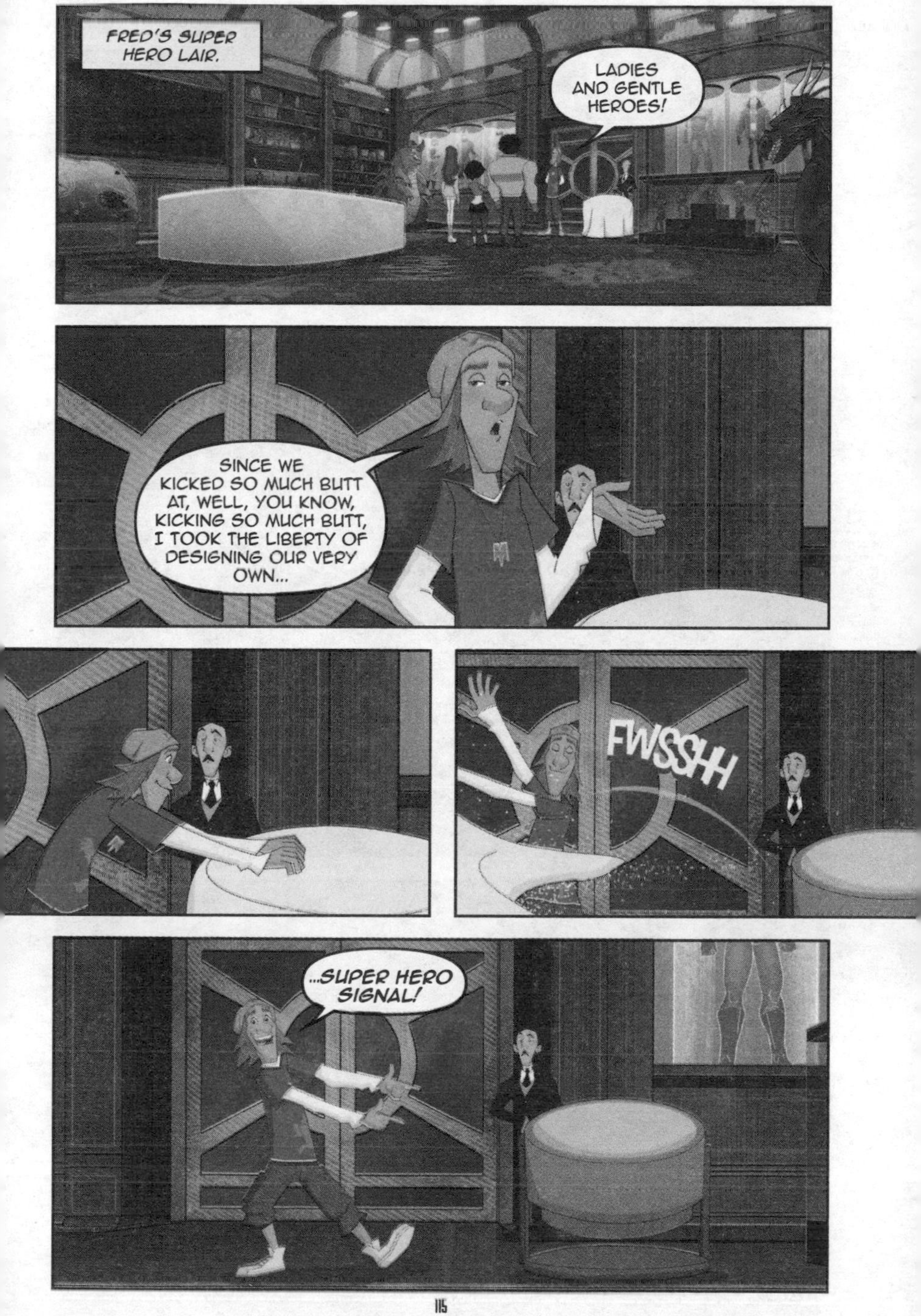
FRED'S SUPER HERO LAIR.
LADIES AND GENTLE HEROES!
SINCE WE KICKED SO MUCH BUTT AT, WELL, YOU KNOW, KICKING SO MUCH BUTT, I TOOK THE LIBERTY OF DESIGNING OUR VERY OWN...
FWSSHH
...SUPER HERO SIGNAL!

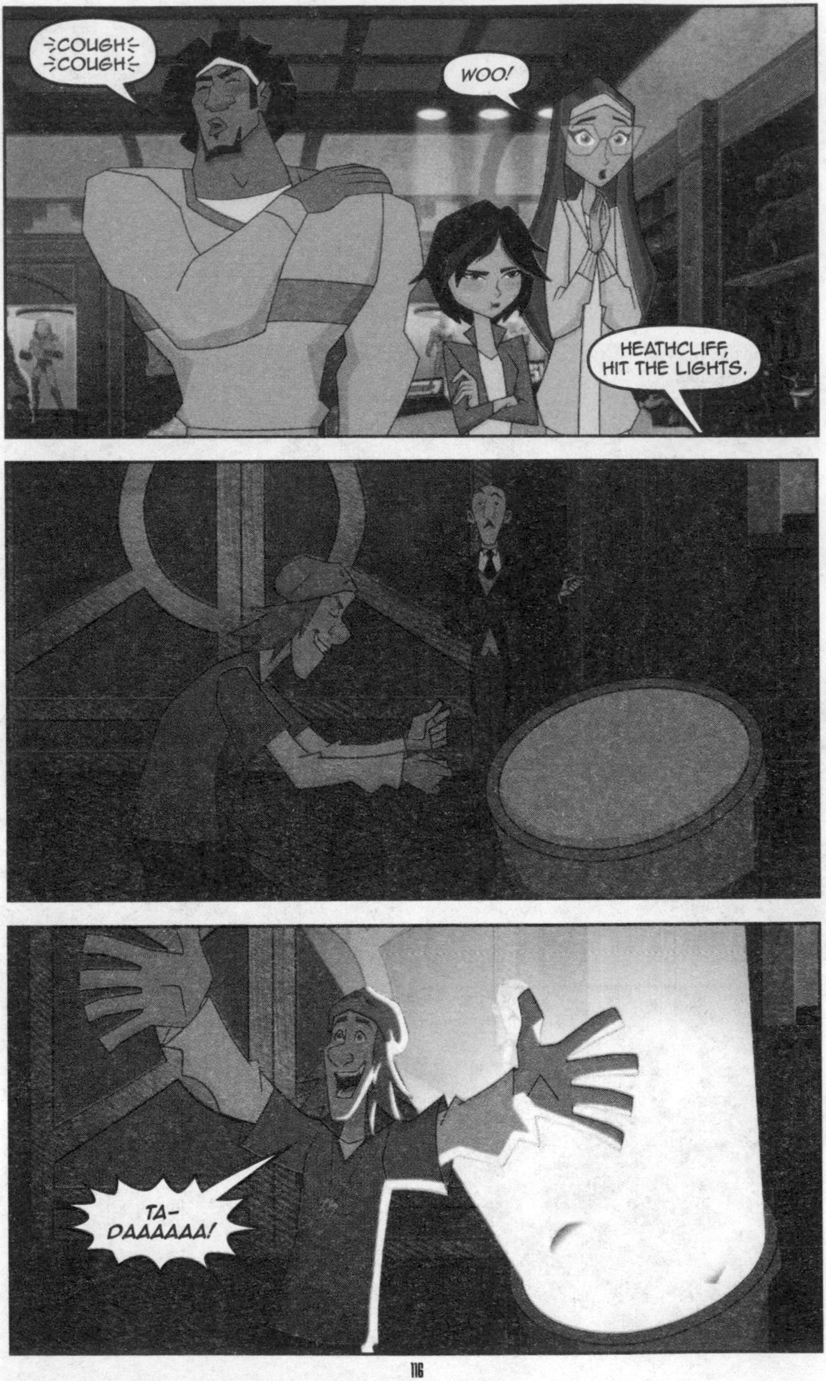
COUGH COUGH
WOO!
HEATHCLIFF, HIT THE LIGHTS.
TA-DAAAAAA!

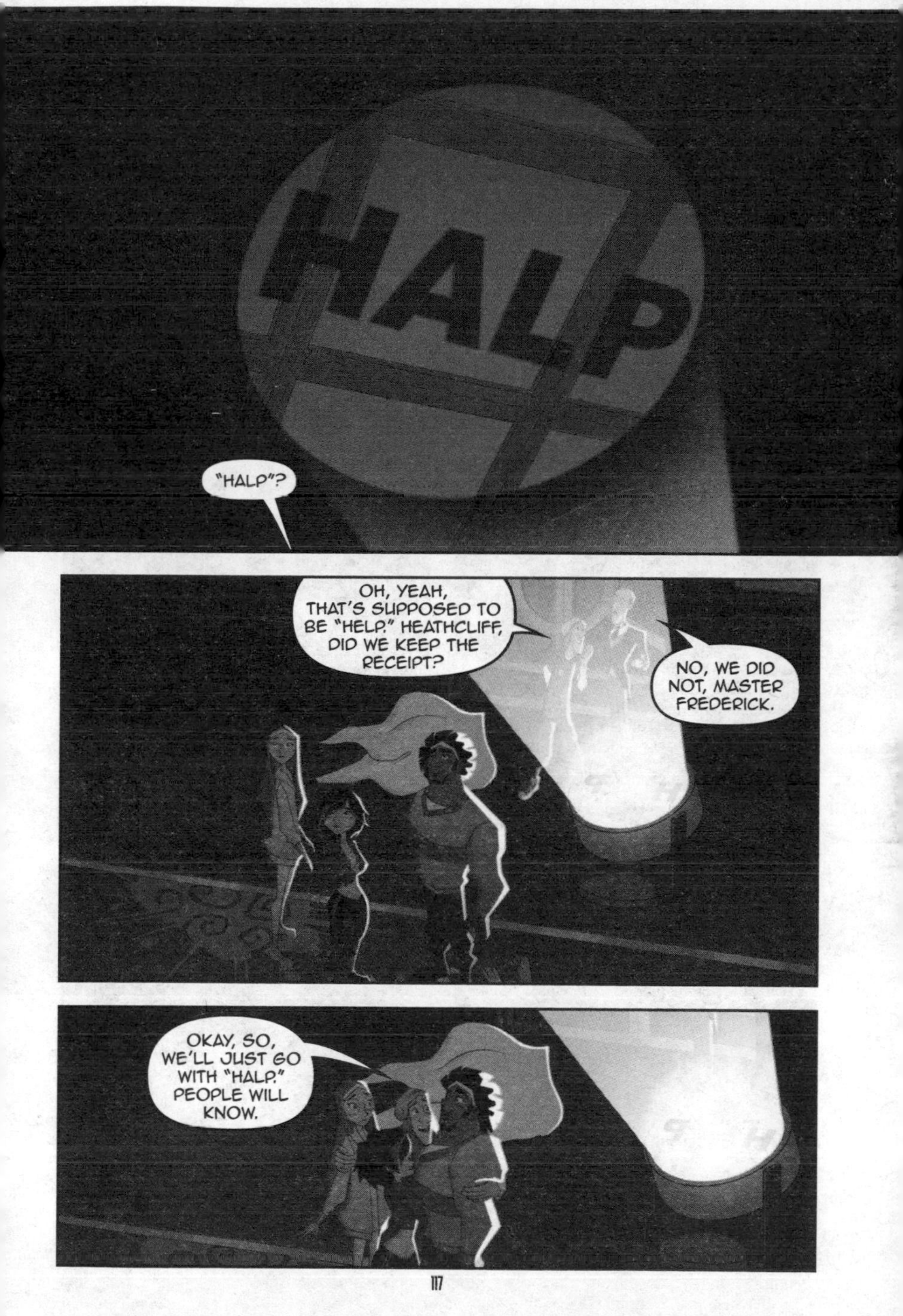
HALP
"HALP"?
OH, YEAH, THAT'S SUPPOSED TO BE "HELP." HEATHCLIFF, DID WE KEEP THE RECEIPT?
NO, WE DID NOT, MASTER FREDERICK.
OKAY, SO, WE'LL JUST GO WITH "HALP." PEOPLE WILL KNOW.

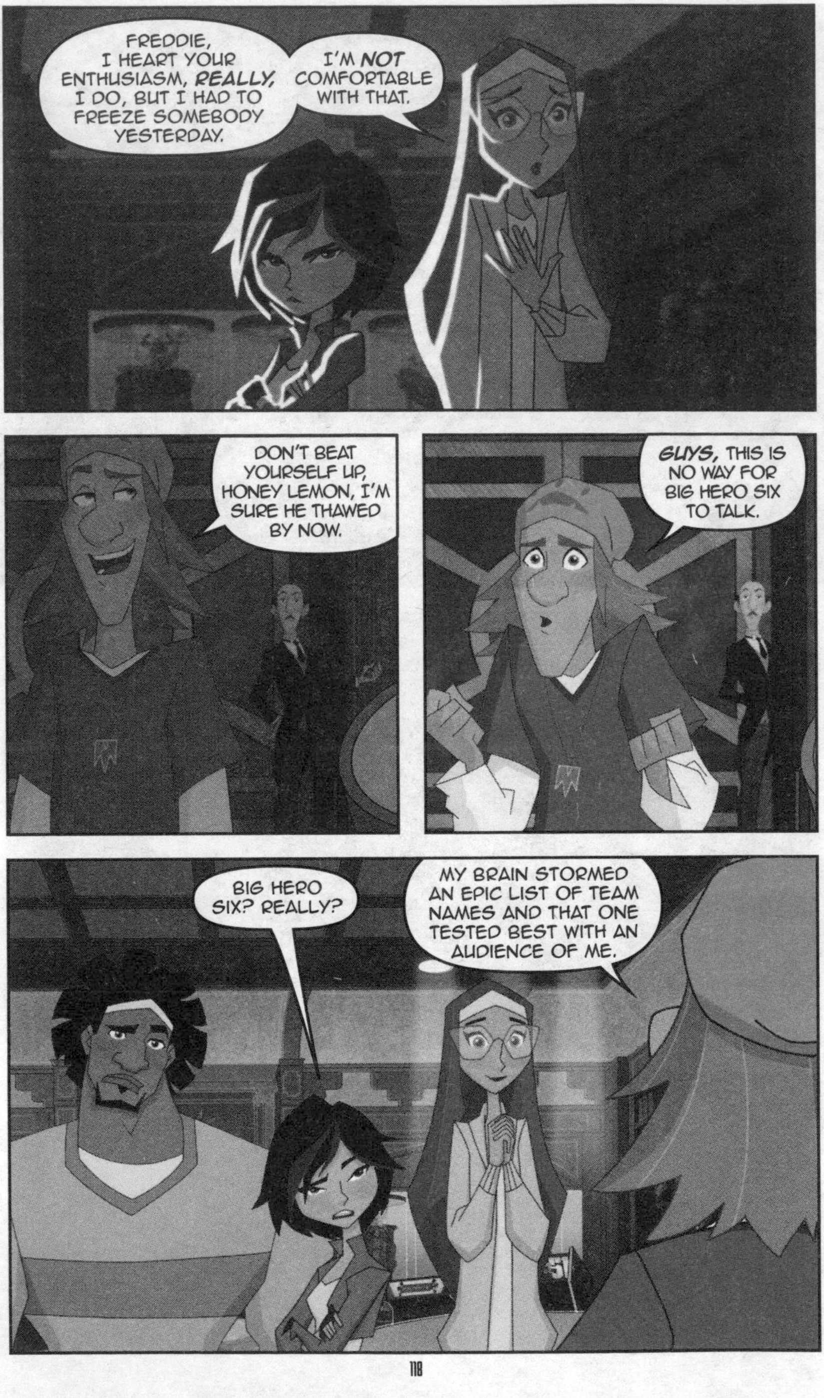
FREDDIE, I HEART YOUR ENTHUSIASM, *REALLY,* I DO, BUT I HAD TO FREEZE SOMEBODY YESTERDAY.
I'M *NOT* COMFORTABLE WITH THAT.
DON'T BEAT YOURSELF UP, HONEY LEMON, I'M SURE HE THAWED BY NOW.
GUYS, THIS IS NO WAY FOR BIG HERO SIX TO TALK.
BIG HERO SIX? REALLY?
MY BRAIN STORMED AN EPIC LIST OF TEAM NAMES AND THAT ONE TESTED BEST WITH AN AUDIENCE OF ME.

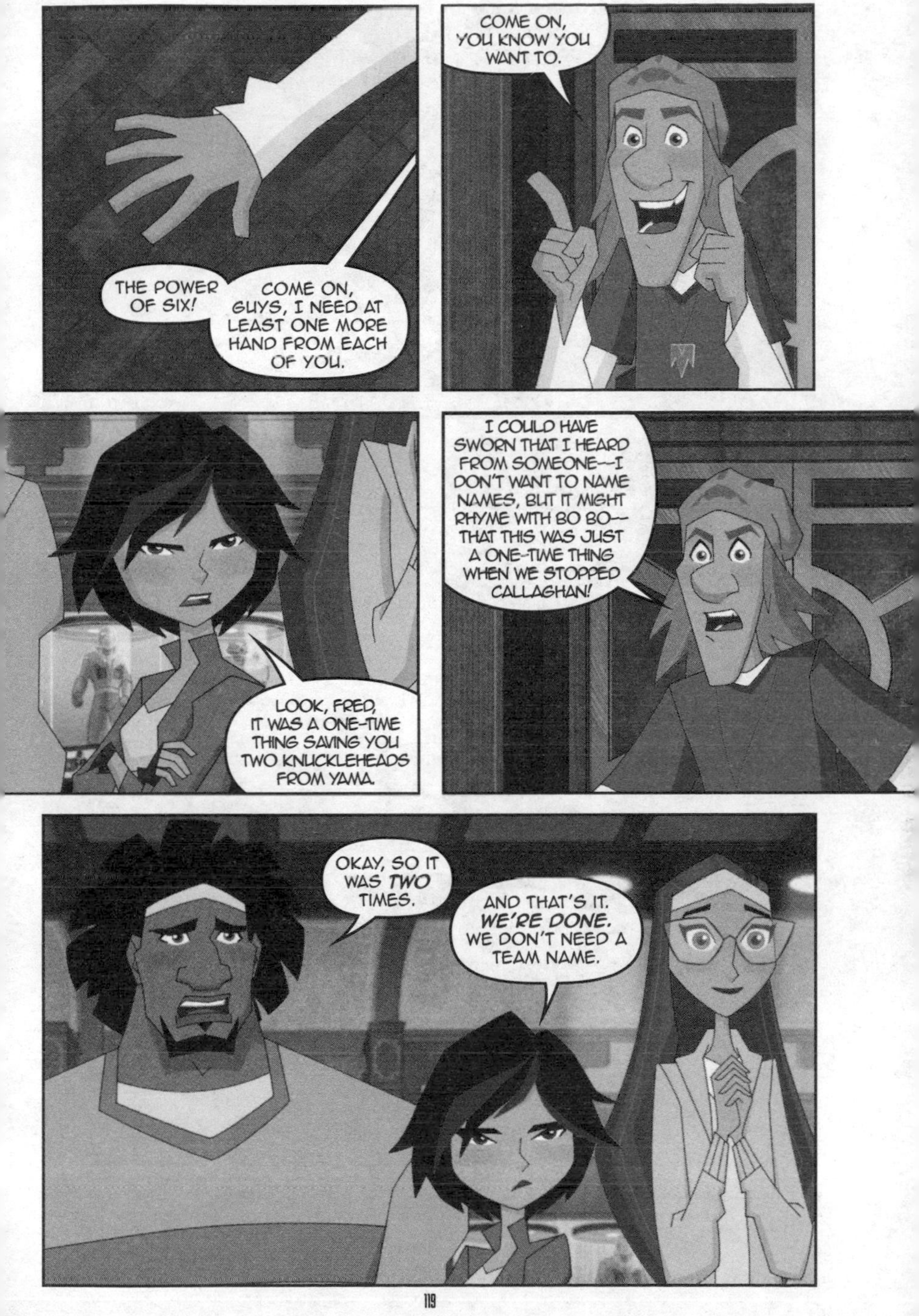
THE POWER OF SIX!
COME ON, GUYS, I NEED AT LEAST ONE MORE HAND FROM EACH OF YOU.
COME ON, YOU KNOW YOU WANT TO.
LOOK, FRED, IT WAS A ONE-TIME THING SAVING YOU TWO KNUCKLEHEADS FROM YAMA.
I COULD HAVE SWORN THAT I HEARD FROM SOMEONE--I DON'T WANT TO NAME NAMES, BUT IT MIGHT RHYME WITH BO BO--THAT THIS WAS JUST A ONE-TIME THING WHEN WE STOPPED CALLAGHAN!
OKAY, SO IT WAS *TWO* TIMES.
AND THAT'S IT. ***WE'RE DONE.*** WE DON'T NEED A TEAM NAME.

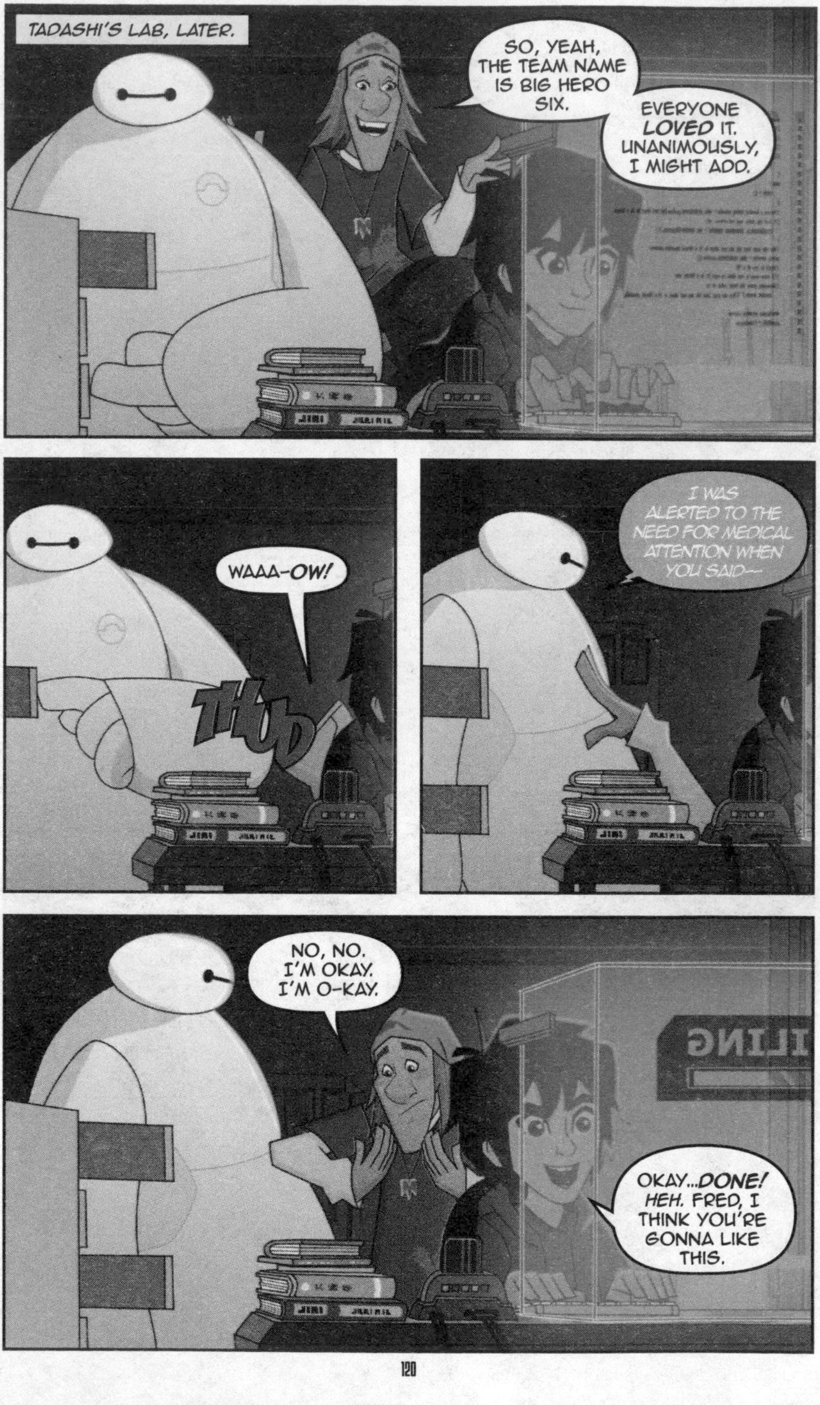
TADASHI'S LAB, LATER.
SO, YEAH, THE TEAM NAME IS BIG HERO SIX.
EVERYONE LOVED IT. UNANIMOUSLY, I MIGHT ADD.
WAAA-OW!
THUD
I WAS ALERTED TO THE NEED FOR MEDICAL ATTENTION WHEN YOU SAID—
NO, NO. I'M OKAY. I'M O-KAY.
OKAY...DONE! HEH. FRED, I THINK YOU'RE GONNA LIKE THIS.

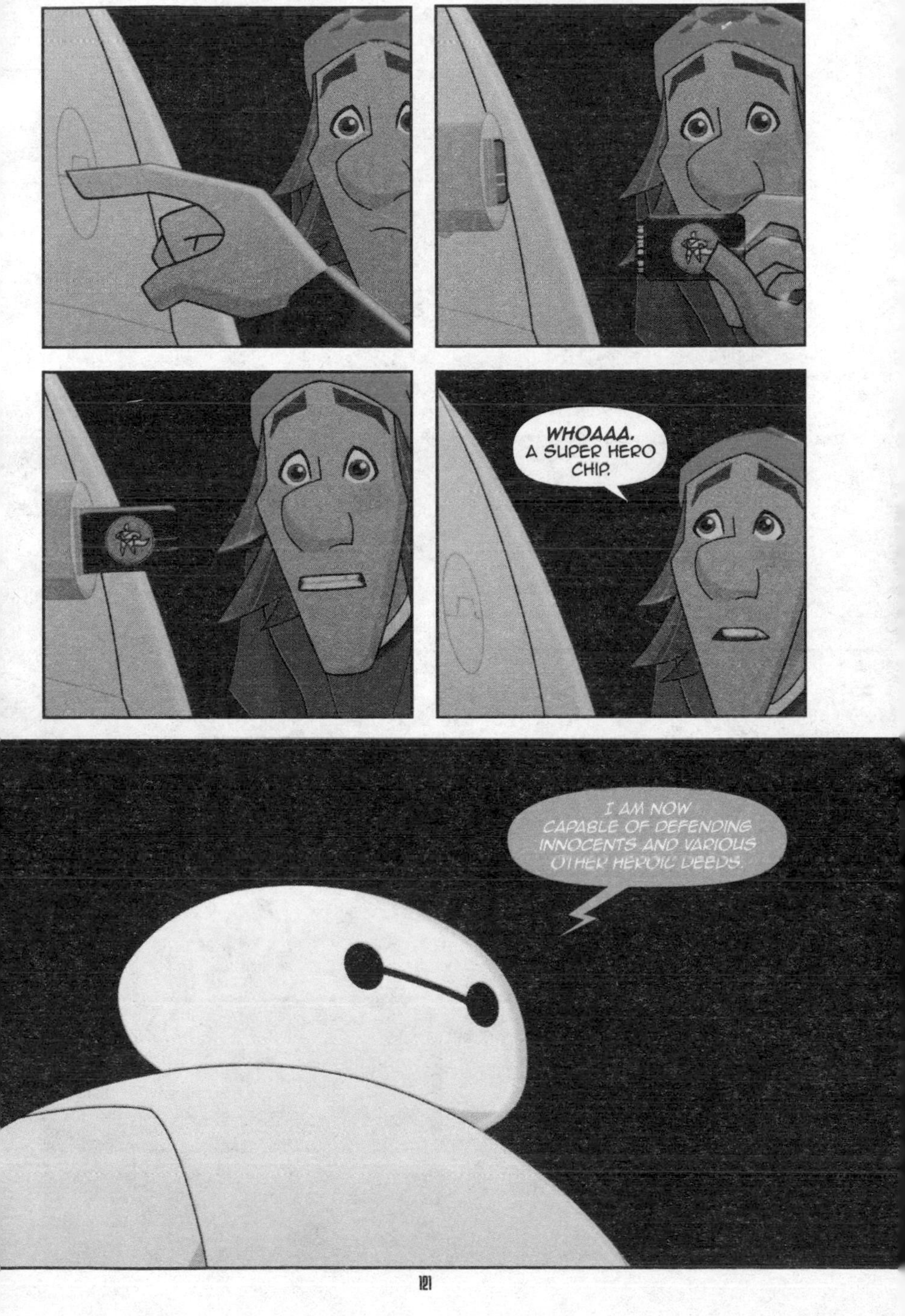
WHOAAA.
A SUPER HERO CHIP.
I AM NOW CAPABLE OF DEFENDING INNOCENTS AND VARIOUS OTHER HEROIC DEEDS.

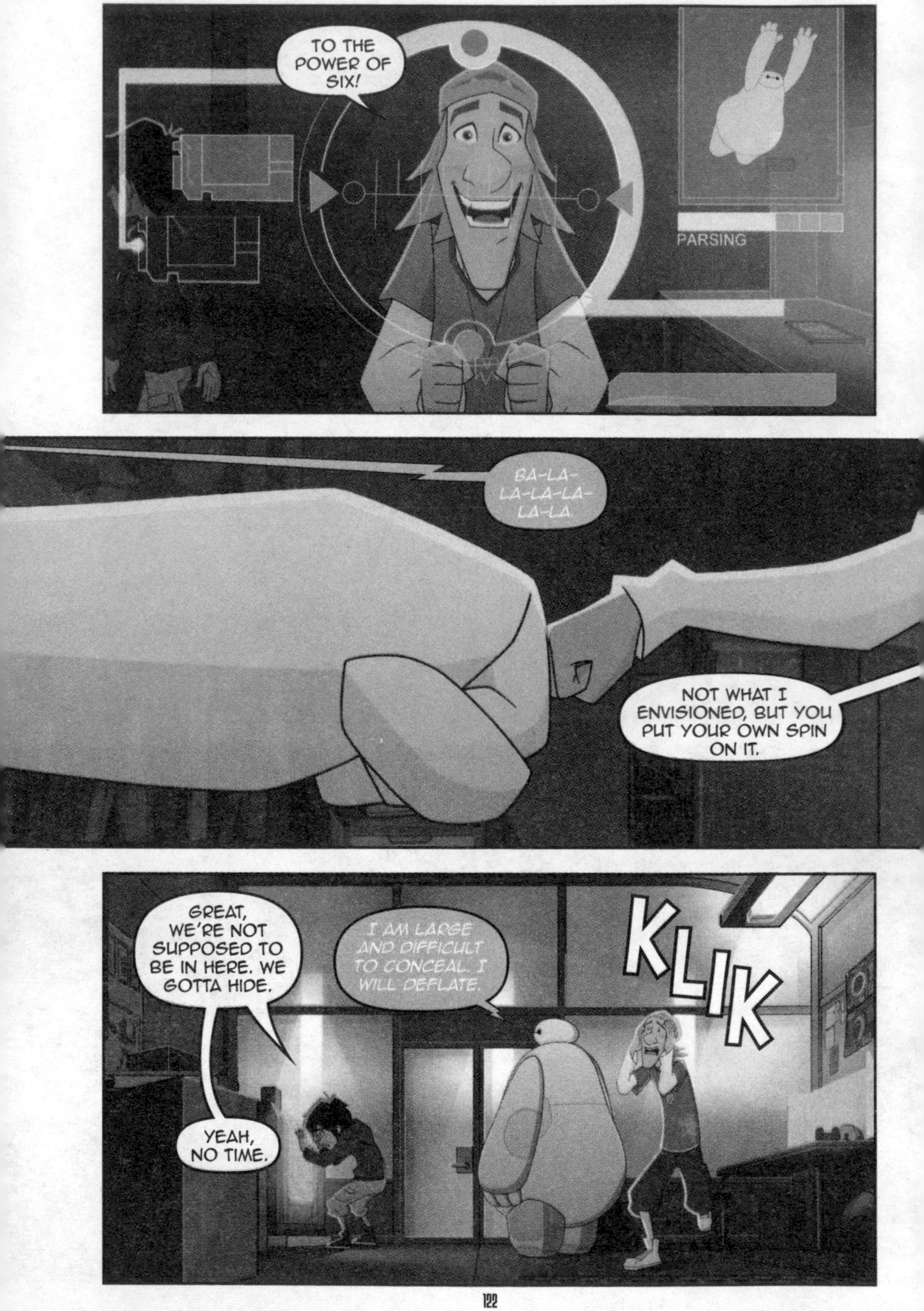
TO THE POWER OF SIX!
PARSING
BA-LA-LA-LA-LA-LA-LA.
NOT WHAT I ENVISIONED, BUT YOU PUT YOUR OWN SPIN ON IT.
GREAT, WE'RE NOT SUPPOSED TO BE IN HERE. WE GOTTA HIDE.
YEAH, NO TIME.
I AM LARGE AND DIFFICULT TO CONCEAL. I WILL DEFLATE.
KLIK

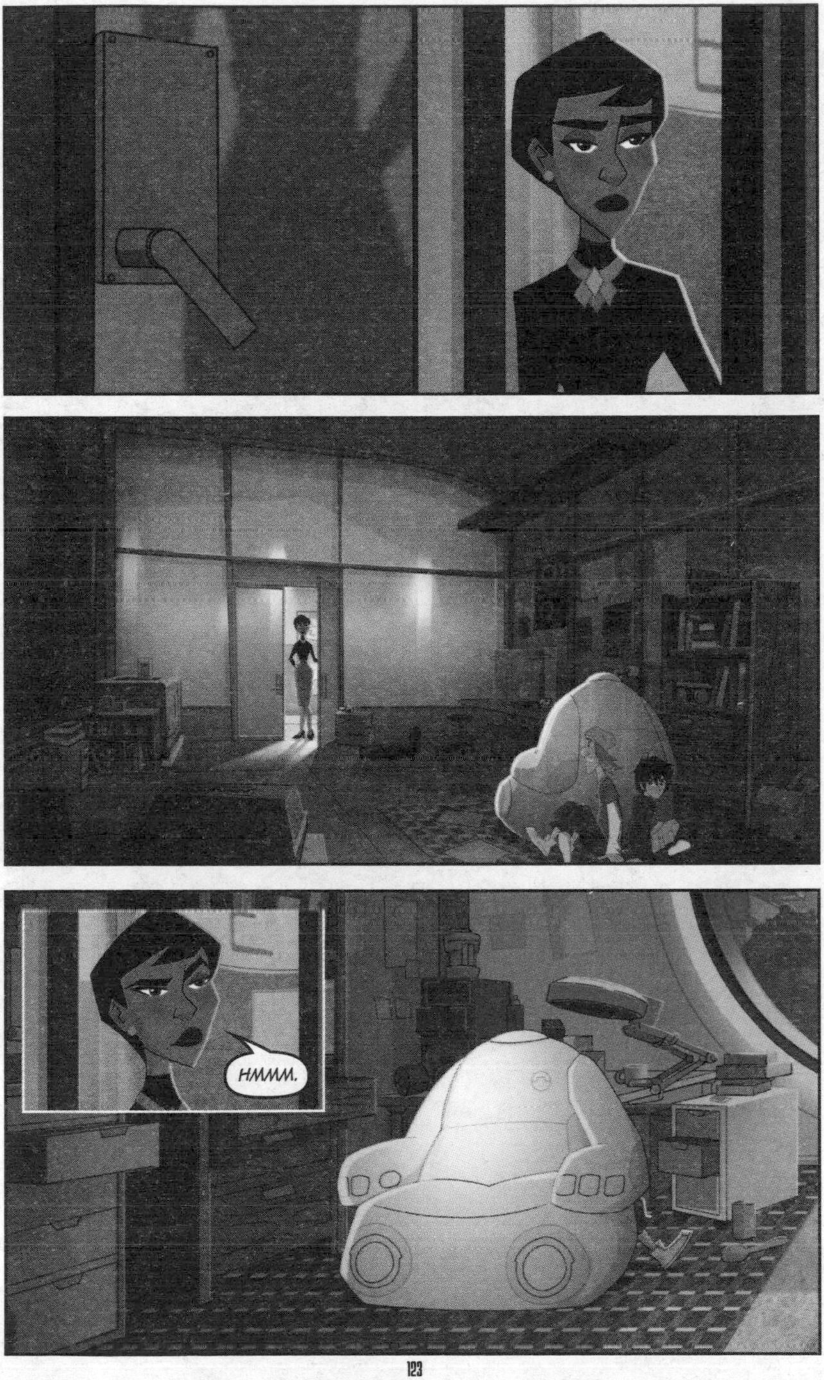
HMMM.

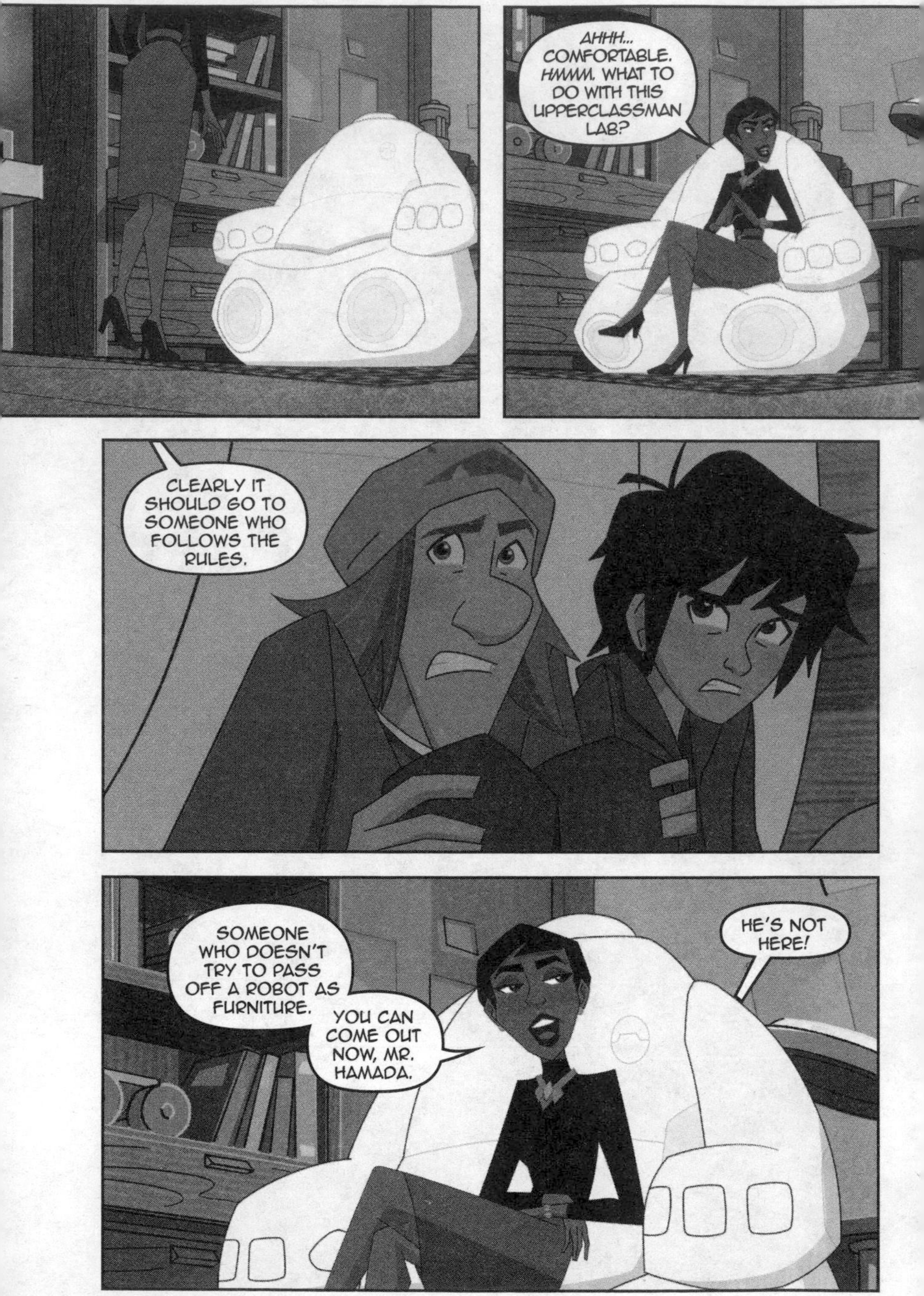
AHHH... COMFORTABLE. HMMM. WHAT TO DO WITH THIS UPPERCLASSMAN LAB?
CLEARLY IT SHOULD GO TO SOMEONE WHO FOLLOWS THE RULES.
SOMEONE WHO DOESN'T TRY TO PASS OFF A ROBOT AS FURNITURE.
YOU CAN COME OUT NOW, MR. HAMADA.
HE'S NOT HERE!

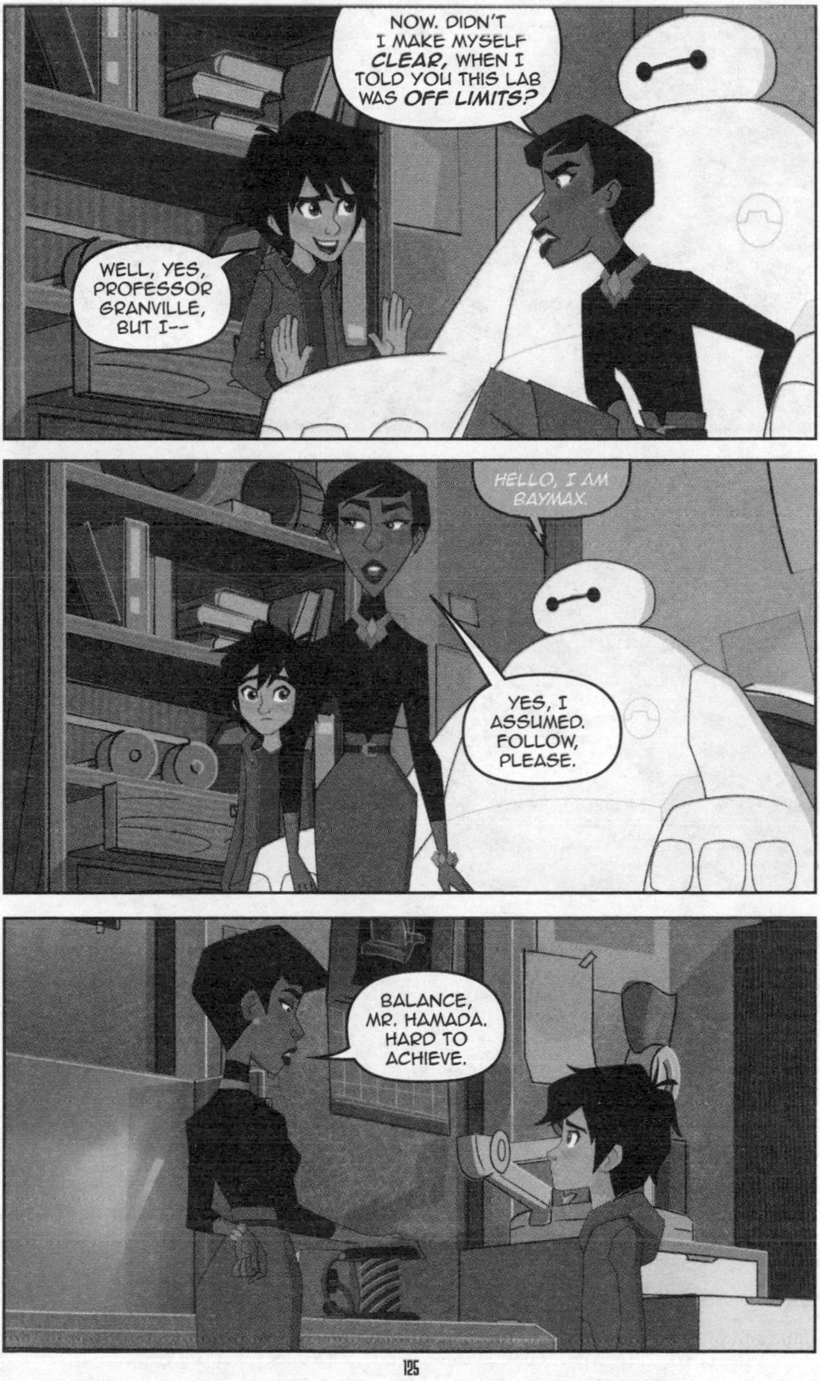
NOW. DIDN'T I MAKE MYSELF **CLEAR,** WHEN I TOLD YOU THIS LAB WAS **OFF LIMITS?**
WELL, YES, PROFESSOR GRANVILLE, BUT I--
HELLO, I AM BAYMAX.
YES, I ASSUMED. FOLLOW, PLEASE.
BALANCE, MR. HAMADA. HARD TO ACHIEVE.

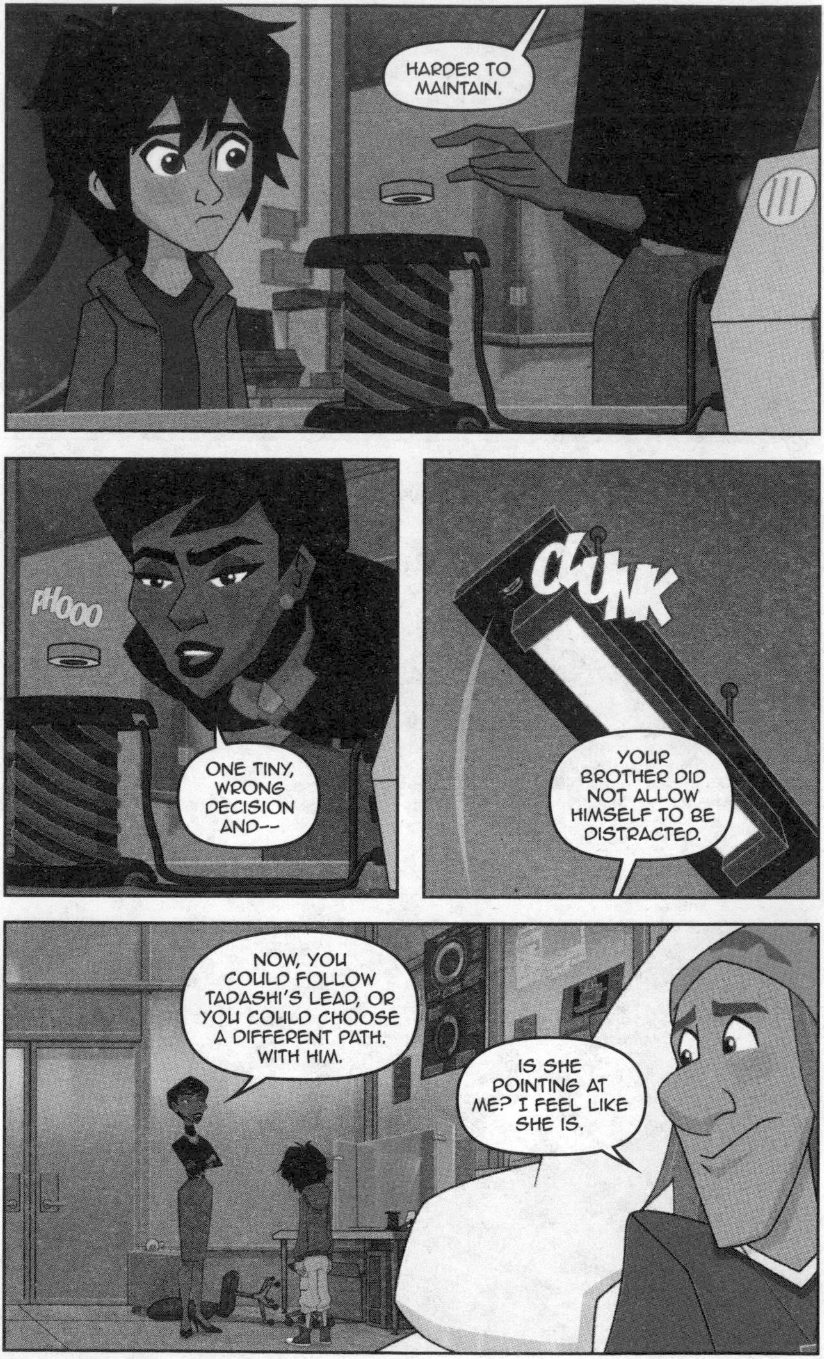
HARDER TO MAINTAIN.
PHOOO
ONE TINY, WRONG DECISION AND--
CLUNK
YOUR BROTHER DID NOT ALLOW HIMSELF TO BE DISTRACTED.
NOW, YOU COULD FOLLOW TADASHI'S LEAD, OR YOU COULD CHOOSE A DIFFERENT PATH. WITH HIM.
IS SHE POINTING AT ME? I FEEL LIKE SHE IS.

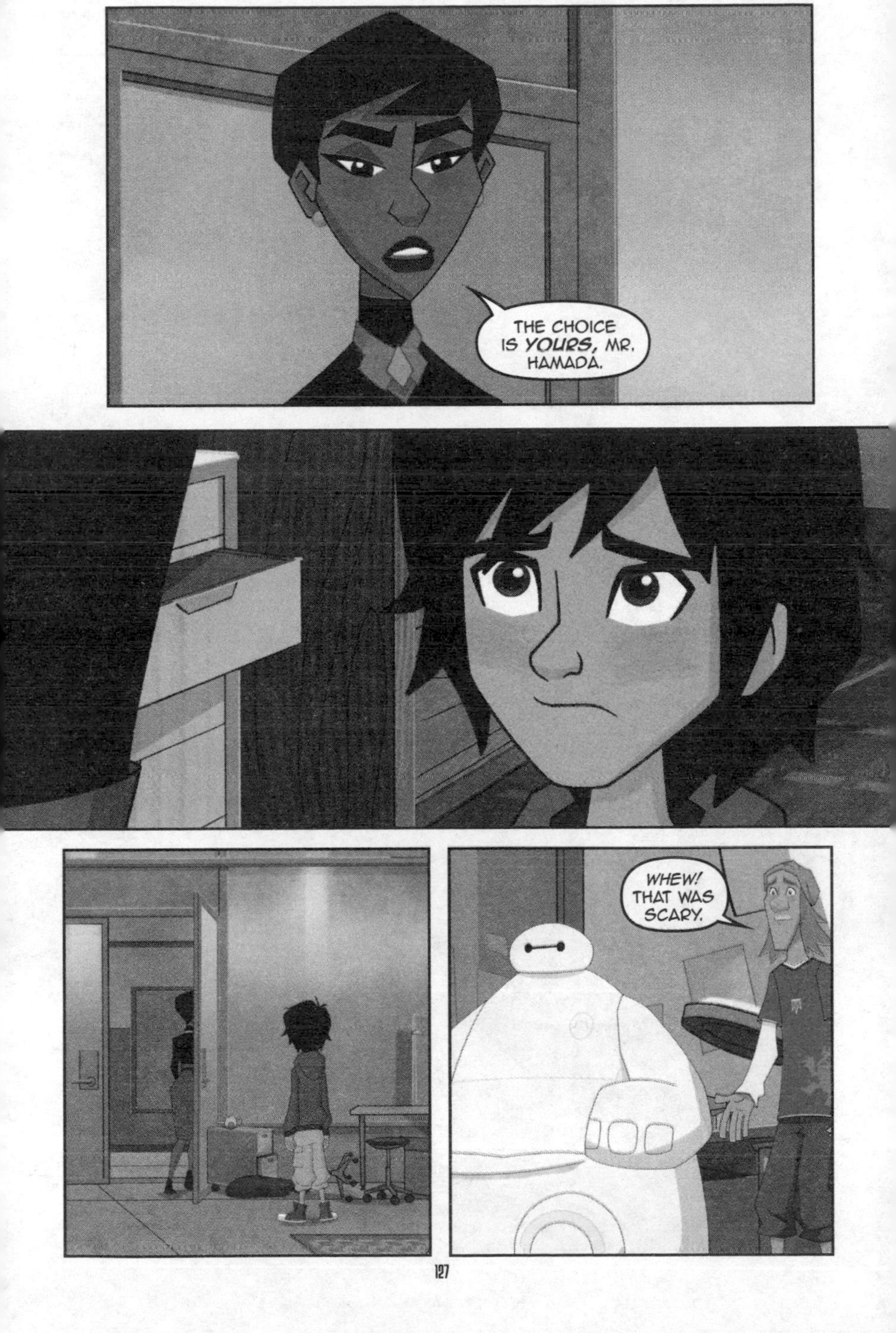
THE CHOICE IS YOURS, MR. HAMADA.
WHEW! THAT WAS SCARY.

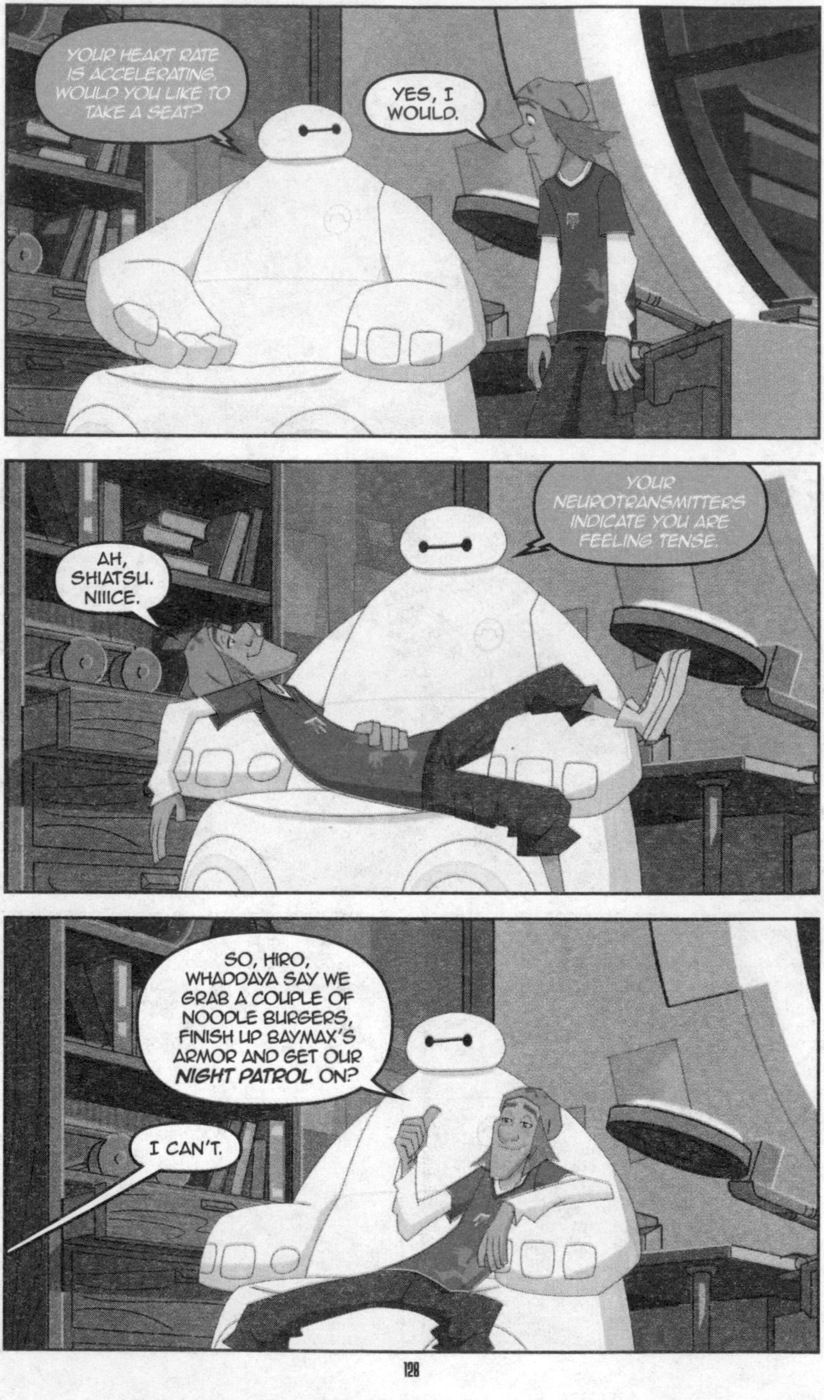
YOUR HEART RATE IS ACCELERATING. WOULD YOU LIKE TO TAKE A SEAT?
YES, I WOULD.
YOUR NEUROTRANSMITTERS INDICATE YOU ARE FEELING TENSE.
AH, SHIATSU. NIIICE.
SO, HIRO, WHADDAYA SAY WE GRAB A COUPLE OF NOODLE BURGERS, FINISH UP BAYMAX'S ARMOR AND GET OUR NIGHT PATROL ON?
I CAN'T.

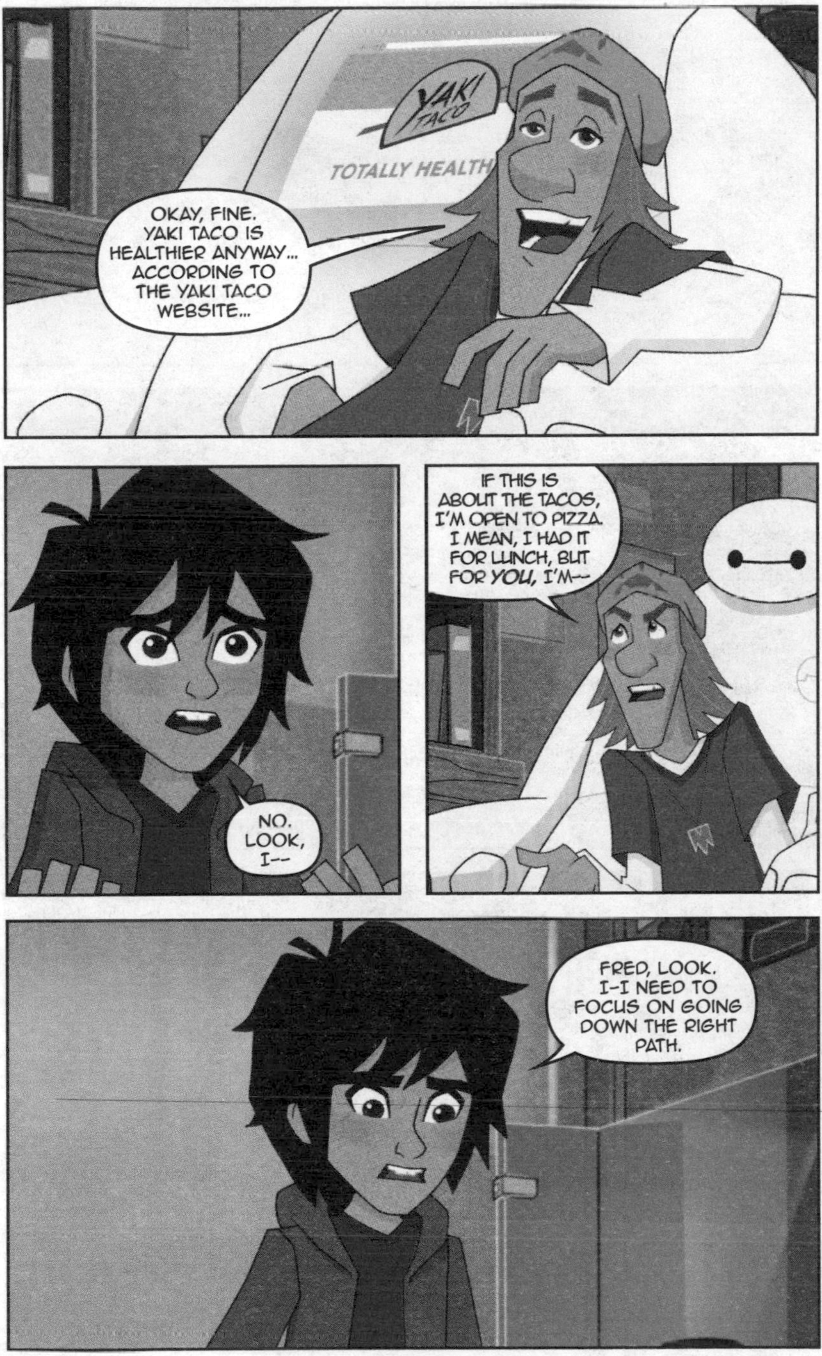
YAKI TACO
TOTALLY HEALTH
OKAY, FINE. YAKI TACO IS HEALTHIER ANYWAY... ACCORDING TO THE YAKI TACO WEBSITE...
NO. LOOK, I--
IF THIS IS ABOUT THE TACOS, I'M OPEN TO PIZZA. I MEAN, I HAD IT FOR LUNCH, BUT FOR *YOU,* I'M--
FRED, LOOK. I-I NEED TO FOCUS ON GOING DOWN THE RIGHT PATH.

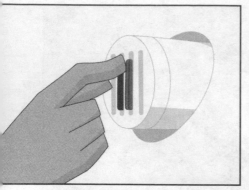

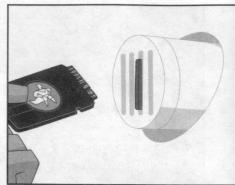

TADASHI'S PATH.

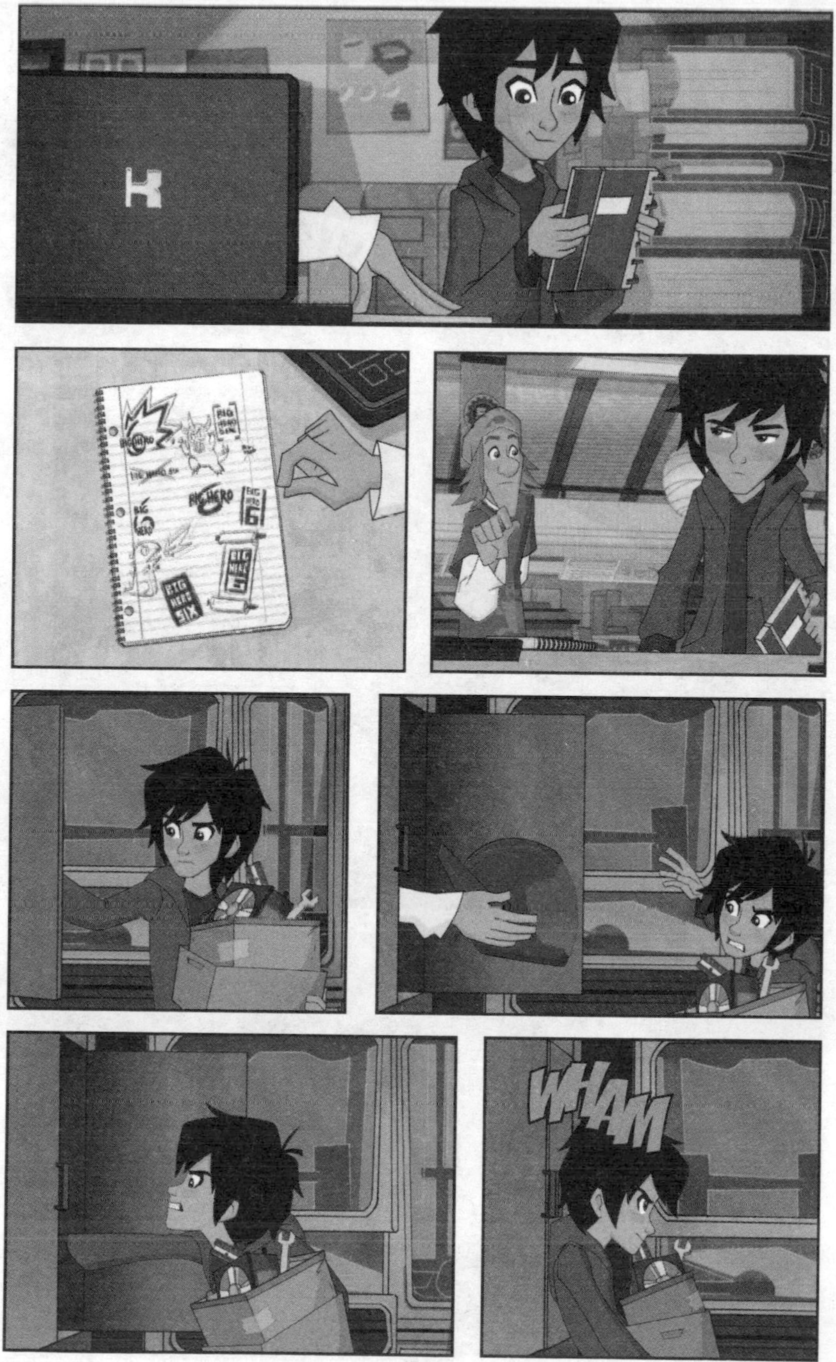
WHAM

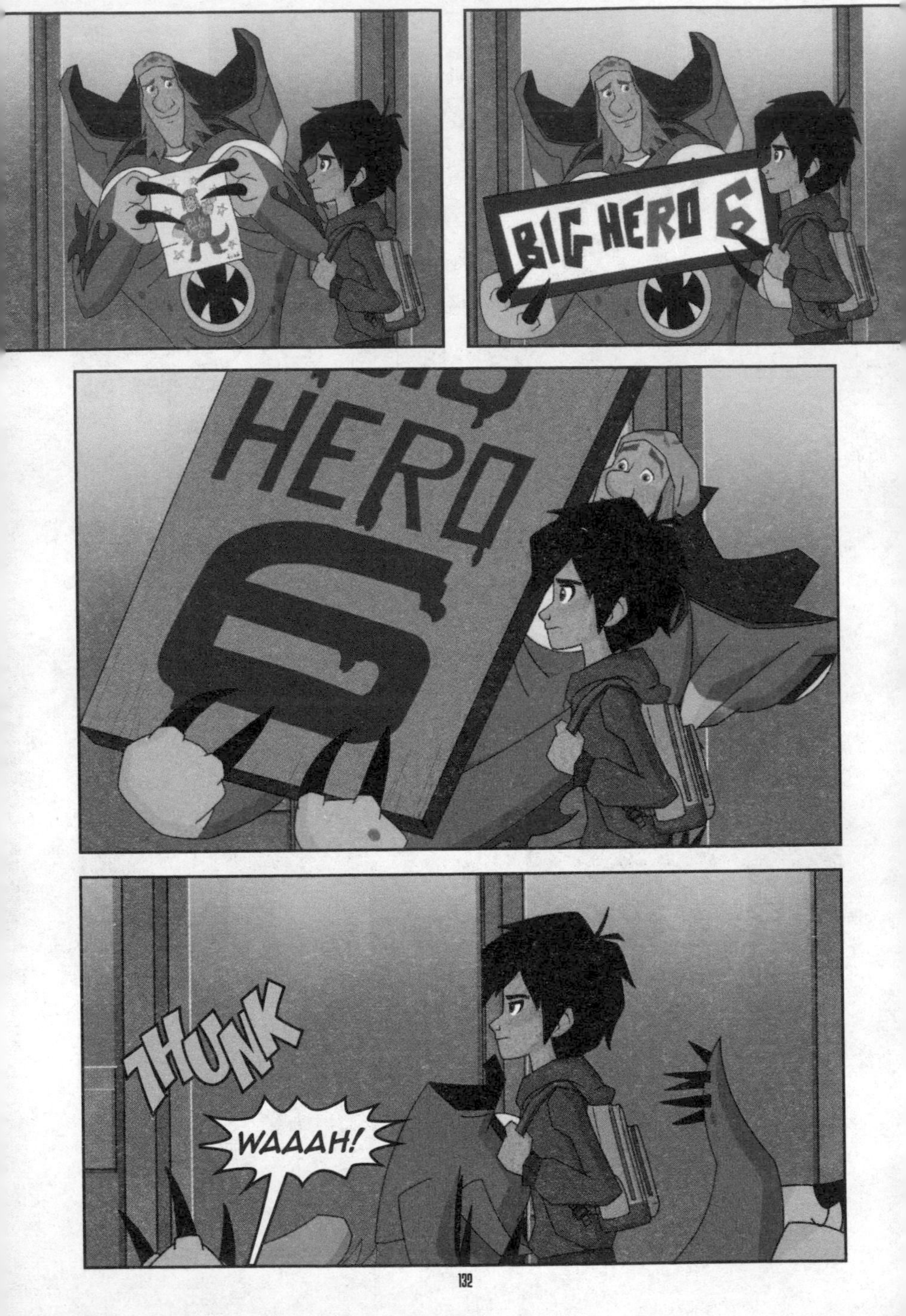
BIG HERO 6
HERO
THUNK
WAAAH!

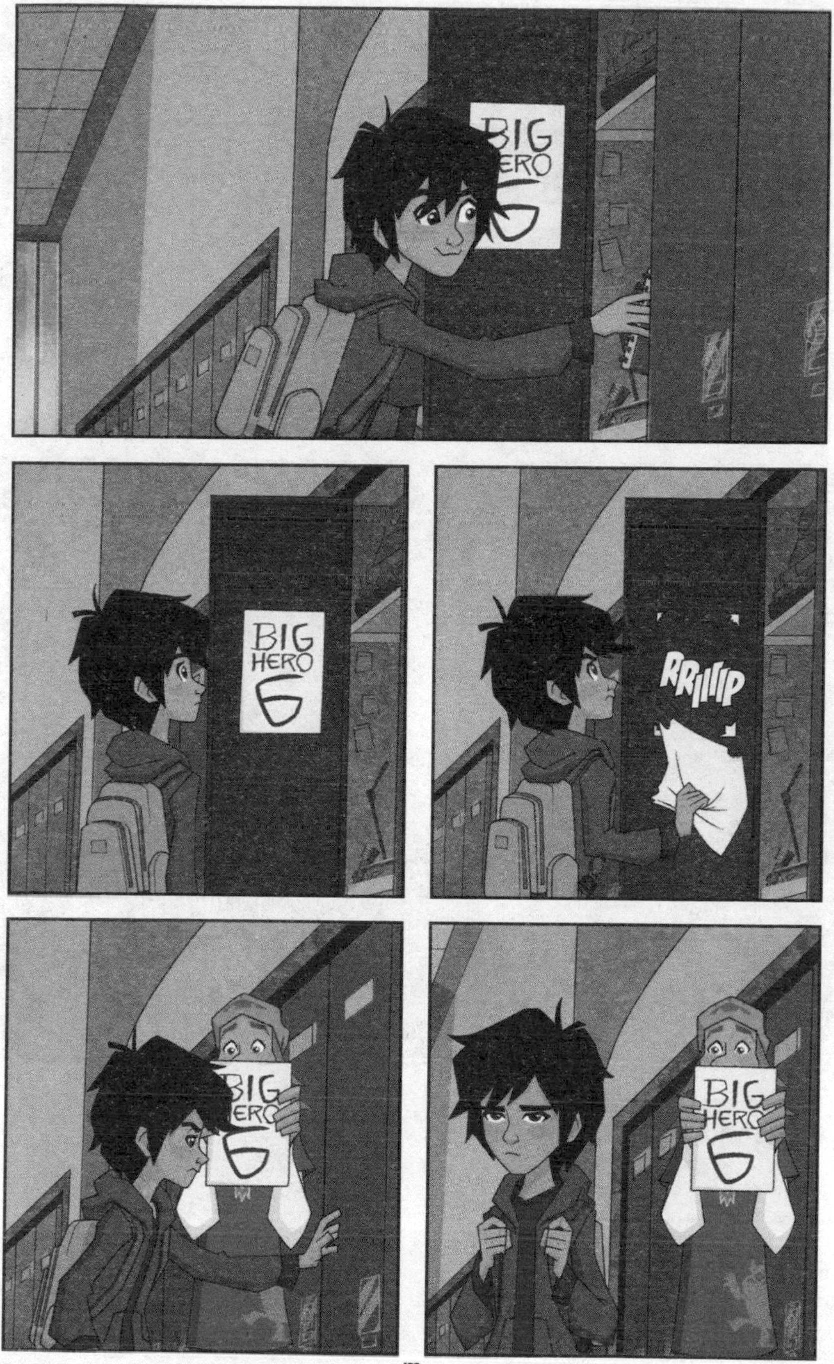
BIG HERO 6
BIG HERO 6
RRIIIIP
BIG HERO 6
BIG HERO 6

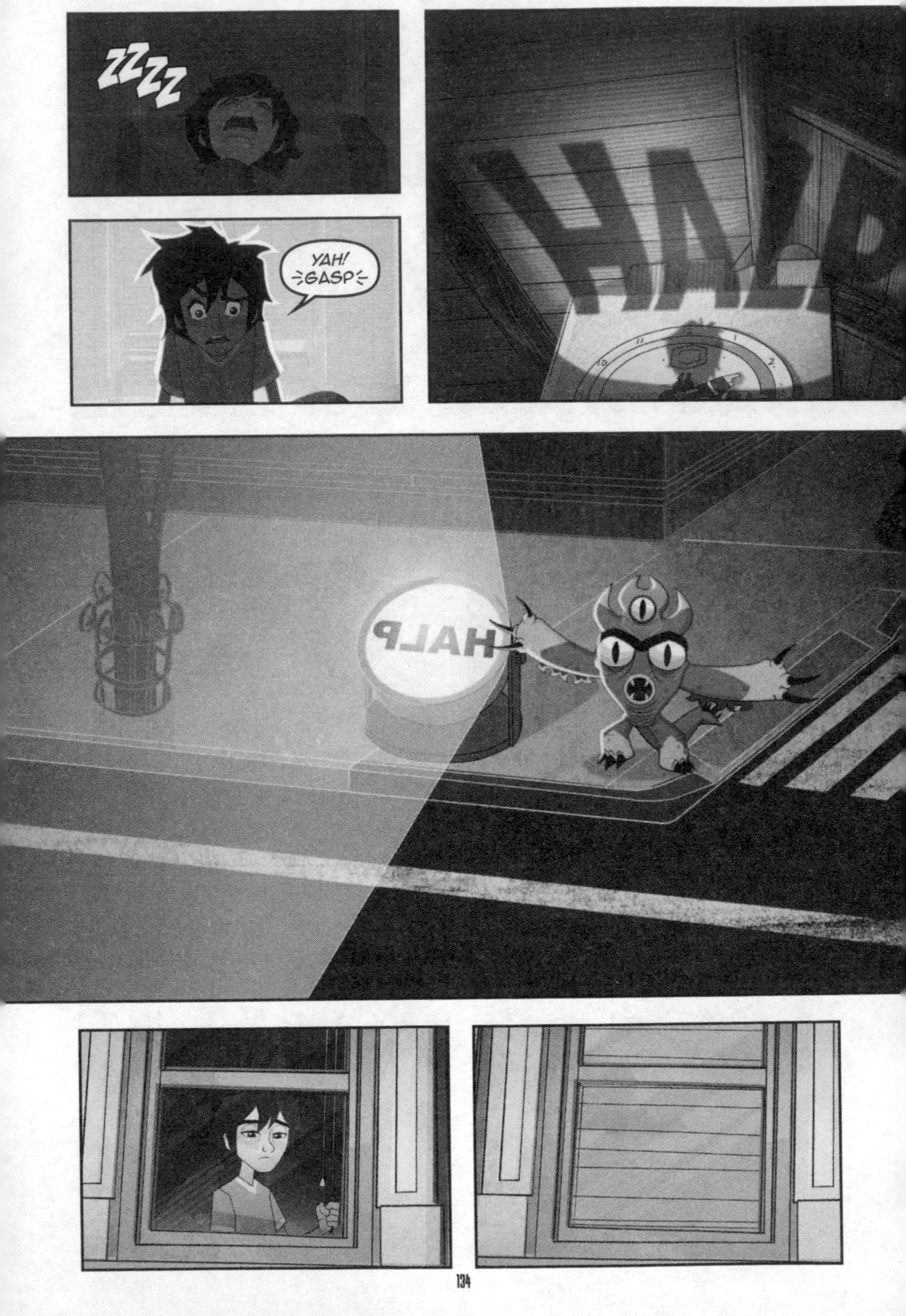
ZZZZ
YAH! GASP
HALP
HALP

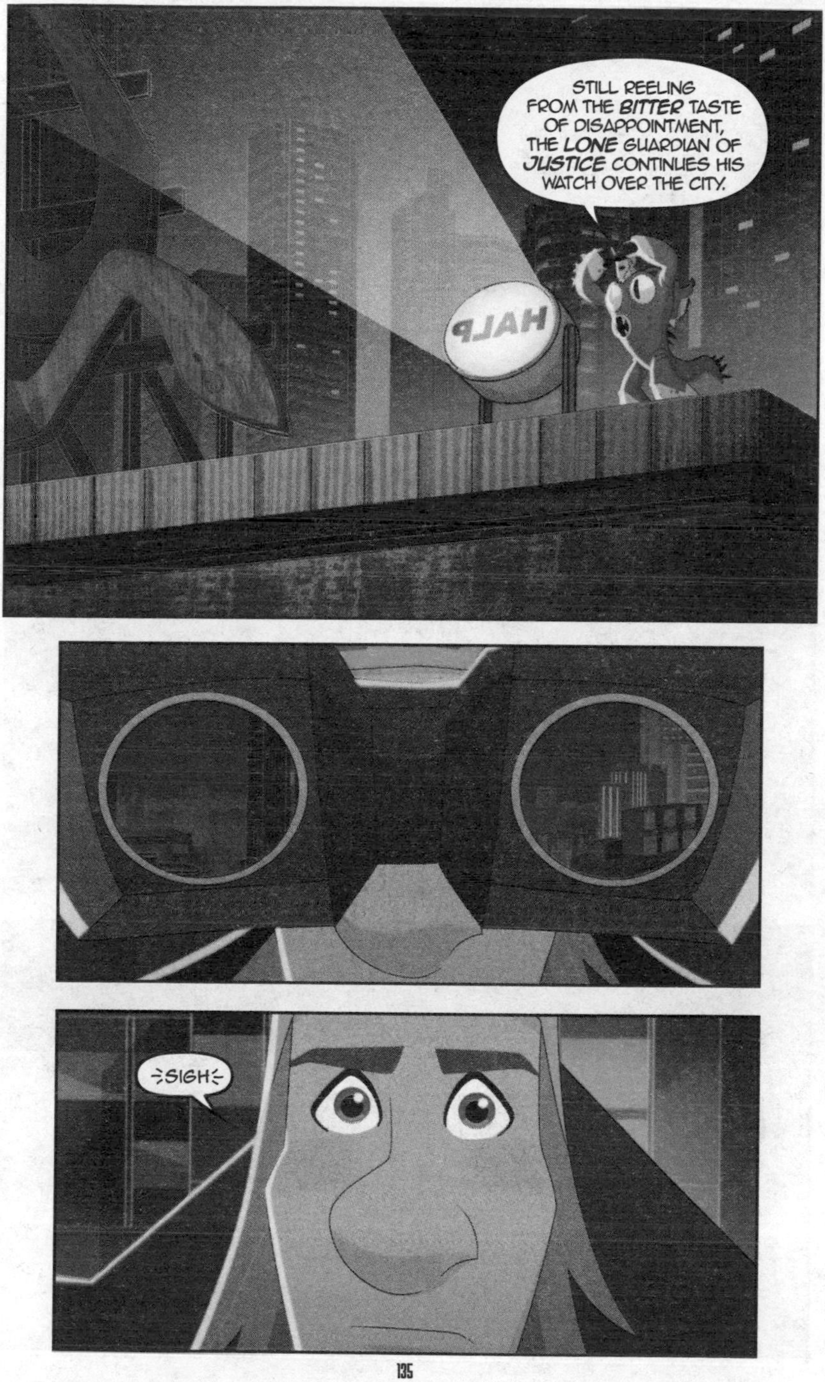
STILL REELING FROM THE BITTER TASTE OF DISAPPOINTMENT, THE LONE GUARDIAN OF JUSTICE CONTINUES HIS WATCH OVER THE CITY.
HALP
SIGH

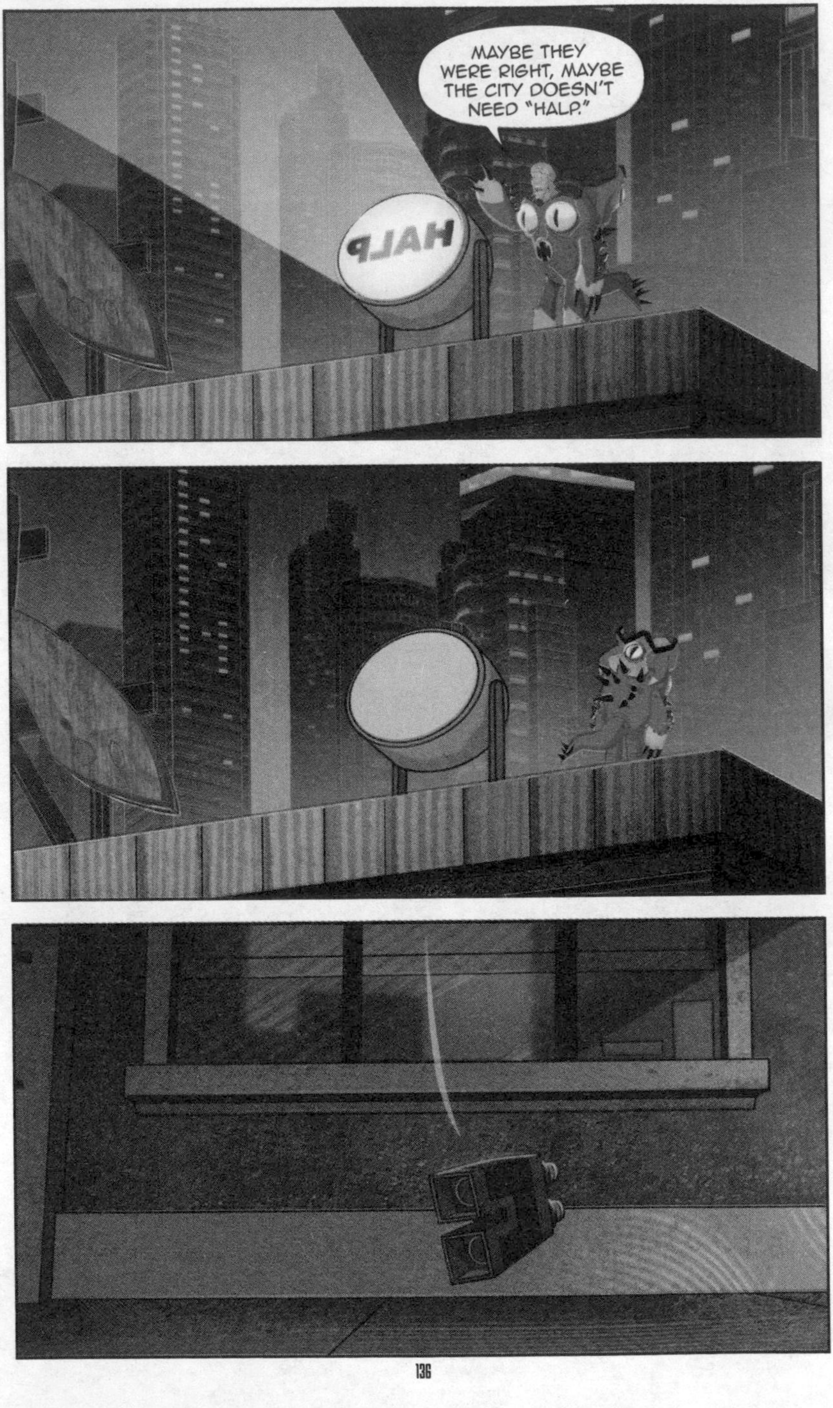
MAYBE THEY WERE RIGHT, MAYBE THE CITY DOESN'T NEED "HALP."
HALP

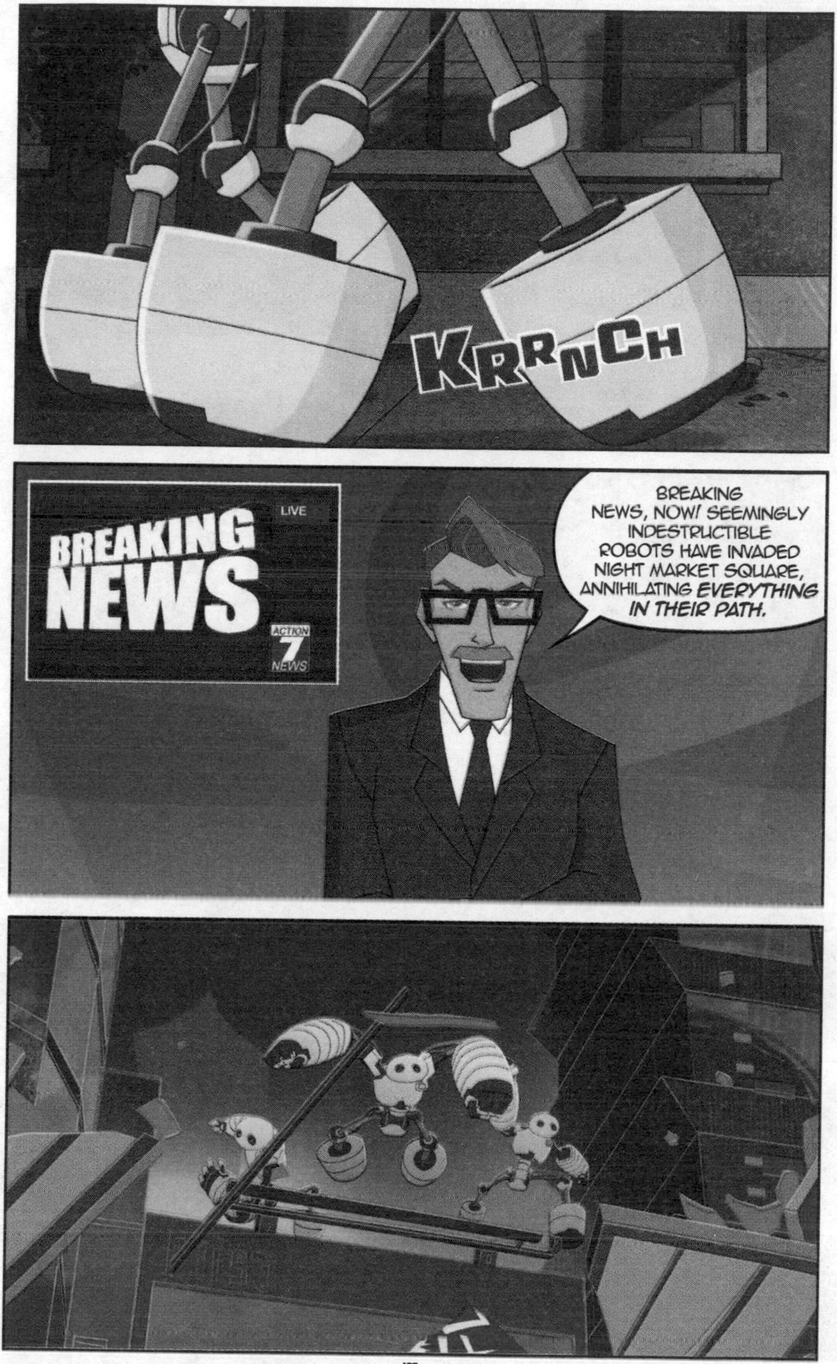
KRRNCH
BREAKING NEWS
LIVE
ACTION 7 NEWS
BREAKING NEWS, NOW! SEEMINGLY INDESTRUCTIBLE ROBOTS HAVE INVADED NIGHT MARKET SQUARE, ANNIHILATING *EVERYTHING IN THEIR PATH.*

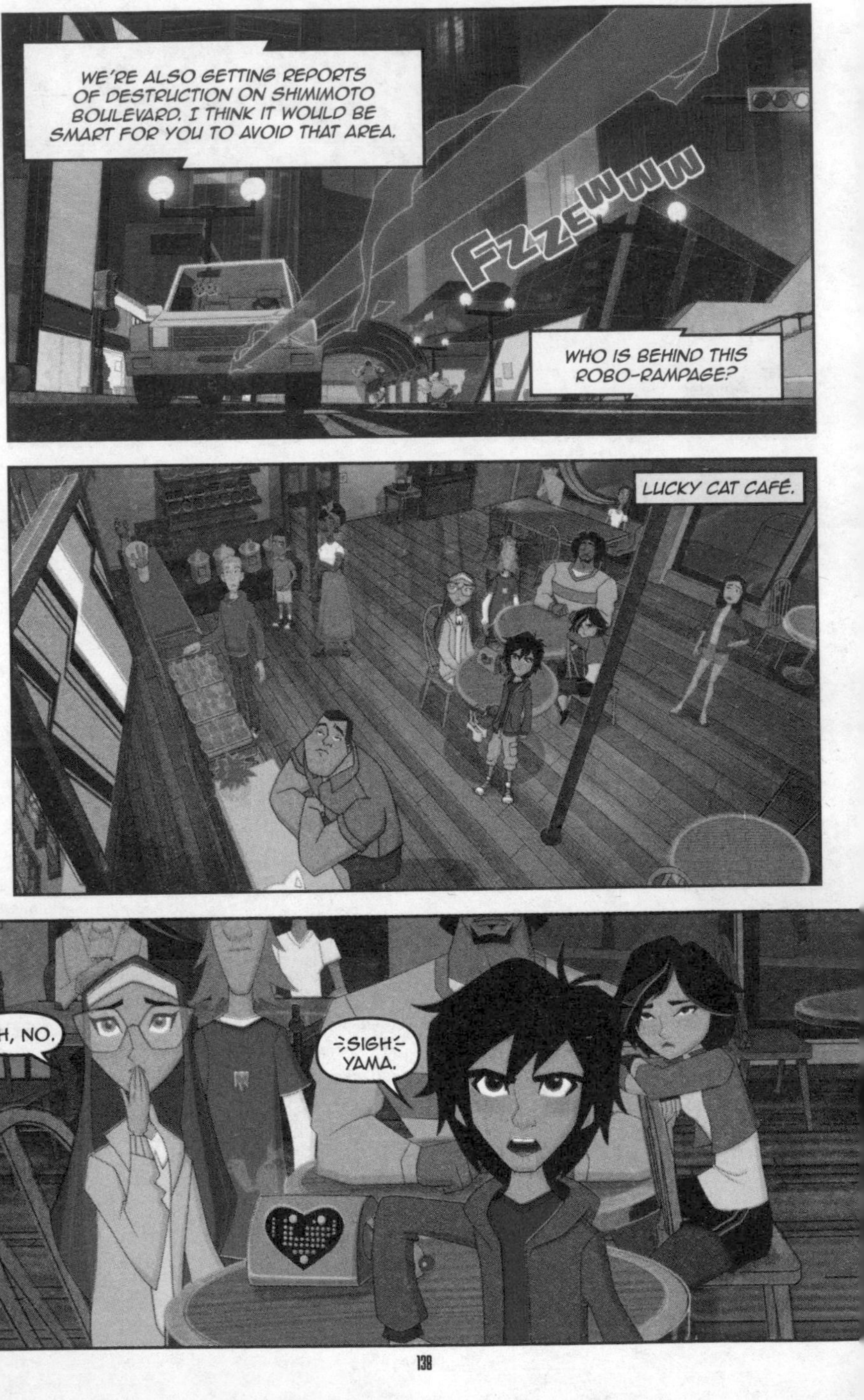
WE'RE ALSO GETTING REPORTS OF DESTRUCTION ON SHIMIMOTO BOULEVARD. I THINK IT WOULD BE SMART FOR YOU TO AVOID THAT AREA.
FZZEWWWW
WHO IS BEHIND THIS ROBO-RAMPAGE?
LUCKY CAT CAFÉ.
OH, NO.
SIGH
YAMA.

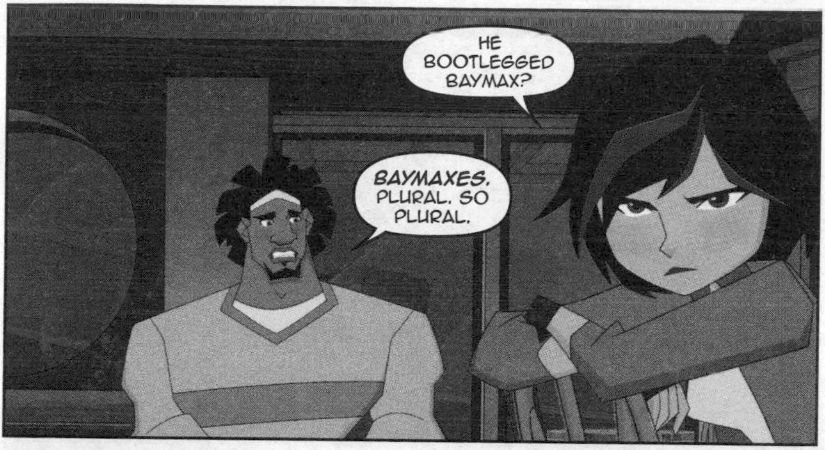
HE BOOTLEGGED BAYMAX?
BAYMAXES. PLURAL. SO PLURAL.

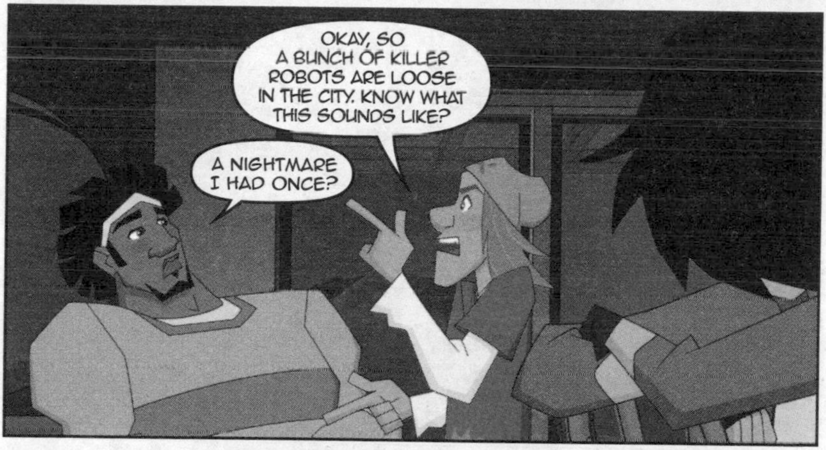
OKAY, SO A BUNCH OF KILLER ROBOTS ARE LOOSE IN THE CITY. KNOW WHAT THIS SOUNDS LIKE?
A NIGHTMARE I HAD ONCE?

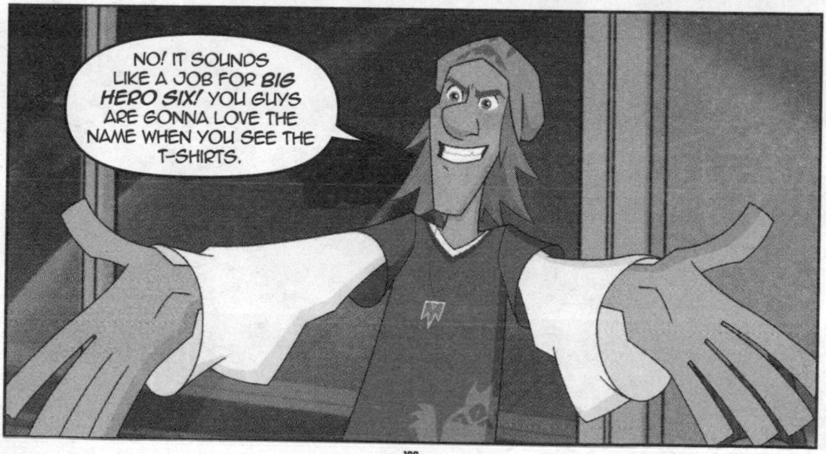
NO! IT SOUNDS LIKE A JOB FOR BIG HERO SIX! YOU GUYS ARE GONNA LOVE THE NAME WHEN YOU SEE THE T-SHIRTS.

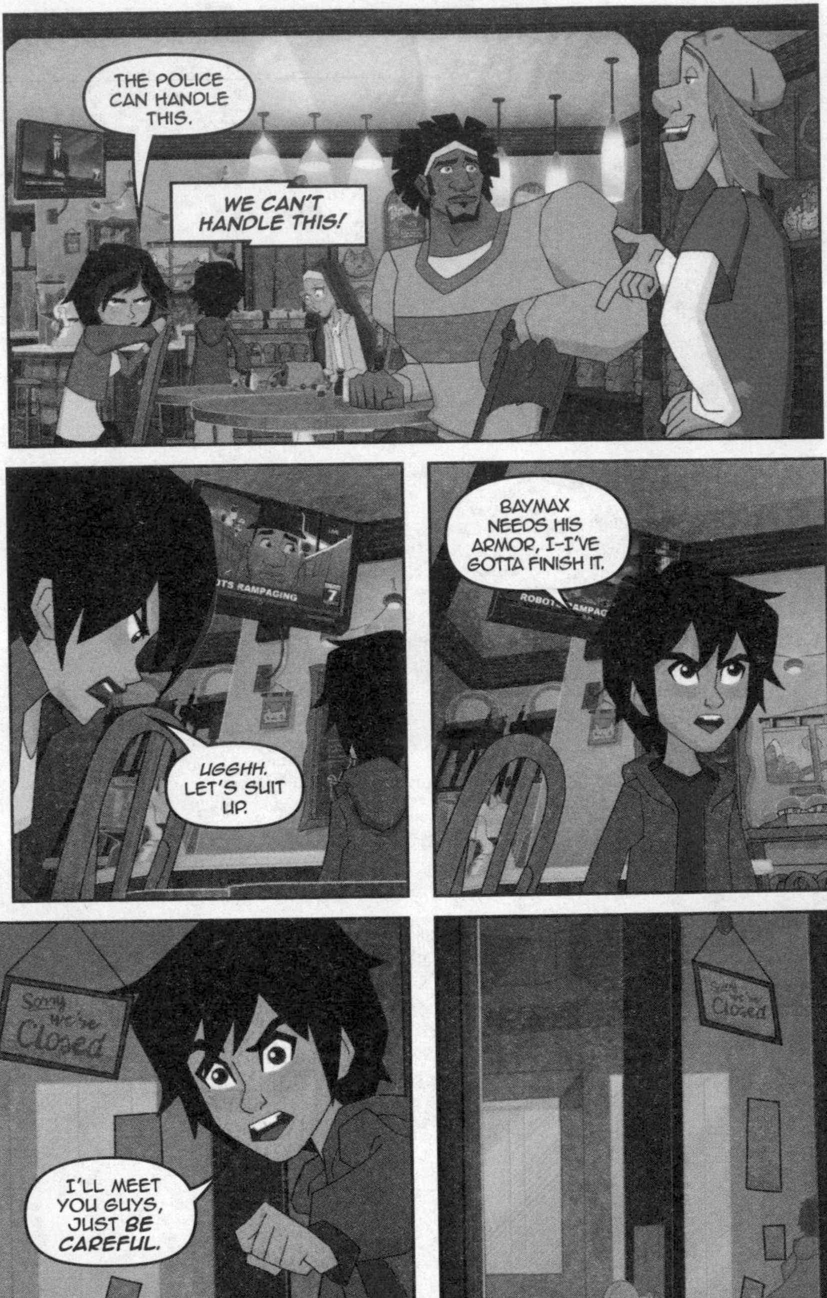
THE POLICE CAN HANDLE THIS.
WE CAN'T HANDLE THIS!
ROBOTS RAMPAGING
UGGHH. LET'S SUIT UP.
BAYMAX NEEDS HIS ARMOR, I-I'VE GOTTA FINISH IT.
Sorry we're Closed
I'LL MEET YOU GUYS, JUST BE CAREFUL.
Sorry we're Closed

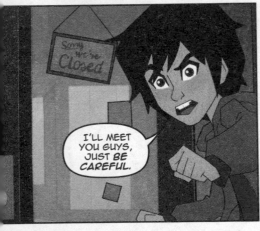

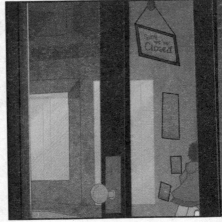

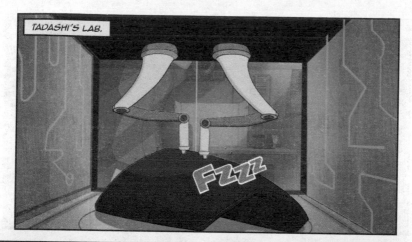

TADASHI'S LAB.

Fzzz

COME ON, COME ON, **COME ON!**

YOU APPEAR TO BE... AGITATED.

YEAH, THE CITY'S UNDER ATTACK.

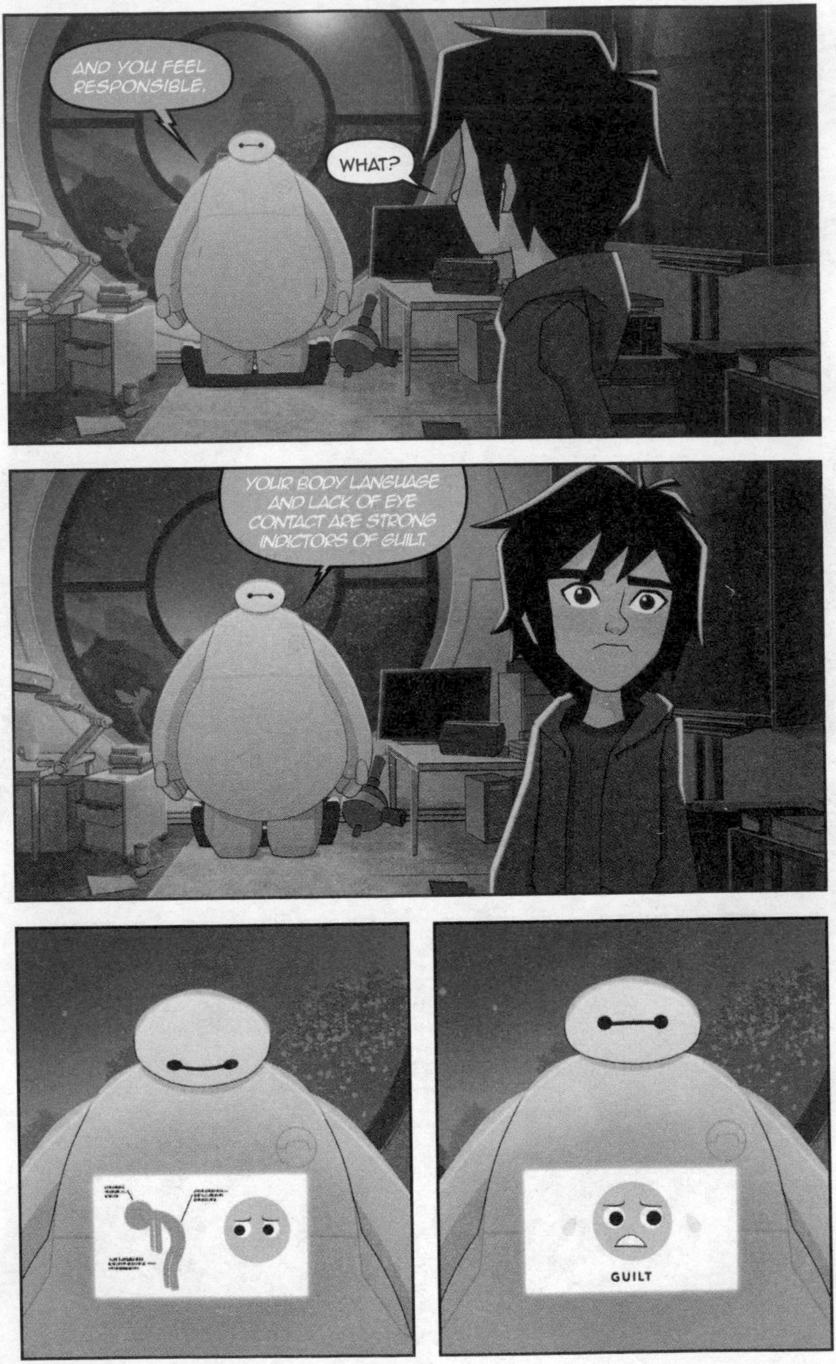
AND YOU FEEL RESPONSIBLE.
WHAT?
YOUR BODY LANGUAGE AND LACK OF EYE CONTACT ARE STRONG INDICTORS OF GUILT.
GUILT

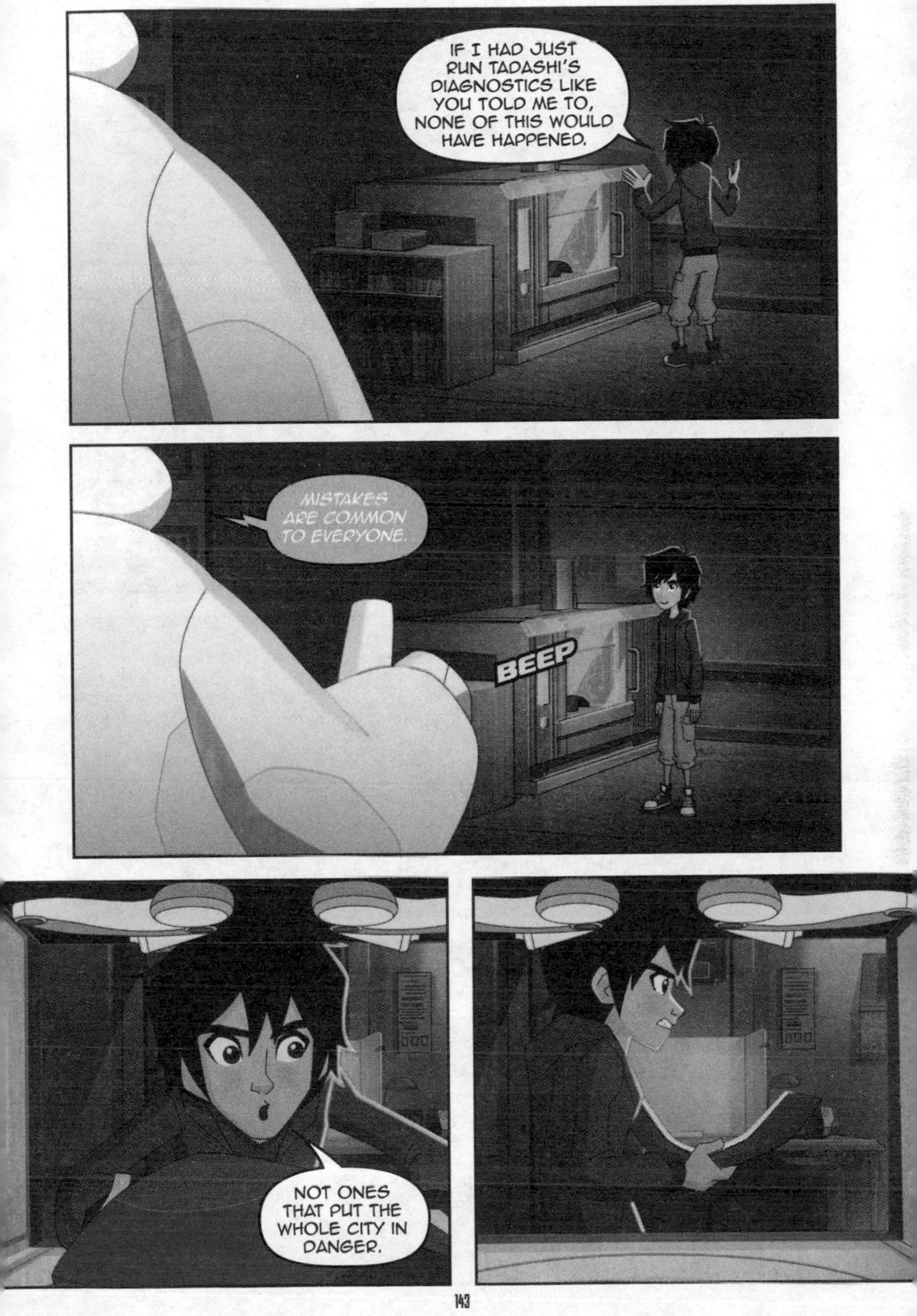
IF I HAD JUST RUN TADASHI'S DIAGNOSTICS LIKE YOU TOLD ME TO, NONE OF THIS WOULD HAVE HAPPENED.
MISTAKES ARE COMMON TO EVERYONE.
BEEP
NOT ONES THAT PUT THE WHOLE CITY IN DANGER.

NIGHT MARKET SQUARE.

AAHHHHHH!

AH! AH! AAAIIEEEEEE!

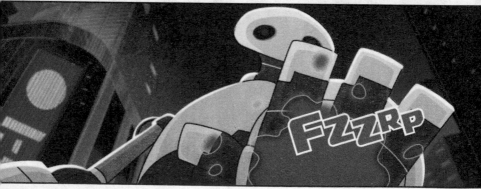

FZZRP

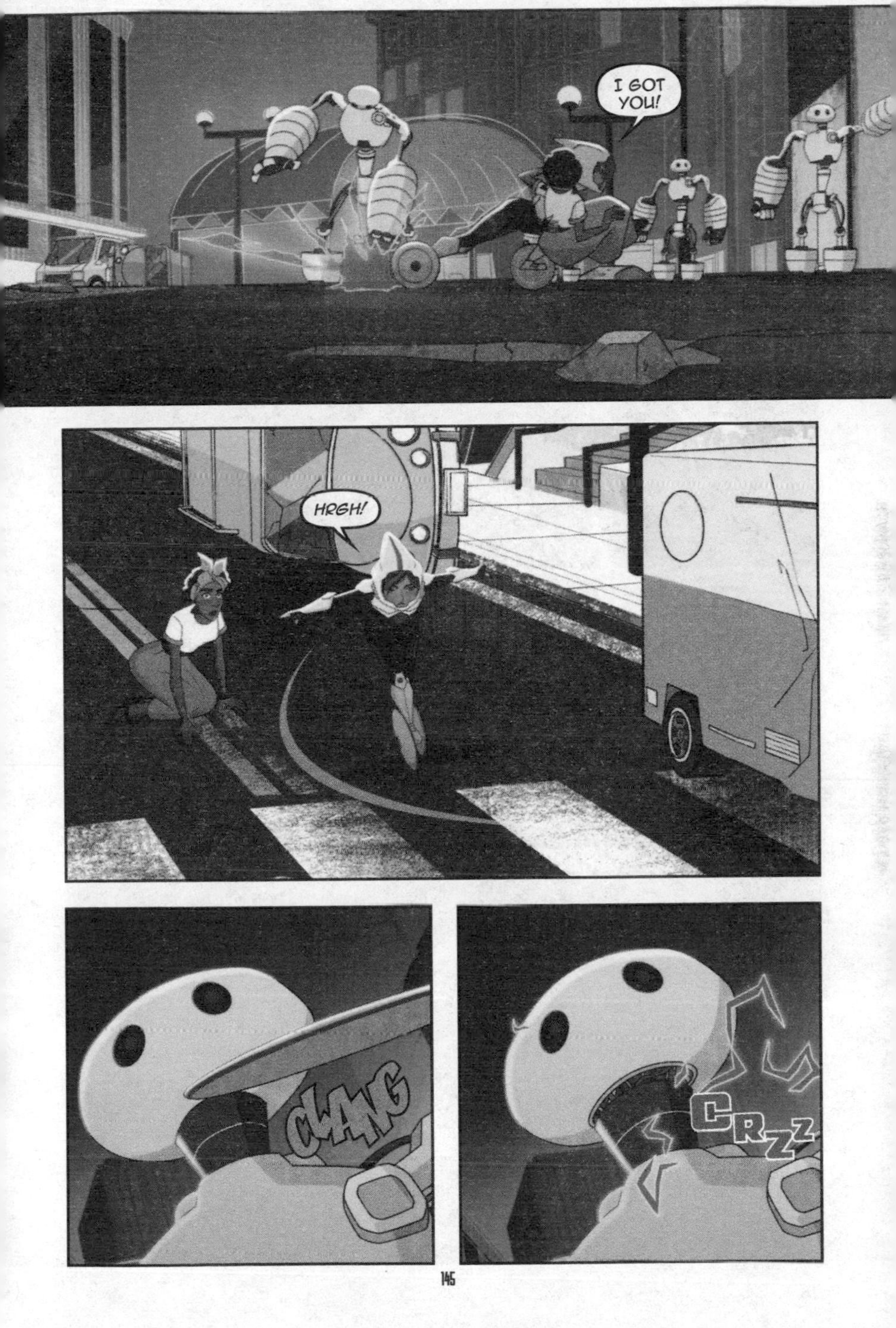
I GOT YOU!
HRGH!
CLANG
CRZZ

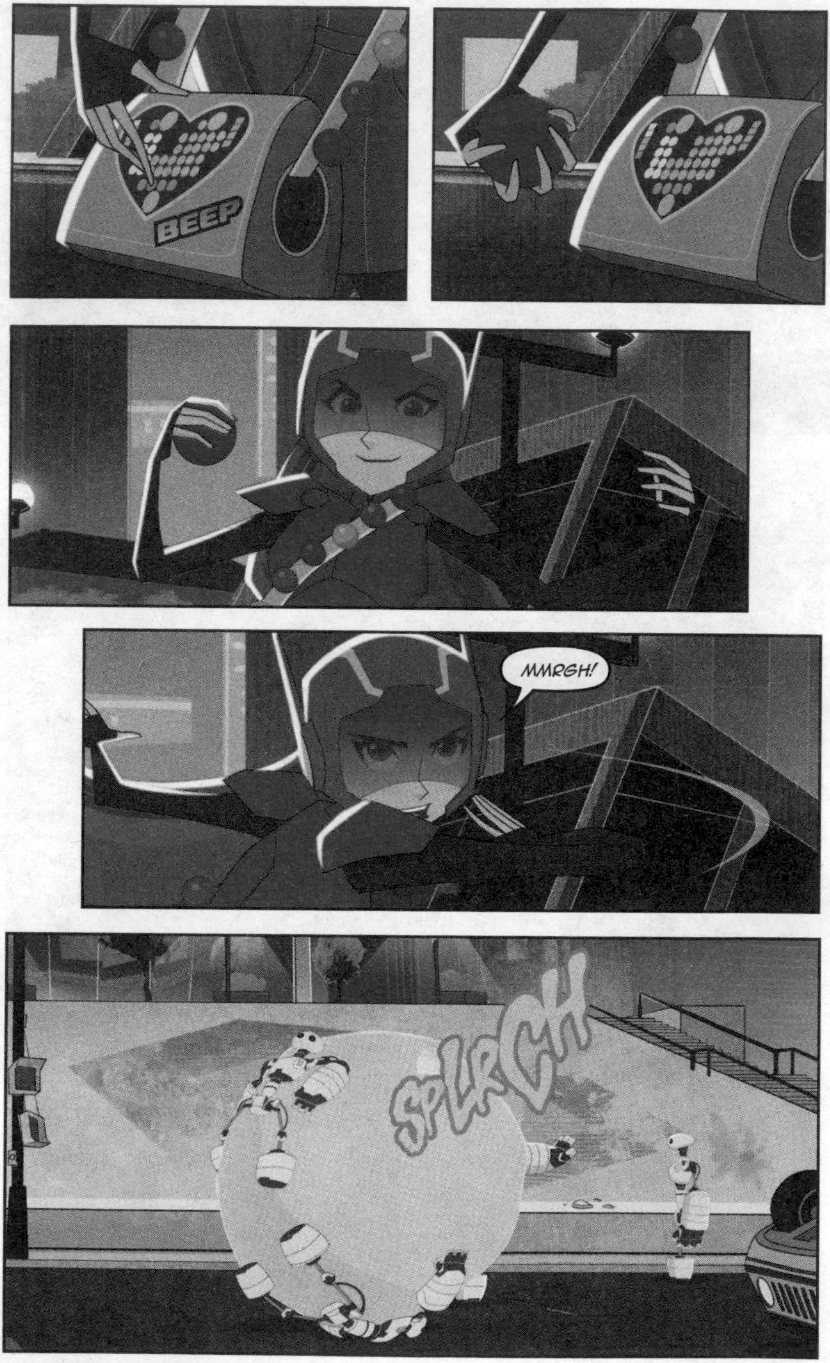
BEEP
MMRGH!
SPLRCH

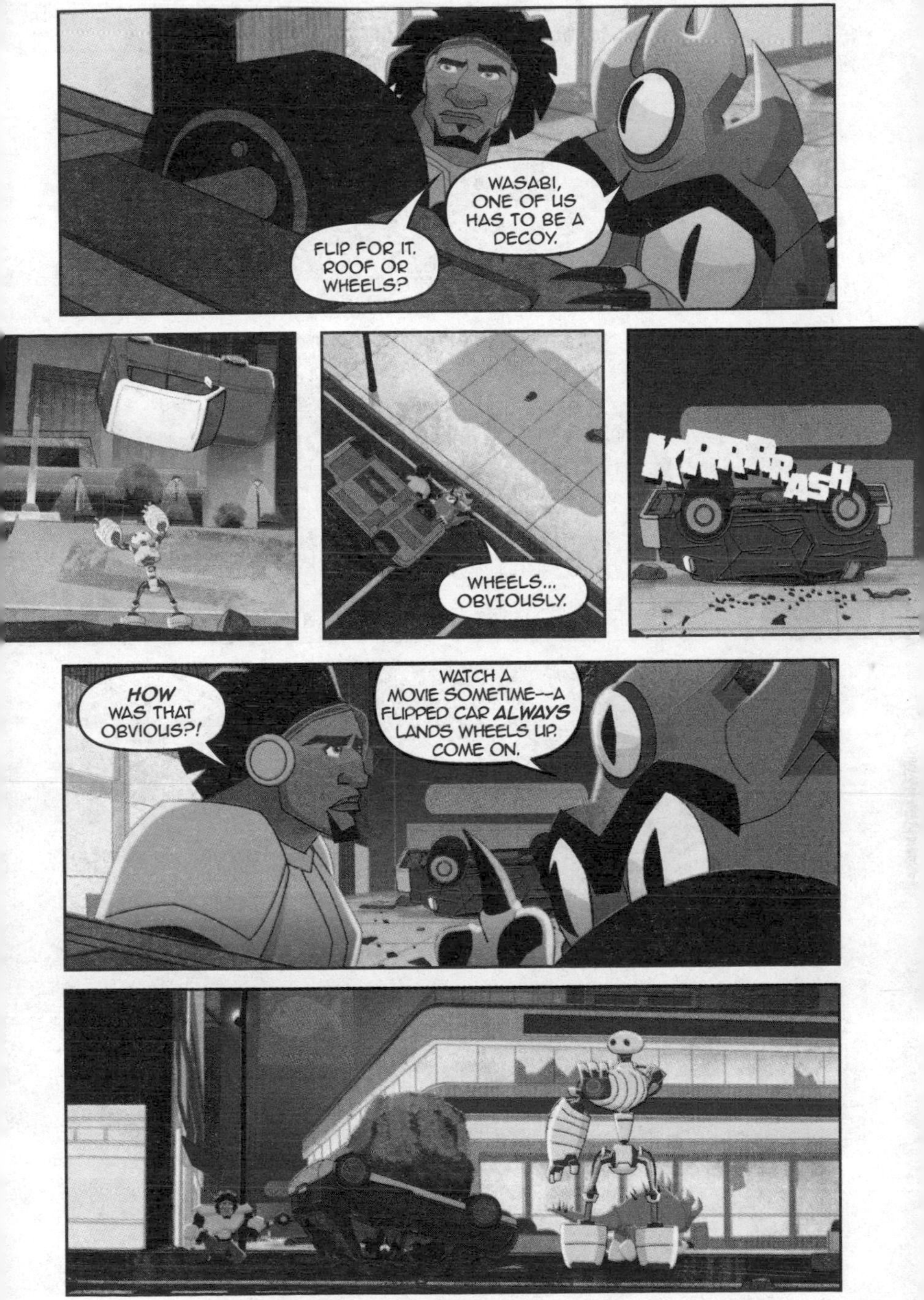
WASABI, ONE OF US HAS TO BE A DECOY.
FLIP FOR IT. ROOF OR WHEELS?
WHEELS... OBVIOUSLY.
KRRRRASH
HOW WAS THAT OBVIOUS?!
WATCH A MOVIE SOMETIME--A FLIPPED CAR ALWAYS LANDS WHEELS UP. COME ON.

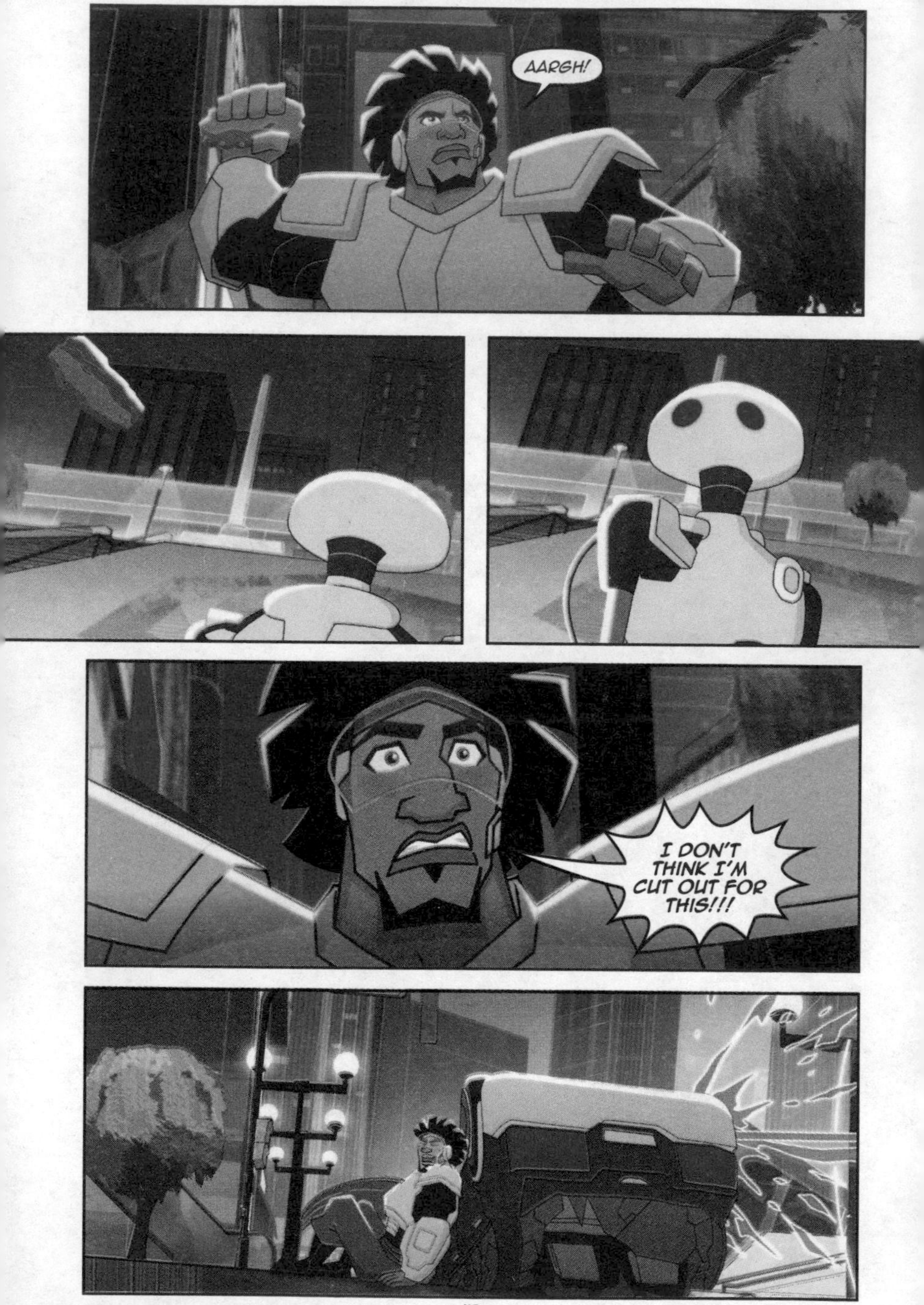
AARGH!
I DON'T THINK I'M CUT OUT FOR THIS!!!

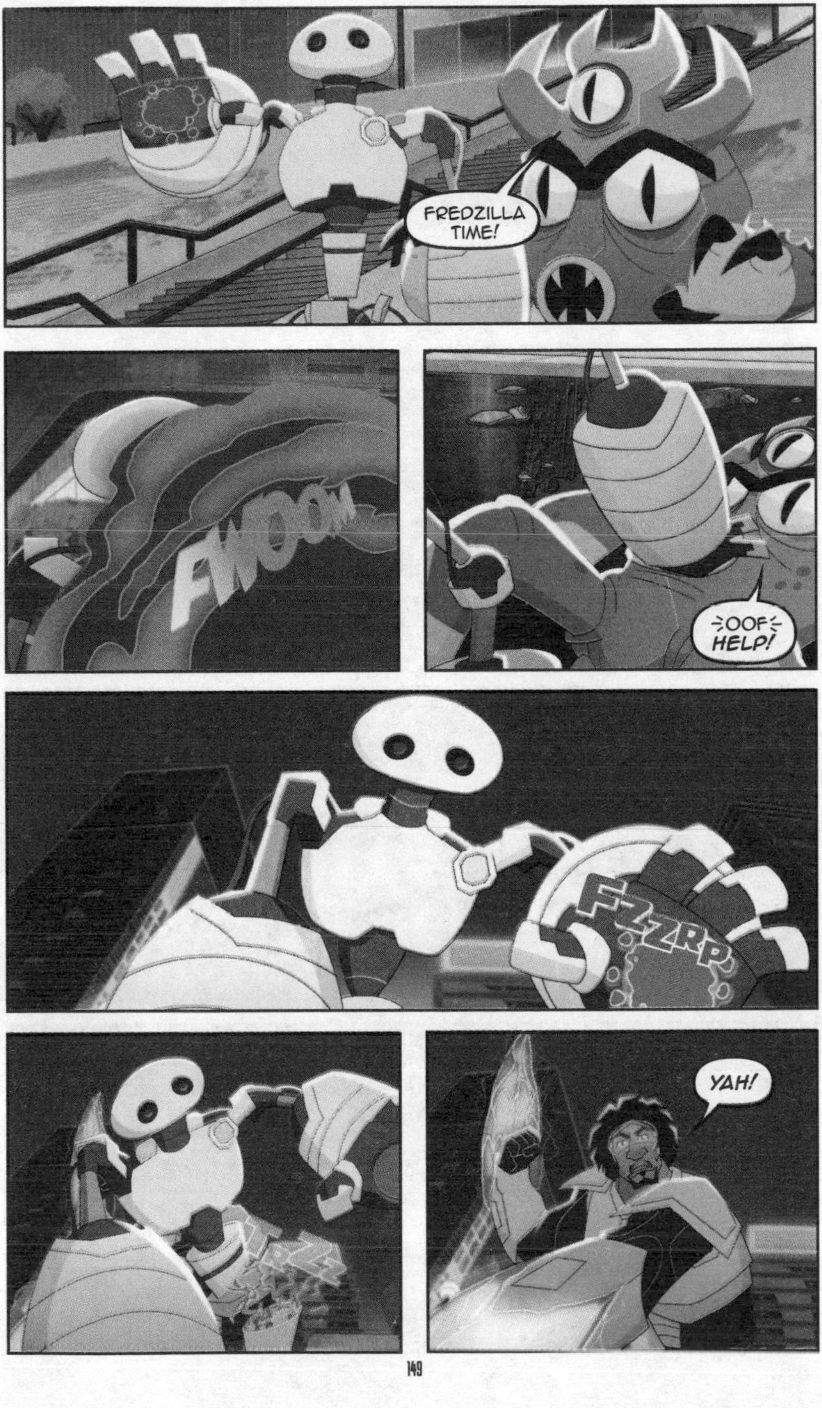
FREDZILLA TIME!
FWOOM
OOF HELP!
FZZRP
YAH!

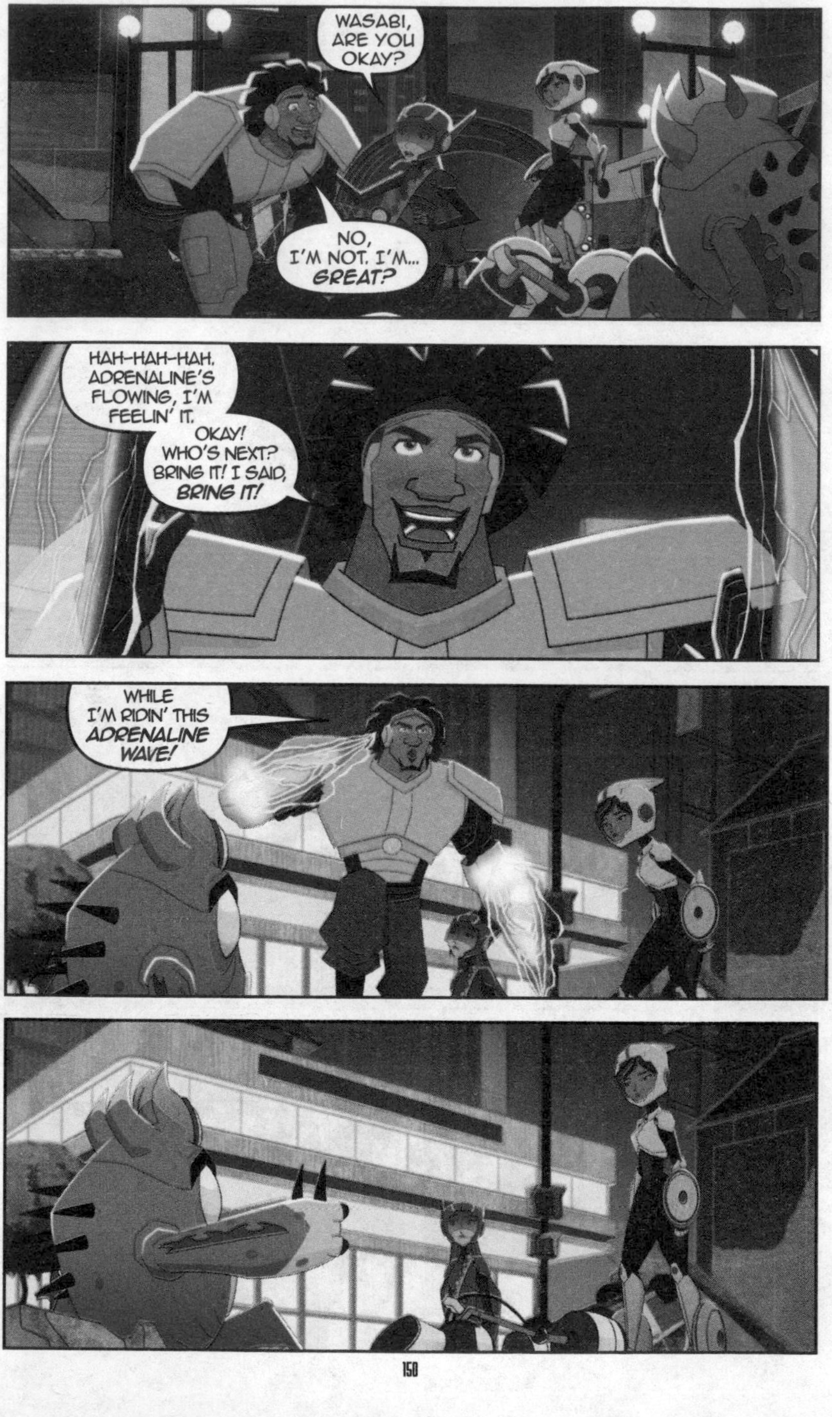
WASABI, ARE YOU OKAY?
NO, I'M NOT. I'M... GREAT?
HAH-HAH-HAH. ADRENALINE'S FLOWING, I'M FEELIN' IT.
OKAY! WHO'S NEXT? BRING IT! I SAID, BRING IT!
WHILE I'M RIDIN' THIS ADRENALINE WAVE!

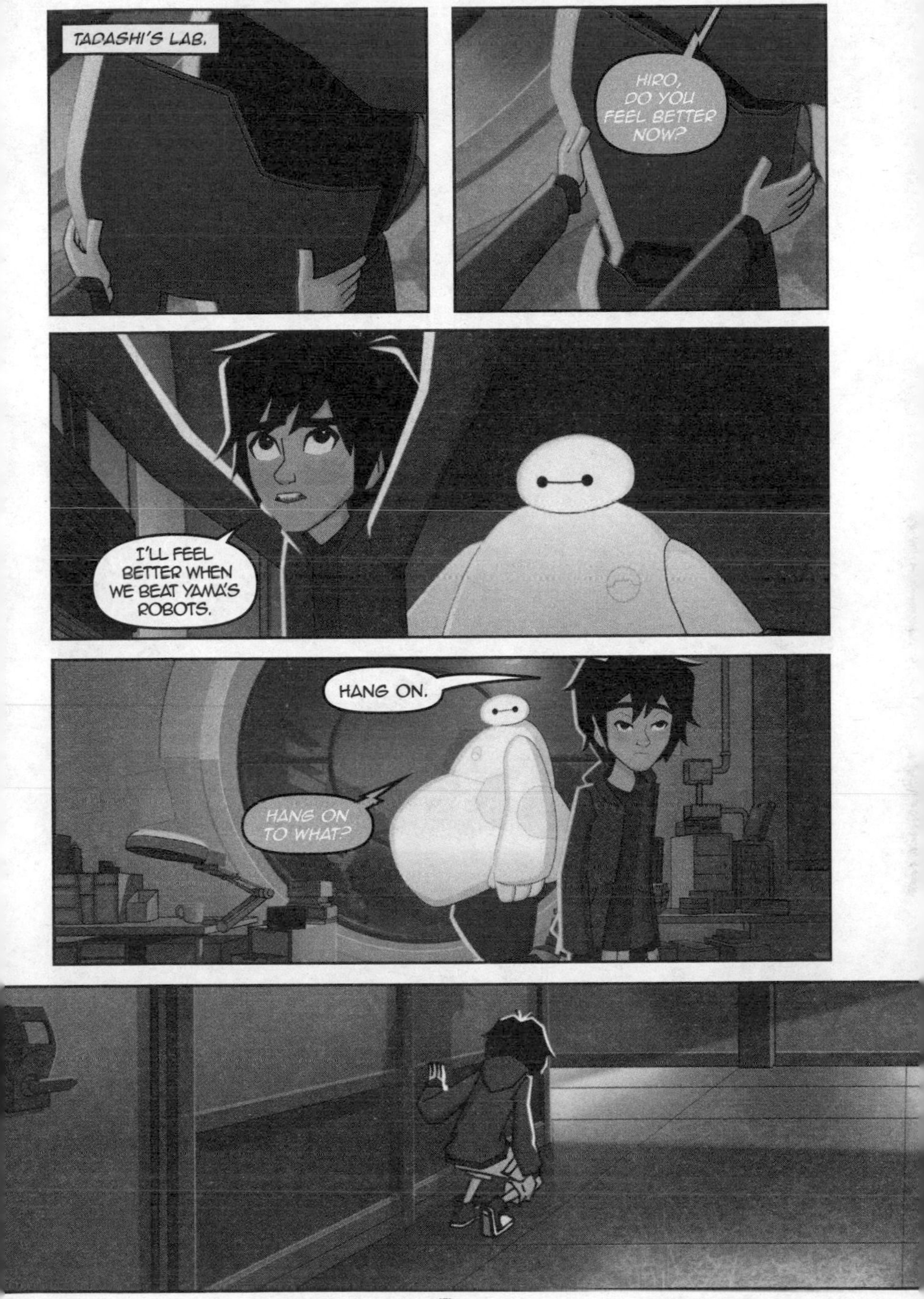
TADASHI'S LAB.
HIRO, DO YOU FEEL BETTER NOW?
I'LL FEEL BETTER WHEN WE BEAT YAMA'S ROBOTS.
HANG ON.
HANG ON TO WHAT?

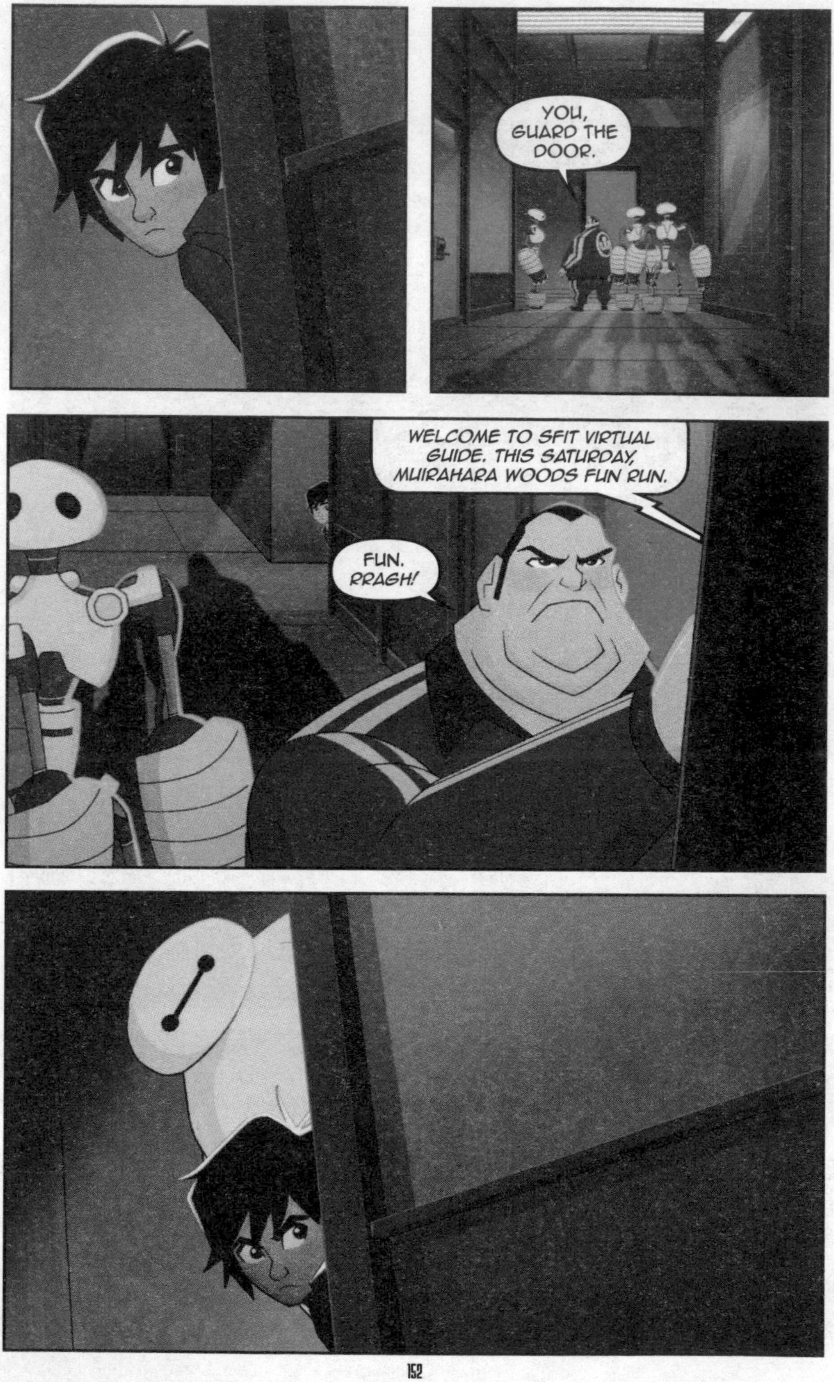
YOU, GUARD THE DOOR.
WELCOME TO SFIT VIRTUAL GUIDE. THIS SATURDAY, MUIRAHARA WOODS FUN RUN.
FUN. RRAGH!

SSSHHHHHHH.

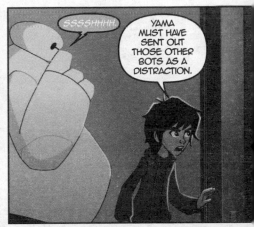

SSSSHHHH.

YAMA MUST HAVE SENT OUT THOSE OTHER BOTS AS A DISTRACTION.

YOU ARE HERE.

HERE? I KNOW I'M HERE! *WHERE* IS *HERE?*

GUYS, YAMA JUST BROKE INTO THE SCHOOL.

I–I THINK HE *REALLY* WANTS THAT THING FROM GRANVILLE'S OFFICE.

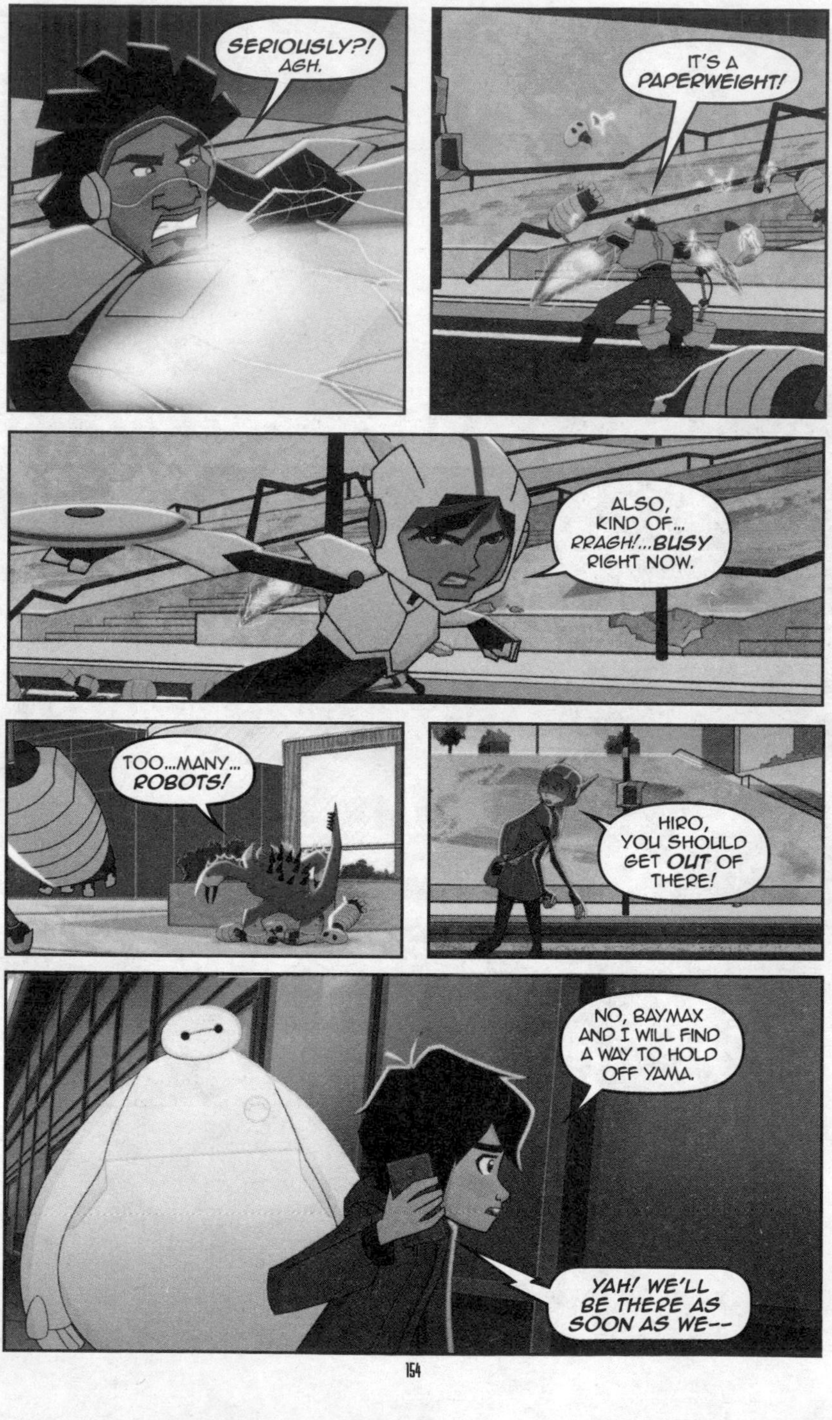
SERIOUSLY?! AGH.
IT'S A PAPERWEIGHT!
ALSO, KIND OF... RRAGH!...BUSY RIGHT NOW.
TOO...MANY... ROBOTS!
HIRO, YOU SHOULD GET OUT OF THERE!
NO, BAYMAX AND I WILL FIND A WAY TO HOLD OFF YAMA.
YAH! WE'LL BE THERE AS SOON AS WE--

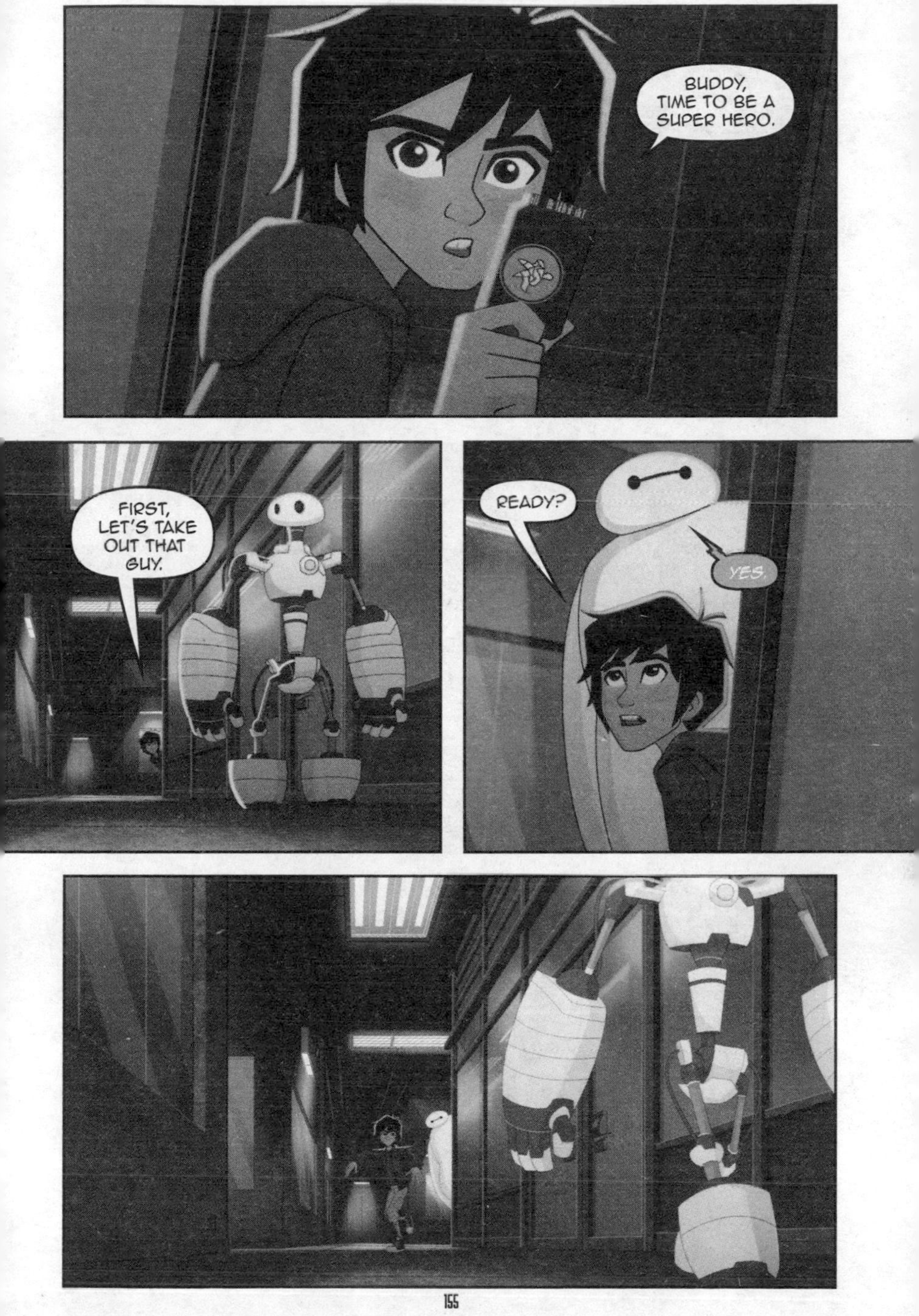
BUDDY, TIME TO BE A SUPER HERO.
FIRST, LET'S TAKE OUT THAT GUY.
READY?
YES.

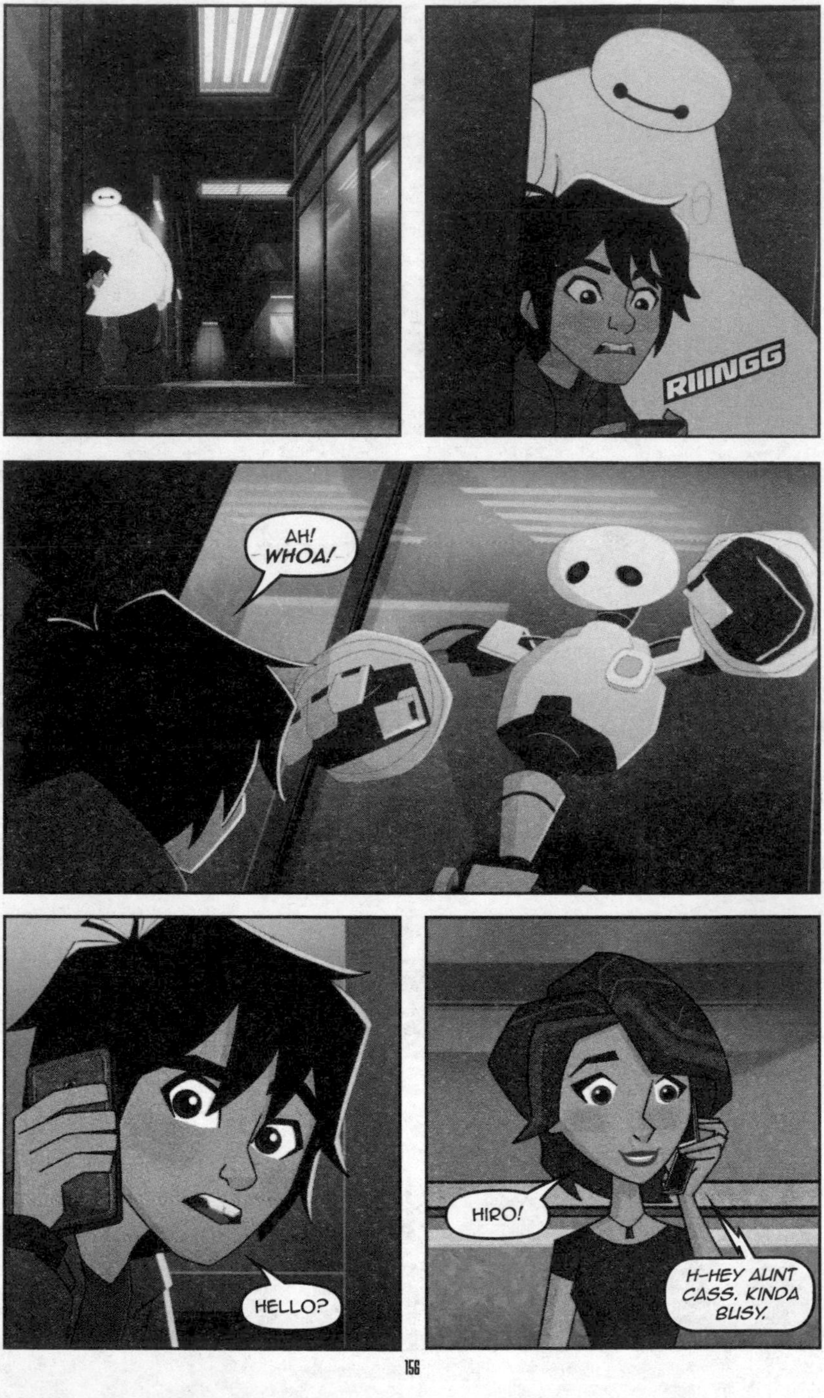
RIIINGG
AH! WHOA!
HELLO?
HIRO!
H-HEY AUNT CASS. KINDA BUSY.

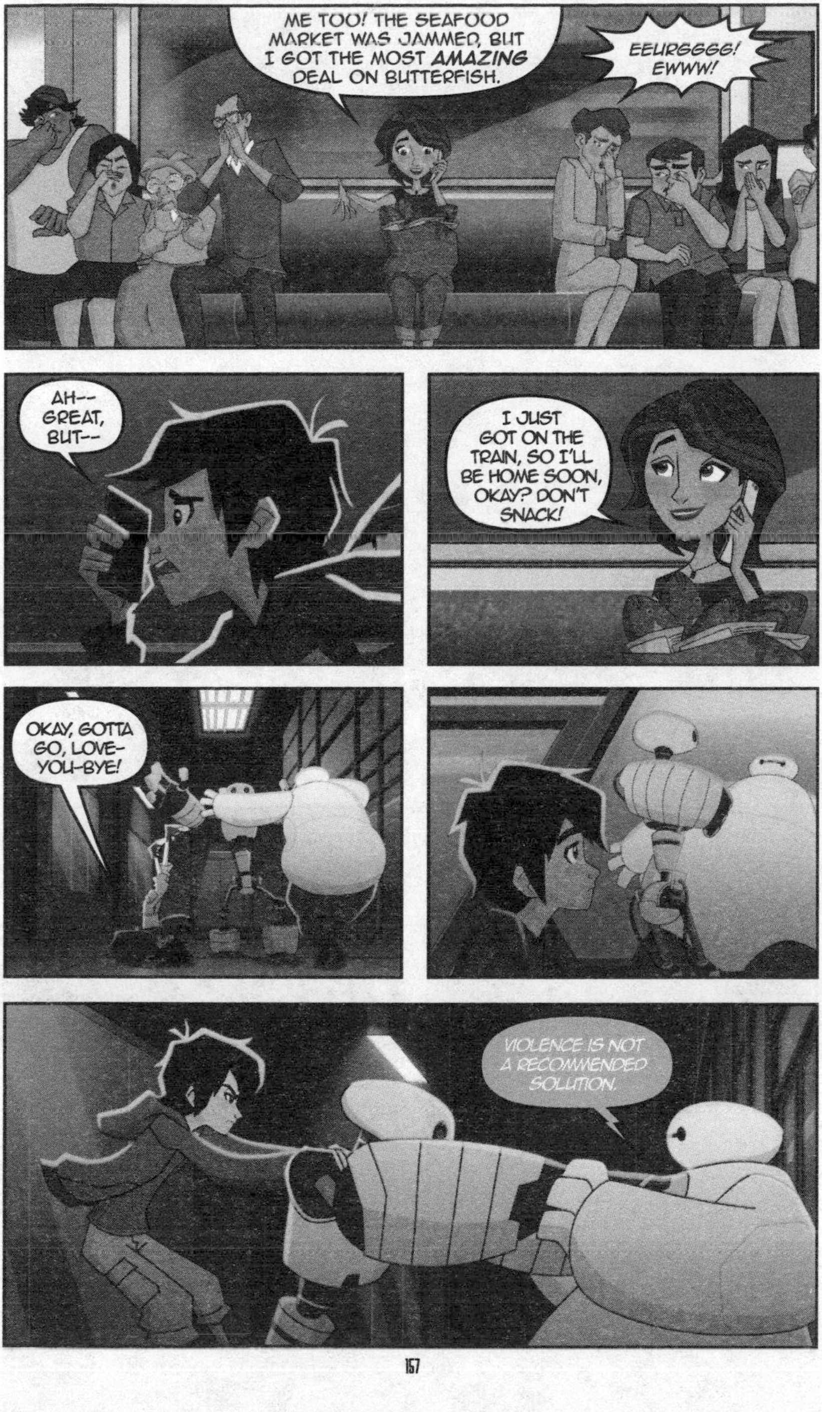
ME TOO! THE SEAFOOD MARKET WAS JAMMED, BUT I GOT THE MOST AMAZING DEAL ON BUTTERFISH.
EEURGGGG! EWWW!
AH-- GREAT, BUT--
I JUST GOT ON THE TRAIN, SO I'LL BE HOME SOON, OKAY? DON'T SNACK!
OKAY, GOTTA GO, LOVE-YOU-BYE!
VIOLENCE IS NOT A RECOMMENDED SOLUTION.

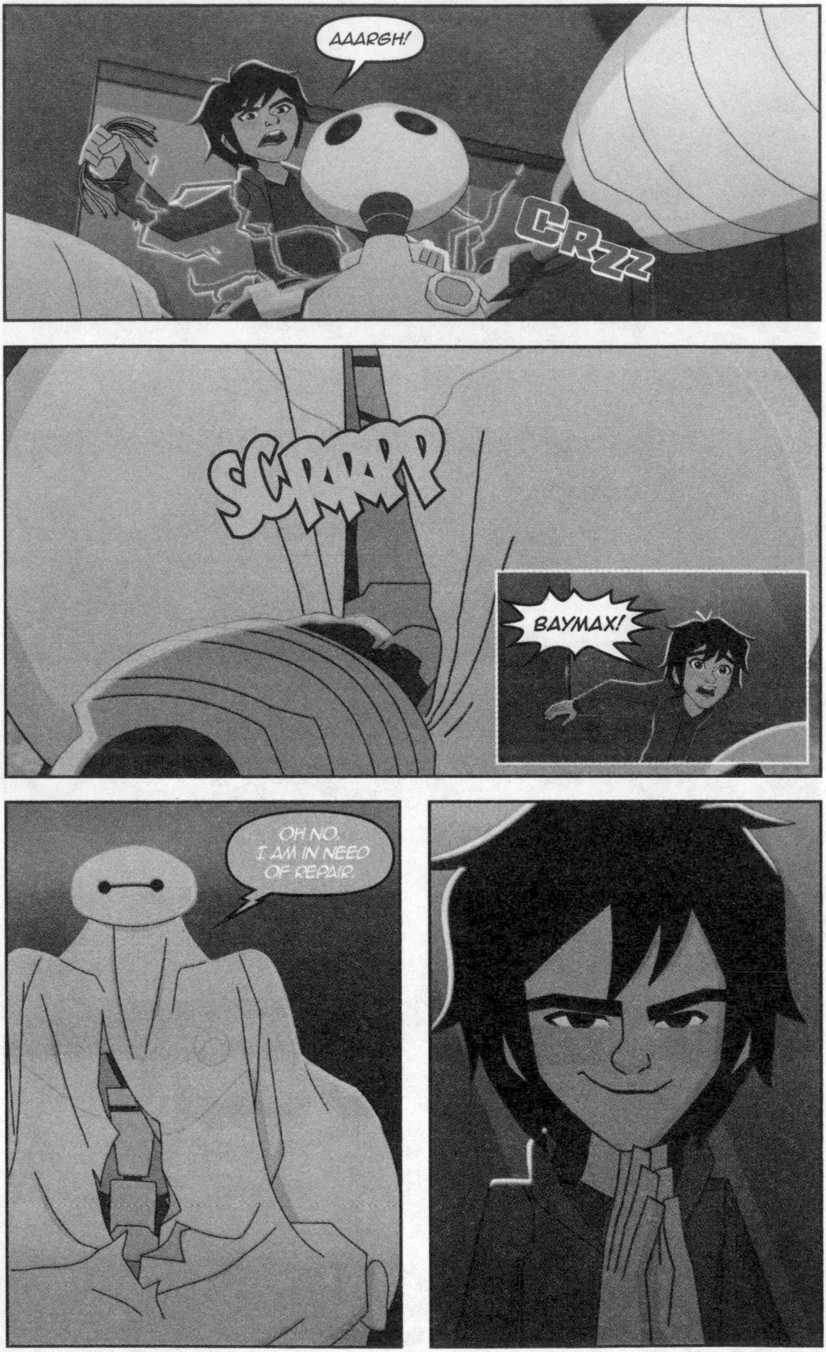
AAARGH!
CRZZ
SCRRRP
BAYMAX!
OH NO. I AM IN NEED OF REPAIR.

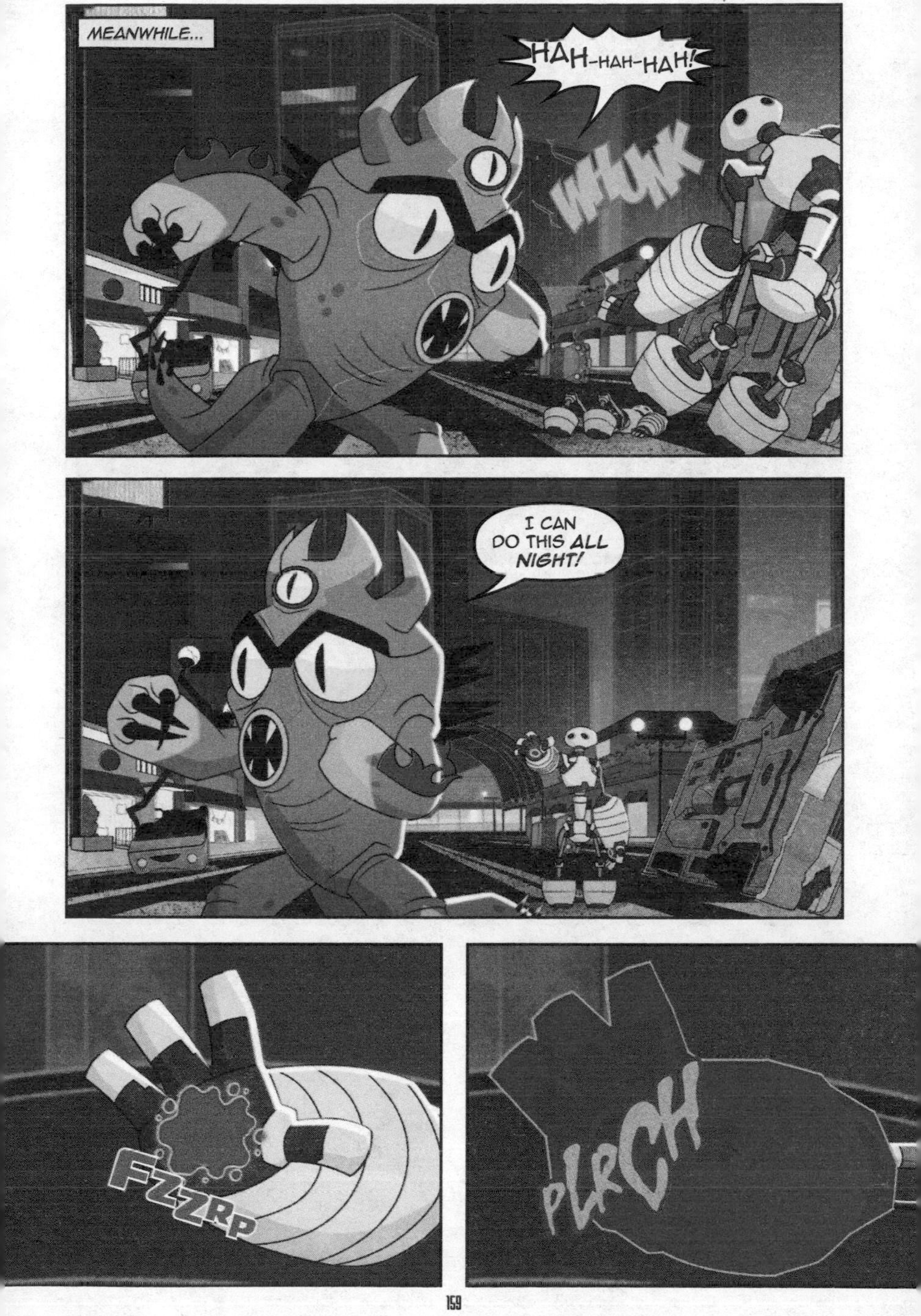
MEANWHILE...
HAH-HAH-HAH!
WHUNK
I CAN DO THIS ALL NIGHT!
FZZRP
PLRCH

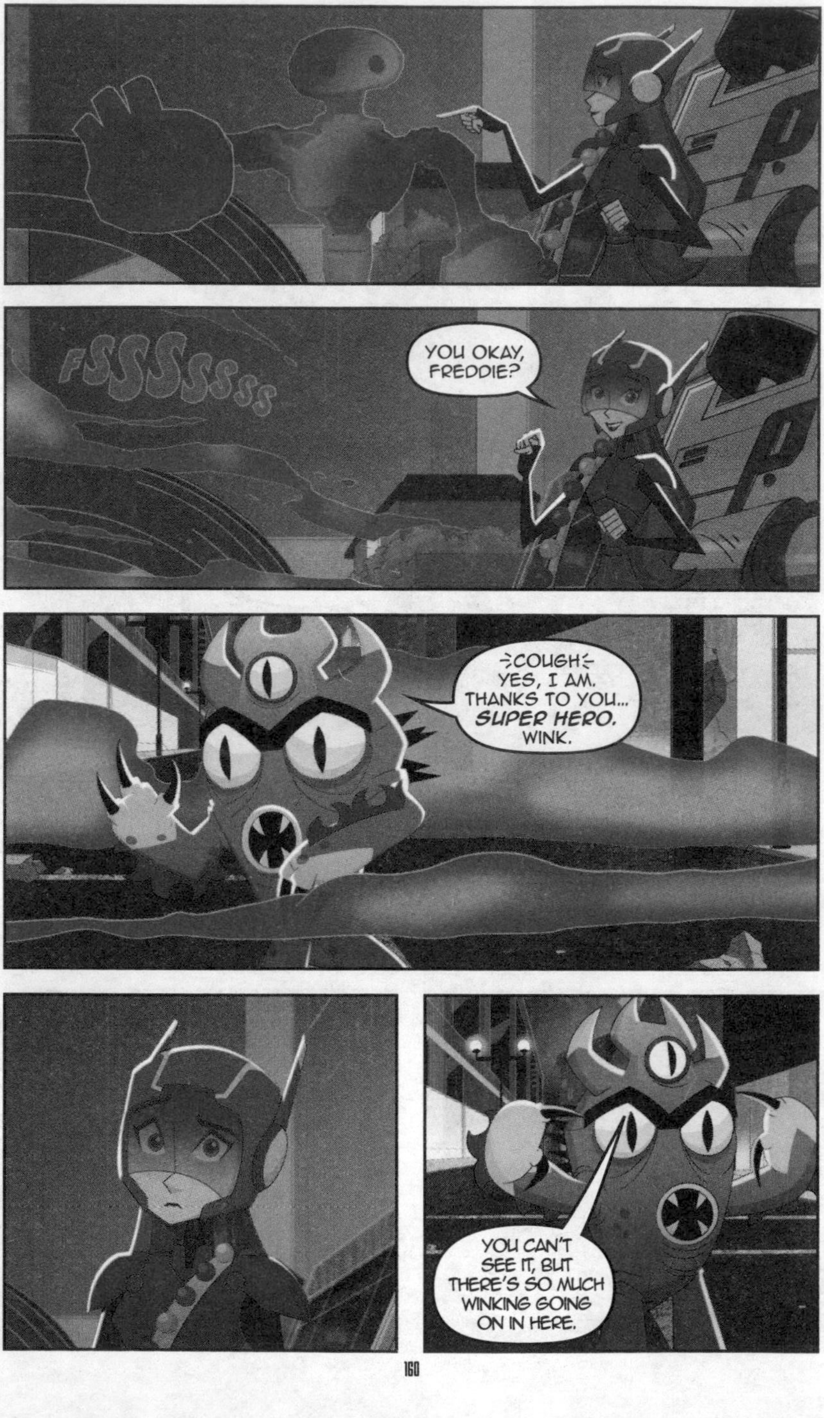
FSSSSSSSS
YOU OKAY, FREDDIE?
COUGH YES, I AM. THANKS TO YOU... SUPER HERO. WINK.
YOU CAN'T SEE IT, BUT THERE'S SO MUCH WINKING GOING ON IN HERE.

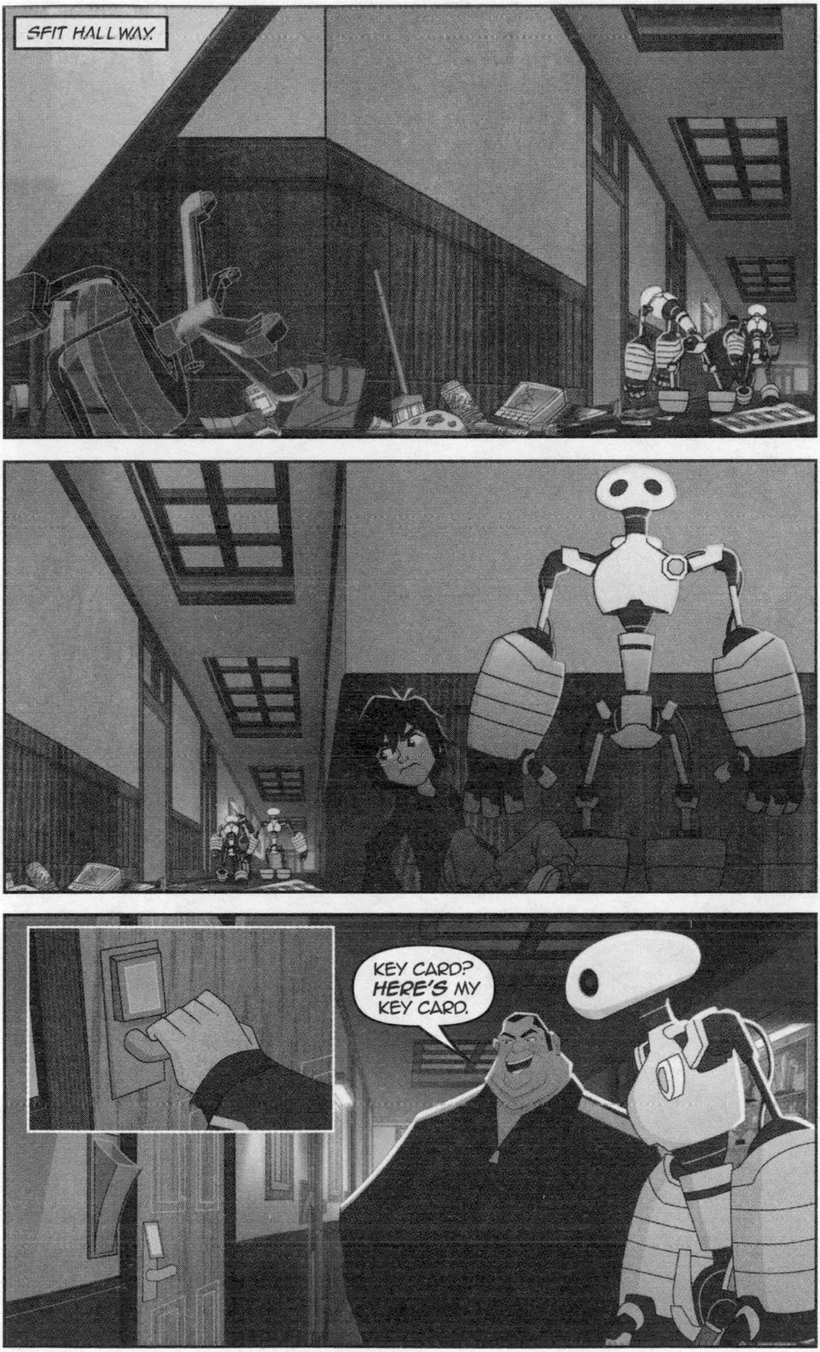
SFIT HALLWAY.
KEY CARD? HERE'S MY KEY CARD.

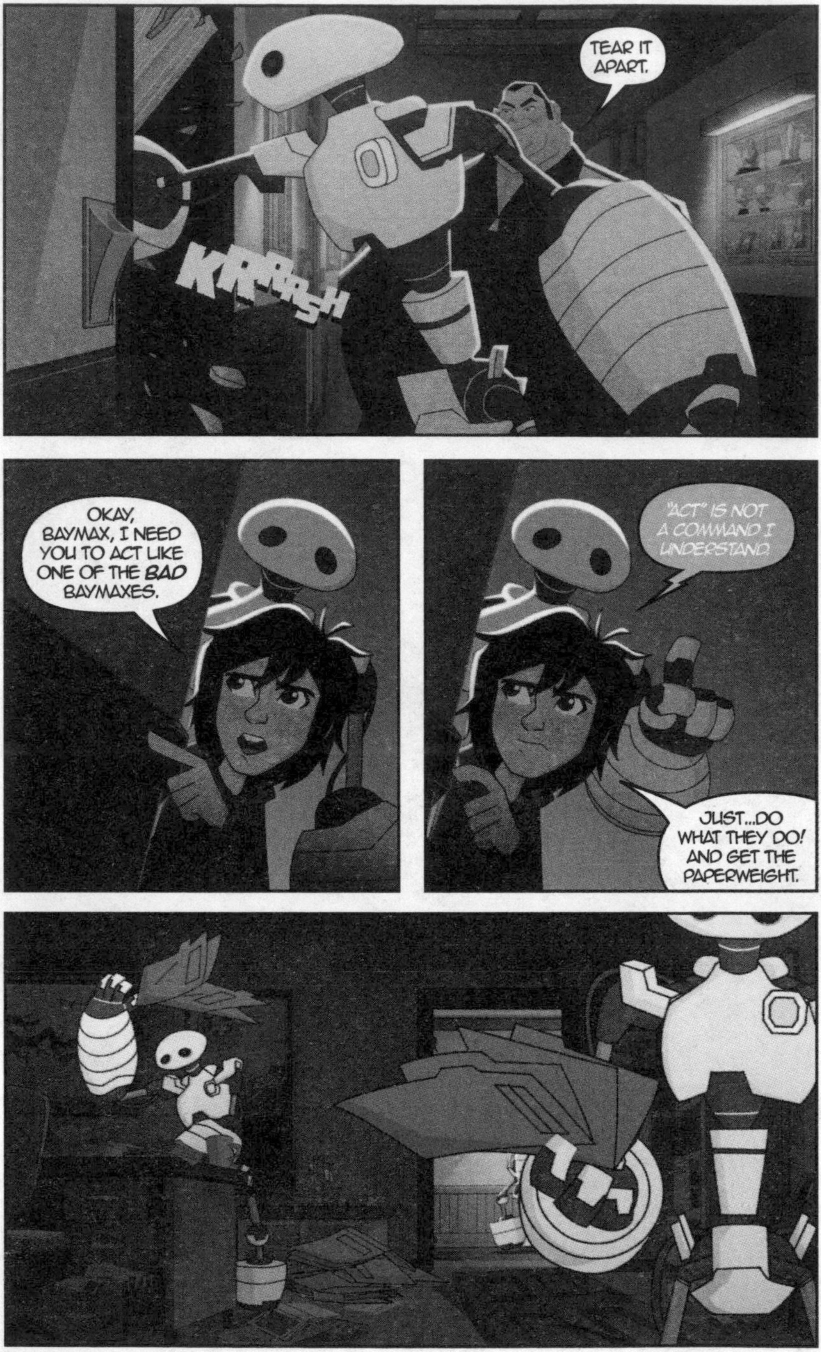
TEAR IT APART.
KRRRASH
OKAY, BAYMAX, I NEED YOU TO ACT LIKE ONE OF THE *BAD* BAYMAXES.
"ACT" IS NOT A COMMAND I UNDERSTAND.
JUST...DO WHAT THEY DO! AND GET THE PAPERWEIGHT.

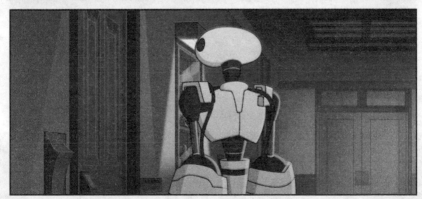

SEARCHING

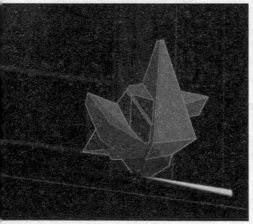

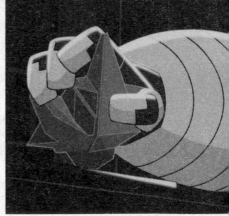

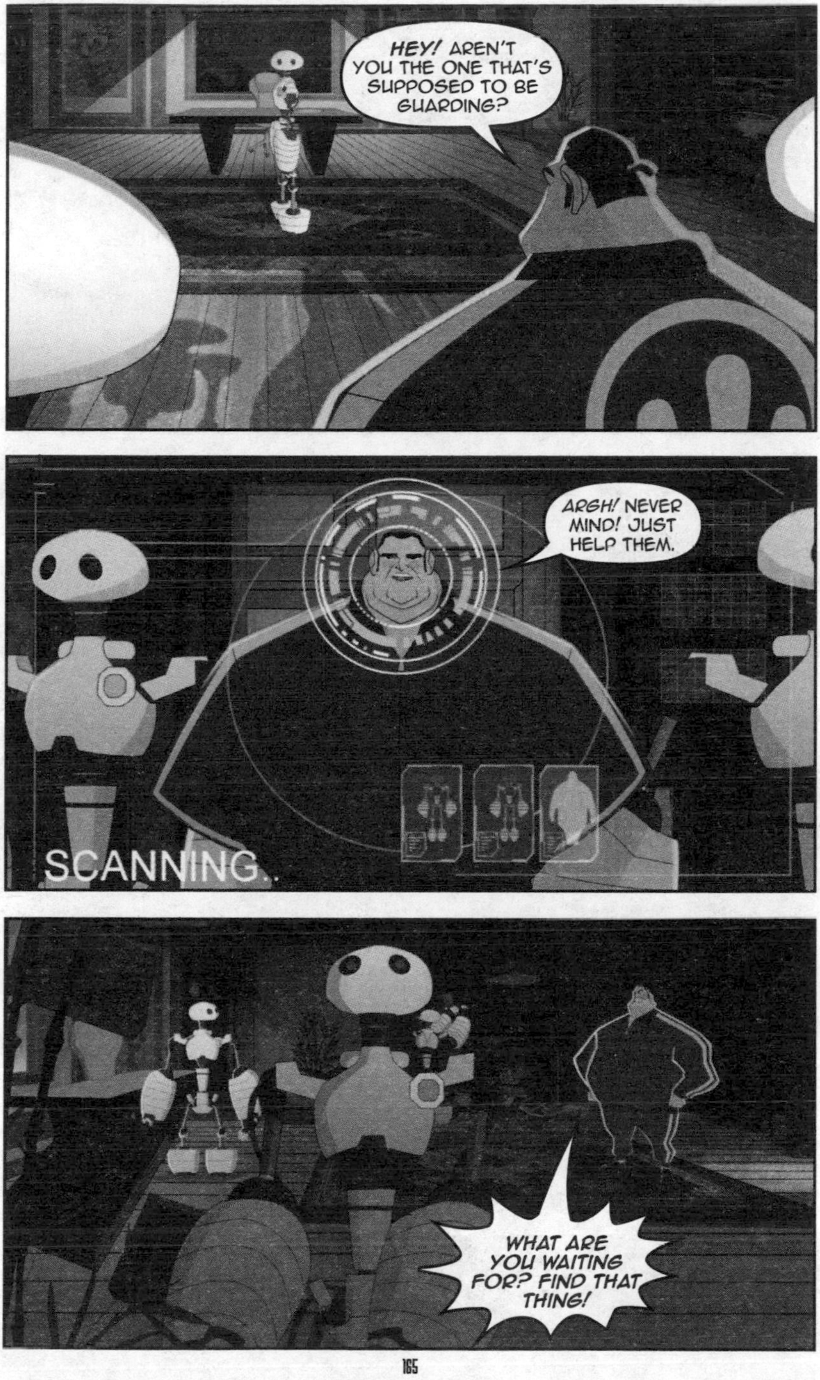
HEY! AREN'T YOU THE ONE THAT'S SUPPOSED TO BE GUARDING?
ARGH! NEVER MIND! JUST HELP THEM.
SCANNING...
WHAT ARE YOU WAITING FOR? FIND THAT THING!

YARGH! AGH!
THUNK
OWW.
WRRRRP
OH NO.

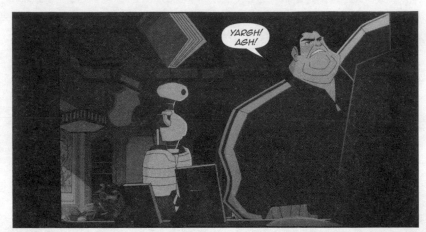

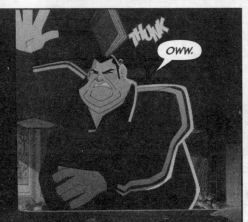

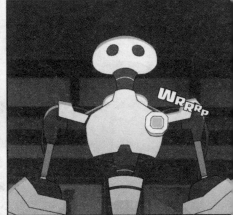

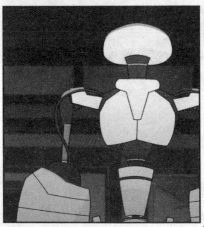

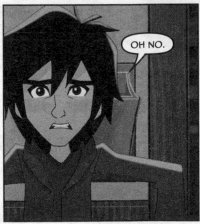

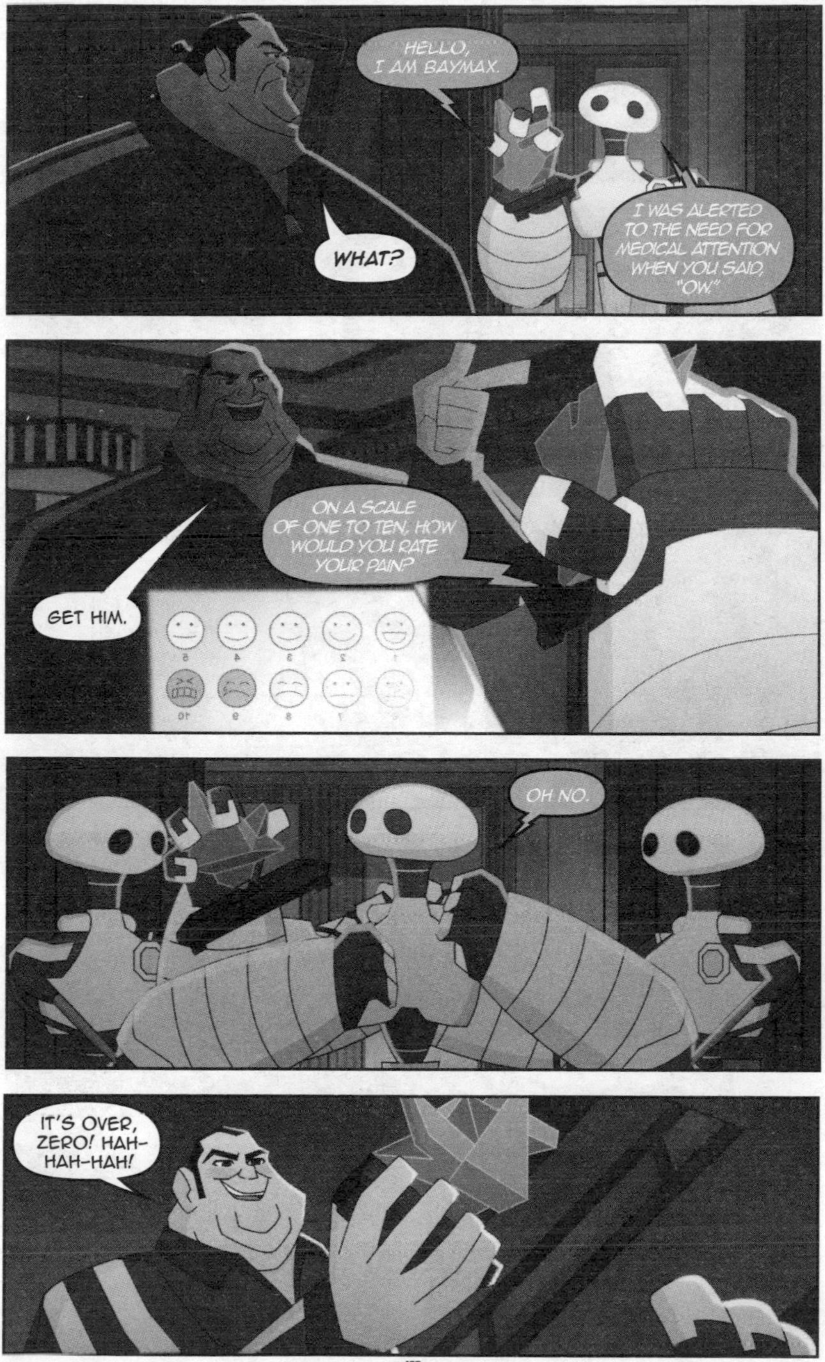
HELLO, I AM BAYMAX.
WHAT?
I WAS ALERTED TO THE NEED FOR MEDICAL ATTENTION WHEN YOU SAID, "OW."
ON A SCALE OF ONE TO TEN, HOW WOULD YOU RATE YOUR PAIN?
GET HIM.
1
2
3
4
5
7
8
9
10
OH NO.
IT'S OVER, ZERO! HAH-HAH-HAH!

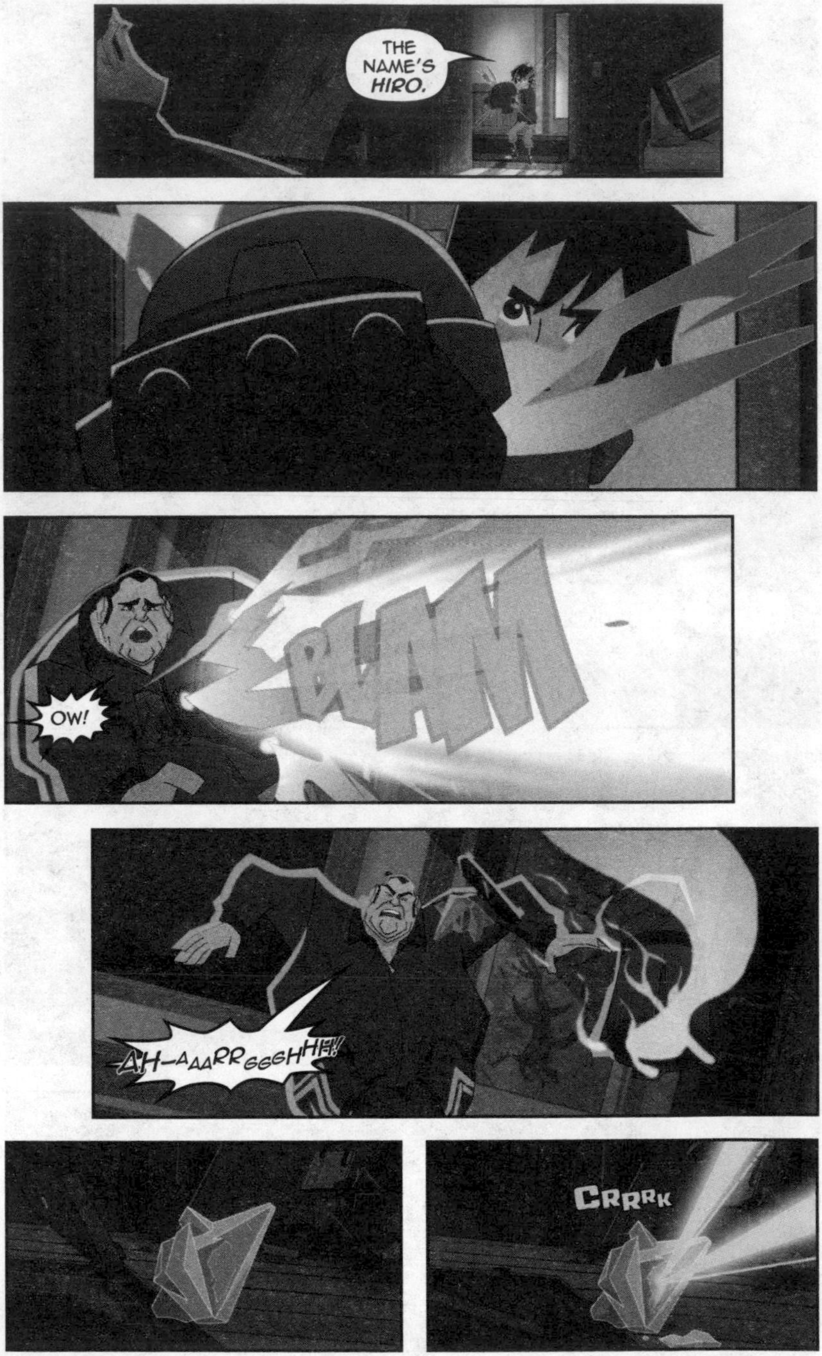
THE NAME'S HIRO.
BLAM
OW!
AH-AAARRGGGHHH!
CRRRK

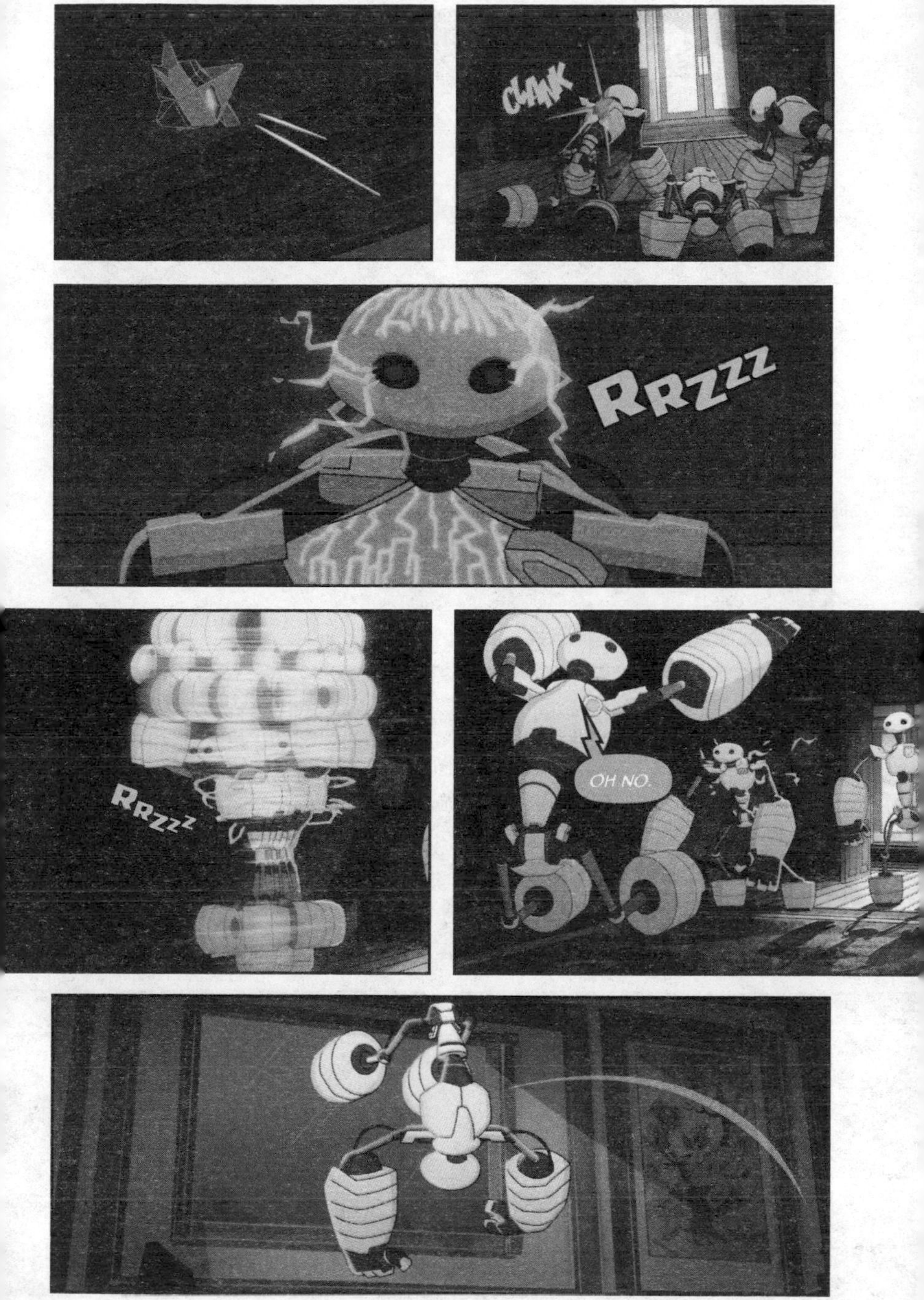
CHANK
RRZZZ
RRZZZ
OH NO.

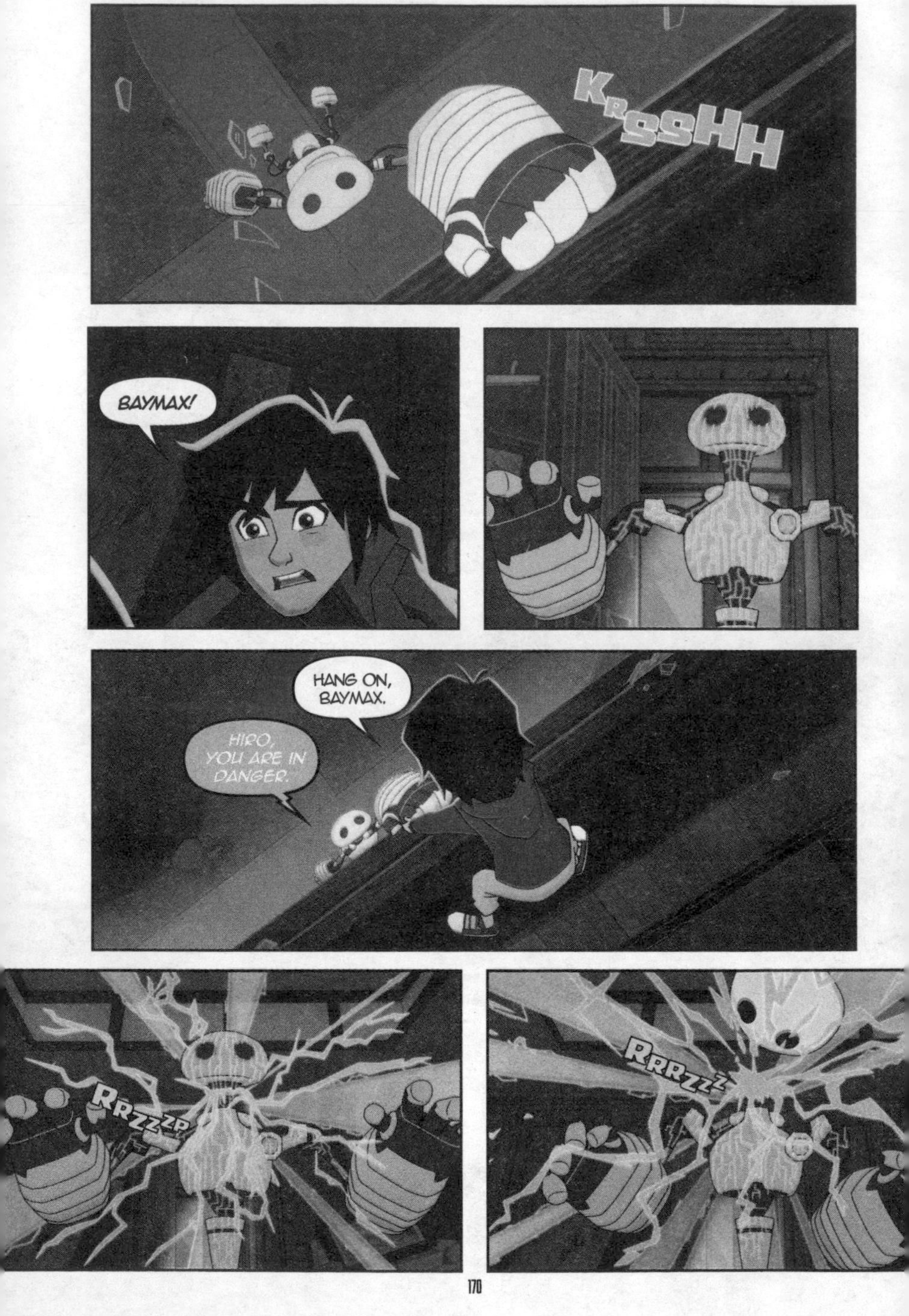
KRSSHH
BAYMAX!
HANG ON, BAYMAX.
HIRO, YOU ARE IN DANGER.
RRZZZP
RRRZZZ

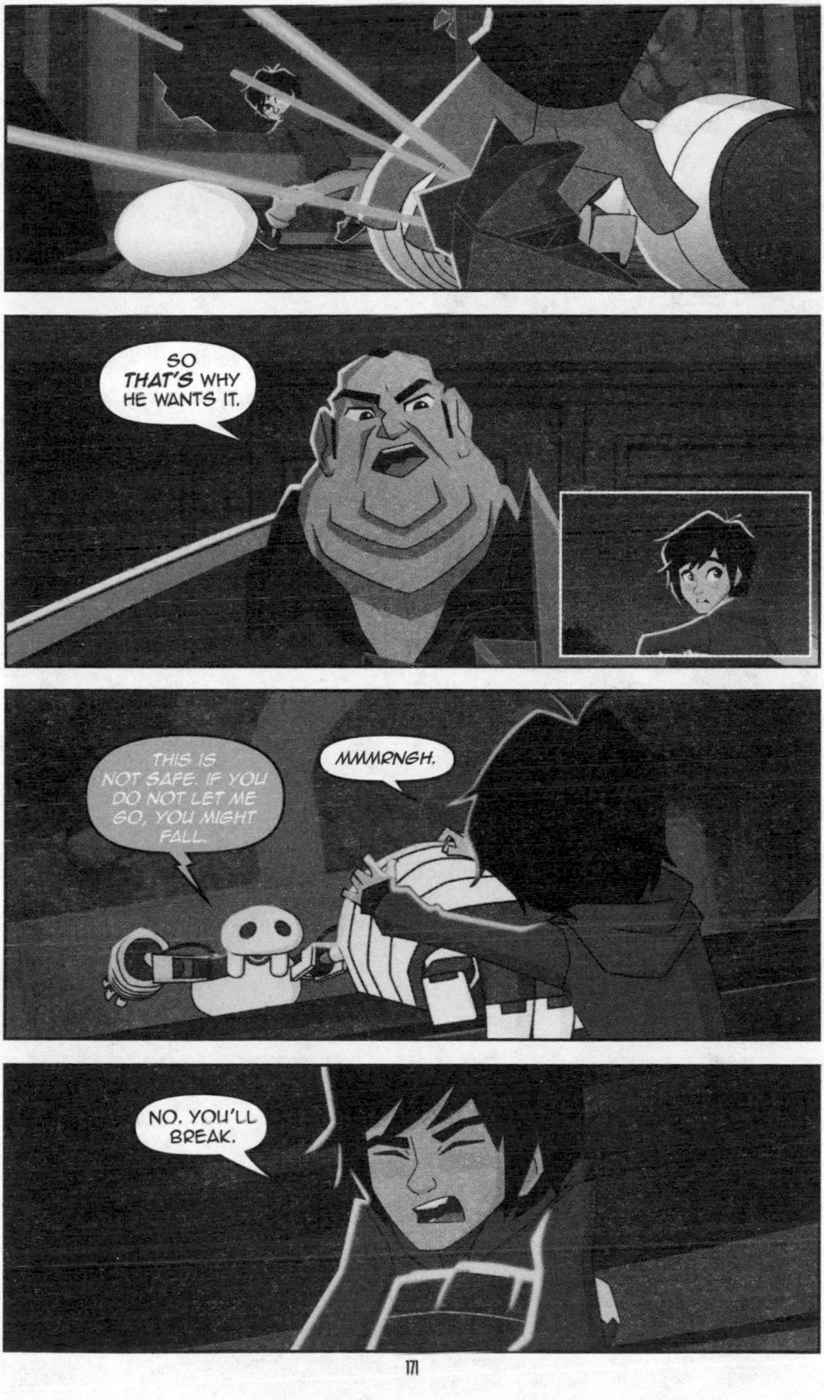
SO THAT'S WHY HE WANTS IT.
THIS IS NOT SAFE. IF YOU DO NOT LET ME GO, YOU MIGHT FALL.
MMMRNGH.
NO. YOU'LL BREAK.

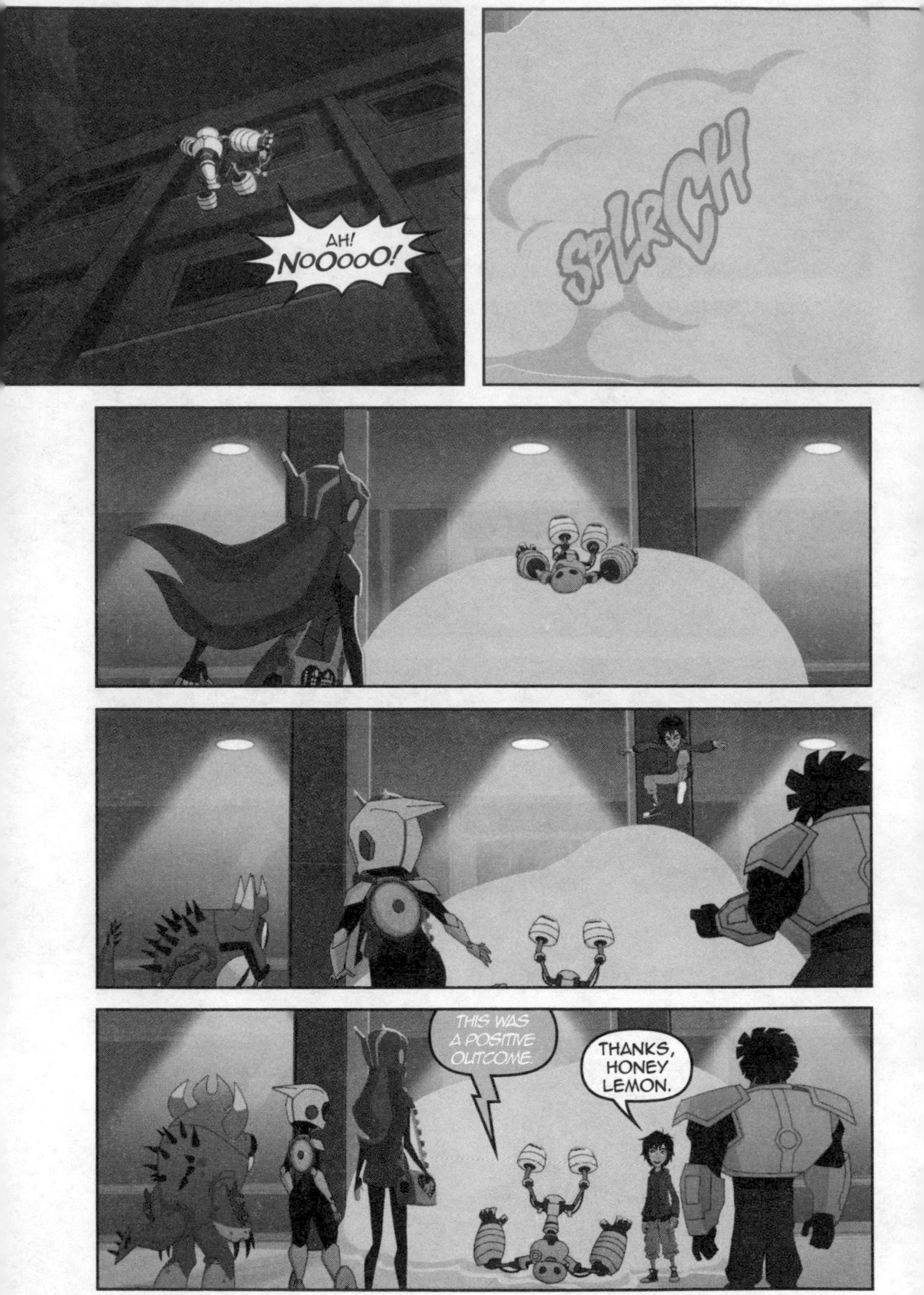
AH! NOOOOO!
SPLRCH
THIS WAS A POSITIVE OUTCOME.
THANKS, HONEY LEMON.

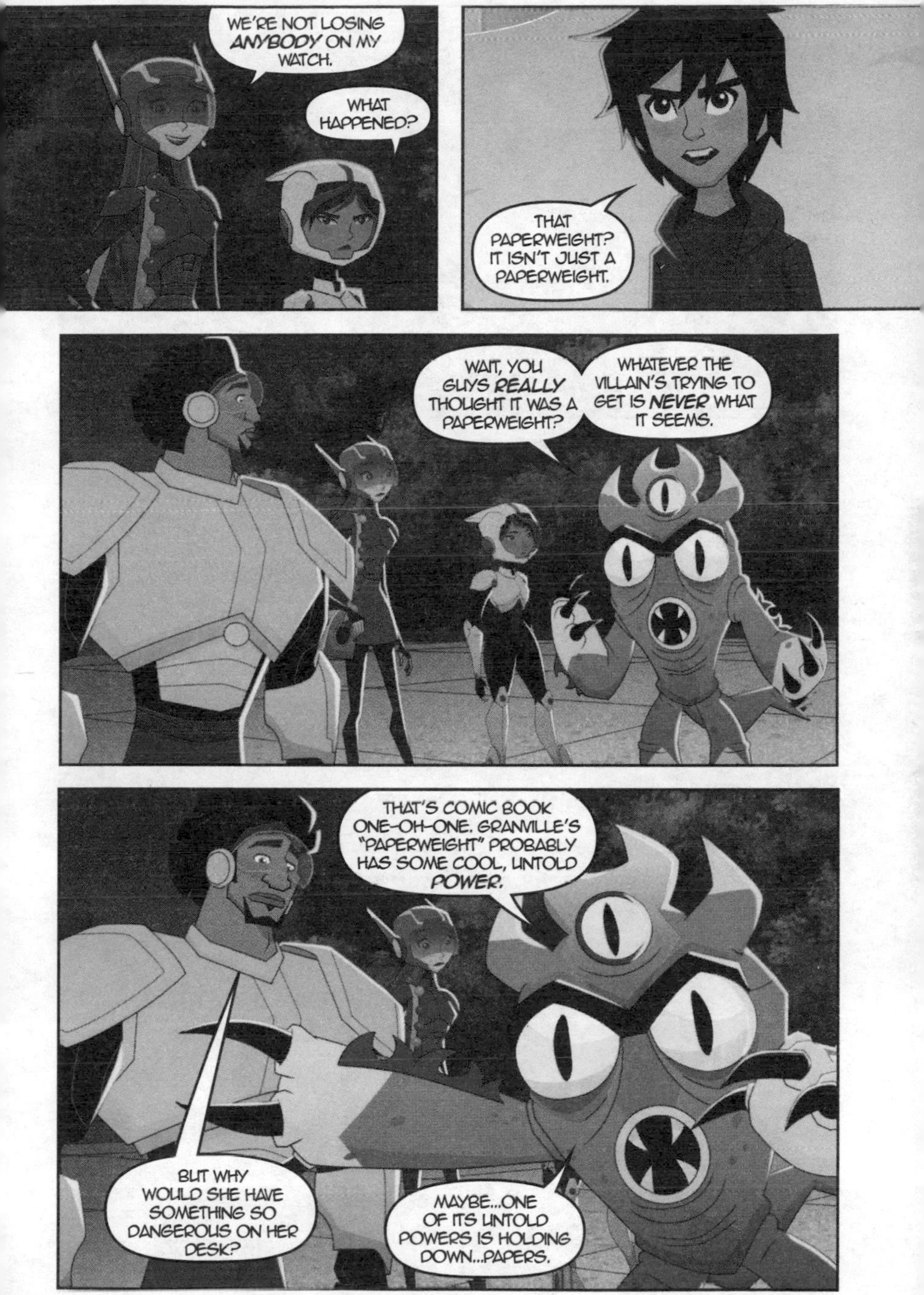
WE'RE NOT LOSING ANYBODY ON MY WATCH.
WHAT HAPPENED?
THAT PAPERWEIGHT? IT ISN'T JUST A PAPERWEIGHT.
WAIT, YOU GUYS REALLY THOUGHT IT WAS A PAPERWEIGHT?
WHATEVER THE VILLAIN'S TRYING TO GET IS NEVER WHAT IT SEEMS.
THAT'S COMIC BOOK ONE-OH-ONE. GRANVILLE'S "PAPERWEIGHT" PROBABLY HAS SOME COOL, UNTOLD POWER.
BUT WHY WOULD SHE HAVE SOMETHING SO DANGEROUS ON HER DESK?
MAYBE...ONE OF ITS UNTOLD POWERS IS HOLDING DOWN...PAPERS.

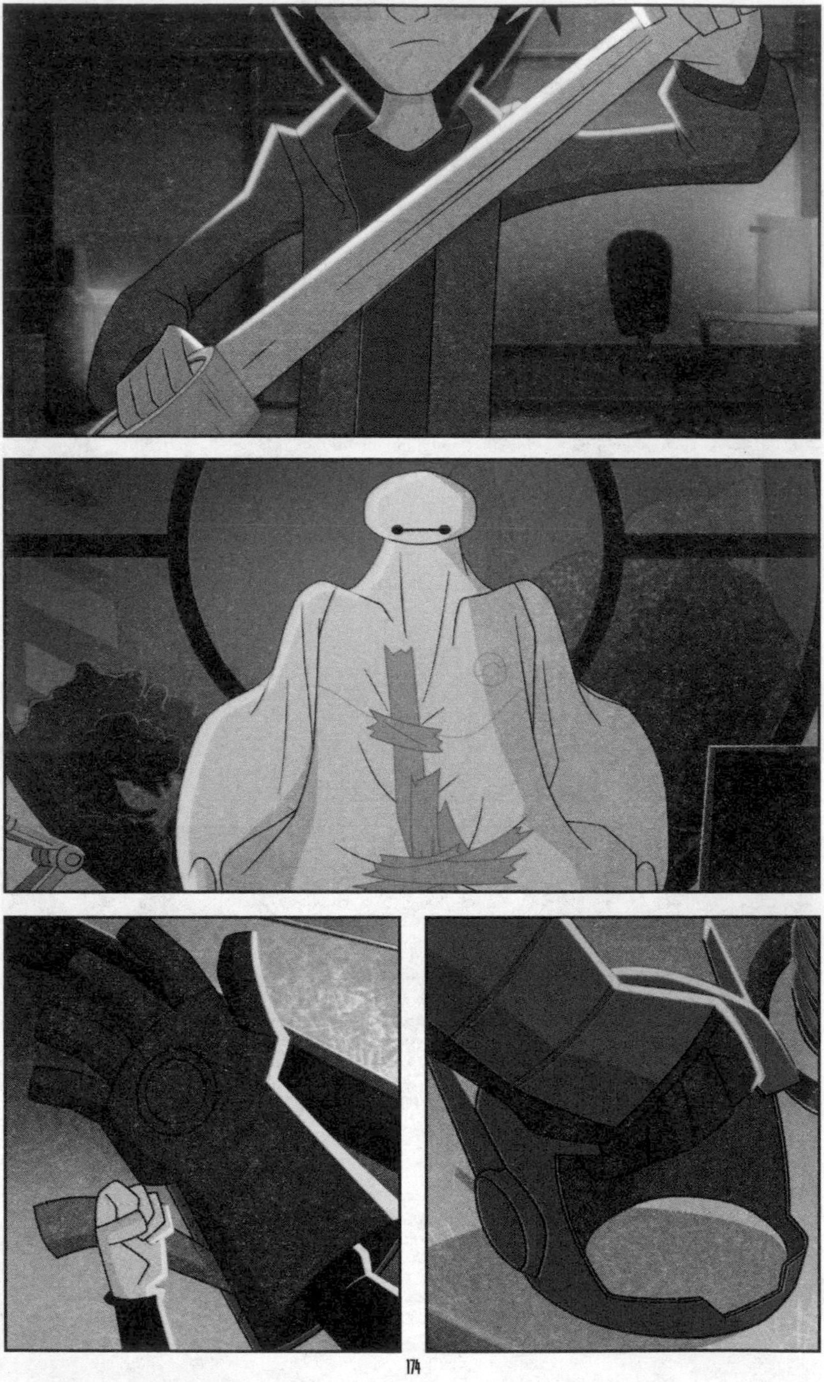

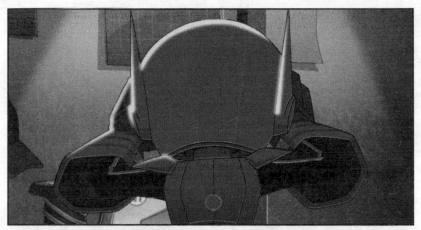

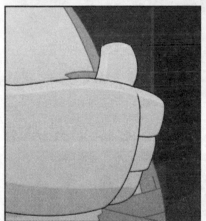

⋟SIGH⋞
I'M GONNA
MAKE THIS
RIGHT.

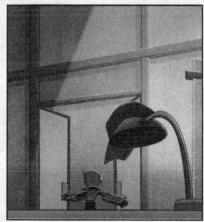

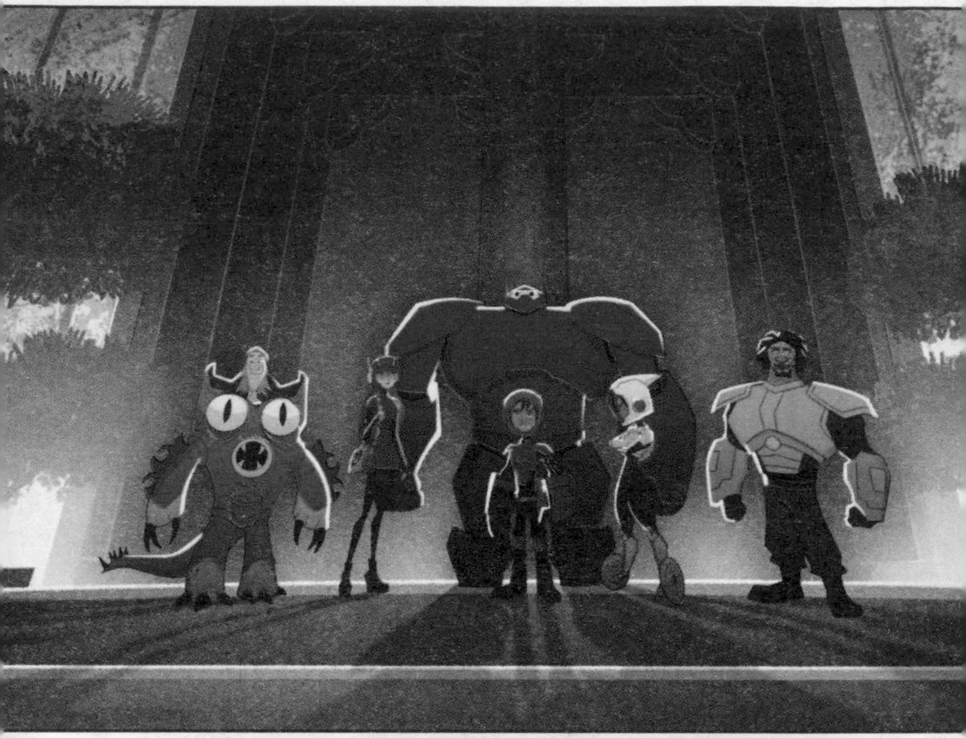

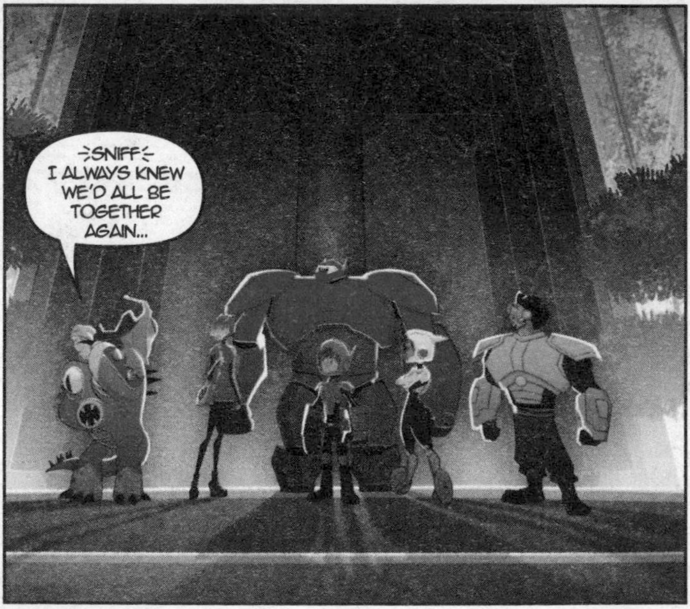

SNIFF I ALWAYS KNEW WE'D ALL BE TOGETHER AGAIN...

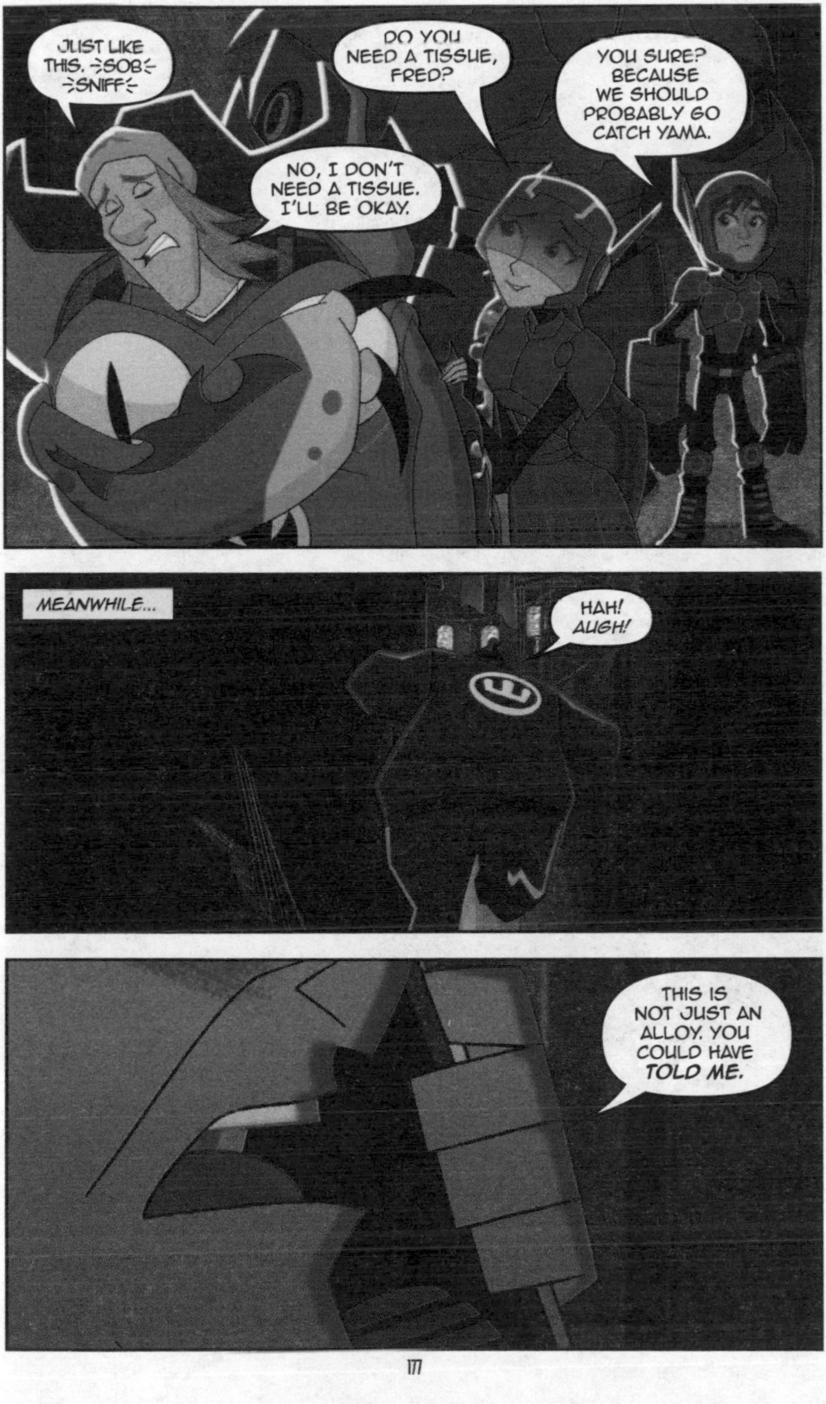
JUST LIKE THIS. =SOB= =SNIFF=
DO YOU NEED A TISSUE, FRED?
NO, I DON'T NEED A TISSUE. I'LL BE OKAY.
YOU SURE? BECAUSE WE SHOULD PROBABLY GO CATCH YAMA.
MEANWHILE...
HAH! AUGH!
THIS IS NOT JUST AN ALLOY. YOU COULD HAVE *TOLD ME.*

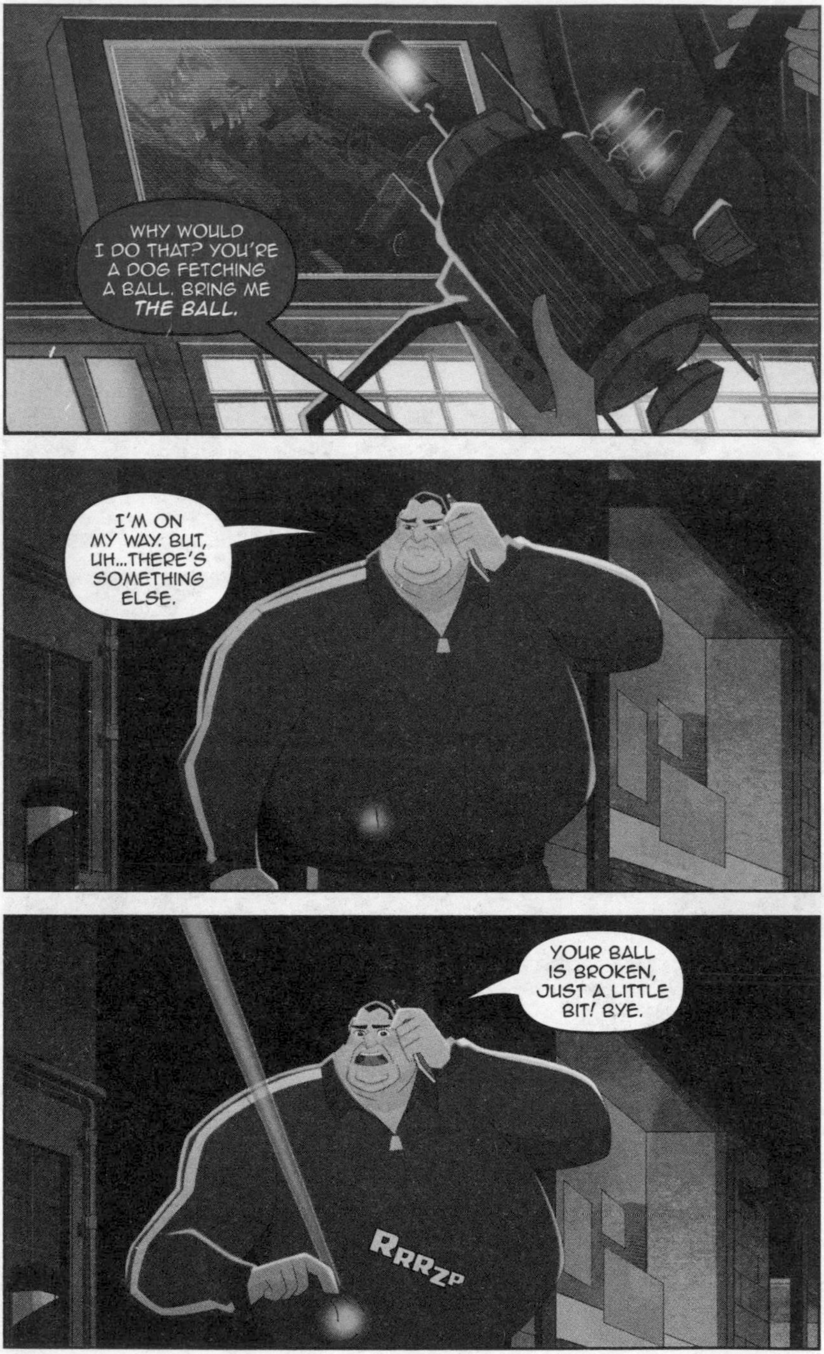
WHY WOULD I DO THAT? YOU'RE A DOG FETCHING A BALL. BRING ME THE BALL.
I'M ON MY WAY. BUT, UH...THERE'S SOMETHING ELSE.
YOUR BALL IS BROKEN, JUST A LITTLE BIT! BYE.
RRRZP

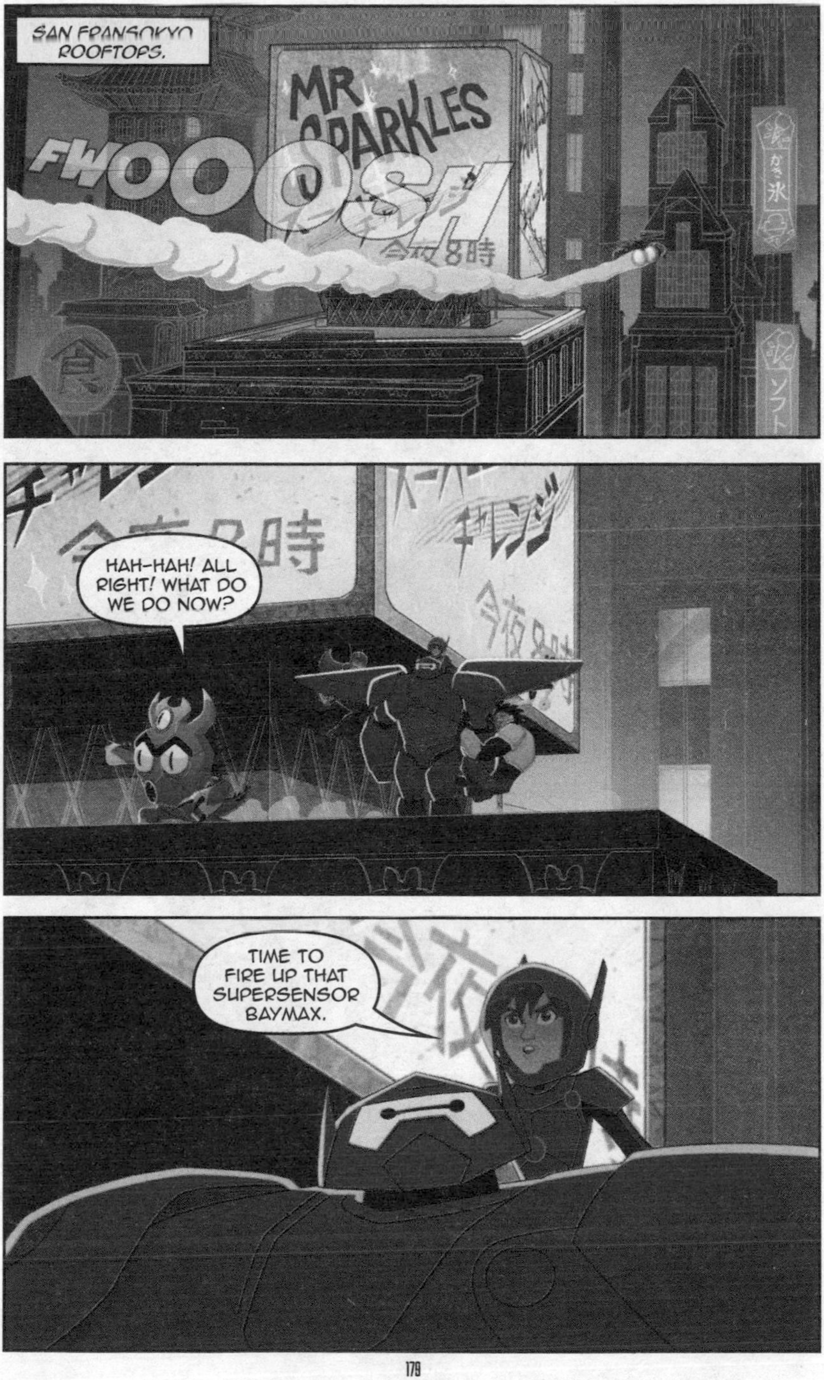
SAN FRANSOKYO ROOFTOPS.
MR SPARKLES
FWOOOSH
今夜8時
HAH-HAH! ALL RIGHT! WHAT DO WE DO NOW?
TIME TO FIRE UP THAT SUPERSENSOR BAYMAX.

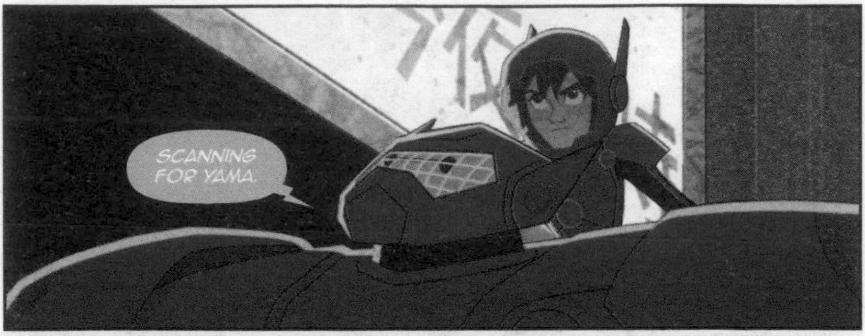
SCANNING FOR YAMA.

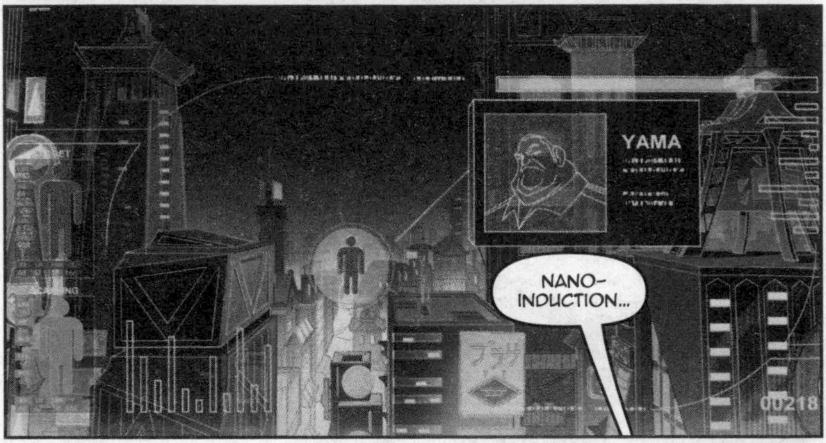
YAMA
NANO-INDUCTION...
00218

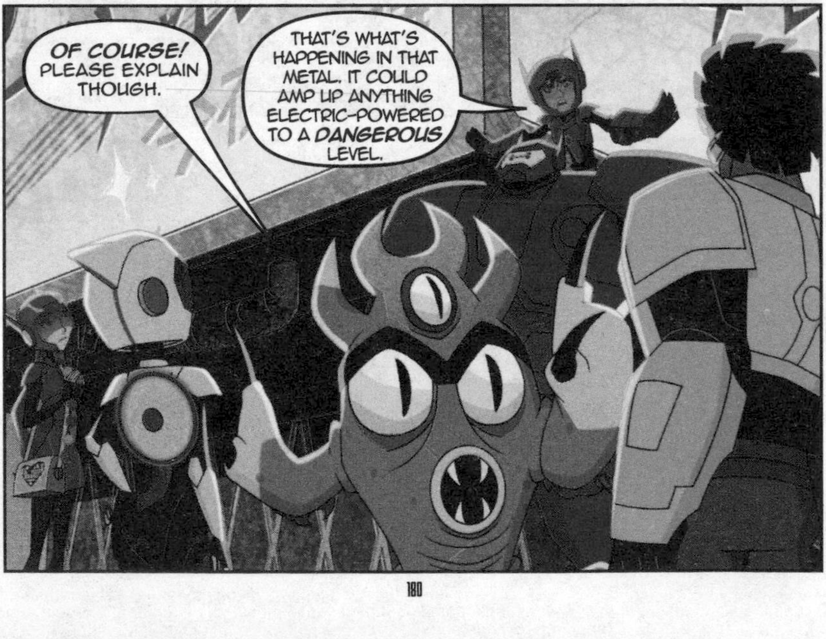
OF COURSE! PLEASE EXPLAIN THOUGH.
THAT'S WHAT'S HAPPENING IN THAT METAL. IT COULD AMP UP ANYTHING ELECTRIC-POWERED TO A DANGEROUS LEVEL.

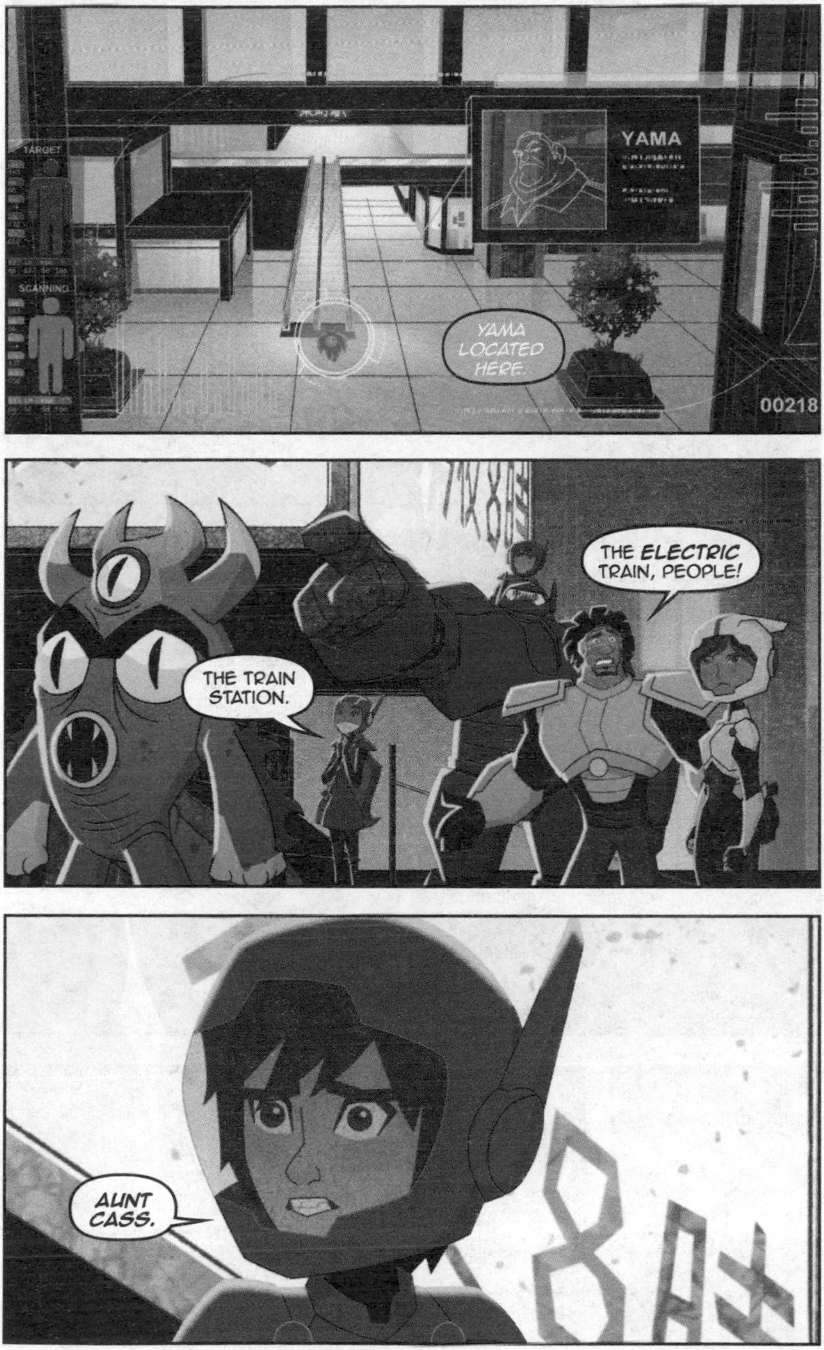
YAMA
YAMA LOCATED HERE.
00218
THE ELECTRIC TRAIN, PEOPLE!
THE TRAIN STATION.
AUNT CASS.

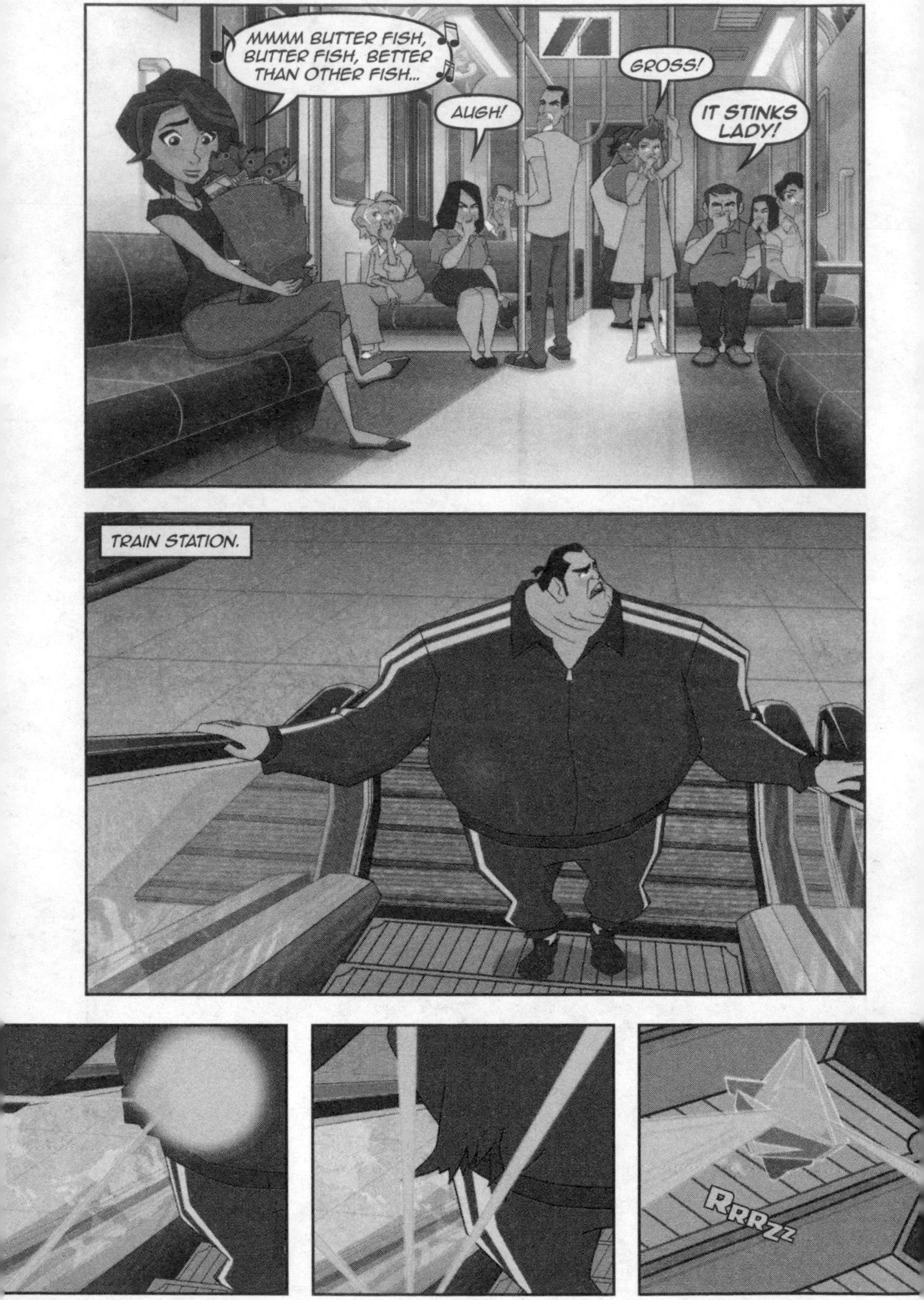
MMMM BUTTER FISH, BUTTER FISH, BETTER THAN OTHER FISH...
AUGH!
GROSS!
IT STINKS LADY!
TRAIN STATION.
RRRZZ

AUUGGGHHH!
AAAHHHHHH!
RRRP
SOUTH STATION
SOUTH STATION
EXPRESS

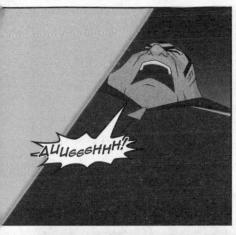

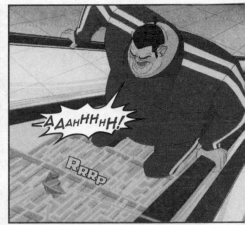

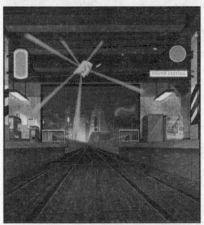

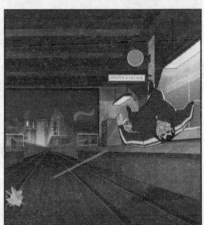

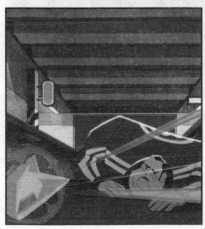

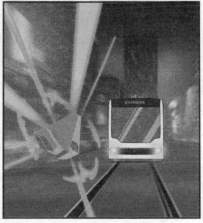

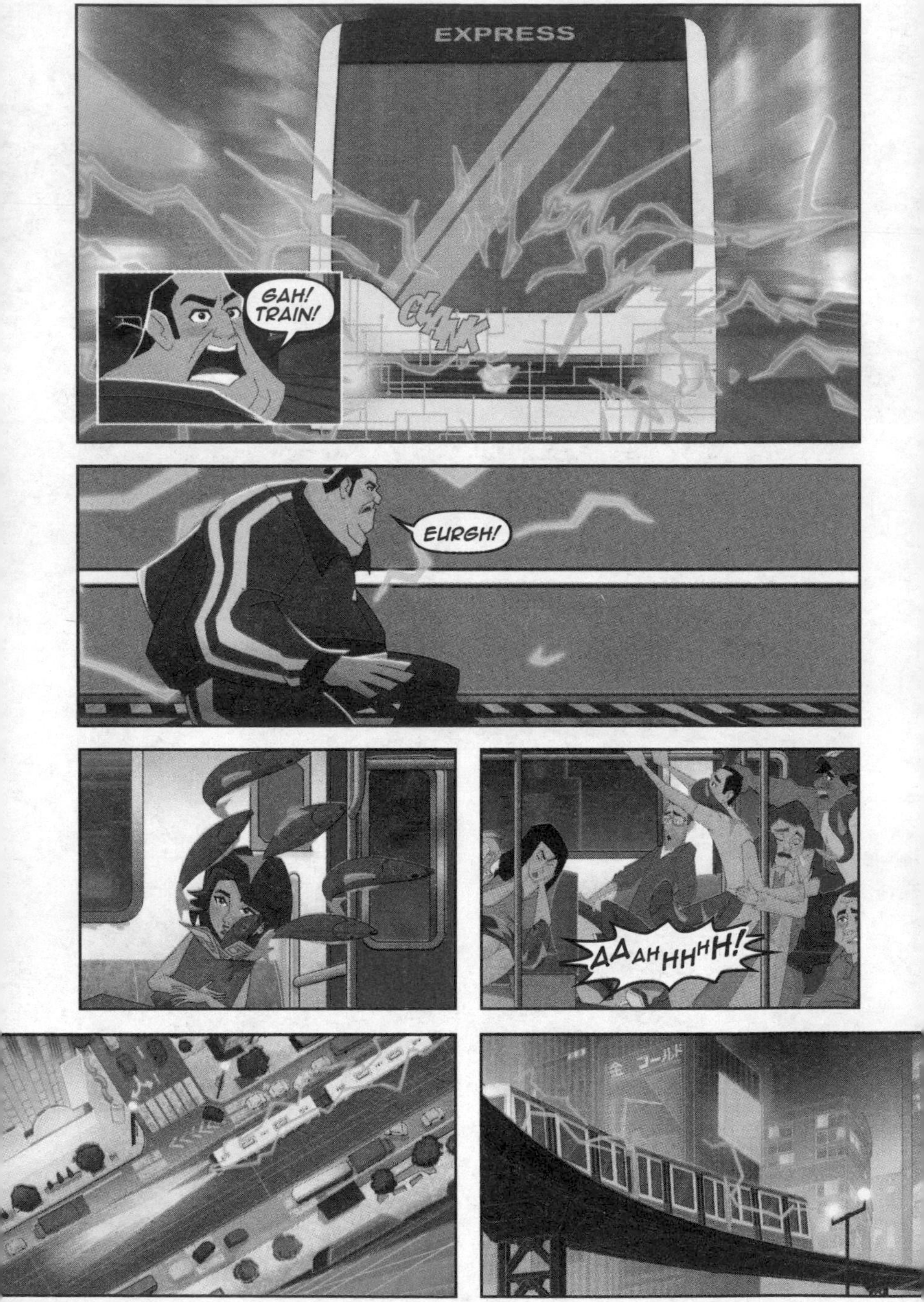
EXPRESS
CLANK
GAH! TRAIN!
EURGH!
AAAHHHHH!
金 ゴールド

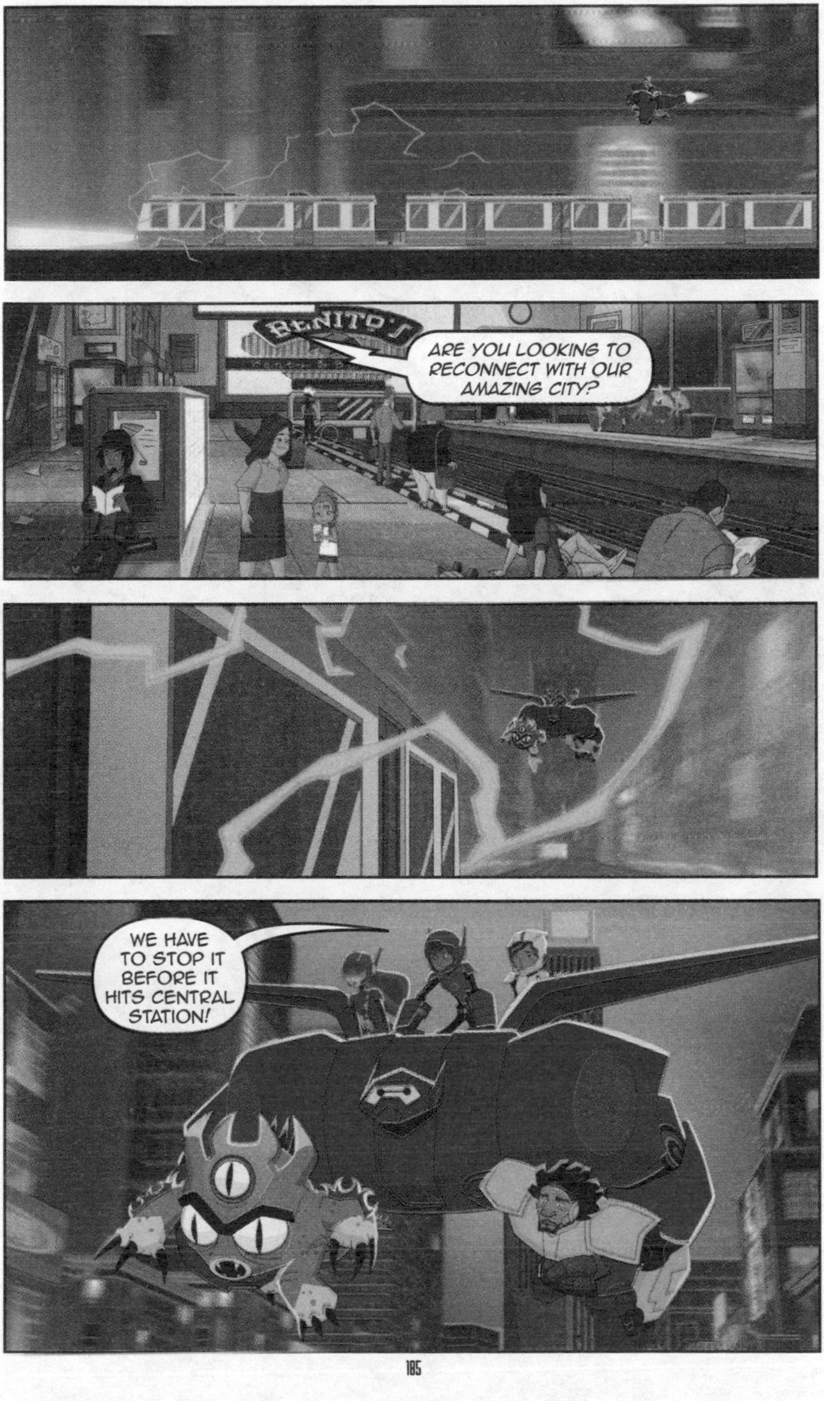
BENITO'S
ARE YOU LOOKING TO RECONNECT WITH OUR AMAZING CITY?
WE HAVE TO STOP IT BEFORE IT HITS CENTRAL STATION!

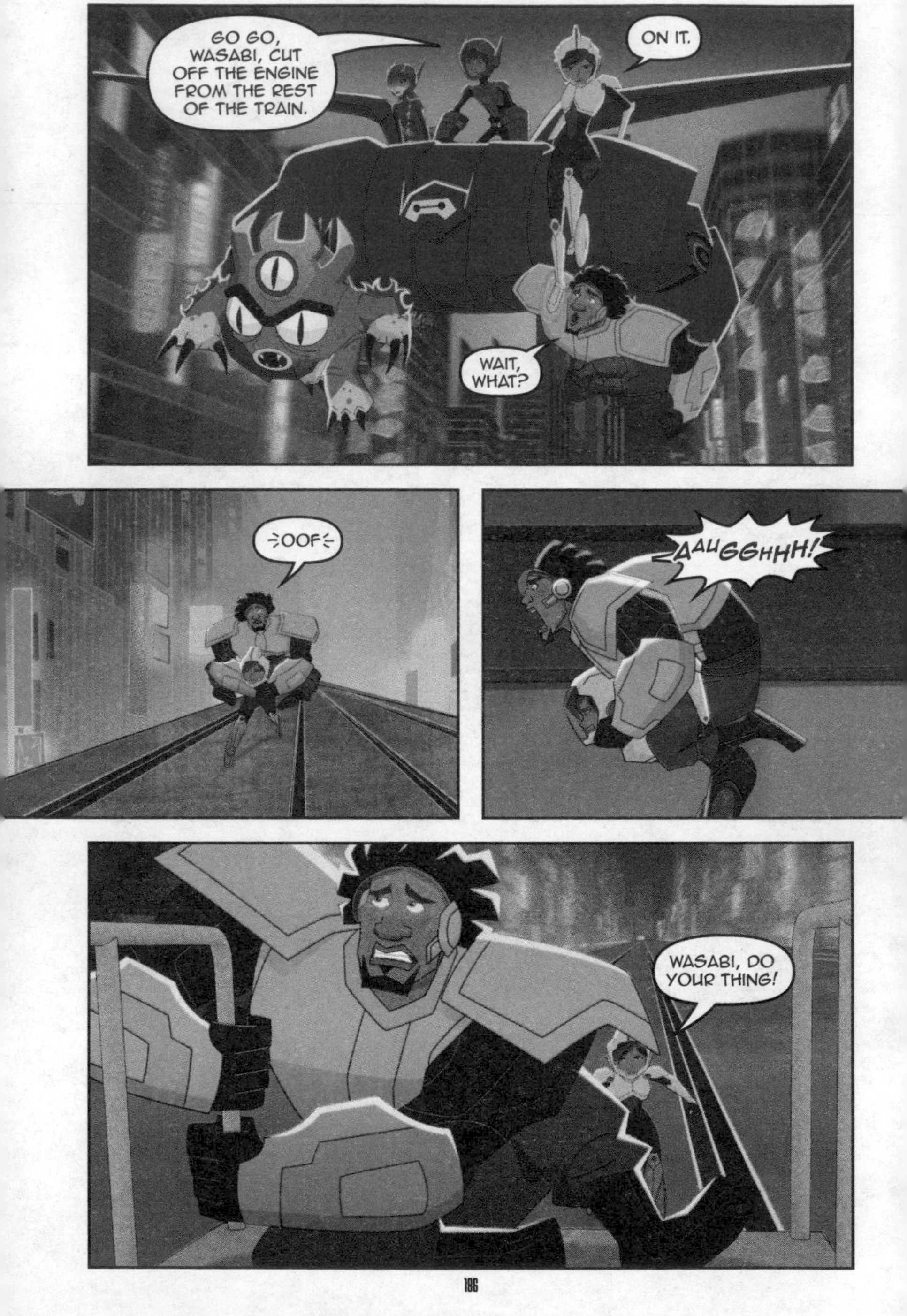
GO GO, WASABI, CUT OFF THE ENGINE FROM THE REST OF THE TRAIN.
ON IT.
WAIT, WHAT?
OOF
AAUGGHHH!
WASABI, DO YOUR THING!

EVEN WITH THE ADRENALINE, I HAVE REALLY *MIXED FEELINGS* ABOUT THIS!

AAAHHHHH!

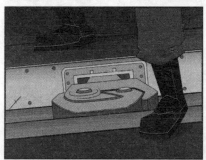

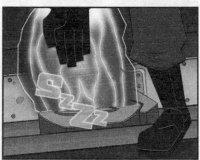

EHH.

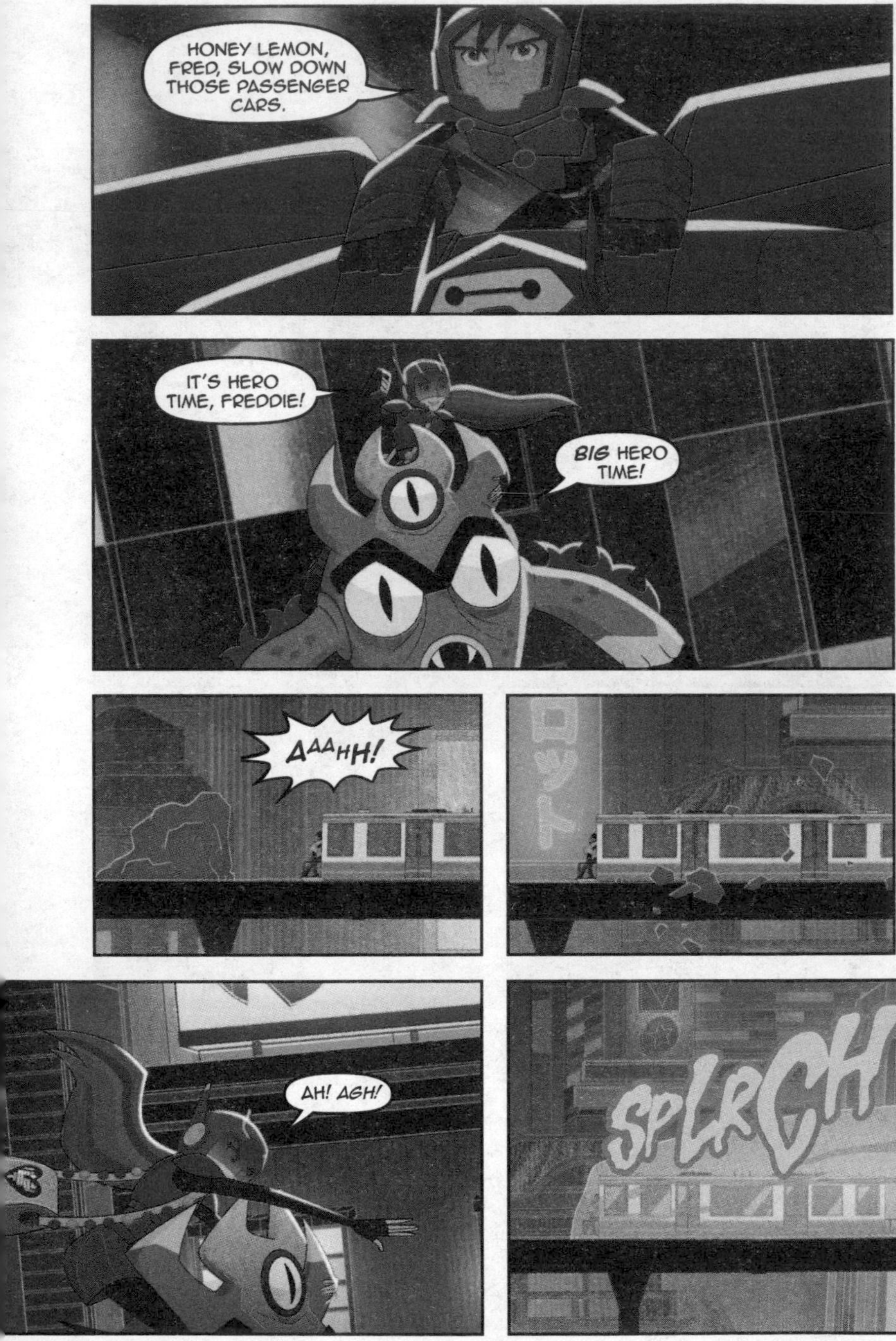
HONEY LEMON, FRED, SLOW DOWN THOSE PASSENGER CARS.
IT'S HERO TIME, FREDDIE!
BIG HERO TIME!
AAAHH!
AH! AGH!
SPLRCH

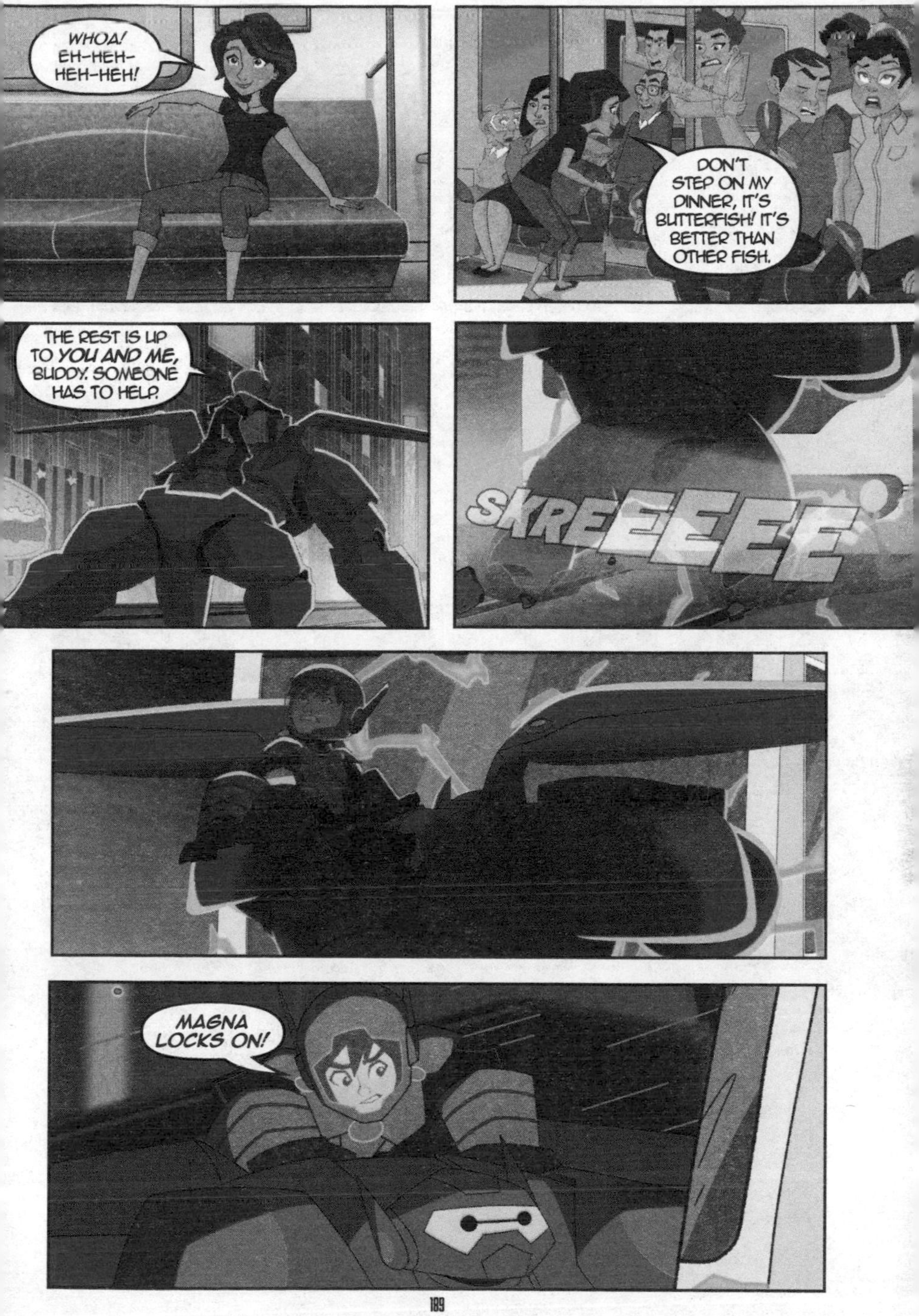
WHOA! EH-HEH-HEH-HEH!
DON'T STEP ON MY DINNER, IT'S BUTTERFISH! IT'S BETTER THAN OTHER FISH.
THE REST IS UP TO YOU AND ME, BUDDY. SOMEONE HAS TO HELP.
SKREEEEEE
MAGNA LOCKS ON!

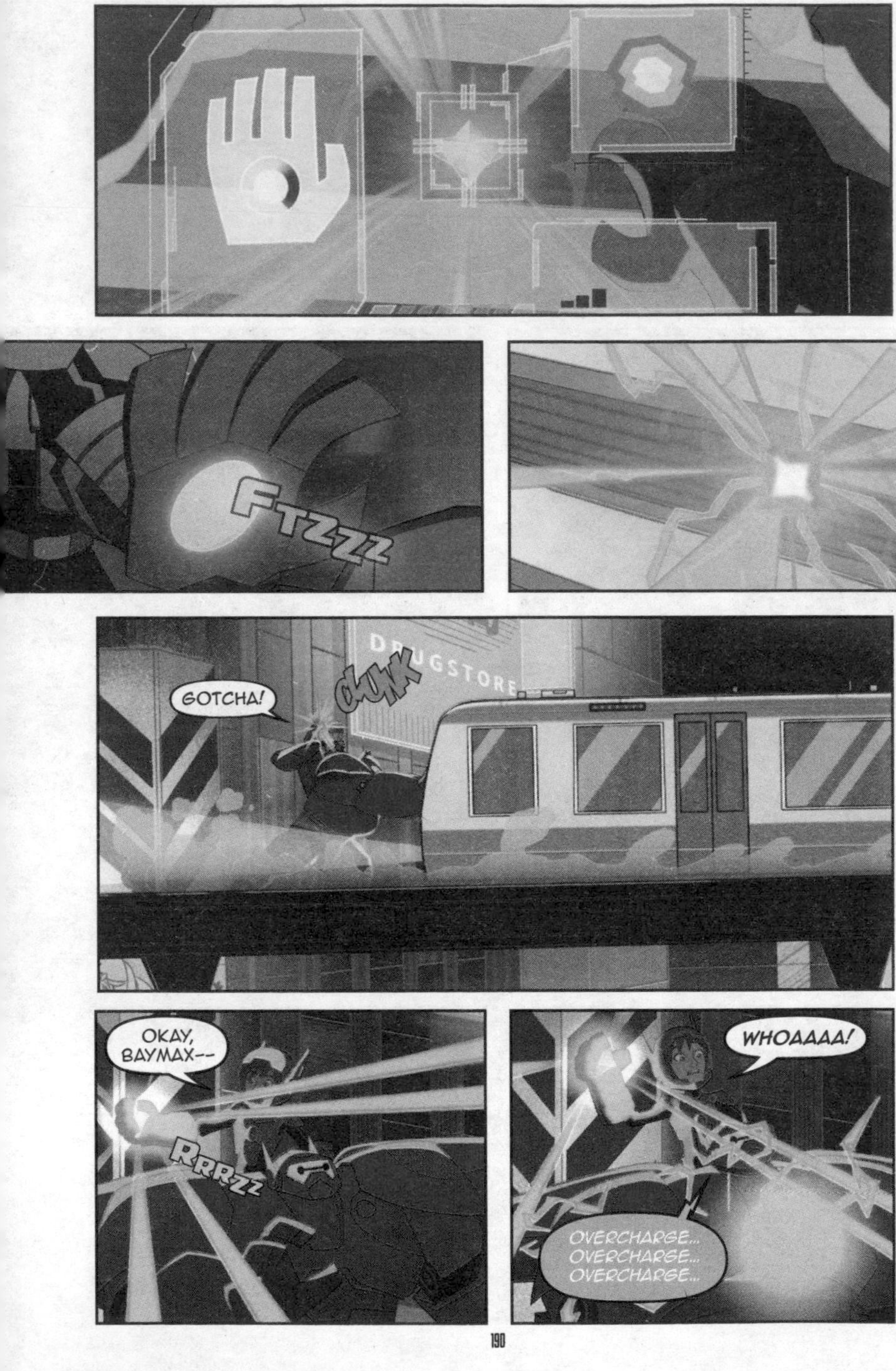
FTZZZ
GOTCHA!
CLUNK
DRUGSTORE
OKAY, BAYMAX--
RRRZZ
WHOAAAA!
OVERCHARGE... OVERCHARGE... OVERCHARGE...

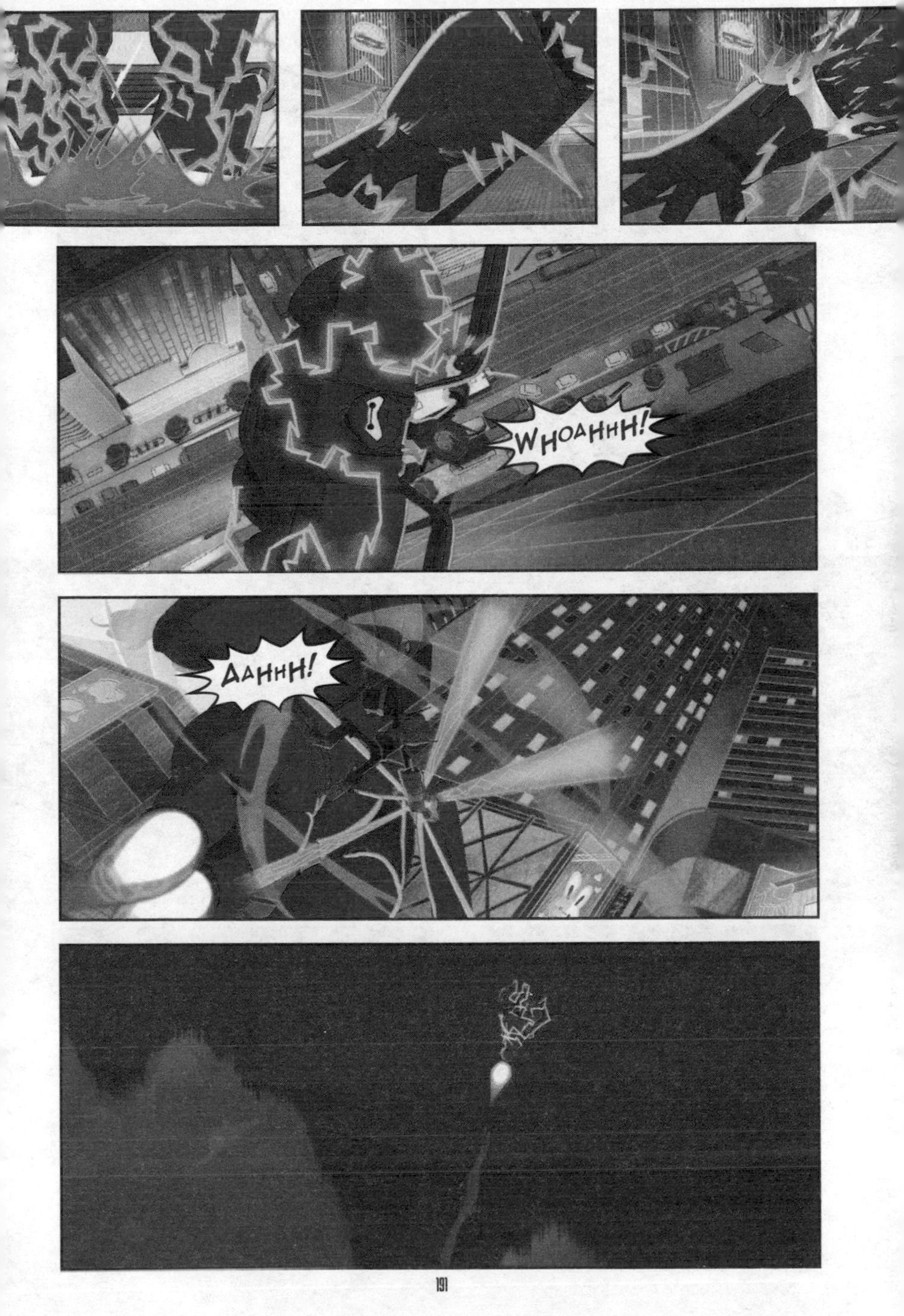
WHOAHHH!
AAHHH!

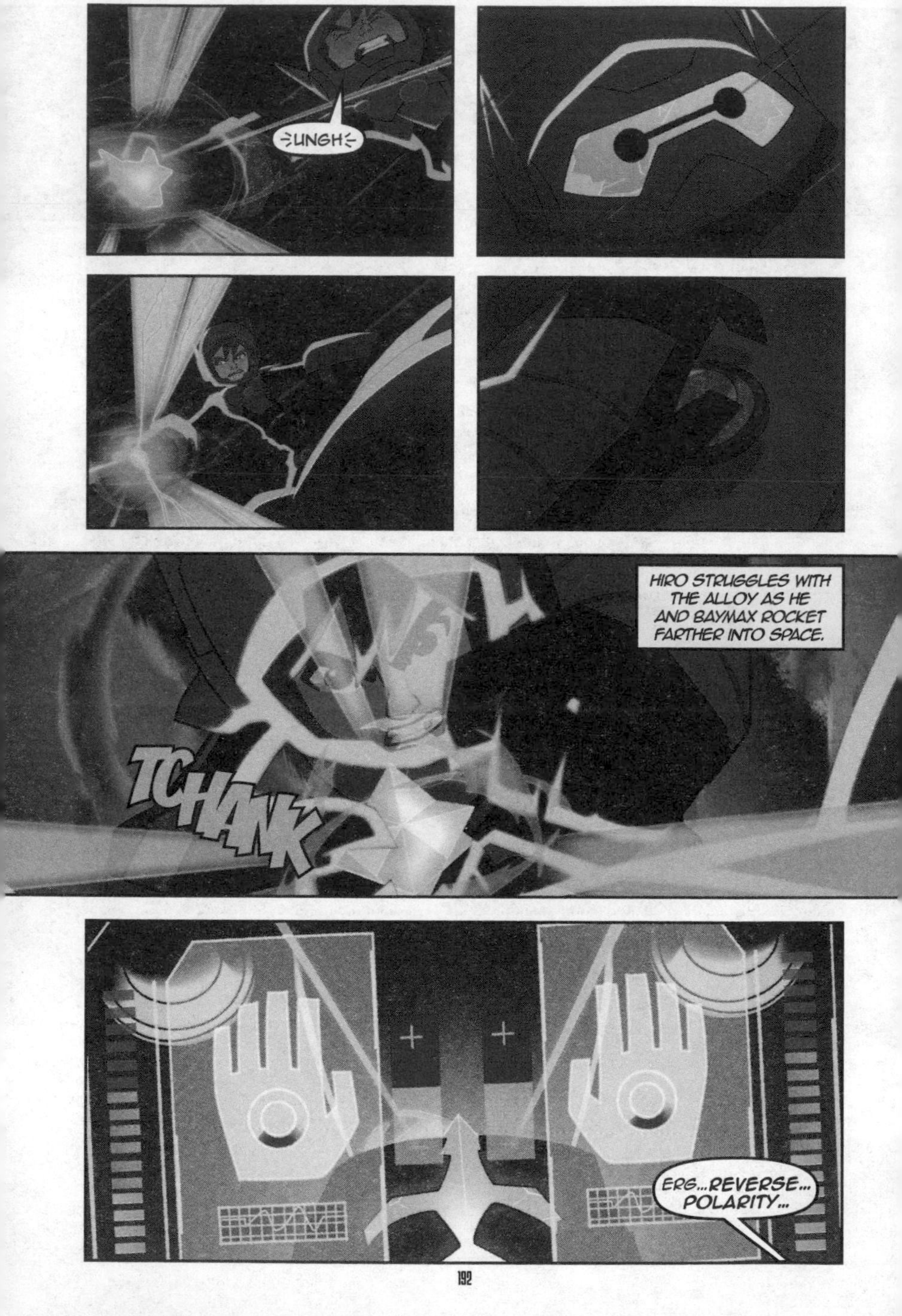
UNGH
HIRO STRUGGLES WITH THE ALLOY AS HE AND BAYMAX ROCKET FARTHER INTO SPACE.
TCHANK
ERG...REVERSE... POLARITY...

PANT
AHHH! AHH!
THOOM
AHH!

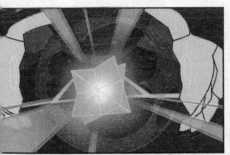

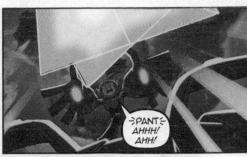

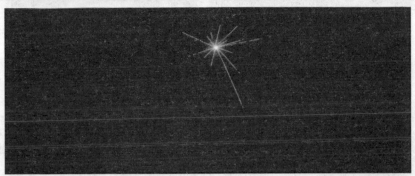

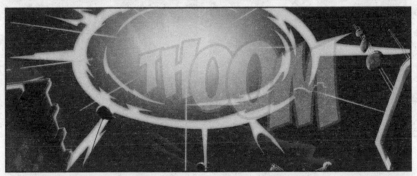

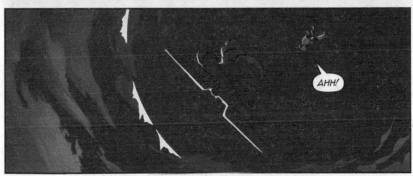

⇉PANT⇇ COME ON, COME ON, COME ON!

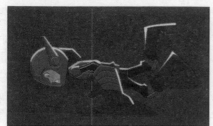

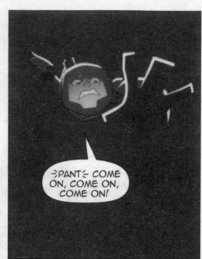

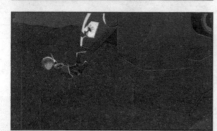

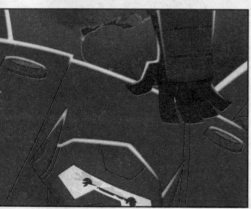

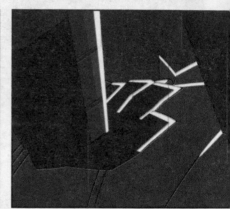

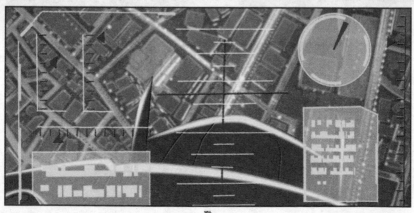

COME ON, BAYMAX!

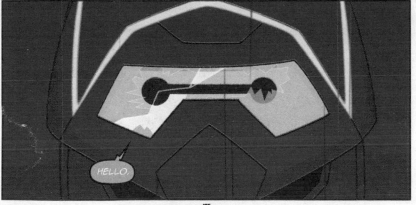

HELLO.

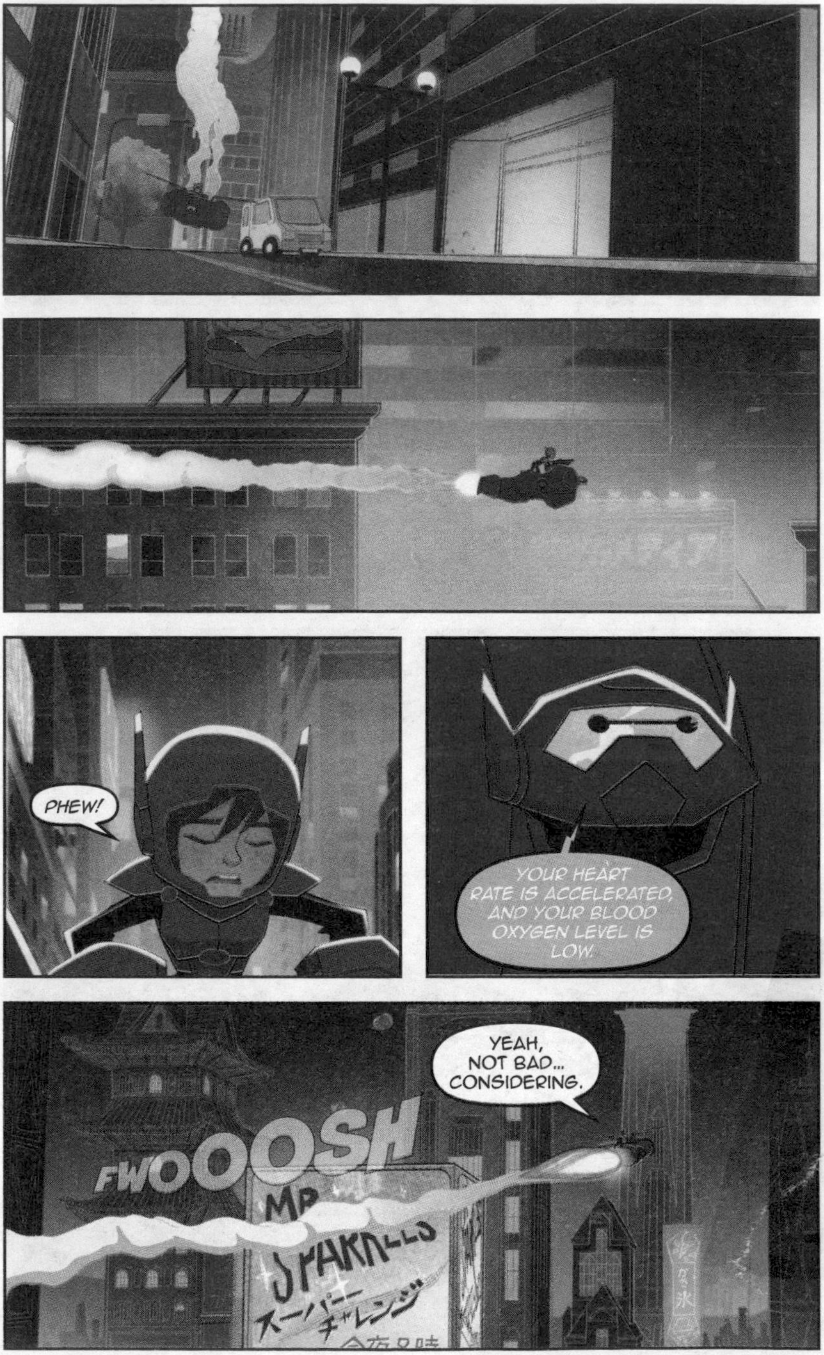
PHEW!
YOUR HEART RATE IS ACCELERATED, AND YOUR BLOOD OXYGEN LEVEL IS LOW.
YEAH, NOT BAD... CONSIDERING.
FWOOOSH
MR SPARKLES
スーパーチャレンジ

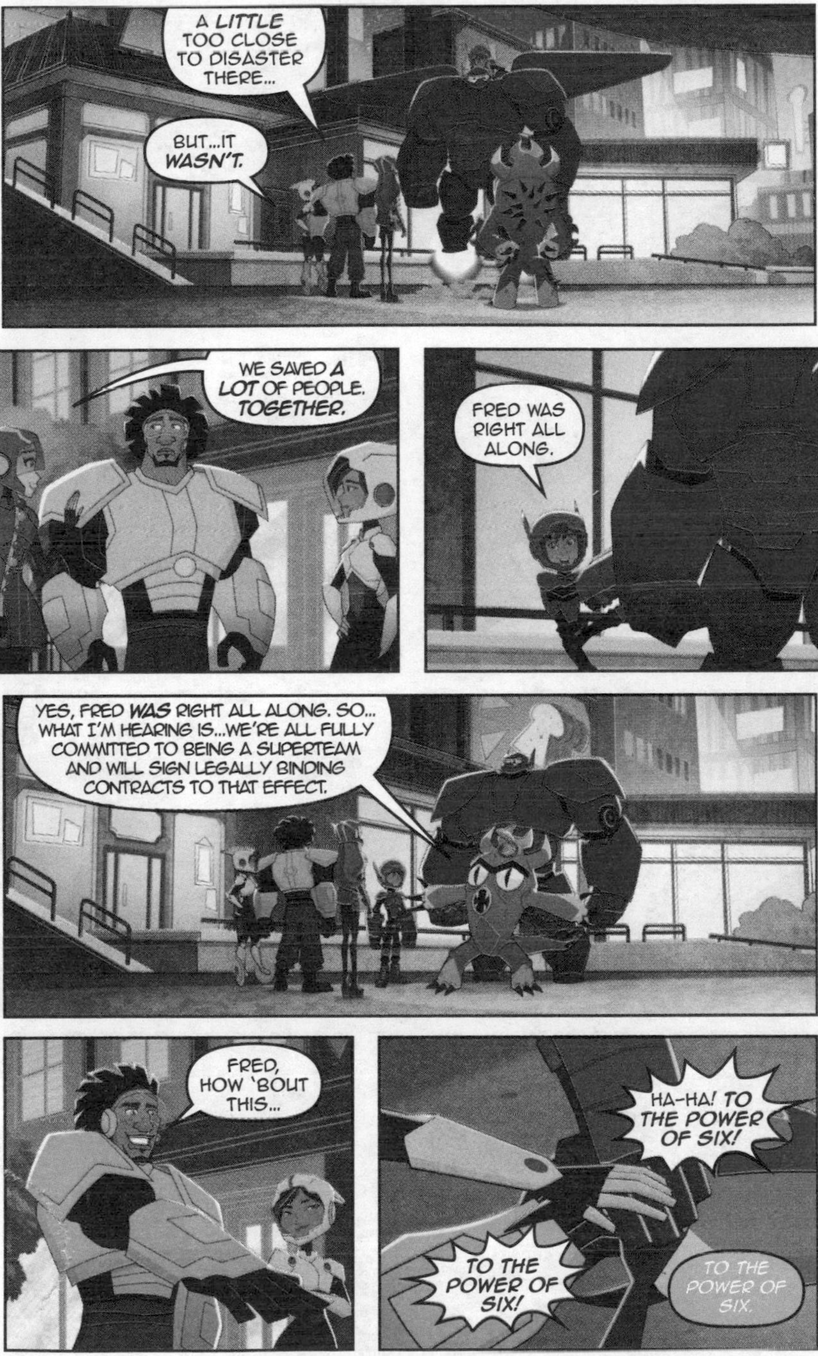
A LITTLE TOO CLOSE TO DISASTER THERE...
BUT...IT WASN'T.
WE SAVED A LOT OF PEOPLE. TOGETHER.
FRED WAS RIGHT ALL ALONG.
YES, FRED WAS RIGHT ALL ALONG. SO... WHAT I'M HEARING IS...WE'RE ALL FULLY COMMITTED TO BEING A SUPERTEAM AND WILL SIGN LEGALLY BINDING CONTRACTS TO THAT EFFECT.
FRED, HOW 'BOUT THIS...
HA-HA! TO THE POWER OF SIX!
TO THE POWER OF SIX!
TO THE POWER OF SIX.

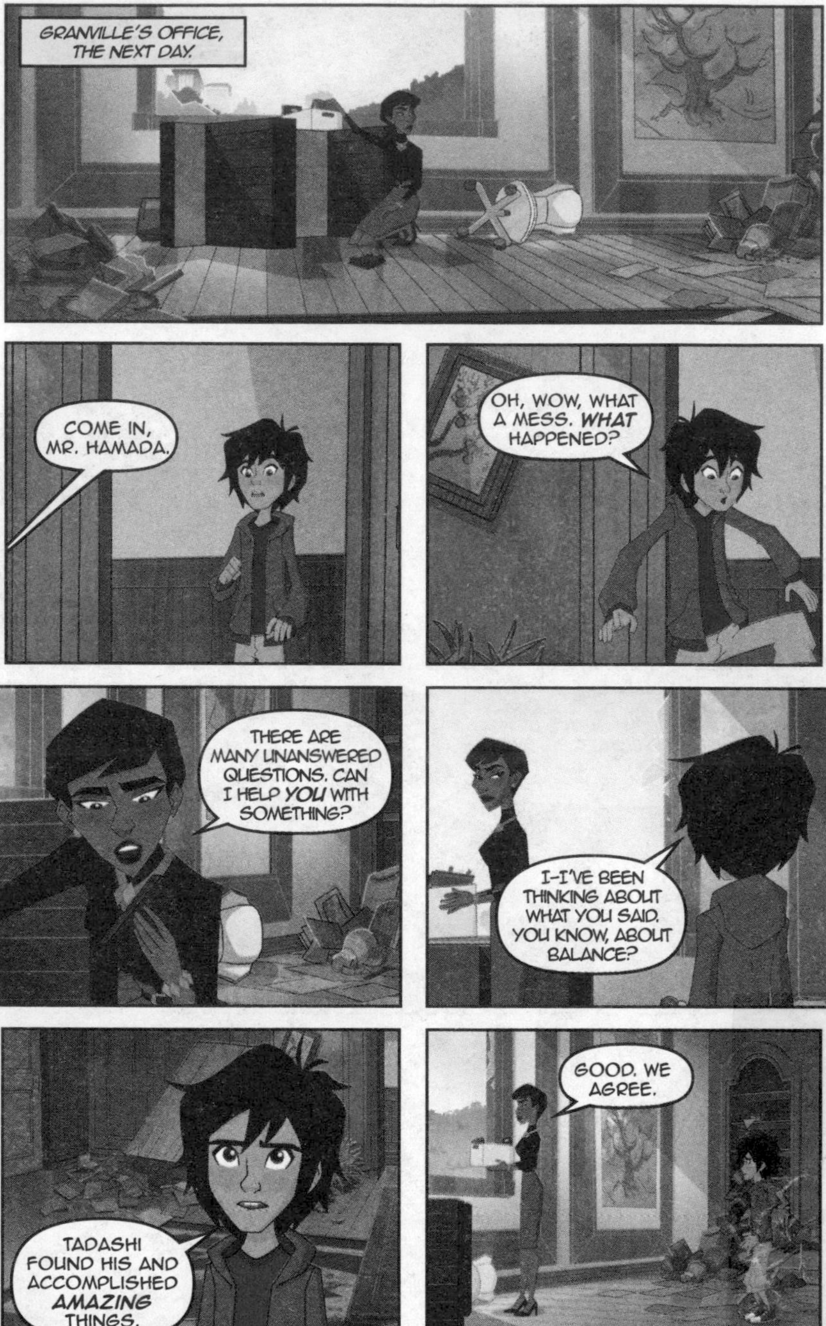
GRANVILLE'S OFFICE, THE NEXT DAY.
COME IN, MR. HAMADA.
OH, WOW, WHAT A MESS. WHAT HAPPENED?
THERE ARE MANY UNANSWERED QUESTIONS. CAN I HELP YOU WITH SOMETHING?
I-I'VE BEEN THINKING ABOUT WHAT YOU SAID. YOU KNOW, ABOUT BALANCE?
TADASHI FOUND HIS AND ACCOMPLISHED AMAZING THINGS.
GOOD. WE AGREE.

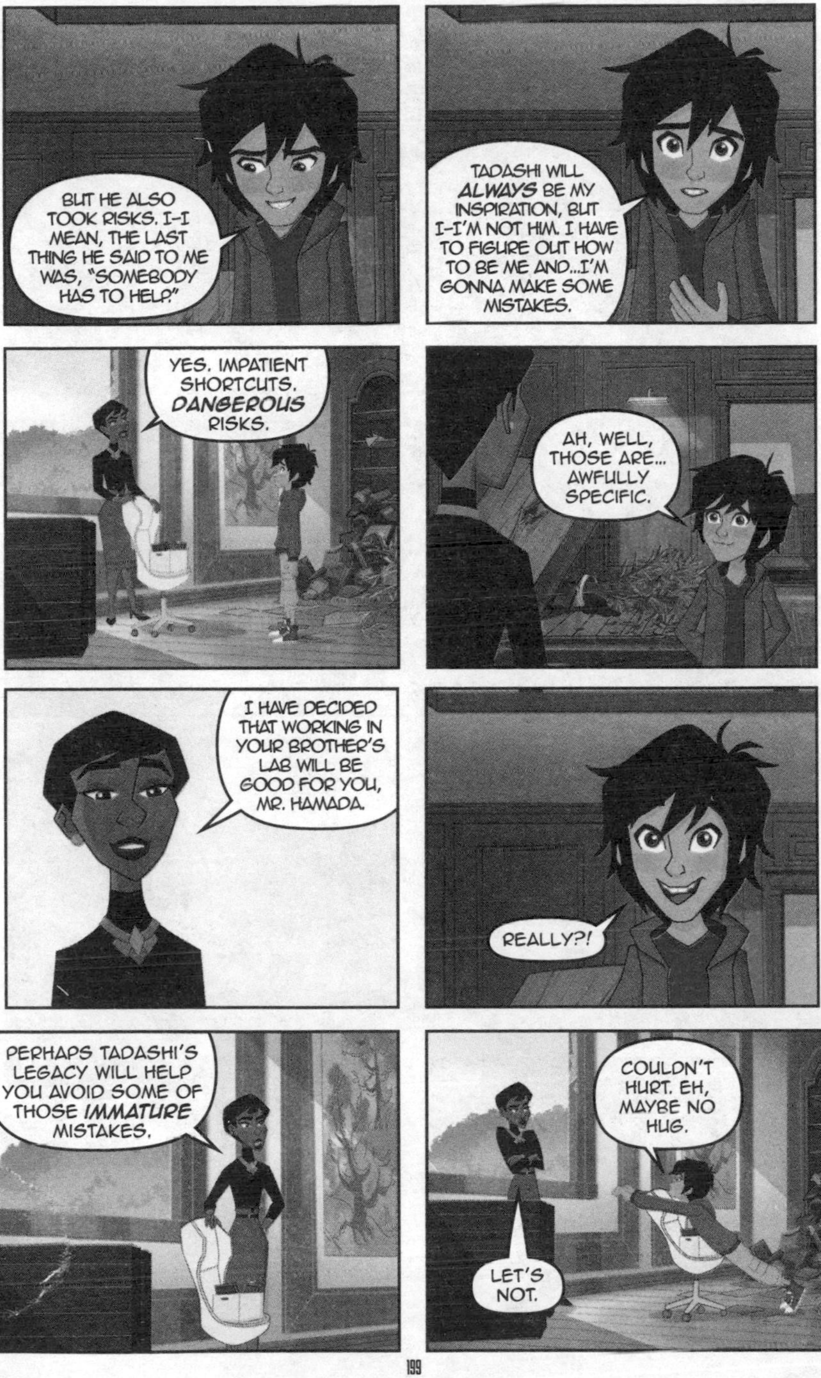
BUT HE ALSO TOOK RISKS. I–I MEAN, THE LAST THING HE SAID TO ME WAS, "SOMEBODY HAS TO HELP."
TADASHI WILL *ALWAYS* BE MY INSPIRATION, BUT I–I'M NOT HIM. I HAVE TO FIGURE OUT HOW TO BE ME AND...I'M GONNA MAKE SOME MISTAKES.
YES. IMPATIENT SHORTCUTS. *DANGEROUS* RISKS.
AH, WELL, THOSE ARE... AWFULLY SPECIFIC.
I HAVE DECIDED THAT WORKING IN YOUR BROTHER'S LAB WILL BE GOOD FOR YOU, MR. HAMADA.
REALLY?!
PERHAPS TADASHI'S LEGACY WILL HELP YOU AVOID SOME OF THOSE *IMMATURE* MISTAKES.
COULDN'T HURT. EH, MAYBE NO HUG.
LET'S NOT.

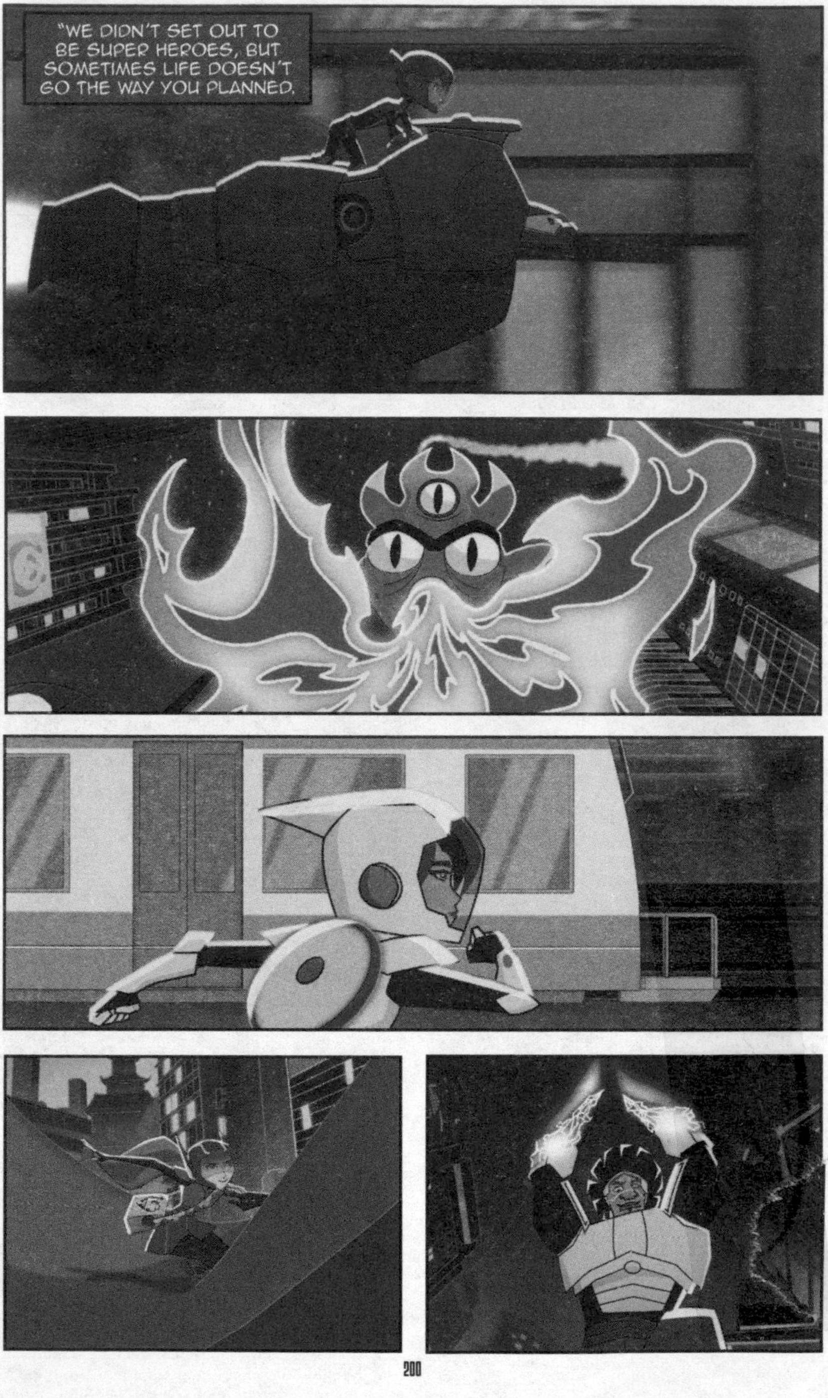
"WE DIDN'T SET OUT TO BE SUPER HEROES, BUT SOMETIMES LIFE DOESN'T GO THE WAY YOU PLANNED.

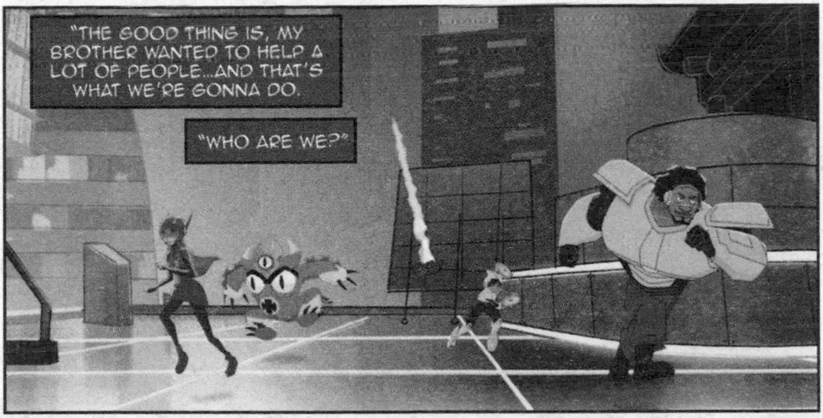
"THE GOOD THING IS, MY BROTHER WANTED TO HELP A LOT OF PEOPLE...AND THAT'S WHAT WE'RE GONNA DO.
"WHO ARE WE?"
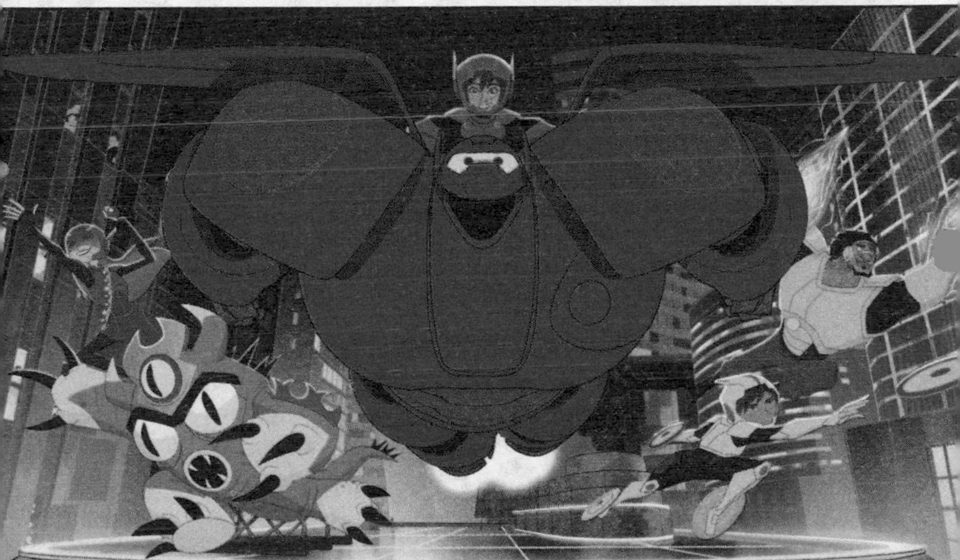
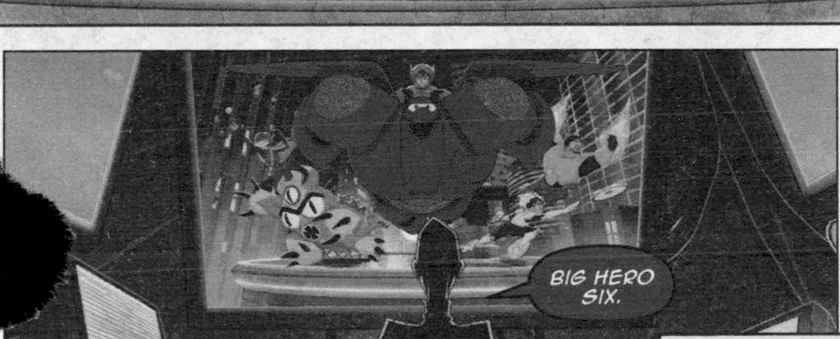
BIG HERO SIX.
TO BE CONTINUED...?

Disney

BIG HERO 6 THE SERIES

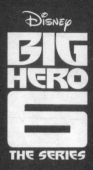

BAYMAX RETURNS

Big Hero 6 Team and Characters Created by
Man of Action

Developed for Television by
Nick Filippi
Mark McCorkle
Bob Schooley

Directors
Stephen Heneveld
Ben Juwono

Writers
Sharon Flynn
Paiman Kalayeh

Executive Producers
Mark McCorkle
Bob Schooley

Executive Producer and Supervising Director
Nick Filippi

Art Directors
Benjamin Plouffe
Christopher Whittier